a good book !

F

M/

i

N

PERJURY

PERJURY

STAN LATREILLE

CROWN PUBLISHERS, INC.

NEW YORK

Published by Crown Publishers, Inc., 201 East 50th Street, New York, New York 10022. Member of the Crown Publishing Group.

Random House, Inc. New York, Toronto, London, Sydney, Auckland
www.randomhouse.com

CROWN and colophon are trademarks of Crown Publishers, Inc.

Printed in the United States of America

Design by Lenny Henderson

Library of Congress Cataloging-in-Publication Data
Latreille, Stan.
    Perjury / Stan Latreille. — 1st ed.
    (alk. paper)
    I. Title.
  PS3562.A7594P4   1998
  813'.54—dc21   97-40653

ISBN 0-609-60138-5

10 9 8 7 6 5 4 3

To Barbara, my wife
and *sine qua non*

Acknowledgments

I wish to thank Ann Patty, my editor, and Jane Cushman, my agent. Their insights and skills made this all possible. I must also express my gratitude to Professor Jeanette Buttrey, who teaches legal research and writing at the Thomas M. Cooley Law School. She was good enough to read the manuscript and offer valuable suggestions, as did her husband, Jim Buttrey, a public defender who practices law the way it should be practiced. My sister, Doris White, also contributed, and, of course, I must mention the encouragement and assistance of my wife, Barbara, who is my biggest fan and toughest critic.

Finally, I have to acknowledge the debt I owe to the legal profession. My association with lawyers and judges has not only provided material for my writing but also immeasurably enriched my life. The law presumes to deliver justice, a divine attribute, and, being merely human, it of course falls short. Yet the quest goes on, inching mankind closer to the light, and therein lies the beauty of the profession.

And whoever hunts for me . . .
God or Devil, will find me hiding
in the thickets of the law.

Robert Bolt, *A Man for All Seasons*

PERJURY

1

DAVEY ALDEN TURNED OUT TO BE ONE OF THOSE WILDFLOWERS that miraculously spring up from the cracks in the concrete. In this case the concrete was the Laffler County Jail, on the outskirts of Kirtlcy, Michigan. The jail was only twenty years old or so, modern by most standards, a sprawling, flat, single-story white building, almost windowless. Inside were society's losers, and Davey Alden.

A chunky, kindly faced matron brought her into the lawyers' interview room, a stuffy cubicle the size of a small bathroom. Davey was dressed in oversized orange coveralls that made her look like a little girl playing grownup. Her reddish blond hair fell below her shoulders in a tangle of curls. She had delicate features and pale skin that was sprinkled with freckles, and she wore only a touch of makeup. Her eyes were blue, but as we talked, they seemed to change shades like the color of a lake on a day when the sun is contesting with the clouds. In those eyes I saw fear, sadness, supplication, and hope. I'd expected a bimbo, I'd found a little girl.

"Did Joel hire you?" she asked when she had taken a seat across from me at the table.

"Are you talking about your husband?" I spoke more sharply than I'd intended. The question made no sense. Joel Alden was the victim—her victim.

"Yes," she said. "I mean . . . I thought he might get a lawyer for me, I didn't know . . ." She raised a hand to her mouth and turned away from my gaze.

I tried to soften my tone. "Mrs. Alden, I've been appointed by the Circuit Court to defend you. Your husband did not hire me. I've never met your husband."

I smiled, and she responded with a tentative smile of her own.

"I'm curious, Mrs. Alden. Why would you think that your husband would hire a lawyer for you—under the circumstances?"

"Joel always handles things like that . . . I just . . ." Then she looked me in the eye again and seemed to gather courage. "No, that's silly. Joel wouldn't hire me a lawyer. Why would he?"

"Precisely. Joel Alden is not going to do anything to help you, Mrs. Alden. I'm the only one who's going to help you from now on. I'm your lawyer. I'm probably the only one you can trust right now. Do you understand?"

I picked up my ballpoint pen and began writing on the yellow legal pad I had placed on the table in front of me. While I wrote her name, the date, and a few other details of the interview, she sat silently across from me. When I looked up again, she was studying me with curiosity and a hint of defiance.

"Are you any good as a lawyer?" she asked. The frightened little girl of a minute ago was gone. Her cheeks had a genuine flush to them and her chin was tilted challengingly.

"I'm considered pretty good," I said cautiously. I was a veteran of hundreds of jailhouse interviews, including dozens with women criminals, so human nature held few surprises for me. But this woman's transformation was atypical. If they are posturing, they usually stick to a single role—bereaved, betrayed, outraged, whatever. Most criminals have neither intelligence nor imagination, so the

2

repertoire is usually limited. Davey Alden showed promise of being different.

She smiled. "Appointed attorneys are not supposed to be very good. They don't work very hard for you. They just want to get the case over with and make a plea bargain. Or so they tell me."

This time the smile was provocative, the kind that good-looking women wear at cocktail parties when they are bored and ready to flirt. She was an actress, I decided, and any scene in which she appeared might suddenly dissolve, kaleidoscopically, into a new one entirely.

"I see you've been talking to the jailhouse lawyers. The truth is that most appointed attorneys do a good job. They—"

"Most?"

Damn that smile.

"Look, sometimes political hacks get appointments, and they couldn't care less about their clients. And some lawyers won't do a good job because they're not paid enough. But poor people usually get pretty good representation. They get a fair shake, and the lawyers who make sure of that get no thanks from society or from the scum they represent."

I put my pen back down on the legal pad and stared at her. I had heard that same fear of appointed lawyers voiced hundreds of times, but never before had I responded with irritation. My annoyance puzzled me.

"Look, Mrs. Alden, you may be accustomed to better and quicker service at the hotels you frequent, but this is not a hotel and I'm not a bellhop. You're in big trouble—the penalty for perjury is up to life in prison—and neither of us has the time to be cute. If you're in a position to retain counsel, then by all means do so. I didn't want this appointment, but until I'm relieved, I have a job to do. The preliminary exam is a week away, and I'm ready to go forward with the interview—if that is quite all right with you."

I watched with satisfaction as her pale complexion turned a shade lighter, making the scattered freckles even more noticeable. She turned away from my stare, and for a moment I thought the tears were about to flow. I wished I'd gone to Judge Olenik and told him that under no circumstances would I take any criminal assignments.

"Will you be able to get me out on bond?" she asked, her face strained. She was a little girl again, and so intense was she in her plea that, perhaps without realizing it, she reached across the table and laid her hand over mine.

"Please, Mr. Brenner, I am so, so sorry. I'm all confused. It's been a nightmare. But I must make you understand how very important it is for me to get out of this jail so I can be with my little girl. She needs me. You must help me."

I retrieved my hand and began writing again on the legal pad. Her hand had been surprisingly cool, and I could still feel its light touch on my skin.

"I'll bring up bond at the exam, Mrs. Alden. We should be able to get a personal bond of some sort. The magistrate who arraigned you set bond at a half-million cash or surety. That's outrageous—unless you've got a criminal record. Ever been convicted of a felony?"

She looked down and shook her head.

"Well, there's no doubt that the bond should be lowered, but I can't make any guarantees. There's not enough time to get into court before the exam, so we'll have to wait until next Tuesday."

She leaned back in her chair in an attitude of surrender and gave me her respectful attention.

"I've got some questions and I want the truth," I continued. "If you lie, I'll end up looking stupid in front of the jury, but you're the one who'll go to prison. I'll go home and have a beer and feel sorry for both of us, and if I get to feeling really sorry, I might write you a post-card in prison. I can't defend you effectively if you lie to me. I trust you understand that."

It was a standard speech. It did not prevent anyone from lying to me, but it put the responsibility for what happened afterwards on the liar's shoulders. At this stage of the game, a lawyer rarely expects or even wants the truth. The truth can blunt a vigorous defense. It can make a liar of an otherwise honest lawyer. Invincible ignorance is the smart lawyer's chastity belt.

"I'll tell you the truth," she said, but from the way her hand fluttered to her throat, I knew that I was not about to hear precisely that. That was all right with me. The fact that she had lied was written irrevocably in the trial transcript that I had reviewed an hour before; in it she was condemned out of her own mouth. The prosecutor did not need anything more. But convention required that I go ahead.

"You're charged with perjury. My question to you is very simple. Did you lie under oath when you testified against your husband? When you said you saw him molest your daughter?"

In her face I saw conflicting emotions struggle for dominance—desperation, hope, mistrust, fear, courage. The truth is never simple for criminal defendants; it is always encrusted with a thousand rationalizations. When she finally spoke, her voice sounded distant and hollow and filled with despair.

"I lied. It was wrong . . . It . . ."

She did not complete her thought, but I'd gotten what I wanted, and I would do what I could for her. Whatever else she might add would only be a gloss to salve her conscience. She could go elsewhere for that. I was not in the forgiveness business.

"All right," I said quickly. "Now we have to talk about the preliminary examination. In a week we go in front of a District Court judge for that hearing. It's a screening process to see if there's enough to hold you for trial. Then you go to a higher court—the Circuit Court—for your jury trial. Frankly, I believe there's more than enough to bind you over for trial in Circuit Court—the trial transcript is really all they need—and I think we'd be wasting our time to insist on an exam. So unless the prosecutor demands one, we should waive it—skip it—and go right to Circuit Court. But I'll argue for a decent bond in the District Court."

"Will I have to have money to get out on bond?"

"Not if I can get a personal bond. But tell me, are you saying that you have no money at all? No money to hire a lawyer or post a bond?"

"I have nothing," she said. "Joel managed all the household money. I had only a small checking account, and Joel took that just before I was arrested. Everything is in his name."

"With your assets, I'm surprised they appointed a lawyer for you at public expense."

"I told the judge just what I've just told you. I have nothing. He said he didn't want to hold things up and would appoint a lawyer for me. He said I'd have to pay the county back later."

"When did your husband file for divorce?"

"Right when I got arrested. Joel filed and got custody of Julie— although the court papers say she is to stay with my mother. Are you appointed for the divorce too?"

"Not a chance. Look, when I talk to the judge about bond, I need to be able to tell him where you'll be living. Have you thought about that?"

It was clear that she had not. She responded with a dejected shrug of her shoulders. Armed with court orders, Joel Alden was back in the family home and calling the shots. He had custody of their daughter and control of their assets. After what he'd been through, it was hard to blame him.

"See if you can wear something nice when you come to court— nothing too flashy, something dignified. We want to make a good impression on the judge when we ask for a personal bond."

I stood up, placed my papers in my briefcase, and snapped it shut. "And think about a place to live. Don't you have any girlfriends? Somebody who can put you up?"

"Joel picked all our friends," she said. "Even those who seemed friendly to me stayed away after Joel was arrested. I guess they didn't want to get involved."

I turned to the window and rapped on the glass. When the matron started moving our way, I turned back to Davey. She looked as if she wanted to apologize for causing so much trouble.

"I'll see you next week," I said. "We've got a lot more to talk about, but there will be plenty of time after the exam."

I watched her walk down the hall with the matron. The barren walls accented her vulnerability. She was beautiful, and I could see how an older man like Joel Alden could lose his head over her.

When I reached my battered old Volvo in the parking lot, I punched in a Doors tape and turned the volume up. The sounds of crazy Jim Morrison drowned out all thought for a while.

2

WHENEVER SCOTT SHERMAN TALKED ABOUT WOMEN, IT ALWAYS seemed to mean trouble for me. When I told him the next day about my interview with Davey Alden, his grin was sly and knowing, as if I were asking him about a Tri Delt he had dated and about whom there was plenty to tell. We might have been sophomores again in Ann Arbor instead of two jaded lawyers on the wrong side of forty.

"The Alden case? You've drawn the Alden case?" He laughed his fraternity-boy laugh. "It's the perfect case for you—the Don Quixote of the legal profession, the defender of lost causes. Davey Alden. Wow!"

"I didn't ask for any assignments," I said peevishly, holding up the pink sheet that formally announced my selection by the Honorable Harold Olenik to defend one Davilon Alden against a charge of perjury. Maximum penalty: life.

"I'm out of criminal work," I added. "I've had it."

"It's not that easy, I'm afraid. No public defender in Laffler County, so we all have to share the burden." The *we* he was referring to consisted of a hundred lawyers in a county of just over 150,000 people.

"Even I have to take them," Scott continued. "They pay so poorly you may as well figure it's all pro bono. Olenik won't pay enough even to cover our overhead. Not to worry, though. It should be an easy in-and-out case."

With a sigh, I sat down across from Scott, who leaned back in his executive chair and studied my annoyance with a look of insincere sympathy. There he sat at his massive oak desk, master of his universe, surrounded by the badges of his success: the golf and tennis trophies, the framed photo of himself and the governor, certificates of appreciation from the Boy Scouts and Big Brothers/Big Sisters, a glamour photo of his new wife, Kitty.

Once again, as he had in our college days, Scott Sherman was about to fill Jack Brenner in on the facts of life. The more things change, the more they stay the same.

Judging from his smirk, I knew I was about to hear about the Davey Alden case in delicious detail. Like any small town lawyer worth his legal pad, Scott knew almost everything there was to know about anybody who counted in Laffler County. No meaningful gossip escaped him. His main intelligence source was Gordy's Donut Shop on Church Street, where the 6:00 A.M. gossip was as thick as the frosting on Gordy's crullers. If you wanted to know what was going on in Laffler County, you went to Gordy's and listened to the plumbers, masonry contractors, and siding salesmen—forget about the Chamber of Commerce types.

"Now, Davey Alden, that's a gorgeous piece of work," Scott began, his face aglow with his image of her. "You're lucky she's in jail. You'll be able to concentrate on the shape of your case, if you know what I mean."

Knowing what Scott meant when it came to women was not hard to figure. It was his favorite topic, and he was clearly enjoying the interruption of a morning of tiresome paperwork. His desk was mounded high with files, mainly blue civil files. Like many lawyers who are good in court, Scott was not a paperwork man. Such lawyers are at their best in front of a jury, painting with a broad brush, and while their absorption of facts in preparation for trial can be amazing, they rarely are outstanding at detail work such as drafting pleadings, contracts, or even letters.

Wisely, Scott, recognizing his shortcomings, had hired an outstanding desk attorney—Ralph Miles, crackerjack researcher, meticulous drafter of documents, and proofreader par excellence. It was a shrewd move. Ralph might leave someday, but he would take few clients with him. Ralph preferred paperwork to people. Scott's specialty was people.

"Seriously, Jack Boy, you've got a tough one. The whole damned town was split when she claimed her husband sexually abused their little daughter. Joel Alden is a big man, not only in this community but everywhere in the state—even in Washington. Millionaires who spread their money around have a lot of chits to call in. You don't fuck with a guy like Joel Alden."

"What's he do? What business?"

"Owns a big construction firm—highways, public buildings, you name it. Does work all over the nation, and he knows how to grease the skids."

"Sounds like the trial was a major screw-up."

"Our esteemed prosecutor, Brad Holtzman, brought the sex case against Joel to trial—only to have it blow up in his face. Jesus!" He shook his head in joyous wonder. Having been the prosecutor himself a while back, Scott was convinced that lesser lights had followed him, and he loved to see his prejudices justified.

"Right in the middle of the trial, Joel's attorney, Syd Masters, gets her to admit that she's lying—that she'd just perjured herself on the witness stand. Not only that, but she'd done it to get rid of Joel so she could be with her lover and get custody of the kid too. It turns out she had been screwing some dentist from Southfield. Like the headline said, the son of a bitch was filling the wrong cavity."

"You think that was her motive?"

"I'm not sure she admitted that—but it was pretty obvious. They subpoenaed the dentist and had him sitting in the front row during cross. He was ready to spill his guts. She had no choice."

"Olenik has the divorce case?"

"Olenik has the divorce. Either he or Frank will get your perjury case when it gets to Circuit Court."

"Frank" was Circuit Judge Francis X. Kane. Since arriving in Kirtley I'd appeared in court only a few times, usually to fill in for Scott when he had a scheduling conflict, but I had picked up a few essentials about the two Circuit judges. Olenik was the schoolmaster: scholarly, kindly to litigants, courteous but demanding of lawyers. Kane was the politician: always a finger in the wind, booming with hearty laughter, eager to let you know that he'd been a *very* successful trial attorney before taking the bench.

I stood up. "How come it's so much fun talking to you?"

"No problem, glad to oblige. Just remember, with Davey Alden you're going to have to keep your pecker in your pocket."

I had to ask. "You just might be speaking from experience, old cock?"

Scott threw up his hands in mock protest. "Not me. Just heard a lot of rumors—and maybe recalled a fantasy or two from when Joel used to bring Davey to the club. You should have seen her in a tight little cocktail dress. Whooee!" The wistfulness in his voice convinced me he was telling the truth. Besides, Scott was not bashful about kissing and telling.

As I left, the phone buried under the files and other debris on Scott's desk began ringing. Kitty, his third wife, was calling to make certain he was coming home for lunch. Kitty knew the dangers of the unstructured lunch hour; she had been his secretary once.

When I closed the door, he was cooing to her like a newlywed.

In the library I pulled volume four of *Gillespie's Michigan Criminal Law and Procedure* off the shelf. It looked as if it had never been opened—a real possibility, since Scott did little criminal work these days. I sat at one end of the long conference table and waved a greeting to Ralph Miles at the other end. Ralph sat behind a stack of documents and several open volumes on contract forms. He returned my smile tentatively. Everything that Ralph did was tentative—except when he was talking or writing about the law.

Gillespie taught me little I did not know already. Perjury was the same whether the liar was in Michigan or Illinois, but the Michigan statute had a nifty twist: if the perjurer has testified falsely in a case in which the defendant could have received life in prison, the perjurer also faces up to life; otherwise fifteen years. Davey Alden could get life.

Perjury prosecutions are rare. Lying is nothing new in the courtroom; only the worst and most convictable perjurers are indicted. Davey Alden had made the mistake of embarrassing the wrong people.

Plus ça change . . . I thought I'd gotten out of criminal law. After seventeen years, I was ready to make the transition to Brooks Brothers suits, button-down collars, and wingtips. I'd left Chicago and criminal law behind. And now, lo and behold, I had the Davey Alden case.

More than three months ago I had left Chicago for good, bitter with the taste of personal and professional disillusionment. My marriage was over, and I'd had my fill of lying criminals with no money.

Not that I was thinking of leaving the law. Sheila might discard our marriage the way she did last year's tax guides—within six months of our divorce, she met and married someone else—but no such tidiness was possible for me. The language and logic of the law, its rhythms and reflexes, were so interwoven with the fabric of my being that there was no separating us now. I would presumably get over Sheila. Not so the law.

Two decades ago, as a student at the University of Michigan, I had been taught that the law is a jealous mistress, that only if she is courted assiduously will she deign to grant her favors. And so it had proven. Over the years I had worked hard, and I grew in experience and skill and sagacity. But in the end I'd learned what generations of lawyers before me had learned, and what those young innocents poring over dusty tomes in law-school libraries today would learn soon enough—the law is no lady.

Determined to eschew filthy lucre and make my mark as a protector of the poor (this was pre-Reagan, of course), I went right from law school to Chicago as a public defender. I would be the voice of the oppressed, the helping hand for those victims we called defendants, the advocate who would make the courtroom echo with the thunderclap of justice.

Alas, my clients proved to be more sinning than sinned against, and rarely anything other than victims of their own greed, lust, and malice. For most of them—murderers, rapists, drug dealers, armed robbers—a lawyer who served justice would be working against them, not on their behalf. What they did have going for them from my point of view was their poverty, and that was enough to keep me in their thrall. A vigorous defense for even the most repulsive of my clients guaranteed justice for all of us, I told myself.

It was enough to keep me going for years, but in the end I burned out. People, not ideals, provide grist for the mill of everyday life, and there was nothing to love in the people I defended. For a long time I consoled myself with the thought that at least I had Sheila, but that turned out to be the biggest illusion of all.

So I honed my skills and gave it my best, no matter what I thought of my clientele, and gradually I was able to think of them hardly at all. I took satisfaction in my victories and lost no sleep over my losses. I was a professional, and like that paradigm of professionalism, the whore, I did not get personally involved.

By the time I left Chicago, my innocence was long gone—lost little by little in the whispered offers conveyed in the corridors outside the courtroom, in the sordid deals struck in the magistrate's chambers under his approving eye, in the endless dissembling in front of judges and juries. I did not lament my loss of innocence. It made me a free man. My ideals had been my chains.

And so I came to Kirtley. Scott Sherman matched my salary and promised a full partnership if things worked out. We'd been fraternity brothers at Michigan, and he had settled in Kirtley, largely, I always suspected, so that he could be near Ann Arbor and the bittersweet memories of coming of age. Scott was the perpetual undergraduate, undaunted in his quest for eternal boyhood, although at forty-two he was balding fast, and the sun-hastened lines in his tanned face were increasingly challenging the grin that held back the years.

Scott wanted to transform me into a civil lawyer—attending all-day depositions, drafting wills and contracts, doing up corporate minutes. Laffler County was growing—*exploding* was the word the newspapers used—and Scott was convinced that a smart local law firm could lop off its share of the new business coming in, instead of watching out-of-county attorneys move in to follow their clients, as was so often the case in growing areas. He had plans, big plans.

Civil law, that's where the money was, the real money, day in and day out. Bill it out at two hundred dollars an hour, and a check was on your desk the first of the next month. It was good, clean business money, the cost of doing business. Unlike divorce or criminal law, the lawyer's fee rarely compounded the tragedy. And if my heart was bonded to the courtroom, there was plenty of that kind of work for me; in fact, my thousands of hours of trial work would be a real asset. I'd have to tone down the irreverence that had become my trademark. A few more haircuts and shoeshines, a couple of dark suits, some white shirts and regimental ties, and I would be in business.

The rich had the right to good lawyers too, Scott reminded me. He needn't have. I was ready to be seduced. With a little help from him, I was ready to burst forth from the cocoon of soured idealism and emerge as a master of the billable hour and the bottom line.

Like the building that housed him, Prosecutor Brad Holtzman was modern, functional, and friendly. His smile as he came around the desk to greet me later that morning displayed the perfect teeth of our generation, his and mine, the people who grew up in the sixties and seventies. He wore a charcoal gray suit and a white shirt with a red flowered tie of the type that was fashionable that year.

Holtzman's office was in the Justice Building, located in the county government complex on the western edge of town. Adjacent to the county jail, it was a new three-story structure that housed all of the county's courts and most of the county's other offices as well. Only two years old, the building was already too small for one of the fastest-growing counties in the nation. Laffler County's claim to that distinction had its roots in the crime rate in Detroit: everybody wanted out of the big city.

Holtzman's smile was well grooved, and the hand that grasped mine had a politician's firmness. A handshake was not enough; he also gripped my arm with his free hand to show that he was giving his all. Only the eyes behind the plastic frames held back; they were wary and appraising. I was surprised that he was not wearing contact lenses.

"Jack, I've been looking forward to this," he said, guiding me to a chair in front of his neat, polished desk. "I understand that you've had a lot of experience in criminal law. Chicago, wasn't it?"

"You've done your homework. Cook County Defenders Office for seventeen years. Too long."

"I'm told they called you Jack the Ripper in Chicago—for your forensic skills, of course." He gave a short bark of a laugh.

"Scott talks too much. I drew a messy murder case and the reporter for the *Sun-Times* wanted to dress the story up a bit. He got carried away. The name kind of stuck."

"Did you get your client off?"

"The jury came back with manslaughter. I guess that was something of a victory."

"Ah, the wisdom of our jurors. God bless and keep them." He shook his head slowly as he contemplated the labyrinthine mind of his typical juror. Then he switched channels and leaned forward to share a confidence with me.

"Jack, I know you've had a lot of experience. You're an old pro and all that, but you are new here. You may find the practice of law different here. For one thing, you deal with the same people all the time, and you have to be able to count on a man's word—strike that, a man's or a woman's word. It's not like the way the defense boys in Detroit or Chicago practice law."

"That's strange," I said. "My experience is that it's the prosecutors who have to be watched. Too much second-guessing from higher-ups. Too many political decisions."

Holtzman dropped his head and stared at me. "Jack, I've heard other things. Some of them unpleasant. An investigation into suborning perjury—you don't have to explain, I know you were cleared. Things like that can taint a man—unfairly, I agree, but that's life."

"Strange, I don't feel tainted," I replied cheerily. "I feel clean and pure. It was a bullshit charge by a crud criminal encouraged by a snake of a prosecutor."

Pleased with himself, the prosecutor leaned back again and smiled at me. I responded in kind, and we sat there grinning at each other like two Cheshire cats. I was beginning to suspect that neither of us would break that pose before quitting time when Holtzman finally said, "You're really here to talk about the Davey Alden case. What are you looking for, Jack? You will find me very reasonable. I'm ready to forgive and forget."

"You'll drop the charges?"

"Ha-ha. I'm glad to see you have a sense of humor. No—no chance of a dismissal. Your client has given the whole system a black eye. A lot of people believed in her, and she screwed them royally. But I'm not being vindictive. I just want to make certain that justice is done."

"Which would be what?"

I noted the satisfaction in his eyes when I took the bait. When prosecutors start talking about doing justice, they are usually thinking about a plea bargain. What puzzled me was the eagerness in his expression as he framed a response.

"Plead on the nose and I'll recommend no more than ten years."

"That's not much of a deal. What judge would give a nice lady like that ten years?"

"Frank Kane would. It's a blind draw but I'm betting that Olenik will disqualify himself if he gets it because he's got the divorce and because he was the judge in Joel's case. Kane's a political animal if there ever was one, and his sentence is a wild card in a case like this. If he thinks there is any mileage in a harsh sentence, that's what he may very well hand out."

"But what if the wind is blowing the other way—our way?"

"Don't hold your breath waiting for a favorable wind. The *Detroit Times* thinks it's a hot story because it shows the other side of the coin—women who falsely accuse men of molesting children. Our weekly—the *Laffler Chronicle*—loves me and is eager to show what a bitch your client is. Kane knows all this."

"So much for justice in Laffler County."

Holtzman turned magnanimous. "It's not that bad, really. Frank Kane is actually a very good judge, and perhaps I exaggerate his political tendencies. But it's only fair that I warn you of the courthouse realities. Tell you what. I want to be more than reasonable. Plead her straight up and we'll recommend a five-year cap. An old hand like you should be able to persuade Kane to go under that. If he insists on more than five years, you can withdraw the plea and go to trial."

"It's a little early to be talking deal, Brad. I just met my client yesterday. It doesn't sound like you have much of a case. It—"

"Just read the transcript," Holtzman said impatiently. "We've got her cold under oath, admitting that she perjured herself." Then he smiled again. "Well, there's no rush, Jack. You've got to look over the terrain. I understand that. A good lawyer has to be careful and not rush into anything. Our offer will be good, let's say until the exam, but it's withdrawn if we have to hold the exam or go up to Circuit Court with no agreement."

It was my turn to smile indulgently. Every prosecutor I ever knew drew lines that no one took seriously. Besides, unless Brad Holtzman was plain stupid—which I did not for a moment believe—he was overeager to cut a deal, and that made me suspicious, especially in a case that everyone said was solid.

I stood up. "Got to be going. I thank you for the time, and I'll take your offer to my client. By the way, if we do go to trial, will you be trying the case yourself?"

"I'll try it if you decide to turn it into a three-ringer," Holtzman replied, not bothering to stand up to see me out. Although he made an effort to hide it, his disappointment was palpable. The politician's smile was still painted on his face, but it was forced, as if he were at the end of a long day of campaigning.

"I'm sure we can work something out," I said cheerily as I departed.

3

WE WENT TO LUNCH AT THE RIVERBEND COUNTRY CLUB IN Scott's new Lincoln Town Car. I sat up front with Scott, and Ralph Miles sat in the back. Scott was in a mellow mood. He had just received a hefty retainer from a Japanese auto parts supplier to nego- tiate the purchase and rezoning of a large parcel of land for the con- struction of a new factory. Today, instead of pretending the Lincoln was a sports car as he usually did, he drove like a father of four on a Sunday outing in the family station wagon.

"It's what I've been saying all along," he said as we turned down Golf Club Road. "Things are changing fast. The Japs are buying up America, guys, and there's a bundle to be made for people who are in the right place at the right time."

I was not focused on making bundles. I was brooding over the Davey Alden case. "I've been here three months. How come I haven't heard about the Joel Alden trial? Why so long to bring the charges?"

Scott arched an insider's eyebrow. "You don't read the local news- papers. Besides, you're new to Kirtley, and this is a touchy case. In a town like this, everybody is related to somebody down the street or around the corner. People don't open up to you yet, and, anyway, you live like a hermit on the lake."

"But Mrs. Alden wasn't charged for four months after Joel's trial. Why the wait?"

"Holtzman had to get the trial transcript typed up before he made his move. And he's gotten cautious. He's still wiping egg off his face. That little gal is like a hand grenade with the pin pulled out."

"What about the kid?"

"Oh, make no mistake. Joel's going after her—a girl three or four years old—and he'll get her. Right now she's with Davey's mother, but the only reason Joel doesn't have her already is that Harold Olenik doesn't want to kick the mother while she's down. Plenty of time for Joel to make his move after the trial."

"Holtzman's talking a deal. What can I expect, bottom line?"

"He says he doesn't deal, but when the chips are down he bargains like prosecutors everywhere—just like I did. But the Alden case I don't know about. He may just feel the need to show the world how tough he is on perjurers. Who knows?"

"I thought I was going to practice civil law," I said glumly. "Answer interrogatories, take deps, do up corporate minutes."

"Right on. We're going to get you cleaned up and in the boardroom yet. This Alden case is no big deal for someone like you. Frankly, you'd probably do well to plead her straight up and get it over."

"Ouch! That would hurt."

"I'd think about it, my lad. Davey Alden has pissed off everybody in this community. Holtzman wants her guillotined so that he can appease the country-club set and Joel's friends, not to mention FAIR—Fathers Against Interrupted Relationships—Jesus, isn't that precious?—which is making a cause célèbre of this case. And that's not all. If Kane is your judge, he just might nail the little lady, especially if he thinks it'll look good in the press, which gave a lot of coverage to Joel's trial. Quite a story."

Scott paused to smile benevolently at his old college chum. Having assured himself that I was absorbing the gruesome details, he went on, "The local women's groups won't help you because they went out on a limb for Davey the last time—and Davey sawed it off. You won't have any friends. A plea bargain with a sentence cap might be the merciful way out for your new client."

I found myself longing for the days when a three-martini lunch was not only deductible but still respectable.

In the Riverbend Country Club dining room, Laffler County's all-male elite, dressed in colorful golfing attire, strutted about like gaudy cock pheasants—slapping backs, trading jokes, sipping martinis, readying themselves for an afternoon on the links. Anyone left in the office on a Wednesday afternoon had to be at the bottom of the pecking order.

Our threesome stood out because of its drabness: we were suited up for business. Ralph did not play golf, I had temporarily given it up while I got my life straightened out, and Scott, having been club champion three times, was choosy about when and with whom he golfed. It was a mark of status to be invited to join a foursome with Scott Sherman.

Ralph and I were already studying our menus by the time Scott finished wending his way through the tables, bestowing and receiving recognition, embracing all with his ready smile and instant recall of names and faces. Many of the golfers were Scott's clients; he had a good start on his goal of improving his market share in the business law area. I saw him chatting with local doctors, a banker or two whom I recognized, and several businessmen. I also saw several lawyers watching Scott with envious eyes. So little threat were they to Scott that he could afford to show up on Wednesdays only occasionally, and then usually just for lunch.

"In case you're interested, that's Joel Alden over there by the wall," Scott said from behind his menu when he was finally seated. "The guy in the purple shirt, holding court at the round table."

Joel Alden was in his mid-fifties, a tall man who was conceding nothing to age: he was well muscled, with only the slightest hint of middle-age spread. I envisioned him lifting weights each morning before showering and dousing himself with Ralph Lauren's Chaps. He obviously paid a lot of attention to his thick, wavy hair, which he wore long and swept back over his ears, and which was combed and sprayed into rigid submission. He had the florid, rough face of the man who either drinks a lot or spends a lot of time outdoors in nasty weather, or both. By the way they attended to his every word, I judged the three younger men with him to be his employees.

When the young waitress arrived, Scott flirted with her outrageously enough to make her blush. We placed our orders and Scott watched her retreat with obvious longing. Shaking his head mournfully, he seemed about to comment on the unfairness of time when he flashed a smile and tossed a wave in the direction of Joel Alden, who had detached himself from his group and was headed our way.

"Scott, there's a matter I've been wanting to see you about for some time," Alden said when he reached our table. He ignored Ralph and me. "I'm working on an agreement to take over a cloverleaf on I-75 near Monroe. The son of a bitch that outbid me looks like he's going under, and they want me to step in and save their asses."

Scott looked both pleased and amused. "Sit down, Joel. Happy to help you out if I can," he said, shooting a sly glance at me. "By the way, Joel, have you met my new associate, Jack Brenner? Jack and I are old college buddies. I believe you already know Ralph Miles."

Alden remained standing. He nodded at Ralph and took my proffered hand. His grip was firm. "Good to meet you, Brenner," he said before turning his attention again to Scott.

"Jack has been appointed by the Circuit Court to handle your wife's case," Scott said. "That may make things awkward if you have to have something done right now."

Joel Alden's eyes met mine and evaluated me for a second or two before returning to Scott. What I saw there told me that he knew very well who I was, and had known before he started across the room. I saw other things in his eyes too—damaged pride, anger, impatience.

"Look, I don't know about this conflict-of-interest crap—with your firm representing my wife and all—but I need you to look into something for me," Alden said to Scott. "I can wait for a while, but not forever. I'm also talking to the State about repaving a stretch of 75 and an overpass bridge up near Saginaw. I may need some advice on that. Got any idea how long it may take to clear the decks on my wife's case?"

"You'll have to talk to Jack about that," Scott replied. "He's the man calling the shots there." Turning to me, Scott waited with a look of innocent interest. He enjoyed seeing me put on the spot. Alden turned to me also.

"That's going to depend on a lot of factors," I said carefully. "What kind of case they have against her, how reasonable the prosecutor will be, how reasonable my client is—a host of factors, and I've only just gotten into the case."

Alden looked irritated. "Any chance I could just hire you, Scott, and not your law firm—in other words, leave Jack out of the picture for the time being?"

Scott raised his eyebrows and hesitated only a fraction of a second. "We really couldn't do that, Joel. We'd have the Bar grievance people down our neck."

"Well, let me know," Alden said to Scott. "I'll wait for a while, I guess. But there will come a point when I'll have to move—and you're the man I want to handle it for me."

"Sure thing, Joel," Scott said. "Jack is an old hand and doesn't believe in spinning his wheels. Your wife is going to get top-notch representation, but Jack is a realist."

Alden glanced at me one last time before taking his leave. On the way back to his table, he stopped to chat at a table full of men who had the well-fed but still hungry look of bankers.

"Why do I have the feeling that he was trying to hire me, not you?" I asked when he was out of earshot. "And why the hell is everybody in such a rush to get this case over with?"

Scott's pleasure at my discomfort knew no bounds. "Easy now, big fellow. Nobody's rushing you, but it does seem to be a quick in-and-out deal." He turned to Ralph and added, "I'm not talking about Jack's sex life," and then continued, "And maybe we can end up with everybody happy."

I was irked. Scott was flirting with conflict of interest, betrayal, selling out—and it was all a big joke. That was the problem with him. He would be outrageous and then retreat under the cover of humor, leaving you feeling like a pompous ass for taking him seriously. Or maybe he was serious. Fortunately, the blushing waitress arrived with our lunch and the topic was put on hold.

Some people insist that their moods are not affected by the weather. I am not one of them. Beautiful days give me a high, and this one was a winner. My frustration with Scott evaporated in the warm August sun. Standing next to Scott's car and gazing out onto the course, I wished Scott and Ralph would take all afternoon to answer the question of the client who had buttonholed them back in the clubhouse. My reverie was interrupted by Joel Alden's voice behind me.

"I'm not a vindictive man, Brenner," he said as I turned. He was wearing his golf shoes and carrying his bag. "Believe it or not, I would take the lady back. I still care for her."

"I do find that hard to believe," I said. "After what she's done to you?"

Alden set his bag down and looked at me. He shook his head slowly and scowled. "You don't understand how it is, do you, Brenner?"

"How what is?"

"How a woman can get under your skin."

"No, I can't say that I do understand," I said. I lied.

I could almost reach out and touch his pain and anger. He wanted an explanation for all that had happened to him, for the destruction his wife had visited upon him. He thought that from my lips should come the answers that his wife owed him, the words that might make the pain bearable. He was wrong. I had nothing for him.

His lips curled in a smile that divided between self-pity and contempt for me. "You think about a woman like that day and night, and about how lucky you are. Then one day—"

He stopped suddenly, clearly uneasy. I was uneasy too. I did not owe him sympathy or understanding. I did owe loyalty to my client. He had endured much, but he would have to go elsewhere for comfort.

Alden shouldered his bag and said, "You tell the lady what I said. We can settle this. All she has to do is be reasonable."

"I'll tell her," I said, but I didn't know what I was supposed to tell her.

"One more thing," Joel said. "Davey tried to screw me royally, but I don't have it in me to destroy her if it can be avoided. I hope you're not going to make a three-ring circus out of this case. I wouldn't like to see you get hurt either."

"That sounds like a threat," I said with a flush of anger that was laced with relief. Anger was so much more manageable than pity.

"Don't try to steal my client!" Scott shouted from across the parking lot. He and Ralph were headed our way.

"Think about it, Brenner. Do what's best for her—and yourself." With that he gave a wave to Scott and strode off toward the first tee. His metal spikes made clicking sounds on the asphalt until he reached the grass. He did not look back.

It was not until we were halfway back to the office that I recalled that Brad Holtzman had also told me not to turn the Davey Alden case into a three-ring circus. The circus apparently was still a big event in Kirtley.

4

THAT NIGHT, AS I LAY OVER AND IN JUDY CUSMANO, MY FACE BURIED in that tempest of thick black hair, tasting the wetness of her brow at her hairline, as yet unable and unwilling to retreat, I had no questions and no curiosity. We clung to each other, deferring the return to earthly reality.

Finally, with a groan that she echoed, I left her and rolled over on my back next to her. Our hands sought each other. We did not speak for a long time.

Judy was so matter-of-fact about our lovemaking that sometimes I was tempted to break the postcoital quiet by cross-examining her about her detachment. Not that I would challenge her right to sexual satisfaction without emotional attachment. After all, she was a modern woman. And me? I was a representative post-sixties specimen of my gender: I was not about to look a gift horse in the mouth.

But something was missing, which was not to say that Judy was in any way deficient in technique or enthusiasm, for she was as passionate and skilled a sex partner as any man could ask for. Not only that, she was attractive, understanding, and undemanding. She was Everymale's dream come true. And yet it was not enough, and I sensed that she knew it too. Our unspoken knowledge perfumed our nights with a hauntingly sweet sadness, and sometimes, for me, something that felt depressingly like guilt.

I had met Judy in the Andan Tavern shortly after arriving in Kirtley. The Andan was a hangout for lawyers and county employees, including social workers like Judy. Bored and lonely, I had wandered in for the happy hour one Friday after work and joined a table of male lawyers who called me over to join them. By the time most of them had drifted off to wives or dates, I was already deep in conversation with two young women at the next table.

One of the two women was Judy, and we went to bed together that night. Judy had a simple and natural quality to her that I found soothing after Chicago and Sheila. She was intelligent without being complex, attractive without being beautiful, and carnal without being common. In the almost three months that we had been sleeping together from time to time, I never told her I loved her—partly because she never seemed to expect it, but mostly, I believe, because she would know that I was lying and would be disappointed in me. I cared for her, and that was enough. She did not demand any commitment beyond that, and in fact seemed not to want anything more. They were good months for me, and for her too, I believed.

The cool of the evening coming in through her apartment window caused me to reach over and pull a sheet over us. When I returned to my pillow, she snuggled close and lay on my shoulder. Often she went to sleep that way, and I would let her stay there until my arm went numb. Once I had even disengaged myself, slipped out of bed, and gone home without waking her. Tonight I was content to lie there holding her, smelling her hair and the faint muskiness of our coupling.

"They're talking about you," she said in her husky, quiet voice.

"What are *they* saying about me?"

"That no one really knows much about you except that you are supposed to be some hotshot lawyer from Chicago or New York or somewhere, that you better watch yourself or Davey Alden is going to eat you alive. Everybody's dying to know more about her—and you, now that you're a celebrity."

In the middle of this breathless recitation she could not resist giggling.

I turned my head and rooted in her hair until I could take her ear in my mouth. Then I proceeded to torture her with alternate nibbling and probing. Laughing, she rolled over until she was on top of me.

"You're confessing, then?" she said. "She's already got to you. You've got the hots for her."

"Confess? Not on your life, lady. I just met her. There's nothing to confess. I'm innocent. I plead not guilty."

"I'll torture you until you admit your guilt—until you tell me everything about her." She began to plant little wet kisses all over my face.

"Keep it up, keep it up. I'll never talk."

Suddenly serious, she raised her head. "You're not worried that she'll get you in trouble or anything?"

"Not unless vigorously defending a client is something you can get in trouble for."

"You wouldn't mess around with her, would you?" The question was so straightforward, so lacking in emotional overlay, so full of genuine concern, that I took her face in my hands and kissed her tenderly on the lips.

"No, I'm not about to mess around with Davey Alden. For one thing, I don't like her type."

"Oh yeah?"

"What does that mean?"

"You're kidding yourself if you believe that. She's exactly your type. Like a lot of men, you go for the helpless woman, and she's good at projecting that image."

"You don't have to worry about me."

"I do worry about you. For lots of reasons. Because you're so desperate to be good that sometimes you're naive. Because sometimes you're unhappy and you drink too much. But most of all because Davey Alden is a dangerous woman."

"Why do you say that?"

"It's hard to explain. She's beautiful and intelligent. I only met her a few times, but she struck me as very bright. It's strange that she would go after a man like Joel. They say he never had a chance once she started spinning her web."

"It sounds like a bunch of jealous women talking."

"That's true. Some of the older women resented her intruding onto their territory by grabbing off Joel. Many women her age were contemptuous because she chose to snare a sugar daddy instead of pursuing a career. But it was more than that."

"Like how?"

"It's strange. I've seen for myself the way she acts at social gatherings. One minute she's the shy little girl and then suddenly she's talking to some guy and being very seductive. Yet an hour later you might find her engaged in a conversation on some deep subject that you know she's given a lot of thought to."

"And you? What did you think about her?"

"I thought she was beautiful in a fragile kind of way—a porcelain doll that might break at any minute. I felt sorry for her."

"What happened when the charges against Joel came out?"

"We social-worker types talked about nothing but Davey Alden— Child Protective Services and Women Against Rape being involved and all—and generally there was a lot of support for her. She was believed. Then, when she admitted to perjury, the sympathy turned to outrage."

"What about you?"

"I couldn't really share the outrage. I know the child's therapist, Andrea Swanson. Andrea couldn't say anything, but hinted that things were not what they seemed. Andrea knew something, but she wouldn't say what."

"I still don't see how all this makes her dangerous."

She gave me a pitying look. "Are you saying you're incapable of being fooled?"

"I've been around the track a few times."

"Just watch yourself, mister."

Then she kissed me long and lingeringly on the lips. Astride me, her long hair covering my face, she made me forget about the Alden case and just about everything else on earth.

5

I WENT BACK TO THE JAIL THE NEXT DAY WITH A SENSE OF FRUSTRA-
tion and foreboding. I had not planned to see Davey Alden again
before the preliminary exam, but too many things were eluding me. I
felt as if I were in a large, empty house and could hear a voice calling
my name, but that each door I opened led only to more emptiness,
and then the voice calling again from another part of the house.

"I'm happy to see you again," Davey said when she was seated. The
sleeves on her coveralls were pulled up, and I noticed that she had
freckles on her arms. Her hands were long and pale and delicate. She
was stunningly beautiful, and I found myself wishing that she would
forget herself again and touch me the way she had the first time. She
did not look like a dangerous woman.

"I had some more questions before the exam. I need to get some
background and some more details."

I removed the transcript of the Joel Alden trial from my briefcase
and placed it on the table between us. It was not a large volume; the
trial had been short. If I expected her to flinch at the sight of this doc-
umentation of her guilt, I was wrong. She glanced at it without
curiosity. She just sat there waiting for me to speak.

I placed a legal pad in front of me and wrote her last name. Then I sat there staring at the paper. I did not know where to begin, because I did not know what I was looking for. So I began with the trivialities that are called vital statistics.

She was thirty-two, Joel was fifty-eight. Married ten years with one child, Julie, age four. They lived in a five-bedroom house behind the Riverbend Country Club, of which they were active members. Joel drove a Mercedes 560 SEL, she a Cadillac Allante. They spent three weeks every January in Aruba while her mother watched Julie. Davey's mother loved Joel; she loved Joel so much that she had not spoken to Davey since the accusations surfaced ten months ago. Julie was now staying in St. Clair Shores with Davey's mother, ever since Davey was arrested three days ago.

"I met Joel while I was waitressing at Riverbend during the summer between my junior and senior years at Michigan State. He asked me out and I went, and I guess he just took over my life . . . I never finished at State. Joel said he didn't want me to. He said he'd take care of me, and he did. He was good to me."

In her earnestness she seemed to be defending her husband, or perhaps herself. As we talked, I noticed how like a child she was in the way she ran through the whole range of emotions—one moment sad, the next happy; excited, then suddenly subdued; hopeful, then despairing. In an attractive woman like her, it was all very intriguing, making it difficult to concentrate.

Joel was a native of Kirtley. His father had founded Alden Construction in the thirties and had prospered by becoming an entrenched member of the Kirtley establishment, back in the days when Kirtley was the only town that mattered in Laffler County. As a civic-minded citizen, Joel's father had been the chairman of the county's first United Way drive, had helped found the First National Bank in Kirtley, of which he'd been the chairman of the board for ten years, and had been a charter member and first president of the Riverbend Country Club. The father had also been a member of the

Laffler County Board of Commissioners when the budget was less than a million (now it was $30 million).

Joel succeeded his father in virtually every one of his business, civic, and political positions, and, like his father before him, used his connections to ensure the continuing prosperity of Alden Construction. Government contracts, like the one to renovate the 1890 courthouse four years ago, helped keep the Alden Construction ledgers glowing with health. But where the father had been content to remain a local eminence, Joel had made Alden Construction a national presence, constructing highways in Texas and Arkansas, dams in Colorado and Arizona, and bridges in almost every state in the union. He moved with ease through the corridors of power, flattering and greasing, making timely campaign contributions here and there, helping out old friends, destroying rivals and enemies when he could.

I watched Davey closely as she told me about Joel and their relationship. The portrait she unwittingly sketched of herself was of a young college girl daring to be free, but in the end fleeing back into the den of parental security by marrying a man old enough to be her father. Yet I could not help noting the insight she showed when she described the Alden family's position within the local power structure. She was not merely parroting something Joel had told her; the analysis was her own. She was more than an ornament.

Judy was right. Davey Alden was a very bright woman who hid her intelligence behind a façade of seductive girlishness. Yet nothing about it seemed calculated. The way she furrowed her brow when she explained Joel's political connections made me think of a grade-school girl delivering a book report in front of the class. When she twirled a reddish lock of hair around a finger and pondered a question with wide eyes, she seemed totally oblivious of the effect it might have. I could not believe that it was all acting.

Davey had grown up as an only child in St. Clair Shores, an eastern suburb of Detroit, next to the Grosse Pointes. I gathered that hers had been a lonely, dreamy childhood in which her father had been her closest friend and confidant. Her mother was a pretty, passive woman from whom Davey inherited her finely sculpted features and ethereal nature. At Lakeview High School she had excelled academically but had not participated in social activities and had seldom dated. The plan had been for her to attend a local community college and live at home, but her grades and the family's meager finances had earned her a full scholarship at Michigan State.

Things had not gone well at State. She had few friends and little interest in her studies. Living in a dormitory, she gained thirty pounds, then lost that and a lot more in a wild swing of the pendulum. Eventually she settled in well enough to hang on to her scholarship. After her sophomore year she got a summer waitressing job at Riverbend and returned the next summer, even working there part-time during her senior year.

And then her father died of a heart attack in October of that year. By then she had already been dating Joel Alden, twenty-six years her senior. Before Christmas she dropped out of school to marry him.

Alden was different from the other men she met at Riverbend. As a waitress serving drinks, she had learned to tolerate the under-the-table grapplers (she was not the type to raise a fuss anyway), but when Joel was present, none of the Sansabelt crowd gave her any trouble, for Joel had developed a proprietary attitude toward her that no one challenged. He had a raw-faced, masculine roughness about him in dealing with other men, but toward her he was invariably polite, even courtly, and he made it clear that he could not only take care of himself but also of her, if she would allow it.

I watched her closely when she spoke about her husband. She talked dreamily that day, as if recounting the events of a life not her own, and when she described the days with Joel before they were married, she spoke of him with a fondness and respect that made her later accusations impossible to understand.

Nothing about this woman made any sense. My distaste for the heinous nature of her perjury clashed with the undeniable attraction I felt for her. I forced myself to look away from her face and down at my sparse notes. My confused feelings made me think of Judy's image of the spider's web.

"That's enough history for now, Mrs. Alden. The big question is why you lied—committed perjury—on the witness stand at your husband's trial. Why did you make up that story in the first place?"

She looked startled—like a child awakened suddenly from a nap. Her eyes widened and her lips parted. It seemed to take her a moment to comprehend my question. Before answering, she studied my face. She did not find what she was searching for.

"I didn't . . . I mean, I have to tell you . . ."

"Was it because of your lover?" Suddenly, unreasonably, I was angry at her. I had read the transcript of the aborted trial. She was a liar.

The cold print of a trial transcript rarely conveys the emotion or drama of the moment, but the small black letters on the white pages in this one did. One could feel the heart of this creature called a trial skip a beat, falter again, and then give one last shudder before dying. Davey Alden had invented a story that was intended to send her husband to prison for a long time.

"It's all right here in the transcript," I said, pointing to the volume of typed pages I had placed before her. I opened the transcript and turned it around so that she could read it. "Look at line fourteen on this page, and what comes after. Read the next few pages. That's what they'll use against you. Do you remember saying those things?"

She continued looking at me. "I don't need to read it," she said. Her eyes searched my face again, and when she finally spoke, her voice was almost a whisper.

"It wasn't true," she said. "I know what's written there, but it isn't true."

"You didn't say those things? Is that what you're telling me?"

"I said those things. But—"

"Mrs. Alden, before you change your story again, please remember you told me the day before yesterday that you did lie on the witness stand."

I never saw a woman look more lonely. She might be a compulsive liar, I thought, but she was not an accomplished one. She did not look as if she expected me to believe her. She sat with her hands clenched tightly in her lap. A lone tear journeyed down a cheek. I felt a sudden, irrational urge to reach out and capture that tear with a finger and to taste it—to know what was hidden in the heart of this strange woman.

When she finally spoke, her voice was without hope. She spoke quietly, but there were a thousand tears in her voice.

"Mr. Brenner, I love my daughter . . . beyond anything that you or anybody else could comprehend. What I did, I did for her. It was my only hope. Oh God, what I did was right . . . it must have been. You see, when that detective questioned me the night before the trial, and when Joel's lawyer cross-examined me, I got confused . . . he made me doubt that I was doing the right thing. I told him I'd made up the date, that I wasn't sure, that maybe . . . I just . . . I didn't know what to do . . . I made a mess of it, and I was afraid."

"You testified that you lied—that Joel Alden was innocent."

That word: *innocence*. Pontius Pilate might have been judged less harshly if he had asked, "What is innocence?" Even the law does not presume to find innocence, only guilt. But Davey Alden was a believer in innocence, for my use of that word seemed to strike a chord in her. She sat up in her chair and studied me for a moment, judging me, making a decision. I felt uneasy at what I sensed was coming, as if a rusty gate were swinging open into a darkened graveyard.

"My husband is not innocent, Mr. Brenner. Yes, I lied about what happened—about dates and times and even about what happened. But Joel Alden is not innocent. As God is my witness, he is not innocent. He is guilty. He did those things. Or he *will* do them."

I rubbed the palm of my hand across my brow. "What are you asking me to believe—that you lied and told the truth at the same time? What jury is going to believe that?"

"I'm telling the truth. You must know that."

"I know no such thing," I snapped. "You took an oath to tell the truth, but you lied under oath. Your husband could have gone to prison for life. That's why your possible penalty is life."

I was confused and exhausted by this apparition that kept disappearing and reappearing in different configurations. I knew with a terrible certainty what decision she had wrestled with a minute ago. Out of desperation she had decided to trust me and to hand over to me her innocence.

Every criminal lawyer's nightmare was happening to me. They are all guilty of something; that's why the system works so well. They may not be guilty of what they are precisely charged with, but they are guilty of something—and that is what plea bargains are for.

In the end I always broke them down, got them to tell me the "real truth." I gave them a speech about plea bargaining and how I would not allow them to take advantage of an offer if they continued to insist that they were not guilty. I watched with grim fascination as they struggled to choose between the need to hang on to their lies and the desire to save their skins. The skins always won.

"I need your help," Davey Alden said. "If I go to prison—if Joel gets custody of Julie—terrible things will happen to her. You've got to prevent that—for her, not for me. I don't deserve anything. I know that. But for her, please!"

"What kind of terrible things? What do you mean?"

I knew. I did not have to ask. I'd been down that dark corridor many times.

"Terrible things. Things that Joel has done—will do—to Julie. Sick things . . . he's sick . . . He touches them in the wrong places. It won't stop. It never does. It only gets worse."

"For God's sake, woman. What are you talking about? Will do . . . has done? Them? What are you saying?"

I think that if I ever came close to hating Davey Alden, it was at that moment. I did not want her case, much less the responsibility for her life. And that was what she was imposing on me—her very existence.

"You must under—"

"What about your dentist friend? The man you were shacking up with?"

"Terry? He didn't . . . ?" Her question died in her throat. I could see the throbbing in her long, elegant neck, and her eyes seemed so very blue, lighter than ever.

"It's all a matter of motivation. You were committing adultery, and you wanted not only to get rid of your husband but also to ensure that you got custody of the kid. That's what it looks like. That's the way the jury is going to see it. The prosecutor will make certain of that."

"It's not the way it was. Oh God, no. I know Joel's attorney tried to make it look that way, but no . . . Terry never . . . I only met Terry after they brought the charges against Joel, and he was never my lover."

"The truth this time?"

"Yes, so help me, God."

"Let's leave God out of it. Things are complicated enough already." If she was telling me the truth about when she'd met Terry Sinclair, and we could prove it at trial, it would kill the prosecutor's theory on why she had perjured herself. Not much, but it was something.

"You said something about a detective coming to the house the night before the trial. Who was he? What did he say?"

She brushed a wayward strand of hair away from her eyes and leaned forward. "It was a Detective Taggett. He was in charge of the case. He said he had received some information . . . that there was something out there that suggested I was not telling the truth, and could I explain it? He was talking about Terry Sinclair. I met Terry through one of our friends—Joel's and mine—who said that Terry had gone through a similar experience and might be able to help me."

"What kind of experience?"

"His two children had been molested by his ex-wife's boyfriend."

"That was it between the two of you? Nothing romantic?"

"Never."

"Joel's lawyer, Syd Masters, questioned you about being seen in a motel room with this guy. What was that all about?"

"I don't know. Well, yes, I did meet Terry one time in a motel. We had planned to meet, and he called me and asked if I would mind picking him up at a motel he was staying at. He invited me in. I stayed just a few minutes while he put his jacket on and used the bathroom."

"Who introduced you to this guy?"

"Jennifer Calkins. She used to work for Joel, but she got married and left, although she stayed in the area. She married a well-off guy, a friend of Joel's. We used to see them every Saturday night at the club. She's divorced now."

She sat back in her chair again and held her hands together as if she were praying. My questions, incredulous as they sounded, must have given her hope. I could see it in her face. She was reading too much into them, but that was to be expected from someone in the pit of despair.

"Mrs. Alden, did Joel ever sexually abuse Julie?"

"No . . . I mean yes, he did. Not all the way, but he fondles her and caresses her in a way that is not right."

"Let me be blunt, clinical. Has he ever penetrated her vagina or rectum for a sexual purpose? Anything like that?"

"No."

"Have you ever seen him touch those areas for a sexual purpose?"

"No . . . I mean, I couldn't prove . . ."

"Then how—"

"A mother knows such things."

"That's not good enough. There must be more. Suspicion is not enough."

"There was a letter. I saw a letter once."

"A letter from whom? What kind of letter?"

"I found a letter in Joel's desk in his den. It was from his daughter. Joel was married before. He divorced his wife twelve or thirteen years ago. They had a daughter—Melanie—who committed suicide when she was sixteen. The girl's letter accused Joel of sexually abusing her. It said he had molested her since she was a child. It was a bitter, hate-filled letter."

"Did you confront your husband?"

"I showed him the letter and he became very angry. He said Evelyn, his first wife, was a drunk and out of her mind. That the daughter was mentally unbalanced too. That Evelyn had poisoned the girl against him. I'd heard about Evelyn's drinking from Joel's friends."

"What happened to the letter?"

"Joel must have destroyed it. The police asked for it, but I couldn't find it again in his desk. They tried to question Evelyn, but she wouldn't cooperate."

"A missing letter doesn't prove anything. It's still nothing more than suspicion."

She went on as if afraid to stop. "One day I discovered some dirty pictures in an old suitcase of his. They were filthy pictures showing grown men and little children. I threw them in his face and he hit me. He told me that Julie was his and that I couldn't do anything about it. He said that if I said anything, nobody would believe me. He laughed at me. He said that if I caused trouble, he would throw me back out in the street where he found me—and he would have Julie all to himself."

"I suppose he destroyed those photographs?"

"I could never find them again."

"How long ago did this happen?"

"Last year sometime. About six months before I went to the police. I lived a nightmare for those months. I never let Julie out of my sight. I moved into her room. Joel laughed at me."

I shook my head. "And so you went to the police and provided them details of a crime that never happened. You made up those details—the dates, the times, all that?"

"Don't you see? It did happen—with his first daughter. And after I found him out, he made it clear in a thousand ways what was in store for Julie. He would hug and kiss her in front of me, and fondle her—nothing ever sexual—and all the while he was laughing at me. In some perverted way he was glad that it was out in the open. He got pleasure out of my fear, and he enjoyed making me grovel. I don't think he violated Julie sexually—I'm sure he hasn't—but he let me know that he was waiting for her to grow up some more, that he was patient, that he could wait for her to ripen like a piece of fruit."

She placed a hand on her chest, breathless from the effort of telling her story. Her eyes, dark now, shone with intensity. The flush I had noticed on her cheeks two days before had returned.

"Mrs. Alden, I have to ask you this. Did Joel have a normal sex life? Did you and he have normal sexual relations? I mean before all this came out."

She stared at me for a moment and then looked down at her hands in her lap. "I don't know what normal is. Joel demanded things of me that I could no longer give. I changed after Julie was born. He was disappointed in me. Don't you see? I was no longer his little girl."

"You never slept with him after you became suspicious?"

She did not answer immediately. Finally she looked up and met my gaze. When I saw what my questioning had wrought in her face, I was sorry I'd asked.

"I thought that if I went to his bed I might save Julie. I did what I had to do, what he'd always wanted and I'd always refused. And when it was over, he laughed at me again. He told me that it wasn't good enough."

I wish I could say that I was filled with outrage. Or that the reason I sat there unmoved was because I did not yet believe her. In fact I did believe her, or was starting to. Her story was so confused and implausible that it had the ring of truth to it. Her desperation was too real to be feigned. But I'd heard many tales of horror like hers. I'd spent my compassion in Chicago long ago. I no longer put much stock in compassion. It had become too professionalized. It paid too well.

"Holtzman wants to cut a deal," I said. "He's already offered a five-year cap."

"What does that mean?"

"That you plead guilty and you won't get more than five years in prison. The judge can give you less, but he can't give you more. Considering that the maximum is life, it's something you have to think about."

She paled at the mention of prison, but she met my gaze evenly. There was a hint of defiance in her face.

"Am I likely to go to prison?"

"I don't know. I think some time in the county jail is likely, and the state prison is a possibility. You won't get life, but you'll get some time. The case is too hot."

"If it means Joel gets custody of Julie, then it's out of the question. I don't want a plea bargain. And he will get custody if I go to jail or prison. Forget about a plea bargain."

I had no reply.

"Is your daughter safe at your mother's?" I asked.

"I think so. Yes, I'm certain she is. Joel is too clever to try anything now."

We talked for a while longer. I briefed her again on what to expect at the preliminary exam. I cautioned her that she must talk with no one, that the press might try to interview her without my knowing, that she must be careful what she said in jail because a confidante might be a plant. I tried my best not to sound too optimistic when we talked about getting the bond reduced.

Despite all my efforts, her eyes were filled with hope when we parted.

That night I took the transcript of Davey's testimony at the Joel Alden trial home and read it once more. Again I had the feeling that something was just beyond my reach—that voice calling in the empty house.

I opened the transcript and stepped into the darkness inside. It was not unfamiliar territory, for public defender work had acquainted me well with human depravity, but, old hand that I was, I was able to put normal feelings aside and read with a trained and dispassionate eye.

The way Holtzman had handled the prosecution of Joel Alden on two counts of first-degree criminal sexual conduct warned me that I must not underestimate the man: he knew his way around the courtroom. Reluctantly, deeply sensitive to the pain he must be causing the mother of the child victim, he'd forced Davey to tell the jury what she had observed—and tell them she did. In graphic detail she recounted how on two separate days she had seen Joel attempt to penetrate his four-year-old daughter, once on the marital bed and a second time in the bathtub. The details Davey used to tell her story added just the right texture. It was credible testimony, the kind that brings back guilty verdicts.

And then came the cross-examination.

Excerpt from transcript of trial in case of People of the State of Michigan versus Joel D. Alden in front of the Honorable Harold L. Olenik. Cross-examination by Mr. Masters of Davilon Alden.

Cross-examination by Mr. Masters

Q. I want to ask you about these terrible incidents, Mrs. Alden, but first I want to ask you something about your past. Do you understand me?

A. I think so. I guess so.

Q. Excellent. And you are going to tell me the truth?

A. Yes, of course.

Q. Good. That means we'll get along just fine.

MR. HOLTZMAN: Is there a question in there somewhere, Your Honor? I thought this was cross-examination.

COURT: *Do you have any questions, Mr. Masters?*
MR. MASTERS: *Yes, Your Honor. I just wanted to make sure that Mrs. Alden and I understood each other.*
COURT: *Well, please proceed.*

Q. *Mrs. Alden, do you know a man named Terry Sinclair?*
A. *Who? I don't . . . What does he have to do with this case?*
Q. *Just answer the question, Mrs. Alden. Did you have any trouble understanding my question?*
A. *No . . . I—*

COURT: *Mrs. Alden, you are going to have to speak up. The stenographer is having trouble hearing you. Please speak into the microphone, and keep your voice up.*

Q. *You did understand my question, did you not, Mrs. Alden?*
A. *Yes.*
Q. *Do you know a man named Terry Sinclair? Please speak up so the jury can hear your answer.*
A. *Yes. I know Terry.*
Q. *Speak up, Mrs. Alden. As a matter of fact, that's Terry Sinclair sitting right there in the front row, isn't it? Right there behind your husband? You do know who your husband is, don't you?*

MR. HOLTZMAN: *Your Honor, he is badgering the witness now. This is uncalled for. I've been very patient up to this point, but I must object to this harassment, this sarcasm. Mr. Masters knows better.*
MR. MASTERS: *I'm the one who's been patient, Judge. Mrs. Alden seems to have trouble telling the truth.*
COURT: *Mr. Masters, you know that vigorous cross-examination is allowed in a criminal case, but you are straining the bounds of the permissible. Get to the point and cut out the speechmaking and the irrelevant remarks.*
MR. MASTERS: *Yes, sir.*

Q. Do you recognize Dr. Terrence Sinclair sitting there behind your husband in the front row?

A. Yes. That's Terry Sinclair.

Q. The "Doctor" stands for "dentist," does it not?

A. Yes.

Q. What is your relationship with him? He's not your dentist, is he?

A. No. He's just a friend.

Q. Just a friend? A friend of both you and your husband, no doubt?

A. No. He was just my friend.

Q. You mean that you socialized with Dr. Sinclair without your husband being present? Just the two of you?

MR. HOLTZMAN: I don't know where all this is going, Your Honor. I object to all this as irrelevant. What's this got to do with the trial of this case?

MR. MASTERS: It has everything to do with this case. If Mr. Holtzman will be patient, its relevance will become abundantly clear. I'd ask that counsel not interrupt me. He's trying to give the witness time to think.

COURT: With your promise to tie all this up, I will let you proceed.

Q. My question was whether you socialized with Terry Sinclair alone— without your husband being present. Just the two of you.

A. Occasionally, yes.

Q. Occasionally. What did those occasions consist of? Dinner? A show?

A. Usually we went to dinner

Q. How about to a motel?

A. No. Never. We never did.

Q. Are you certain about that?

A. Absolutely. We were just friends.

Q. Do you remember that you went out with Terry Sinclair last June first? That the two of you had dinner at a Holiday Inn?

A. I—I don't know. I may have. No, I didn't know him then.

Q. Let me help you with your memory, Mrs. Alden. This is a copy of a motel registration slip—the Holiday Inn in Farmington—and it shows that a Mr.

and Mrs. Terrence Sinclair registered there last June first. Would you happen to be the Mrs. Sinclair referred to on that occasion?

A. No—I don't think so. I mean, I never—

Q. Mrs. Sinclair—I mean, Mrs. Alden—please think carefully. You are under oath. Terry Sinclair is here to testify that you and he registered and stayed there not only that night but on many other occasions—

MR. HOLTZMAN: I must object to these tactics, Your Honor.

COURT: Objection overruled.

Q. Not only will Terry Sinclair say that you and he spent many a night at that motel, Mrs. Alden, but so will the young woman who worked the night desk and remembers you very well. Do you want to change your testimony?

A. No. Yes—I mean, I did spend the night there with Terry. No, I didn't. It's a lie. Never—

Q. Terry Sinclair was your lover, wasn't he? You were committing adultery with Terry Sinclair.

A. That's not true.

Q. You had sexual intercourse with Terry Sinclair. Correct?

A. But we didn't, he was not—

Q. As a matter of fact, Terry Sinclair and you were longtime lovers and you wanted to marry him, didn't you?

A. Oh my God, that is not true. No . . . it's—

Q. You wanted to be with Terry Sinclair permanently, but your husband was standing in the way. You would have to give up the comfortable life—and that you could not do. Isn't that the truth of the matter?

A. No it's not. Terry and I . . . Julie was—

Q. Not only would you lose Joel's money, but you also feared that you'd lose custody of Julie. You realized that you had to get rid of Joel. That's the truth of the matter, isn't it, Mrs. Alden?

A. No . . . no . . . that isn't it at all—

Q. It isn't? Then let's hear the truth. What is the truth? Was your relationship with Terry Sinclair a one-night stand?
A. You don't understand. You're twisting things. I—I—
Q. I understand all too well, Mrs. Alden. Let's turn to these charges of sexual abuse by your husband, Joel. You fabricated those stories, didn't you?
A. No. That's not—
Q. You lied about those two incidents when you testified just a few minutes ago, didn't you?
A. I—
Q. Isn't it true that you never saw your husband sexually abuse his daughter Julie last March fourteenth or May third or on any other day?
A. It's not what you think. It's just that—
Q. Your testimony was all perjury, wasn't it?
A. Joel wanted to . . . he said . . . I had no way—
Q. Answer the question, Mrs. Alden. You made up those stories about Joel molesting his daughter, didn't you? Your stories are nothing but lies.
A. I had to get someone—
Q. Did you hear me, Mrs. Alden? You never saw Joel Alden sexually abuse his daughter, did you?
A. I don't . . . Oh God, it's true. I never saw it.
Q. You lied.
A. I lied.
Q. No further questions.

MR. HOLTZMAN: If it please the Court, I need a recess. I am caught by surprise, Your Honor.
MR. MASTERS: I am moving for a dismissal.
COURT: I'll have the jury go to the jury room. Do not discuss the case, ladies and gentlemen.

Davey Alden was guilty of perjury. Of that there could be no doubt. My job should be simple. Squeeze the best possible deal out of

Holtzman and get my client to take it. They all said no at first; they all said they were innocent. In the end, of course, they all took a deal. It made sense.

But nothing made sense in this case. Davey was both guilty and not guilty. She was a perjurer, but she told the truth. Irrationally, I not only believed her, but I believed *in* her. I could no more hand her over to Holtzman than I could deliver her daughter Julie to Joel Alden. I sat looking at the last page of the transcript for a long time. There would be no plea bargain.

6

THE NEXT DAY I SPENT ON THE PHONE, WORKING SCOTT'S CIVIL files. I persuaded a claims manager for a hard-nosed insurance company to pay big to get out of a case in which a customer fell into an uncovered septic tank outside a bar. I smooth talked an inexperienced lawyer into settling a slip-and-fall for thousands less than it was worth. In another case I threatened to run the other lawyer ragged with motions and depositions; he was not impressed.

When I'd had enough, I decided to go home to start the weekend early. It was a warm, sunny day and I could see no reason why the cocktail hour could not start at four o'clock instead of the traditional five.

I turned left at Main Four Corners under the Kirtley National Bank clock and headed east down Monroe Avenue. The large brick homes, shaded by massive oaks and maples, reminded me of some of the old Chicago suburbs like Barrington. Many of the houses dated back to before the turn of the century, some to before the Civil War. These same homes showed up in old photographs on display in Kirtley's downtown shops and restaurants. Links to the past were important these days. Stained, faded photographs of old houses and great-grandparents were hanging everywhere in stores and restaurants downtown—unless, of course, the ancestral photos showed folks too obviously just off the boat.

Kirtley and environs were holdouts against the press of suburban sprawl. As the county seat, Kirtley managed to maintain its own starched-collar identity and had so far escaped the invasion of half-million-dollar homes that were popping up everywhere in the eastern part of the county. Thirty years ago the typical Laffler County citizen owned a pickup and a small asbestos-sided ranch. Now, at least in the eastern part of the county, it was a toss-up between Saabs and BMWs, and new homes under a quarter-million were hard to find. Only staid old Kirtley held out against the advancing armies of modernity. It clung stubbornly to the illusion of history.

I drove toward the place I thought of as home these days: a cottage on Spring Lake, ten miles northeast of Kirtley, just off Old Plank Road. Spring Lake was too small a body of water to dignify with such a title, but I loved it because there were no motorboats allowed and no public access. In days gone by, the lake had been a summer retreat for Kirtley's business and professional people, in the time before air conditioning, before freeways made Michigan's fabled north country so accessible. Most of the cottages had now been winterized and sold off to retirees from Detroit and others with no need for space. Scott Sherman owned one of the cottages and had agreed to rent it to me for a nominal sum.

Maggie, my Labrador retriever, greeted me with an alarmed bark followed by an effusive, tail-wagging apology. Dogs are such politicians, and I, like voters everywhere, always fell for Maggie's fawning you're-the-one-who-counts welcome.

I let Maggie outside for her afternoon toilet and inspected the cottage for damage. Maggie was a year old and housebroken, but given to chewing up things to relieve her boredom. Exhibit One was the striped couch facing the picture window that looked out over the lake—the couch with the stuffing torn out of one of the arms.

Satisfied that the household furnishings had suffered no new abuse, I tossed my briefcase onto the couch and began mixing a martini, not too dry, on the rocks with three olives. I dropped the olives into my glass with a flourish and peeked out the kitchen window at the cottage next door, where Mother Superior lived. Her red Ford pickup was not there yet. Had she been home, I would have prepared a very dry martini in a frosted long-stemmed glass with Plymouth gin, straight up with a twist of lemon, and awaited her arrival.

Mother Superior was Dr. Ann Mahoney—physician, spinster, missionary, lover of good gin, bass fisherwoman, and the villain who undermined my feeble efforts at pounding some learning into Maggie. The nickname I had bestowed on her was a reference to the years she had spent doctoring with Catholic missionaries in Africa and Latin America. She had nothing in common with the starched stereotypes of convent superiors so popular in the Bing Crosby movies. My Mother Superior was loud, crude, irreverent to the point of being blasphemous, and an absolute delight to be with if you were not easily embarrassed.

Most impressive, however, was her ability to knock down two martinis and regularly deflate my alcohol-inspired arguments on life, love, God, and, sad to say, even the law. Worse, she did the same thing when we were drinking lemonade. My only hope was to outlive her. She was seventy, I was forty-two.

We had nothing in common, as I frequently reminded myself, and yet within weeks of my moving in, we were close friends, despite my suspicion that we were locked in an unacknowledged battle for my soul, the existence of which I doubted and the possession of which her God coveted. So far, neither side had budged in our metaphysical tug-of-war.

I let Maggie back in and changed into jeans and a blue sweatshirt with a maize M on it. Then I took my drink and sat on the couch. Maggie jumped onto the couch and laid her head on my lap. When I stroked her head, she sighed contentedly. Sipping my martini, I watched the late-afternoon sun shimmer on the lake. My thoughts, as they always did at such times, returned to Sheila and our marriage. At first, in the months after I finally admitted that it really was over, the regrets had swarmed like angry wasps, their attacks painful and crippling. With the passage of time I had gained a measure of control, and it was a mark of my progress that I could schedule my periods of self-pity during nonbusiness hours.

"Why do you have to analyze everything to death?" Sheila had asked on one of our last evenings together. "It's over. It happens to millions of people every year. Just let it go."

Sheila was an accountant and took comfort in statistics. Years before, she'd explained how CPAs allow for a margin of error of two percent or so, which in a giant corporation might mean giving or taking twenty million dollars. I remember joking about how useful lawyers find experts who can kiss off a few million dollars. I had no premonition that one day I would be one of the millions lost in Sheila's margin of error.

The crunch of tires on gravel interrupted my postmortem. Ann was home from one of her missions of mercy to the big city. She was semiretired, which meant that a day or two a week she saw patients at a hospice in Detroit. More than once I'd accused her of racism. White people needed medical care too.

"I don't care about color, you lizard," she had replied one evening, savoring my parry over her frosted glass. "I go to Detroit's inner city because I prefer the company of prostitutes, pimps, addicts, and felons. When you live next door to a lawyer, you learn to be choosy about your company."

Hearing Ann's pickup, Maggie jumped off the couch and ran to the door wagging her thick otterlike tail. I got up and plucked a frosted glass from the refrigerator. By the time Ann and Maggie had completed their ritual greeting, I was sloshing gin onto ice cubes in a pitcher. After I had tossed a lemon twist into her glass and poured a martini, I handed Ann the glass and we sat down at opposite ends of the couch and looked out over the lake. Maggie jumped up between us and put her head on Ann's lap.

"This is my one regret in this wasted life of mine," Ann said, petting Maggie as she took an appreciative sip of her drink. She was a nondescript woman with short gray hair; her attire rarely varied from what she wore today: green hospital scrubs and practical brown shoes. Her idea of dressing up was to put on an acrylic jogging suit. I doubted that she owned a dress. Her plebeian face was leathery and lined from too many years in the sun. In a hospital she could easily have been mistaken for an orderly or a janitor. I had once called her "frumpy, dumpy, and grumpy."

Ann Mahoney might look like a scrubwoman, but she was a first-rate physician—as I had learned one day when she stitched up a bad gash in my hand after I broke a window I had been trying to wash.

"Regret?" I said. "You have regrets? You mean not having a dog?"

"That's it. Dogs are content to be dogs. They never aspire to be human. They accept their creaturehood. Unlike humans, who insist on being gods."

"Doc, you're too metaphysical for me today. She's just a stupid dog, and a poor specimen at that. And she's perfectly capable of deceit, infidelity—look at her now—and sloth. She's a tramp."

Ann laughed and stroked the dog's adoring face with a gentle finger.

"What's the problem?" I asked. "Bad day in the big city?"

Ann's years rarely showed, but today you could count every one of them. Her energy level was usually so high that I was always surprised to be reminded of her age. It made me feel vulnerable.

"What is it about our society that breeds such meanness?"

She looked expectantly at me. She had a habit of doing that, as if we were coconspirators. Her dark eyes frequently glinted with amusement at some secret joke that apparently only she and I shared. In fact, I had no idea what she was thinking about, and at times I resented her unspoken assumption, whatever it was. She was a gallant lady, and I loved her dearly, but we started from different premises, she and I, and never the twain would meet.

"Everybody's mean these days," I said. "Especially if they're dying."

Her weariness and discouragement today were unusual. They were poisoning the pleasant languor of the lakeside cocktail hour.

"I'm not talking about hospice patients. I'm talking about the so-called living. So much hate, so much violence, especially among the urban young. It's different, Jack. Different from what I saw here forty years ago. The violence is so gratuitous and so vicious."

"Ah, a failure of love, no doubt."

"Exactly." She missed my sarcasm—or chose to treat it as beneath notice.

"Love—a four-letter word," I added.

"Don't sneer. Someday, Jack, you will have a chance to love, really love, and it will be the beginning of life for you."

I thought of Sheila. I changed the subject.

"Did I tell you that I've got the Davey Alden case?"

"That poor woman."

"Just my kind of case. Greed, perjury, adultery, perversion—all failures of love."

"Now you're beginning to understand," she replied, with an uncharacteristic lack of conviction. Her discouragement today was disquieting. On any other day she would have eviscerated me by now.

"You're hopeless," I said. "Tell me about child molesters. All they need is love?"

"God only knows what makes such men do the things they do, but, yes, in the end, it too comes down to an inability to love. Other people are only objects."

"With all due respect, Doctor, that's nothing but psychospiritual horseshit—something we seem to have an abundance of these days. You ought to write a book."

"Bad day yourself?"

"You've got it, sister. Let's drink to a better day tomorrow, and the day after that."

"And the next day too, and the one after that."

We held our half-empty glasses up toward the lake and toasted the better tomorrows. As evening approached, various insect hatches started the fish feeding, and for a long time we watched the rippling circles in silence.

"Ready for another one?" I asked at length, holding up my empty glass.

"Not today. I'm having dinner with some old friends in Ann Arbor."

"Bring me back a doggie bag—for me, not for that useless lump. I've got to rustle up my own grub tonight, and if my cooking is as bad as usual, she'll end up getting it all. I'll need sustenance."

After giving Maggie a final hug, Ann headed out the door and up the hill toward her cottage. The spring was back in her step, and before she went inside, she waved goodbye to Maggie and me. Maggie finally turned away from the door and, without so much as a glance at me, threw herself into a shameless heap in the corner. With a sigh, I began mixing another martini. At least I had cheered the good doctor up. Always a helping hand, that was me.

On the way to the office on Monday morning, I passed the Laffler Chronicle Building on Granite Street. On an impulse I made a U-turn and pulled into the parking lot. In the lobby of the county's only newspaper, I was greeted by a massive blond woman who looked as if she would welcome a diversion. From a sign on the counter I gathered that her job was to take want ads, answer questions about papers that didn't get delivered, and deal with pests like me.

"Do you have a morgue here?" I asked.

"Wrong building. You want the county building over on Lightly Drive." She gave me a conspiratorial wink before returning to her paperwork.

"I'm sorry. I mean a newspaper morgue." I didn't know whether to be embarrassed or amused. My big city press jargon was not impressing her.

"We haven't got a morgue here," she replied, struggling to suppress laughter. Her jowls trembled with the effort. Finally the shaking stopped, her tiny red lips parted, and she half shrieked, "The only stiffs we have here are those who don't pay their bills." Then she erupted into melodious peals of laughter that ended only when she stopped to dab at her eyes with a Kleenex.

"I mean a place where you keep newspaper clippings or back copies of your paper," I said. "Where I come from, we call that a morgue."

"Not here we don't. What back copies you interested in?" She continued to dab at her eyes, and the continued trembling of her chins made me fear another explosion. Finally she seemed to gain control.

I told her what I wanted, and she turned out to be helpful and efficient. She even forgave me for not laughing at her joke. Before long I was seated at a table and studying *Chronicle* issues for the last ten months. I had never visited the land of the weekly newspaper before. I found dull coverage of school board and city council meetings, duller write-ups of an ongoing landfill controversy, and, dullest of all, reporting on the nice things that happened to people in the community.

The reporting on the court system provided the only spark of interest for me, and even that was tainted by bad writing and a blissful ignorance of how the courts operate. But apparently the *Chronicle* had hired a new reporter just before the trial of Joel Alden, for about then there was a marked improvement in the writing and the accuracy of the coverage. Also, the timidity that I detected about reporting Davey Alden's accusations disappeared and the stories took on a punchy, let-the-chips-fall-where-they-may quality. The new reporter was named Larry Semczyk, and he walked in the door while I was reading his account of Joel Alden's trial.

"Larry, here's a man that wants to know about the Alden trial," said my blond friend behind the counter. I turned to meet the reporter, and my gaze quickly skipped over a very thin young man with thick glasses, whose stoop-shouldered diffidence belied the possibility that he might be the author of the tough articles I'd just been reading. But he was the only other person in the lobby and there was a reporter's steno pad in one bony hand. It was he.

Larry Semczyk turned out to be the most painfully shy person I'd ever met; he seemed absolutely incapable of looking me in the eye. He also was intelligent, knowledgeable about the legal system, and courageous in handling his crippling shyness. Soon we were seated in a booth in the coffee shop next door, where I discovered that so long as he was talking shop, Larry, if not loquacious, was at least not tongue-tied. I played no games with him, and in return he was open with me, sharing with me his file of clippings from the *Detroit Journal*, the *Detroit Times*, the *Lansing State Journal*, and the *Ann Arbor News*.

The Alden case had received regular but not in-depth coverage in the big city dailies until Davey Alden broke down on the witness stand. Before then the slant was best summed up in this *Detroit Journal* headline: LAFFLER "PILLAR" CHARGED IN CHILD SEX ABUSE CASE. All of the papers carried the story on the first or third pages for the first day or so, then relegated it to an inside spot until the trial.

When Davey Alden admitted lying, the press and the ax-grinders went wild. "The Alden case is a tragic example of the shortcomings of the legal system in dealing with the very real problem of child sexual abuse in our society," intoned the *Ann Arbor News* in an editorial. LAFFLER LEADER CLEARED, WIFE ADMITS LYING, headlined the *Times*. Fathers Against Interrupted Relationships called for new legislation in Lansing to require corroboration in all sex-abuse cases. A feminist professor in Ann Arbor was quoted as saying that wives were justified in using any means necessary in freeing themselves from the yoke of male oppression. After a week or so the story disappeared, but Davey's arrest for perjury several months later gave it new life.

"I think the *Times* is going to play it up so they can blunt criticism from the dads' groups that say women are getting preferential treatment in everything these days," Semczyk said.

"What's your impression of how Brad Holtzman is handling all this?" I asked.

"The prosecutor is eating crow these days. When he took on Joel Alden, he took on the establishment in Laffler County, and now he's eager to get himself back in the good graces of Alden and the other bigwigs in the community."

"He tells me that your paper supports him a thousand percent."

"That's our editorial policy."

"And you?"

"I'm just a reporter."

"And you?"

It was the first time I saw Larry Semczyk smile.

"Do I have to answer that question?"

"You can take the Fifth Amendment if you want—or maybe in your case it would be the First Amendment."

He looked at me quickly and then looked down again. "I think Brad Holtzman had no choice but to charge Joel Alden. In today's political climate he dared not disbelieve a woman like Davey Alden, but I think that, once committed, he relished the thought of knocking off a kingpin in the power structure. He was so dazzled that he forgot Mrs. Alden might be lying—and he forgot what Joel and his money might be able to accomplish through Sydney Masters, his attorney. Now those two have Holtzman sitting up and begging like a puppy dog."

"What do you mean—Joel's money?"

"Joel's money enabled him to hire a private detective to uncover his wife's relationship with another man. A typical criminal defendant couldn't do that. It makes you wonder."

"What do you know about her lover?"

"Not very much. He disappeared right after the trial. He was a dentist in Southfield. That much I know because I looked it up in the phone book. His office said he went on a vacation in Europe."

"Tell me about Masters."

"Very influential in Republican politics, and a very hard-nosed lawyer. The kind of guy other lawyers love to hate—but you never really know if that is because he's a skunk or merely because he's so successful. Lots of political connections in the county and in Lansing. He's especially influential in township politics in the county. He knows the right people."

"What about Davey Alden? What was your impression of her?"

Semczyk looked pained. "I believed her right up to the end. She was so . . . so beautiful, so credible . . . To this day I still don't believe that stuff about her and that dentist." He raised his head and looked me in the eye for the first time. "I suppose I'm not being very objective. A reporter should be more cynical about people."

"Did you ever get a chance to talk to her?" I asked gently.

"Once or twice I chatted with her in the hall. She seemed so fragile. It was as if she didn't belong in our world. My only consolation is that I don't think my faith in her colored the stories I did. I think I played it straight in what I wrote."

Having just read his coverage, I was able to reassure him that he had been objective. Then I added, "What if I told you that I believe Davey Alden is innocent? That she told the truth about Joel Alden? That I have faith in Davey Alden despite what happened at Joel's trial?"

"You're her lawyer."

"Not just as her lawyer. As a person."

Semczyk smiled into his coffee cup. "Then that makes two of us who are fools."

"Maybe. I intend to get her acquitted. No plea bargain, no deals."

"That's going to be tough. That would mean that the jury has to believe Joel is a child molester. How can—"

"No comment. Everything's off the record for the time being."

Semczyk nodded his agreement as he studied my face. I could see that he wanted to believe me. Davey Alden had left her mark on him too.

We talked for another twenty minutes about the politics of Laffler County and the preliminary examination scheduled for the next day. Some of what we talked about I had already learned from Scott and other sources, but Semczyk added a fresh perspective. He had been here only a few months longer than I. I was amazed by his grasp of detail and nuance. He put me to shame.

When I left, I promised to keep him posted on anything that I was free to divulge. Outside, as I struggled to find the right key to unlock the door of my beloved Volvo, I reminded myself of an old adage:

Never trust a reporter in search of a story or a lawyer in defense of a client.

7

ASSISTANT PROSECUTOR SANDRA MCCLELLAN HAD BEEN LAWYER-
ing too long. The eyes that greeted me the next morning were as
warm as a prison sentence. The many tight little crevices around her
mouth definitely were not smile lines.

Like most prosecutors who stay with it a while, she was no longer
capable of real outrage. That's reserved for new prosecutors, the
youngsters who wear their self-righteousness like shiny breastplates.
Old prosecutors only simulate outrage, and then only in front of a
jury. Their workaday demeanor outside the courtroom is usually one
of boredom and mistrust.

I found McClellan in the waiting room outside the office of District Judge Susan Kashat. The furniture in the office and in the courtroom reflected the lower status of the District Court compared to the
Circuit Court where Davey Alden's case would eventually be tried.

"You're Brenner?" She barely glanced up from the three-month-
old *People* magazine she was studying. After I had confessed my
identity, she finally raised her eyes and gave me a look that was calculated to make me feel like a fecal specimen under a microscope. It
didn't work. As a defense lawyer I was accustomed to being treated
that way.

She tossed the magazine aside and stood up. She did not offer her hand or even trouble to tell me who she was. That didn't bother me either. A pretty receptionist at the front desk had told me which prosecutor was assigned to the case. She had rolled her lovely brown eyes when she mentioned McClellan's name.

"You going to take the deal or what?" McClellan asked. She was about my age and wore her brown hair straight and cut evenly all around, like a Vassar girl's. She wore no makeup. She should have.

"Let's talk about it," I said, gesturing toward the hallway. I had in mind a stroll toward the coffee machine. McClellan acted as if I'd invited her to lunch at a topless bar.

"I haven't got any time for bullshit," she said. "I've got five exams scheduled for nine, and you're the only defense lawyer who's bothered to show up on time. If you want to talk, let's do it. Our judge wants to get going."

As if on cue, the phone on the secretary's desk buzzed and Judge Kashat's grandmotherly secretary picked it up, listened for a moment, and then replaced it.

"You two will have to quit your bickering and go tell it to the judge," she said. "She wants you in her office now."

"Oh Christ," McClellan muttered, picking up her file and slamming her way through the secretarial gate toward the closed door beyond. I was a step behind, and the gate swung back and smacked me on the knee. Despite the pain, I managed to keep up with the prosecutor. As I passed the judge's secretary, she rolled her eyes just as the pretty young clerk down the hall had.

Judge Kashat was a small, black-haired woman in her mid-forties. She had large dark eyes, and her face displayed what I hoped was empathy. With her hawkish Middle Eastern nose and long face, she was not a good-looking woman in any conventional sense, and probably had never been considered pretty even as a young girl. All the same, there was a quality about her that gave her an undeniable elegance. She reminded me of a museum fresco of an Egyptian queen.

Taking a seat next to McClellan across from the judge, I prayed silently that what I was finding attractive about this woman in the black robe was character. I sensed immediately that McClellan disliked her, and that gave me hope.

"You may want to think of disqualifying me," the judge said after introductions and small talk about my life in Chicago. "I assume you know that Joel Alden had a preliminary exam in my court. I listened to Mrs. Alden's testimony and ordered him to stand trial in Circuit Court. I believed Mrs. Alden's testimony."

"That may not be a problem," I said.

"I must say that I do not appreciate what she did, not only because she fooled me, which she did, but more because of what she did to undermine the system. Despite all that, I still think I could be fair."

"Your Honor, if you believe you can give my client a fair shake, that's good enough for me. But I see no reason for an exam in District Court. My plan is to waive exam and go right to Circuit Court for trial."

"You're not taking Holtzman's offer?" McClellan asked.

"No, and I see no reason to burden the court with an exam this morning."

"Don't do us any favors, Counsel," McClellan said.

I noticed that she had a run in her stocking and was tempted to point it out to her, but discretion prevailed. I ignored her comment, and so did the judge.

"Does the prosecutor want an exam?" the judge asked McClellan.

"The People will not demand an exam."

"It's up to you, Mr. Brenner," the judge said. "I just wanted you to know that I would listen to any arguments you might want to make on disqualification. If you want to waive exam, that settles it. If you're ready—"

"Judge, I would like to make a motion to reduce the bond. Frankly, I think that a personal bond is in order here. I—"

"Not a proper motion at this time," McClellan interjected, discarding her bored look. "He's got to make that motion in writing—"

Judge Kashat held up her hand. "Now, Sandra, you know that I always allow bond arguments at exam time, even if exam is waived. But let's not argue it here. Let's go on the record and you can make your objections in the courtroom."

The judge turned to me. "Have you had a chance to talk with your client yet this morning, Mr. Brenner? No? Well, why don't you talk to her in the courtroom—I'll ask the deputy to bring her in for you—while Sandra and I sort out the rest of the morning's files. Be sure to have your client sign a written waiver before I take the bench. Pick up a form from Alice as you leave."

Thus dismissed, I made my way to the courtroom and took a seat at the defense table. The half-dozen defendants and spectators in this courtroom sat in gray molded plastic chairs; the counsel tables were fake wood and had aluminum legs.

All this was a far cry from the old marble-floored courthouses found in most of the major cities in America. Irish, Italian, and German immigrants had built courthouses that rivaled their churches. At first I assumed it was because of respect for the law; later I came to realize that graft and greed often played a role in the building of those lavish palaces of justice. Maybe the taxpayers in Laffler County were just luckier.

The courtroom door opened, and a brown-uniformed deputy brought Davey Alden in and steered her toward me. Davey's face was pale and strained, but she smiled gamely at me as I sat her down at counsel table. She wore a gray wool suit with a cream blouse. Had she carried a briefcase, she might very well have been taken for a nervous young lawyer appearing in court for the first time.

I could not have asked for more; she did not look as though she belonged in jail. She had been taken to jail in the jeans and sweatshirt she'd been wearing at the time of arrest. Since then, Joel had taken control of everything, even her clothing. But for the kindness of her part-time cleaning lady, Davey would have had only those clothes today. Shortly after Davey's arrest, that lady had sneaked a few clothes out of the house and kept them until Davey needed them. As far as I could tell, she was Davey's only remaining friend in Kirtley.

"You look all right," I said. "I know you're nervous, but you won't have to say much of anything today, so try to relax. I've got a form for you to fill out." As she was signing the form giving up her right to a preliminary examination, I asked her if she had been able to line up a place to live in case she was released on bond.

"I don't have anywhere to go," she replied. "Joel's got the house, and I wouldn't go back there even if I could. My mother has Julie, and she's on Joel's side. Our friends were all Joel's friends, and they won't want to get involved."

"Look, Mrs. Alden. I've got to be able to tell the judge that your situation is stable—that you have ties to the community, that you are the kind of person who will show up for trial. That means family, children, a place to live."

"I'm one of the homeless now," she said. The look on her face said she was confident I could handle the situation.

"I'll do what I can," I said curtly, regretting my sharpness when I saw a shadow pass over her face. Then I regretted my regret. What the hell was wrong with me?

I glanced around the courtroom. More people were coming in. The deputy who had brought Davey in had taken a seat in the back and was reading a newspaper. A lawyer I recognized was engaged in earnest conversation with a young black man—no doubt persuading him to take a deal McClellan had offered. I saw Larry Semczyk in the back with the other spectators. I waved and he smiled but did not approach us.

As I looked around, the door opened and a balding man in his thirties slouched in, surveyed the room with barely concealed contempt, and quickly zeroed in on Davey and me. This had to be a reporter from one of the big city dailies: hard-bitten, cynical, and ready to let one and all know that he found the hicks outside Detroit (it might as easily have been Chicago or L.A. or Philadelphia) amusing if not outright laughable.

I feared the worst. I'd gotten along well enough with most of the crime reporters in Chicago, but a few were downright dangerous in their ignorance or malice. This one looked like trouble.

I turned to Davey and went over her rights again in the hope that the reporter would leave us alone. Although I was not out to make an enemy of the press, I saw little advantage for Davey in extensive press coverage of her case. Lawyers and judges tend to grandstand for the press. Davey's best hope was for the community and the press to lose interest in her.

"Counselor, I'm Bob Ripley from the *Times*."

I looked up but remained seated. The balding man who had just entered stood next to us. I accepted the hand that was offered and returned the introduction.

"I'd like to talk with your client"—he smiled appreciatively at Davey's good looks—"and get her side of the story. With your permission, of course."

We were saved by the bell. A chime rang as a uniformed bailiff entered from a door next to the bench. Everybody rose. The bailiff called the court to order, and Judge Kashat took the bench. Simultaneously, Sandra McClellan entered through the main door and headed toward the table next to ours. I muttered something that may have sounded like agreement to Ripley and turned my attention to the proceedings. In response to Davey's inquiring look, I whispered another warning that under no circumstances was she ever to talk to the press—in person, on the phone, in writing, or even in her dreams.

The judge called our case first. Davey and I took our places at the lectern and went through the ritual of giving up her right to a preliminary examination. Then we turned to the question of bond. It had been set at $500,000 cash or surety when Davey was arrested.

"Your Honor, I'll oppose any bond change," McClellan argued. "Any reduction must be based on change of circumstances or on an abuse of discretion by the magistrate who set the bond."

I smiled winningly at the judge. "Your Honor, as you know better than I, the purpose of bond is to ensure the appearance of the defendant at trial," I said. "In cases involving violent crimes, the safety of the public may come into play—but I am certain that Ms. McClellan is not claiming that Mrs. Alden is a dangerous criminal who is about to kill or maim anyone."

I sensed that the judge was sympathetic. It was an unusually high bond, even allowing for the fact that perjury cases like this were rare. I knew enough not to call into question the competence or honesty of the magistrate who'd set the bond; I couldn't be sure that he was not the judge's campaign manager or third cousin. Only really dumb lawyers buck the system that way without knowing who all the players are. Small-town courthouses can be quicksand for the lawyer with an undisciplined tongue.

"Your Honor, please keep in mind that the potential sentence in this case is life," the prosecutor said. "This defendant may not be a mad dog killer, I agree, but she has in fact maimed the system. Mrs. Alden no longer has a home in Laffler County. She is separated from her husband. She has no employment. I believe the danger of flight is very real. My office has received information that she has threatened to flee the jurisdiction with her child, who, by the way, has been removed from her custody."

"That's preposterous," I shot back. For as long as I had been practicing law, it was always thus. As soon as the pendulum starts to swing, lawyers get desperate and the truth gets mangled.

"Your Honor, I'd like to know the source of the tip about my client's plans to flee. I dare the prosecutor to produce anything to substantiate such an allegation."

Judge Kashat ignored McClellan. She'd been around and knew that if the prosecutor had anything other than rumor or speculation, we would have heard it.

"If bond is granted, where would your client live?" she asked me.

What I did next was inexcusable and totally inexplicable for an old hand like me. I knew better than to get involved personally. I knew all about maintaining professional detachment. I had learned all the lessons when I was still in knee pants in the law. What I did was a living example of how we humans make decisions deep inside without bothering to inform the miserable outer shell that walks and talks and thinks it is in charge.

"Mrs. Alden will be residing on Lakeview Drive in Clare Township, at the home of Dr. Ann Mahoney," I improvised. "I am assured that she has a place to stay there as long as she wishes."

Although I had consulted neither Ann nor Davey, I was not lying to the judge, for, if anything were true under the heavens, it was that Ann Mahoney would not refuse shelter to this homeless defendant. The puzzle was not that I was being presumptuous, but rather why I had put myself in the tenuous position of being Davey Alden's babysitter by moving her in next door. I would like to say that I lost my head in the heat of battle, but I was too experienced for that to happen.

Before McClellan could continue the argument, Judge Kashat made her ruling.

"I believe that personal recognizance would be in order under the circumstances," she said. "I'm convinced that Mrs. Alden is not going to go anywhere. Her child is here in Michigan, and I see no risk that she would not appear for trial. Like defense counsel, I'm at a loss to explain why the bond was set so high in the first place."

And that was it. A court clerk filled out a form, Davey signed it, and in minutes she was on her way back to the jail with the deputy to get her personal effects and be processed out. I waved a cheery goodbye to McClellan and, on the way out, whispered to Semczyk that I would

call him later. Then I ducked down an unfamiliar corridor and out a
back door into a parking lot.

I had taken about three steps into the parking lot when Ripley of
the *Times* suddenly loomed up ahead of me, materializing from
between the cars.

"Nice work, Brenner. It's clear you've been around. I like to see a
real pro work over the locals. It's good for their sense of proportion."

He stood blocking my way, wearing a grin that said there was no
escaping him: I was his next journalistic meal. Outside of pushing him
aside or indecorously trying to step around him, I could not avoid
talking to him. Besides, although I was not eager to keep media attention on Davey Alden, there was no point in antagonizing the press
deliberately.

"Thanks. Getting the bond reduced was the easy part."

"Hey, don't play Mr. Humble with me," he said with a poke at my
shoulder. "I've been around too, Counselor, and I know a real street
fighter when I see one. Knee 'em in the balls and hit 'em when they're
down, eh?"

He had moved closer to me to better communicate his spirit
of camaraderie. He had an elongated face that made me think of
an editorial-page cartoon. I didn't feel like his comrade, or, for that
matter, like much of a street fighter, but I grinned appreciatively. If I
could have pulled it off, I would have given him a conspiratorial wink.

"Look, Brenner, I'm looking for a story and you want to get your
client off, right?" I must have nodded because he continued on. "I see
no reason why we can't work together. That way, nothing I write will
hurt your client—because we'll be working together—and you yourself benefit personally because, let's face it, good publicity never hurt
a lawyer."

He must have seen something in my face because he added quickly,
"Not to mention that your client may benefit from some sympathetic
ink, right?"

"I see no reason why we can't work together," I replied. "If you want the truth, I believe you'll find this a gripping story. Excuse me. I've got to get over to the jail now, Bob—it is Bob, isn't it?—but let's get together to work out some ground rules—like what will be on the record, that sort of thing."

He looked disappointed. "Sure, that'll be great," he said vaguely. "How about a quote now on waiving the exam and getting the bond reduced?"

"Sure," I said with enthusiasm, delighted to get off so lightly. "Let's just say that Judge Kashat showed real fairness and wisdom in her bond ruling today. Now that Mrs. Alden is free, we can work on her defense more effectively. We've got a lot to do to get ready for trial."

"That's fine, Counselor, I can use that, but I need something with more meat. What kind of strategy can you possibly have for a defense, when the lady admitted on the stand under oath that she lied? If there ever was a hopeless case for a lawyer, this has got to be it, right?"

I replied with what I hoped was a look of confident cunning. "I can't reveal my strategy to the press, can I, Bob? If I do that, I'll have no surprises to spring on the prosecutor, will I?"

"Off the record, then."

"No can do. Client confidences. I'm sure you can appreciate that. But I'll talk it over with my client, Bob. I can promise you that."

While we talked I'd managed to sidle around him, and I started toward the jail with him tagging along.

"Who is this Dr. Ann Mahoney? I don't recall hearing her mentioned before."

"An old friend. She's got a heart of gold."

"A friend of Mrs. Alden's or yours?"

"Well, both of ours, to be precise." Precise is the last thing I wanted to be at that moment.

We were almost to the jailhouse steps. Never did Moscow Modern look so warm and inviting. But before I could make it, Ripley stopped me with a hand on my arm.

"Isn't that address you gave to the judge near where you live? In fact, it's only one house away from yours. I looked it up in the phone book. Isn't that going to make your client your next-door neighbor? A very good-looking neighbor, I might add."

I managed to extract my arm and flee up the steps into the building. As I entered, he was eyeing me like a wolf watching a crippled caribou.

We were silent as I headed my car out Old Plank Road toward Spring Lake. From time to time I sneaked a glance at Davey, sitting at my side. Looking straight ahead, she smiled like a young girl on her way to visit a favorite aunt in the country. She had removed the jacket of the gray suit. I could see the lacy contour of her bra through her blouse.

Occasionally her expression changed and she would frown momentarily, but always the smile returned to match the beautiful August day we were passing through.

For much of the trip I too was lost in thought, and my thoughts were jumbled. I'd never realized how carefully I had lived my life before this day. As a public defender I had readily identified myself with the bold ones, the liberals who fought to preserve what was left of idealism and purity in America. Heedless of the opinions of either the masses or the elite, we were the few, the daring.

Now that my reckless courtroom gesture had placed me on a path that led to places unknown, driven by motives that were yet a mystery to me, I was profoundly uneasy. I realized how sheltered I had been in Chicago with Sheila. Far from living on the cutting edge, I'd been insulated from the chaos surrounding me. The cornerstone of my existence had been predictability. No longer.

"Is this where you live?" Davey asked as we crunched up the driveway to Ann's cottage.

"No, this is Dr. Mahoney's home," I said quickly. "I live over there, but you'll be staying with her until we can get you some more suitable place to live."

We got out of the car and stood between the cottages, looking out over the lake. A light wind rippled the dark blue water. A few yards offshore, a half-dozen Canada geese paddled quietly away, watching us suspiciously. At the far end of the lake, a hawk circled lazily overhead.

"This is so beautiful," Davey said, brushing aside a tendril that the breeze had displaced. "You must love it here."

I muttered something inaudible as I reached inside the car for the paper bag that contained all her earthly possessions. I led the way up to Ann's cottage, which sat on a small bluff overlooking the lake. The key to the front door was in a flowerpot.

Once inside, we stood in silence looking around the house. Artifacts from Ann's African and Latin American sojourns were everywhere, among them a carved wooden zebra mask that hung above the fireplace in the living room. Three bookcases were filled with works on medicine, anthropology, and religion.

"Why don't you sit down, Mrs. Alden?" I said. "I'll try to reach Ann to let her know what's up." I wasn't as confident as I sounded. Any normal person would resent being imposed upon by a neighbor in such a manner. My only consolation, indeed the wellspring of my hope, was that Ann Mahoney was not any normal person.

"That might be a good idea, and please stop calling me *Mrs. Alden*," she said with a teasing smile. She sensed my embarrassment. After taking a seat on Ann's couch, she crossed her legs, rearranged her skirt, and sat primly with her hands on her knee, watching me.

After fumbling around for a few minutes in the area of Ann's phone, I found the number of the hospice in Detroit. When I got her on the phone, I explained the situation.

"Of course she can stay, you big jerk," Ann said. Her voice was laced with laughter, as if she too sensed my uncharacteristic awkwardness. "I could use some company for a while, although she may find me a rather dull companion."

"I doubt that."

"Well, she's welcome. Find a place to put her things. She can use the bedroom on the east side. You'll find linens in the cedar chest there—or at least a sleeping bag. Here, let me talk to her. Put her on."

I handed the phone over to Davey. Within minutes they were chatting excitedly about Davey's stay. I heard talk about shopping for food, discussion of Davey's wardrobe or lack thereof, and a schedule for sharing the chores.

"What a marvelous woman," Davey said when she had replaced the receiver. "She even said I could borrow some of her clothes until I can get some of my own. These may be a bit dressy for everyday wear."

A look of pain passed over her face.

"What's the matter?"

"Julie. When can I see her? I can't stay here like this." She'd stood up to talk on the phone; now she sank back down onto the couch.

"You have no choice," I said. "At least for the time being. Once you get a lawyer to handle the divorce for you— "

"I don't know any lawyers. I have no money. I don't even have any clothes besides these and what's in that bag."

"You're not penniless. Your husband is a wealthy man, and a court will order him to pay for a divorce lawyer for you. You can get into court and challenge the temporary custody order. The one thing that you cannot do is sit here and brood."

"I'd like to see my daughter," she said. She looked at me with the same mixture of hope and despair that she had displayed in the jail. A moment ago she had been an attractive, perky young woman amused by my sudden awkwardness, and now reality had given the kaleidoscope a twist, and she was a portrait of tortured shadows.

"Look, Davey, I need time to think. I've got some ideas, but I've got to think them through."

The truth was that I had no ideas and I needed time to come up with some. Although my experience and my natural cockiness led me to believe that divorce law was not much of a legal challenge, the fact remained that my experience was limited. I had watched hundreds of divorce cases argued by others, and I'd handled a few motions for Scott—that was it. She needed another lawyer to handle her divorce—anyone other than me. I was in deep enough with her criminal case.

"Can't I at least see Julie?" she asked. "I know my mother will take good care of her—but she won't believe anything bad about Joel. If he ever gets full custody . . ."

"Take it easy. He won't. We'll get you over to see your daughter as soon as possible. First we've got to get you some clothes and a car, not to mention some money to live on."

"I know I'm a lot of trouble, but—"

"Ann will be home by dinnertime," I said in my best command voice. "Why don't you get busy with some of the chores you and she were talking about? I've got some appointments at the office this afternoon. We'll talk tonight."

My suggestion that she get to work seemed to placate her. When I left, she was checking out Ann's clothing in the bedroom. I wanted to make my escape before she got a good look at Ann's wardrobe.

As I opened my car door I noticed a black and white sheriff's patrol car at the bottom of the driveway. Standing next to it, staring up at Ann's house, was a tall, blondish deputy with mirrored sunglasses. When he saw me he unhurriedly got back into his vehicle, backed into the road, and drove slowly off. Davilon Alden, threat to public safety, was apparently under surveillance.

8

WHEN I PASSED SCOTT SHERMAN'S OFFICE THAT AFTERNOON, HE watched me with a smirk on his face. That smirk followed me down the hallway and into my office, and taunted me throughout the afternoon. I dictated an answer to a complaint on a railroad crossing accident, talked on the phone to the niece of an elderly widow about a will, and dictated three letters. Finally it became too much to bear. I jerked open my door and barged into Scott's office.

"All right, out with it!" I demanded.

"I'm sure I don't know what you're talking about," Scott answered, his day complete now that I had blinked first.

I knew Scott only too well. We both laughed, loud and long enough that Sherry, Scott's twenty-year-old knockout receptionist, poked her head in to see if we were all right, frowned at our grins, and fled as if she feared something contagious.

"You son of a bitch," I said. "You dirty-minded SOB." As was so often the case with Scott, I wanted to be angry, but I couldn't get up a real head of steam.

"Whatever happened to Judy Catalano—or Catano, or whatever her name is?" he asked.

"Cusmano."

"Yes, that's it. I thought you'd found a main squeeze there."

"Judy and I are very close friends," I answered stiffly.

"You're sleeping with her, aren't you?"

"None of your business, dickhead!"

Scott giggled. He knew he was being crass, but such a fluffy consideration would never be allowed to spoil his fun. Fortunately he chose to change the subject—more or less.

"Well, don't say I didn't warn you, Jack Boy. Now you've gone and done it."

"Done what?" I asked, curious to know what he'd heard. Davey had been released on personal bond only a few hours ago. News traveled fast in Laffler County, and it seemed always to travel first to Scott Sherman.

"I told you that girl is a temptress. You better watch it or she'll have you tied in knots with those curly red tresses of hers."

"Knock it off, Scott. I'm serious. This woman tells a plausible story. Christ, I don't know, she may be lying, but there's something else up—"

"Up? I'll say there is, and we both know what it is."

This was the way it had been with us ever since our college days, when I started to think about something other than getting laid: Scott laughing, me stewing over his superficiality.

I was getting up to leave when Scott got serious.

"Let's get this case wrapped up and make some money. You're an old pro. Hell, that's why I recommended you for the job. Little did I know what I was letting the firm in for."

"You recommended me for this job?" Scott's eyes narrowed momentarily, and I could see that he regretted his indiscretion. "Why would you do such a nasty thing to an old Sig brother?"

Scott responded with the sly look that I knew so well. How many times had I been taken in by him in Ann Arbor during our undergraduate days? Conned into hauling the Sigma Chi party kegs when it was his job. Duped into a double date so that he could ingratiate himself with some lovely whose roommate needed help. Or the many times he'd begged to use my class notes just before exams, and then left me hanging by failing to return them when I needed them.

All of this was the stuff of nostalgia now, memories made fond by the mists of time, but I had learned a thing or two in the years since, and I was not about to play the fool again for Scott Sherman.

"I happened to be in Olenik's office with Brad Holtzman," he said, "when the subject of who was going to represent Davey Girl came up. Someone said an old hand was needed, one who knew how to exercise client control and cut the best possible deal for her. Somehow your name came up and I had to admit that you were the best."

"I'll return the favor someday."

"Look, old buddy, this firm is on a roll, and it would be a shame to screw things up now. Get rid of the case, plead the lady out. Joel Alden is ready to abandon the big boys downtown and go local. You heard him. A client like that could make a small firm like this. Joel's got too much business for Syd Masters to handle. If we can get our nose into the tent, there'll be no stopping us."

"You've got to be kidding," I said, but he was grinning again, and the mockery in his look made it seem churlish to challenge his motives.

"Hey, lighten up, guy," Scott said. "And remember your old buddy when you reach the Promised Land. You don't have to shit me, old bean. I can understand how you might want to get your ashes hauled— although I do think you might do it more discreetly."

"Screw you," I said as I left. As usual, I couldn't be certain whether I really was angry with Scott or not. Despite his cynicism, I was confident that my motives were upright. Davey Alden needed me. I was her only chance. I believed in her.

I left the office early enough so that I could stop by the county clerk's office to look at the Alden divorce file. Then I headed home through Kirtley's version of the five-o'clock rush hour, which meant a delay of three minutes getting through the Main Four Corners. It was a sign of my acclimation to the Kirtley environment that I found myself grumbling over a three-minute tie-up.

The sunshine deserted the day somewhere between the clerk's office and the Main Four Corners, and by the time I was headed north out Old Plank Road, it was raining. Lightning jabbed at the sky, illuminating the white faces of the cattle in the farm fields along the road.

It was still raining when I turned into the common driveway for Ann's home and mine. Ann's pickup was not there. A light shone in her window. I parked my Volvo next to my cottage, went inside to let Maggie out, and dashed through the rain over to Ann's place. Maggie raced around me in delight. Her day was really just beginning.

I opened the door to Ann's covered patio and was greeted by a Mozart concerto. After knocking on the door to the living area and receiving no response, I opened the door and entered, leaving Maggie behind on the patio. I shouted a greeting as I went in.

Davey Alden sat on the couch with her legs folded under her and a book in her hands. My shout startled her and she dropped the book to the floor. Her look of concern turned to relief when she recognized me.

"I'm sorry if I frightened you," I said over the swelling of the music flowing from Ann's sound system.

"No, that's all right," she replied, rising and turning the volume down. She wore a pink jogging suit that was too large for her but still managed to be flattering. The glow of femininity about her, a mixture of self-consciousness and vulnerability, softened everything around her. Somehow her very presence made Ann's house more attractive.

"You seem to have found something to wear," I said. "I don't recall ever seeing that outfit on Ann."

"I don't think it's ever been worn. Dr. Mahoney—Ann—seems to have modest taste in clothes except for this piece."

She pulled at the waistband of the jacket and twirled around to show it to me, smiling mischievously at her parody of a fashion model.

"You look all right," I said quickly. I turned away and stepped over to Ann's stereo. "You must be an incurable romantic," I said, holding up the cassette box for the Mozart Concerto No. 21. "This is the *Elvira Madigan* theme. Do you know the movie?"

"She was in love with a Swedish nobleman," she shot back. "It was a doomed love, and in the end they had to die. Did you think I wouldn't know?"

I bent over and picked up the book she had dropped. It was a novel by Graham Greene, *The Power and the Glory*, a fiftieth-anniversary edition in hardcover. The inside covers contained reproductions of portions of the handwritten original manuscript.

"I'd expect Ann to have a book like this," I said. "Better be careful. Ann's a professional Catholic. That kind of stuff can be catching."

"It's very sad and gloomy."

"I think I read it back in college. Greene was obsessed with salvation and damnation."

"I read somewhere that he was obsessed with God's mercy. That he insists God is more interested in mercy than in justice."

"God probably decided that mercy was needed after he let the lawyers take over the justice game," I said.

We both laughed at that. Lawyer jokes are always safe. I handed the book back to her.

"You don't care for the Catholic beliefs?" she asked.

"It's not that. They produced Ann, they can't be all bad. I just don't feel the need for any religion. Faith is a virus I've never succumbed to."

"Everybody has a religion. They just call it something else. I suspect that the law is your religion."

"Maybe once, but not now."

"What's that I hear? The barrister disillusioned?"

I smiled gamely—and a little uneasily. I found this different Davey fascinating. This was neither the distraught mother nor the ethereal woman-child I'd rescued from jail. This was a flirtatious, lively, thoughtful woman.

"It's a living," I said. "I don't really know anything else."

"I'm sure you're very good at it." Her smile contained a mixture of encouragement and irony.

"I try," was all I managed to say.

She fell silent, and I could not think of a way to refuel the conversation. Outside, the rain fell steadily. Inside, the Mozart concerto concluded and the only sound was the rain on the roof.

Davey's face clouded over.

"Did you try to call your daughter?" I asked.

She brightened for a moment. "Yes, I talked to her this afternoon right after you left. She asked when her mommy would be coming home."

The cloud returned. "My mother said she would have to check with Joel before I could visit with her," she added.

"We'll see about that. Is there any possibility that you could move in with your mother while we wait for trial?"

"I know she'll never allow it. She thinks I did a terrible thing in reporting Joel."

"She doesn't believe you?"

"I don't know. No, she doesn't. She could never let herself believe something like that."

"She sounds like a strange woman. After all, you are her daughter."

She smiled sadly. "You don't know my mother."

The sound of Ann's pickup brought a warning bark from the forgotten Maggie. The bark turned into squeals of delight at the sounds of the truck door slamming and Ann's approach.

"That's Ann—and there's a lady named Maggie that I want you to meet," I said.

Of course the three females, as members of that gender are wont to do, hit it off immediately. No ceremony, no cautious circling, just instant rapport. Before long, Ann was seated on her couch, sipping her martini with Maggie beside her. Davey was in the kitchen broiling three small steaks, while I stood at the kitchen counter putting together a salad.

"You've got to have a plan of action, Jack," Ann said. "You've got to lay out a game plan."

"Sure thing, Coach."

She was quick; it had taken only a few minutes of explanation for her to grasp the complexities of Davey's criminal and domestic litigation. She accepted Davey's situation without question, as she had my decision to bring Davey here, next door to me.

"Don't be impertinent, my friend. You may be the F. Lee Bailey of Laffler County, but divorce cases take just plain common sense."

"I'm not handling the divorce, just the criminal case."

"I don't understand," Davey said, "why you can't represent me in both cases. I want you to."

"Bluntly stated, your criminal problems are enough to occupy one lawyer. Common sense dictates that I concentrate on what I do best—practice criminal law. I'll tell you what little I know about divorce, but that's it."

"Well, that's settled," Ann said. "You'll take on her divorce case until someone better comes along. That shouldn't be too long a wait."

"I didn't say—"

"Shut up and let's eat."

Over dinner I told them what I had learned in going through Davey's divorce file at the courthouse. I did not tell them that Ralph had given me a crash course on Michigan divorce practice and that the analysis of Davey's situation was not entirely my own. Davey filled me in on what had happened in the divorce so far.

Represented by Sydney Masters, Joel had played it smart by moving out of the house and fully supporting Davey and Julie while his own criminal case was pending. He'd paid all the household expenses and provided Davey five hundred a week to spend, a paltry enough sum considering his wealth, but enough for her to get by. Lulled by that fact, Davey had not even consulted with a lawyer about filing for divorce before Joel's criminal case was resolved.

When the tables were turned and Davey was arrested, however, Joel had not hesitated. Masters filed for divorce and got Judge Olenik to grant temporary custody of Julie to Joel, with the understanding that the child would live with Davey's mother until Davey's perjury trial was over. Davey was temporarily frozen out—no living allowance, no attorney's fees, nothing. That was why she'd needed me, a court-appointed attorney. I assured her that it was only a temporary setback and that she had a right to support and attorney's fees in both the divorce and criminal cases.

A temporary injunction tied up all their financial assets, but I'd found nothing giving either one exclusive possession of the family home before the divorce was final.

"Does that mean I can go to the house and take out my things?" Davey asked.

"I don't see why not. I wouldn't recommend that you do it while Joel is there, but it's your house as much as his. I'd go right in and take out anything that is personal—your clothing and anything that's indisputably yours."

"How will I get there? I don't have a car."

"I'll take you out there tomorrow," I said with a lack of hesitation that surprised me. I was supposed to be an adviser, not a participant. I looked at Ann. "Can you come with us? I'd like to have a witness just in case Joel's lawyer—" I stopped to ask Davey, "Do you know Sydney Masters?"

"Joel always gets him for the nasty stuff."

"Just in case Joel's lawyer claims that the place was looted."

"I can be there," Ann said, clearly relishing the air of conspiracy at the table. "But are you certain that you can do this without the permission of the court?"

"Davey will not be disobeying any court order. It would be better to get a court order, but it would take a week to ten days to get a hearing. A little self-help under these circumstances makes good sense. I can't see a judge getting too upset over Davey taking what he'd be certain to give her anyhow."

The calm of our conversation belied the gravity of the situation: a criminal defendant facing a life offense; a lawyer who had thrown detachment out the window; and an aging doctor who did not know when to quit or how to say no.

Ann looked puzzled. "Does the fact that the judge ordered Julie to stay with Davey's mother mean that he doesn't trust Joel—that he wanted to protect the little girl?"

"Highly unlikely. Orders such as these are *ex parte*, which means that they are signed without a hearing. In other words, Davey didn't get a chance to be heard. Such orders are handled like that because any delay might be harmful. My guess is that Joel's lawyer wanted to create an appearance of fairness, knowing that Davey's mother was in Joel's hip pocket. Judges automatically credit grandparents with great wisdom and the purest of motives."

"Do we have any chance of changing custody right away?" Davey asked quietly, placing her fork along the edge of her plate.

I avoided looking at her and spoke instead to Ann.

"I wish I could say for certain. Some judges always assume that little girls should be with their mothers, but that's not politically correct today, nor is it in accord with the law. Nowadays it depends on who has been the child's primary care-giver, which would seem to give Davey an edge, but then you must factor in the unusual circumstances of this case—Joel's acquittal, the charges pending against Davey, the clever ploy of enlisting Davey's mother on Joel's side— and when you do that it's hard to say what a judge would do."

"What are the chances if you file a motion to change custody right away?" Davey asked.

"As I said, I'm not the one to do it. Your divorce lawyer will know better how to handle it."

"Davey wants someone she knows and trusts," Ann said. "I say you should take it on."

"I can't."

"What about a car for Davey?" Ann asked. It was a strategic retreat. I was certain I had not heard the last of the subject.

"If the Allante is titled in Davey's name"—Davey nodded in response to my inquiring look—"and we find it at the house, we'll take it. There's no court order giving Joel possession of it, so it's Davey's to take. We have to keep in mind that Joel will probably cancel the insurance, so your lawyer will have to include that in his motion."

Davey was glowing with renewed hope. Ann raised her glass and toasted the success of our foray on the morrow. I basked in the warmth of their approval. With Ralph's help, I'd been able to come up with a game plan, one that impressed at least Davey and Ann.

I was grateful that neither of them asked about my game plan for the criminal case.

9

WE WERE ON THE ROAD BEFORE NINE THE NEXT MORNING, WITH Ann at the wheel of her rusting Ranger pickup, Davey in the middle, and me next to the window. I had slept poorly the night before. My tossing and turning brought Maggie to my bedside several times to demand an explanation with her wet nose. I finally gave up and rose before dawn. Now I was grumpy from lack of sleep.

"You drive this thing like a garbage truck," I complained after my head had hit the ceiling of the cab for the fourth time. The private road that led to our cottages looked and felt like an antique washboard.

"For the leader of this raid into enemy territory, you demonstrate a singular lack of leadership," Ann replied sweetly, fighting to keep the pickup on a straight line. "Where be your cheerful demeanor in the face of fear, that contemptuous disregard for danger, that patient willingness to suffer any adversity and bear any burden in the cause of justice?"

Davey turned to see how I was taking the doctor's gibes, and a wisp of her hair tickled my face. I looked into her freckled face and grinned. I had never been this close to her before, and suddenly I became conscious of how crowded we were in the front seat of the little truck. My leg was resting against hers, and I carefully moved it away, a difficult thing to do in the cramped, bucking cab.

Within minutes we were driving past the Alden Construction Company. Davey spotted Joel's black Mercedes parked in front. She gave a little gasp of excitement when she saw her Cadillac Allante parked alongside the building. It was inside a tall chain-link fence, the gate to which was open.

"Now out to the house," I said. "Quickly, quickly, good doctor."

The Alden home was located off Hibner Road, on the sixteenth fairway of Riverbend. The five-bedroom Cape Cod sat on five mani-cured acres and was easily the most impressive home on that road. We drove up the asphalt drive and parked in front of the double-doored garage on the side of the house. Davey dug her key out of her purse and within minutes we were inside.

While the women were upstairs packing Davey's suitcases, I looked around. Like Scott, Joel Alden was a trophy collector. On the mantel above the living room fireplace, a swordfish was displayed. A trophy case in another corner of that room was filled with golf awards and photos of Joel in various foursomes. It seemed that anybody who played with Joel ended up in his trophy case. I found Joel's spoor everywhere on the first floor, and nothing of Davey. It was as if he had carefully vacuumed up any hint of her existence here. Or had it always looked that way?

The biggest trophy of all I found in Joel's den. Across from a desk littered with bills and correspondence hung a good-sized portrait of a reclining nude. It was a painting of Davey, and it was obscene.

The slender figure, tangled red hair, blue eyes—they were all Davey's, but as I stood there, transfixed, I realized that it was not really Davey. It was different, but I could not put my finger on it. Something about it made me profoundly uneasy. There was a volup-tuousness in the way she was posed and in the way the light and shad-ows accented her figure, but it was not my aesthetics that were disturbed. Finally I realized that it was her face—no, her eyes—that disturbed me. The body, the mouth, the smile were those of a courtesan, but the eyes . . . they made it all obscene.

I heard the women talking at the top of the staircase, and then they suddenly fell silent. Still puzzling over the portrait, I turned to leave the den.

A uniformed deputy, with his gun drawn, stood in the doorway leading to the kitchen. He had his eyes on the women struggling with suitcases. The revolver was at his side, but when he saw me it came up and pointed in my direction.

"Well, well, good thing I had an eye on the place," he said. "Buddy, you freeze right where you are. Ladies, why don't you leave that luggage right there and come down here."

"Take it easy, Officer," I said. "This is the Alden home, and this lady is Mrs. Alden. The other lady is Dr. Ann Mahoney. I think you had better put that gun away and back off."

"And who might you be?" There was a snotty edge to his voice. I was suddenly angry—at myself for being here, at Joel Alden for being what he was, at the deputy for being so in love with the thrill that his gun and badge gave him.

"My name is John T. Brenner," I said. "I am Mrs. Alden's attorney—and I remind you again that this is her house."

He looked at Davey standing halfway down the staircase in her pink jogging suit and then back at me. I saw a flicker of doubt in his eyes. I was certain that he recognized Davey.

"Let's see some ID, Mr. John T. Brenner," he said. He was the tall, sandy-haired man I had seen at the bottom of the driveway the day before. He looked as if he worked out a lot in front of a mirror and dreamed of slamming suspects against a brick wall. He eyed me hungrily.

"You put that gun back in your holster and I will show you some identification, Deputy. Then I suggest you leave before you get yourself arrested for trespassing."

We stared at each other for what seemed like a full minute. I had no trouble reading his thoughts, and they were not polite ones, but finally, reluctantly, he replaced his .357 in its holster. At that I slowly reached into my back pocket and pulled out my wallet.

I walked from the den doorway toward the deputy as casually as possible, and as I did so I smiled broadly at the women and told them to bring the suitcases down and put them in the truck.

The deputy looked as if he was about to countermand that order, but I distracted him by handing him my State Bar identification card and business card. He seemed most impressed with the business card, which showed my association with Scott Sherman, but the look in his eyes said he was still hoping that I would give him some excuse to spread-eagle me and slap the cuffs on. The tag on his uniform said he was Deputy Gilbert F. Rollins.

"Now, Officer, I would suggest that you leave us to our affairs and go on about your business. We appreciate your attentiveness to duty, but we do not need any assistance in carrying the bags."

"I think we should call Mr. Alden before you go anywhere," he said. "There is something fishy about this. She shouldn't be here. She doesn't live here anymore."

"Why don't you go back to your patrol car and call to see if there is a restraining order against Mrs. Alden coming into her own house. And if you want to call Joel Alden, by all means do so, but we don't have any more time to waste."

With that I moved past him to the stairs where the women—Davey looking frightened, Ann noncommittal—had paused again. I grabbed two of the four suitcases they were carrying and gestured with my head toward the door. They complied with alacrity, and we were outside and tossing the bags into the bed of the pickup before the deputy recovered his wits.

"Hold up there," he ordered from the doorway. "You're not going anywhere before I clear this with Joel Alden."

"Get in the truck," I ordered. When they did, I turned to our tormentor, took a step toward him, and said, "You don't get it, do you, Rollins? Mrs. Alden is undergoing the tragedy of a divorce and has returned to her home with her attorney and doctor to pick up some clothes and personal effects. She has accomplished that chore despite your interference and harassment."

I was on a roll. "Now listen up. If you say one more word about stopping us from leaving these premises, I am going to draft a multi-million-dollar complaint and sue your ass from here to kingdom come. And by the time the federal civil rights people get done with you, you'll be lucky to get a job as an assistant janitor."

His eyes oozed venom, but again he backed off, and without another word he stalked to his patrol unit, reached inside for the microphone, and started talking.

"Is that what they mean when they talk about silver-tongued lawyers?" Ann said as we headed down the driveway.

"What does the initial *T* in your name stand for?" Davey asked with a brave little smile. We all laughed with relief and excitement.

"Take a different route back to Alden Construction," I said when we were about a mile down the road. "If I'm not mistaken, Joel Alden will be burning up the road in a few minutes on his way out to the house."

With Davey acting as navigator, we took the back roads to Alden Construction. As expected, Joel's Mercedes was no longer there. The gate to the yard that contained the Allante remained open. I had Ann park to one side of the gate. Nobody was about.

"I trust one of those keys in your purse is to the Cadillac," I said to Davey.

"I'm sure that I have it here—yes, it's right here." She held up the key with a trembling hand, but I could tell she was shivering with anticipation, not fear. She was still riding the wave of the excitement from our raid on the Alden home. We both were. I had not yet come down from the rush of adrenaline from my confrontation with Deputy Rollins. Only Ann seemed collected.

"Don't hand the key to me," I said, laughing and opening the door to let her out. "I'm already too close to the line between attorney and litigant. It's your car. You go get it."

"She won't be trespassing?" Ann asked.

"It's her car, and arguably she has an interest in the business as the sole stockholder's wife." Then, to Davey, "Go for it, lady."

In a matter of seconds she was into the yard, jabbing at the door lock with her key, and then inside the car, starting the engine. "Go, lady, go," I whispered as she threw the Cadillac into reverse, squealed backward across the yard, and then roared through the gate and down the highway. Ann took off after her but soon fell behind.

"She's getting accustomed to taking the law in her own hands," Ann said, watching the Cadillac pull steadily away from us. She added, "Has it occurred to you that you may have opened a Pandora's box?"

"That's what lawyers do," I replied.

It must have been just before dawn when Davey came to my bed. Despite the two bottles of wine I shared with Ann and Davey at our victory party, the day's excitement had left me unable to sleep. When I finally did drift off, I dreamed of Davey. And suddenly Davey was there, and it was no dream. I heard Maggie let out a harrumph, and, still half asleep, I saw Davey in the moonlit room and felt the bed move as she slipped between the sheets and laid her head back on a pillow, inches away from me. Whatever she was wearing when she came into the room, she'd slipped off before she came to me, and when she entered my bed she brushed against me. Her body was cool and soothing to my fevered flesh.

"Yes," she whispered, and it was the only word she uttered that night.

Resisting the pull toward reality, clinging to my dream, I turned toward her, desire mounting in me. I reached over and gently ran a finger over the outline of her face, and found, to my surprise, that it was wet with tears. Something deep inside me recoiled in horror, and suddenly the night was cold and real.

I drew back. "What is this?" I said. "What are you doing?" So strong was my desire, so bitter the return to reality, that my voice cracked with frustration and shock.

I slipped out of bed and stumbled over Maggie in the darkness. I groped for my clothes on the chair where I'd tossed them.

"Davey, this isn't what . . . You're my client . . . I didn't know—"

But she was gone, slipping away into the night while I struggled with my clothing. I closed my eyes and saw her again for that fleeting moment in the moonlight, saw the whiteness of her flesh where the tan left off. It could not all have been a dream.

I reached over and touched the pillow where her head had lain. It was wet with her tears.

10

DAYLIGHT BROUGHT A CLARITY THAT SHOULD HAVE BEEN COM-
pelling. My first thought was that I had to get out of the case. A dedicated member of the permissive generation I might be, but I did not
get romantically involved with troubled women whose freedom and
sanity depended on me.

In any community there are always lawyers who are willing to collect their fees on the office couch. I was not one of them. In Chicago
we all knew who they were and viewed them with contempt. We all
nodded approvingly when we heard of their downfall. "He who lives
by the sword dies by the sword," said one wit.

I told myself that it was all my fault. It never occurred to me to
blame Davey. I was lonely and she was dependent and vulnerable. I'd
sent out the wrong signals. The smart thing to do was to go to her,
apologize for the misunderstanding, and convince her that she'd be
better served by someone with more professional detachment.

Getting out of the case would have been the smart thing to do, but
it was not what I did. On the day I took Davey home with me to
Ann's, I'd crossed a river into uncharted territory with no idea of what
lay ahead. Only much later would I come to the knowledge that this
had been my last real chance to turn back before I lost my bearings.

I got ready for work, planning to be gone before either Davey or Ann was astir. As I headed out the door, briefcase and jacket in hand, to my surprise I saw Davey kneeling in Ann's garden, her fingers probing the rich soil around the flowers in front of Ann's patio. I set my things on the car hood and went over to her.

She stood up at my approach and held up blackened hands.

"I don't think you'll want to shake hands this morning," she said cheerfully.

"Davey, we've got to talk about what happened. We—"

"That was exciting. That deputy was scary, but I'm glad we got my things. Now I won't have to impose on poor Ann—"

Gently taking hold of those soiled hands, I said, "I'm talking about last night. I don't think that I can go on—"

"We had quite a celebration, the three of us, didn't we. I bet the neighbors—"

"Dammit, I'm talking about you climbing into my bed. I—"

I stopped at the look on Davey's face. There was pain, humiliation, and even anger. Reflexively, I started to take her into my arms.

"No!" she cried.

With that single word she threw off my arms, whirled, and ran into Ann's house. I stood there stunned, unable to move. Across the lake a chain saw jumped to life, breaking the morning stillness. In the distance a crow called. Finally I turned and walked slowly to my car.

No, she had said. Only one word. I remembered the night and the single word she'd whispered then: *yes*.

For the rest of the day I attempted to sort it all out. Davey's conduct was a puzzle, but mine was equally baffling. At odd times during the day I would stare at the phone and decide to call Davey and tell her I had to withdraw. But something always intervened and the call was never made.

I could not confide in Scott. Subjecting Davey's strange behavior to his prurient analysis was out of the question. Besides, the gleeful condescension in another of his "Jack Boy" lectures would be too much to bear.

The next day I again left for the office at dawn and stayed late. I took Maggie to work and kept her in my car under a shade tree in Scott's parking lot, letting her out several times during the day for a quick romp. When I got hungry I hopped in the car and Maggie and I treated ourselves to a Quarter Pounder with Cheese, one for me, two for her.

I attended the deposition of an ER doctor who was being sued for malpractice. He had diagnosed a heart attack as bursitis and had advised the patient to take aspirin. The man had dropped dead six hours later. I was the doctor's lawyer, but a few minutes into the deposition I was wishing I could change sides. My client was arrogant, uncooperative, and dead wrong. He ignored all my advice and gave away the case in the deposition. The plaintiff's attorney was ecstatic. I made a note to advise the insurance carrier to get ready to pay big money to get rid of the case.

The following day I met with the widow of a wealthy businessman who had divorced his wife of thirty-five years, married a woman thirty years younger, and died of a heart attack in the arms of the new bride while on a honeymoon cruise in the Caribbean. I had to explain to the attractive young widow that his failure to rewrite his will meant she would receive much less than she might have if he'd been able to see through the romantic haze and plan ahead. She didn't care. The money didn't matter. She had genuinely loved the man. Civil law had its surprises too.

I found an excuse to work over the weekend. Once I bumped into Ann in the driveway and learned that Davey had driven to St. Clair Shores to visit her daughter. She'd also spent a day with Ann at the clinic in Detroit. I asked if Davey had hired a divorce lawyer. Not yet. I repeated that I could not take on the divorce.

An encounter with Davey could not be avoided indefinitely. There was work to do on her case. On Sunday night I took some medical releases for Julie and Davey over to Ann's and asked Davey to sign them. I was strictly professional as I explained that the documents would allow their doctors to release their medical records to me.

Although I did not show it, I was more pleased to see Davey than I would have cared to admit. She was wearing white tennis shorts with a powder blue top, and her legs were tanned. I begged off joining her and Ann for a drink, telling them that I had to get an early start in the morning. That day and into the next week I was polite, discreet, and correct when I joined them to talk business or just to be neighborly.

Ann seemed amused by my new demeanor. Davey seemed to take my detachment in stride. It was as if the encounter in my bed had never occurred. Occasionally, in those first few days, perhaps to assuage wounded male pride, I wanted to get Davey alone and remind her about that night, but the garden incident warned me off. I said nothing.

It had never happened. That was how we finessed the problem. I finally embraced the idea that it was all a dream. A dream of the over-heated imagination of a lonely man in proximity to a needy, beautiful woman.

Davey, Ann, and I returned to our easy, friendly relationship. I would not have to sever the strange bond that had been forged between us after all.

11

THE NARROW RIBBON THAT DIVIDED THE ROAD WAS A WHITE ROPE pulling me inexorably toward Joel Alden. For the hundredth time I asked why he had called and why I'd accepted his invitation to come to his home.

Although I wanted to interview Joel, I didn't have much hope that he'd agree. It is a rare victim who will meet with the defense attorney before trial. There is nothing to gain and much to lose. Yet here I was, less than a week after getting Davey freed on bond, on my way to Joel Alden's house.

Turning up the tree-lined asphalt drive, I reminded myself that the meeting was not without risk to me. I had the right to interview Joel in the criminal case, but if I took on the divorce case I would have to work through his lawyer. I reminded myself that I wasn't Davey's divorce lawyer, but it could be argued that my previous visit to Davey's house had put me smack in the middle of it. This trip could bring me in front of the Grievance Board.

I had been puzzled by the silence since our raid on Joel's house. Could this be his response? What did he think he could gain by talking directly with me? I could only speculate about Joel's motives, and for my part, I only knew that I could not reject Joel's invitation, and it had little to do with the need to interview witnesses. It had everything to do with Davey and the way my life was starting to focus on her.

I parked my Volvo next to the open garage doors, glanced at my watch to assure myself that I was on time for our meeting, and stood waiting. Joel's black Mercedes was parked inside. I half expected him to emerge from behind his car to greet me.

I heard gunfire—two shots in quick succession from behind the house. My mouth felt dry, and I wondered if I ought to get back in my car and drive away. I walked around to the back of the house.

The man behind the house had his back to me, but I recognized Joel—a big man, heavy, powerful. He held an over-and-under shotgun pointed in the direction of a cat-tailed swamp behind the house. I paused when he kicked at something on the ground. Two little orange saucers flew up and out toward the swamp. Joel shouldered the shotgun and snapped off two quick shots, neatly dusting both.

"You're a deadeye," I shouted to his back.

He turned and surveyed me coolly before issuing a smile that was more acknowledgment than greeting. The shotgun was cradled in his arm with the muzzle pointing out toward the swamp.

"I don't miss very much," he said as I approached.

"I can imagine."

"Pour yourself a drink," Joel said, pointing to bottles of Beefeater and tonic on a table between two white wooden lawn chairs. "Then you can toss me some passing shots."

"I thought guns and booze don't mix."

"That's for fools who can't hold their liquor—amateurs."

I declined the drink, which brought a frown to my redfaced host. In his line of work, real men drank together; my refusal meant either that I was less than a real man or that I intended to insult him.

"Well, if you're not going to drink, make yourself useful by pulling this cord here when I tell you to." He pointed to the steel contraption at his feet, a launcher for his clay pigeons. While I watched, he loaded in two orange clays and carefully pulled the spring-loaded arms back.

Then he walked off about twenty yards to the side and toward the swamp, and stood facing in my direction. I held the cord in my hand, waiting for his signal.

The seconds ticked by, and my mouth began to get dry again. Joel stood there with an amused grin, looking in my direction.

"Pull!" he finally shouted, and I jerked at the cord.

With a metallic twang, the launcher rocketed the two saucers out toward the cattails and across Joel's front. His movement was a blur as he shouldered his weapon and again blasted his targets into powder.

"Your turn," he shouted, reloading.

"No, thanks. Guns aren't my cup of tea."

"Come on. All you can do is miss."

"No, thanks."

"Just not your cup of tea, eh?"

I did not answer.

After placing the shotgun down in a wooden rack next to the lawn chair, Joel picked up a half-full tumbler from the table and beckoned me toward the house. We crossed a brick patio and entered through a sliding glass door. A sense of unreality gripped me as we crossed the living room: I had been in the house before only for a matter of minutes, yet I felt I knew the place, every dark nook and cranny of it, and I understood only too well that places as well as people can be evil.

Joel led me into the room with the painting of Davey, the portrait with the obscene eyes. He gestured toward a comfortable-looking leather couch and began freshening up his gin and tonic at the wet bar across from the desk. I did not look at the painting.

"I hope you're not afraid of booze as well as guns," he said.

"I'll have a beer—whatever you have."

I popped open the can and guzzled half of it in one gulp, surprised at how thirsty I was. Then I sat looking at Joel, who took a seat in a matching leather chair across from me.

"So Davey has convinced you that I'm a child molester," he said. I could not tell if his weathered outdoorsman's face was windburned or flushed with self-righteous anger.

"Your wife is my client," I said cautiously. "I'm paid to advance her cause."

"Do I look like a goddam pervert?"

"I don't know what child molesters look like," I replied. "They come in all shapes and sizes."

"Are you saying I molested my daughter?"

"Did you?"

He smiled and looked out the glass door at the patio behind me. It was a summer evening and as dusk began to settle I could feel the coolness coming from the swamp.

"That was a boneheaded maneuver you pulled the other day," Joel said. "You're lucky Rollins didn't blow you away. That boy scares even me sometimes."

"You talk like he's your employee. I thought he worked for the sheriff."

"Deputies are underpaid. Let's just say I provide them with an opportunity to earn some extra income on their own time. Security guards and that sort of stuff. They tend to appreciate it."

"Rollins is brainless, but I'm accustomed to his type. Although usually they're the inmates, not the keepers."

"I've put the situation in the hands of my attorney, Syd Masters. He'll be in touch."

"I'm not handling the divorce. Mrs. Alden will be hiring another attorney."

Alden brushed the subject away with a contemptuous wave of his hand. "In some cultures, adult men have a duty to introduce young girls into sex," he said. "I can see that you disapprove, but what the hell do you know about such things?"

"I've met a lot of perverts in my time. I've been around."

"You don't know anything. Forcing a child to have sex is a crime. But teaching sex to a young girl who is willing and healthy isn't wrong. It's normal. When a young girl reaches thirteen or so, she becomes sexual. Unless you brainwash her, you'll never convince her that having a pleasurable orgasm at that age is sex abuse. All these taboos are the result of religious intimidation. They're unnatural. Sex is natural. Just wait and see. The taboos are going to fade away."

"Fade away? I doubt it. But who knows? I try to keep in mind that today's pervert is tomorrow's minority group member. Maybe some-day your preferences will have constitutional protection."

"Who the hell are you to judge me—you and all those other hyp-ocrites—when everybody knows you're fucking my wife?"

"Am I?"

"Why not? Everybody else is."

We sat there for a while in silence, each appraising the other. His anger over his failure to convert me was a pose. Joel Alden did not care what I thought. No one would believe me if I said he'd virtually confessed to me. In a way, he wanted to confess to me, not out of any sense of guilt, but from a need to feel superior to me, to impress upon me that the knowledge would do me no good, to make certain I understood that my moral pretensions were just that—pretensions.

But he did not confess. He had said enough to make me under-stand, and that was all that he wanted. Unlike most child molesters I'd dealt with, Joel was confident, even aggressive.

"You're being a damned fool, Brenner."

He took another sip from his drink and eyed me with pity.

"Let's cut the shit, shall we?" he said. "There's no reason why Davey should have to spend another day in jail. I know for a fact that she can get a plea bargain that will guarantee that."

"And the child?"

He was smiling, but I noticed that when he spoke, his hands gripped his glass tightly. His knuckles were white, and for a moment I thought the tumbler was about to shatter.

"Julie will have to come live with me. She's my daughter, and Davey has forfeited her right to her. No judge with an ounce of sense will give her custody. Even if you get her off, she'll still lose Julie."

"Thanks but no thanks. We'll take our chances in front of the court."

"Julie will be safe with me. I don't want to do her any harm. I love that little girl."

"The same way you loved Melanie?"

That did it. His eyes clouded over in a vain attempt to hide the corruption lurking inside. He closed his eyes and seemed to be struggling within himself. Then he consciously made himself relax. He smiled softly.

"More bullshit. I'm not going to touch the kid, but I do want that cunt Davey to wake up in the middle of the night sweating and screaming when she thinks about what might be happening."

Strangely, his relaxed expression did not change. It was almost benign. He set forth his rationale of revenge with detachment, without passion, and the pure evil of it made me dizzy. My knees felt weak, and a paralysis spread upward into my groin and stomach. After a long pause, I finally pulled myself together and managed to stand up.

"It's not going to happen that way," I said as calmly as I could. "Not only am I going to get Davey acquitted of perjury, but you've convinced me to take on the divorce case too. You won't get custody, you won't even get visitation."

My decision to take on Davey's divorce surprised Alden. It surprised me too.

"Let me tell you something, Alden," I said. "I feel sorry for most of the criminals I defend. Oh sure, they're guilty, but what the hell, we're all guilty of something. But there's one kind of scumbag I and the rest of humanity have never been able to identify with—the piece of human garbage that sexually abuses little children. With your kind, no one can say, 'There but for the grace of God go I.' Never. You have ceased to be human."

"You're nuts, you're crazy," Alden said, rising. "You're bad for Davey. You're going to take her down, and you're going down with her."

"We'll see."

Joel's chapped lips curved in a pitying smile.

"Did you know that your precious Davey has been sleeping with half the men in Laffler County? You and I should be on the same side. We've both been fucked in a special way by my wife."

I looked up at the painting of Davey and quickly away again. But Joel had caught it. His smile broadened and his eyes glowed with enjoyment.

I let myself out the patio door. Joel did not follow me out. He was still smiling when I slid the glass door closed behind me.

Sydney Masters called me at the office before nine the next morning. With cobralike coolness he told me that unless Davey returned the Allante to Joel Alden within the next several hours, he would bring her before the Circuit Court the next Monday and ask Judge Olenik to hold her in contempt of court.

He also accused me of unethical conduct in interviewing his client Joel Alden, and threatened to file a grievance with the State Bar.

I responded in the time-honored fashion—with a threat of my own.

"Good luck, Syd—may I call you that? You'll need luck because I suspect that when Judge Olenik, who I understand is a very fair judge, hears how you threw this lady out into the street with only the clothes on her back, and then bamboozled the court into giving your client custody, he very well may find you and your client in contempt instead of Mrs. Alden."

"You're new here, Brenner," Masters replied. "The word is that you don't know crap about civil law and even less about divorce law. You're in over your head on this one. Olenik will not put up with the kind of stuff you pulled here. You're liable to find yourself in jail with your client if you don't watch out."

So it went. He hinted that if I knew what was good for me I would catch the next bus for Chicago. The same to you, fella, I replied, more or less. I also told him what he could do with his complaint to the State Bar.

A day later a messenger delivered to the office a copy of a motion drafted by Masters accusing Davey, me, and an "unknown female subject" of breaking and entering the Alden home and stealing valuable items, "including but not limited to priceless art objects and paintings." It asked the court to hold all three of us in contempt for those crimes and for stealing the Cadillac Allante. It also requested that restrictions be placed on Davey's visitation privileges with Julie because of "threats by the Defendant to kidnap the child and flee the State of Michigan to escape pending felony charges for the capital crime of perjury." Finally, it sought monetary sanctions against me personally for unethical conduct in fomenting a criminal break-in and the "looting" of the Alden home.

Scott was upset that I'd decided to handle Davey's divorce. Considering that he'd stuck me with Davey's perjury case, his anger seemed out of place.

"Nobody said anything about the divorce," he said. "What the hell do you know about divorce? I've got too much other work for you to do to waste time screwing around with Davey Alden's divorce. Get somebody else."

"The lady needs help," I said testily. "The two cases are intertwined. If she loses the perjury case, she won't get custody and the pervert wins."

"Look, I've got bigger fish to fry than a goddam divorce case. We both do. You're not thinking straight. You're going to screw things up—big things."

"I'm not going to stand back and let them steamroll this lady. I'm not going to turn my back on her."

I felt foolish even before the words escaped my mouth. Don Quixote indeed. I should have said that once I tapped into Davey's share of Joel's wealth, I would be bringing in a lot of money to the firm. Anything but noble naiveté.

Suddenly Scott was smiling again. Putting his arm around my shoulder, he said, "Look, I understand that Davey may need a lawyer to put the divorce case in order. It needs to be put on hold until the perjury case is over. But, for Christ's sake, get the criminal case pled out and be done with it. Then somebody else can finish up the divorce case."

I nodded dubiously.

That having been settled to his satisfaction, Scott cheerfully warned me to be careful. Masters was known to be reckless, he said, and would do anything to win. Ralph Miles told me some horror stories about Masters and warned me to watch my back.

With those cheerful notes ringing in my ears, I reluctantly called Davey to tell her what we faced the next week. I would bring our own motion for custody and to force Joel to resume support for her. She listened without comment. I could tell that she did not care to know the unpleasant details. She seemed content to leave things completely in my hands. I sensed that she was turning herself over to me with total trust.

Although I was immersed in Scott's files, I found time to draft and file a petition for a change of custody and temporary alimony that would be heard at the same time as Masters's motion. I made several attempts to talk with Davey about her legal problems, but again she only half listened. She was in my hands. I would take care of her.

At times, Davey's blind faith made me uneasy. I was in the position of a man who holds in his hands a tiny nestling, all lightness and heartbeat, and who is paralyzed by the responsibility for such a fragile existence, who wants it to be free but is afraid to release it into a threatening world.

In the week that followed, I saw Davey almost every day at Ann's, and the three of us had dinner together several times. Once we went into town, and while Ann shopped, Davey and I played tennis on the high school courts. She surprised me by beating me 6–3, 6–4, 5–7. I marveled at her competitiveness. I won the last set only by forcing myself to keep my eyes off her and on the ball.

On another evening, Davey and I went fishing in Ann's rowboat. Davey made herself a comfortable spot in the bow by laying out three orange life jackets on the wooden seat. She wore earphones for the Walkman that lay on the seat next to her. Whenever she caught me watching her, she smiled and moved her head with the music. She wore cutoff jeans over a bathing suit, and it was difficult not to notice her tanned legs and freckled shoulders. Remembering Joel's accusation, I tried to concentrate on my favorite part of the lake, the undeveloped north shore with its spruce trees interlaced with white birches.

I told myself that I was merely enjoying a respite from the pressures of the law in the waning days of summer. I vowed that it would be all business once we really got going on Davey's criminal and divorce cases. I told myself a lot of things, but none of them changed the fact that for the first time in years I looked forward to getting home and laughing and arguing with people I loved to be with.

12

CIRCUIT JUDGE FRANCIS X. KANE PRESIDED OVER HIS COURTROOM
with a mixture of royal disdain and bonhomie. With his square
jaw, broad forehead, and heavy mane of white hair, he looked like a
judge. Cecil B. DeMille would have cast him as Moses, perhaps even
as God.

From time to time Kane would interrupt a lawyer with a flick of his
finger and make his ruling, signaling the clerk to call the next case
while the losing lawyer was still sputtering. Occasionally he recognized a lawyer from days gone by, when he himself had been a practi-
tioner, and he became jovial and clubby, reminiscing at length about
some of his trial triumphs. Then, almost as an afterthought, he would
rule on the motion, usually in favor of the attorney with whom he had
been trading war stories.

Davey and I stood for a moment just inside the door, watching and
listening. This was the courtroom where Davey's perjury case would
be tried. Unlike the haphazard decor of the District Court, solemn,
solid oak dominated the Circuit courtroom—the raised bench, the
witness box, the counsel tables, the jury box, and, of course, the bar,
that communion rail separating the faithful from the priesthood of

lawyers. Behind the judge's bench was the Great Seal of the State of Michigan, flanked by the American and Michigan flags.

The room was a steambath of emotions. Greed, fear, hate—they were all present and accounted for on the tense faces of the lawyers and litigants. We squeezed into one of the pews. Not many church pews were as filled as these.

This was motion day in the Laffler County Circuit Court, the time set aside each week by the two judges to decide interim disputes in the thousands of civil, criminal, and divorce cases filed each year. Who should get to stay in the house until the divorce was final? Who should pay whom support? What was the prosecutor hiding?

These were the skirmishes, the probing actions, the commando raids in that endless trench warfare known as a lawsuit. Later would come the trial—legal Armageddon.

Only a handful of the cases would ever be tried; most of the disputants would be reasoned, coerced, or bludgeoned into settlement. But of course they did not know this as they sat tense and sweaty, waiting for their case to be called. They were here to do battle. They were here to get their money's worth.

This was the lawyers' opportunity to display their wares, and they put on a good show—posturing and bickering, arguing, accusing, and alleging, evading and avoiding—all the while invoking the name of Lady Justice as they vented their clients' pent-up rage and malice.

In the divorce cases, husbands and wives learned to their dismay that everything they had ever said or done in the course of the marriage could and would be used against them in a court of law. Every excess, indiscretion, or dereliction became a club in the hands of opposing counsel.

On motion day the judges listened patiently or indifferently, according to their personalities, as each side catalogued the sins of the other. Husbands against wives, employers against employees, citizens against their government. Everybody against anybody.

Arguing their motions, the lawyers sneered their way around the courtroom, complaining, it seemed, mainly about one another: phone calls unreturned, interrogatories unanswered, offers spurned, agreements broken, misrepresentations and misconduct, mischief and mayhem. So vociferous were the attorneys in their tirades against each other that it was hard to remember what their motions were about.

We were scheduled to appear in both Circuit courtrooms this day—in front of Judge Kane for an arraignment in the perjury case, in front of Judge Olenik to do battle in the divorce case. By filing a piece of paper, I could have avoided this appearance in front of Kane, the only purpose of which was to ascertain that Davey understood the charge against her, but I had to be at the courthouse for the divorce case anyhow, and besides, I wanted this hearing, brief and meaningless as it might be. It was a way to get the feel of Kane's courtroom with Davey sitting beside me.

Kane had drawn Davey's case, and although the jury ultimately would decide her fate, the trial judge would make a hundred rulings before and during trial that could seal that fate before the case ever got to the jury. He could admit or exclude vital evidence, allow or forbid important arguments to the jury, sustain or overrule objections. With the slightest arch of an eyebrow, he could cast doubt in the jurors' minds about the competence and honesty of either lawyer. I wanted to get a reading on the man under that black robe.

Meanwhile, we sat and watched the parade of other cases. Davey appeared bemused by the tragedies and comedies being acted out before our eyes. She wore a flowered dress with a long skirt, and I noted that the other men in the room always gave her a second glance. From time to time she looked at me, and I smiled reassuringly.

For the most part we did not talk. I was determined to maintain my detachment, especially in a professional setting like the courthouse. Last week had been wonderful, but this was the real world for me—the courtroom. Davey needed me, and I should never forget that all was for naught if we lost her criminal case. She would be saved by my skills as a lawyer, not by the warm glow of our relationship.

Finally our case was called. *"People versus Davilon J. Alden,* Case Number one-eight-nine-nine-three-dash-FC," shouted the clerk. I led Davey to the lectern and put my appearance on the record.

"The defense has not filed a written waiver of arraignment?" Judge Kane asked the prosecutor seated at the table to my left, ignoring me.

"No, Your Honor," replied the prosecutor, a young man who looked as if he was just out of law school.

The judge frowned and looked at me. Then he looked at Davey. The quick glance around the courtroom that followed helped confirm my impression that he had recognized the case. He was wondering if the press was present.

"You're practicing in this county now, Mr. Brenner?" His Honor asked.

"Yes, I'm associated with Scott Sherman. Moved here from Chicago. Seventeen years with the Cook County Defenders Office."

"Well, you've got a lot of experience, Mr. Brenner, but you have to learn that we seldom actually conduct open-court arraignments anymore. Most lawyers file written waivers."

It was a reprimand.

"Yes, I'm aware of that, Your Honor. I wanted to take this opportunity to familiarize myself with your courtroom."

A patrician eyebrow was raised momentarily, but Judge Kane apparently decided that I was not being impertinent. He thumbed through the file impatiently and then commenced the ritual.

What followed might have been in Latin and in Gregorian chant for all the meaning the exchange had for Davey, who all the same looked impressed by the proceeding.

"Have you and your client received a copy of the information?" intoned the judge.

"Yes, and we waive a reading of the information and stand mute to the charges," I responded.

"The Court will enter a plea of not guilty on behalf of the defendant."

"Thank you, Your Honor."

"Bond will be continued in the manner previously set, and pretrial and trial will be set within forty-five days."

Forty-five days was rushing it. I was tempted to protest but decided it would be fruitless. Everybody wanted this case done with.

"And, Brenner, be sure to file a written waiver next time," he said as I started to guide Davey out. His tone suggested that I was being let off easy.

"I'll remember, Your Honor."

Sydney Masters was standing with Joel Alden among the little knots of people outside the courtroom of Judge Olenik. We had no chance of avoiding them, so I sailed right in. Davey hesitated momentarily, but she stayed beside me.

"You must be Masters," I said, nodding recognition to Alden as I offered my hand to his lawyer. Joel's malevolent stare caused Davey to shrink back behind me.

Masters was a big man, a full head taller than the rest of us. He radiated physical strength. His heavy-lidded eyes were as cold as a December dawn. He accepted my proffered hand and attempted to crush it, but his timing was off. Forewarned by Ralph Miles, as soon as I felt his huge grip start to close on my hand, I slipped my hand down his and circled his fingers. I squeezed just hard enough to let him know that I was up to his bully-boy tactics. I also moved closer to him and grinned up at his sullen face. He mumbled some sort of greeting. I released his hand and stepped back.

"I'm going to ask for sanctions for having to bring my motion to get Mr. Alden's property back," Masters said. "Olenik will stick it to you if he thinks you have violated the spirit of his orders."

"I'm glad to hear you say that," I replied. "A few days ago, Sydney, you were talking about the letter of the law. Now I see that this has been downgraded to a spirit-of-the-law violation. We're making progress."

"Look, smartass—"

"Are you prepared to change custody to Mrs. Alden, have your client move out of the marital home, and agree on a fair figure for alimony?"

Masters stepped forward, but I refused to give ground. Looming over me, he said, "You've got a lot of nerve, Brenner. The word on the street is that you're doing a lot more than giving Mrs. Alden legal advice. Now you want my client to pay for it?"

"You've got a filthy mind," I replied. "Keep it up and I'll knock you flat on your ass."

Masters smiled. Round One for him. Not only had he managed to make me angry, he'd put on a good show for his client. When their clients are present, many divorce lawyers make a practice of insulting both opposing counsel and the other spouse; it's good for business.

"No need to lose your temper, Brenner. Let's be professional about this."

I turned and escorted Davey into Judge Olenik's courtroom. So much for lawyers as peacemakers, I thought. When we were seated, I could see the pulse in Davey's neck throbbing. I resisted an impulse to touch her hand in reassurance, but she read my thought and smiled gratefully.

Judge Harold Olenik looked out at the faces in his courtroom with eyes of infinite sadness. I had heard that he was in his fifties, but he looked twenty years older. The skin on his melancholy face sagged like dripping candle wax. When he asked a question of a lawyer or made a ruling, his voice was hoarse, played out. Yet, despite his weary demeanor, his questions were sharp and his rulings concise and sensible.

"*Alden versus Alden*, File Number four-five-four-three-seven-eight-dash-DM," announced the judge's clerk from her desk next to the bench. She was a breathless blonde who called each case as if it were the next chapter in a thriller she was reading.

I made it to the lectern first and took command of it before Masters and his client got past the bar. We put our appearances on the record. Masters and Alden took seats at the plaintiff's table next to the jury box. Davey sat down at the defense table.

"Your Honor, this is a case in which the wife has been charged with a serious felony and she—"

"I'm familiar with the background, Counsel. Give me a summary of what brings you here today."

"We are asking you today to set aside an *ex parte* custody order you signed. Additionally, we want an order requiring the husband to resume the support he provided his wife before her arrest. She has been cut off without a penny. We are also requesting that the plaintiff husband vacate the marital home so that the child and her mother, my client, can live there."

"We have a counterpetition," Masters said without rising. "We are asking the court to hold the defendant in contempt for violating this court's orders by looting the marital home of priceless furnishings and artifacts."

Because of his size I'd expected Masters to be loud, but he was a mumbler in the courtroom.

The judge took a minute to study our petitions and then told me to proceed.

And we were off. I decried the way that Masters had waited until the day before the arrest to get a custody order signed without notice or a hearing. I told the judge how Joel had cut Davey off financially as soon as she was arrested. Masters interrupted me to deny that Davey had been the primary caretaker of Julie, suggesting that she was seldom home and had left Julie in the care of a maid most of the time. I protested his interference with my presentation; he accused me of attempting to mislead the judge on this busy motion day; I countered that his original motion for custody was perjured and that his current allegations about looting the Alden home were total falsehoods.

Finally, Judge Olenik put his hand up and called time out.

"Let me understand, Mr. Brenner. Your client is not in the marital home at present, is that correct? Well, then, where does she reside?"

Masters snickered, bringing a frown from the judge. I heard Masters whisper, not loud enough to be heard by Olenik, "She's shacked up with her lawyer, Judge."

"Mrs. Alden lives right here in Laffler County with Dr. Ann Mahoney, Your Honor."

Masters was on his feet. "Your Honor, counsel is attempting to fudge the issues. As a practical matter, the custody order grants physical custody of the child to Mrs. Alden's mother. It is not true that Mrs. Alden is deprived of her child. She can see her child anytime. The order—"

"I can read, Mr. Masters," the judge said. He looked at me. "Tell me about your alimony request, Mr. Brenner."

I argued that Joel Alden earned in excess of a million dollars a year and had an estimated personal net worth of more than ten million (I was making wild guesses because Davey had only the vaguest notion of Joel's finances), that Davey had no job skills with which to maintain the standard of living to which she had become accustomed during her marriage, and that her husband could hammer her into submission in this case unless she received help from the court in the form of an order for alimony.

"She can always get a job," Masters interjected, earning another frown from the judge. Lumbering to his feet to avoid further antagonizing the judge, Masters stepped over to the lectern and, as he continued talking, attempted to edge me out of the way. I refused to budge. I wasn't finished.

"It would be therapeutic for Mrs. Alden to find employment," Masters said. "It might help keep her mind off the felony perjury charges she faces. Where she's going, Judge, she won't have to worry about a standard of living."

And so it went for almost twenty minutes, Masters attempting to cloud the issues, and me (I am proud to say) sticking more or less to the facts because I felt they were so clearly on our side. At some point Masters got to take over the lectern and argue his motion, and it was my turn to interrupt and protest.

When I got a chance to take the lectern again, I vehemently denied that anything had been taken from the house except Davey's personal effects. I pointed out that there was no court order restraining her from entering the marital home. I waved around a copy of the certificate of title proving that she was the owner of the Cadillac Allante.

Finally the judge cut us off and made his ruling.

"Although I do not approve of self-help measures in the context of a hotly contested divorce, I cannot say that there was any violation of my *ex parte* orders," Judge Olenik said. "Mr. Brenner, I will not find you or your client in contempt, but I must caution you against intemperate advice to your client and impulsive action by either of you."

It was my day to get reprimanded.

"On the issue of child custody, this court sees no reason to change the present custody order. Mr. Alden has enlisted the assistance of the maternal grandmother in the present unsettled circumstances— wisely, I believe. Mrs. Alden finds herself in difficult straits, and, to put it mildly, her life is unstable at the present time. However, she is entitled to liberal visitation, and at the first sign of any attempt to interfere with that visitation I will react harshly, I assure you."

Pausing to adjust his half-frame reading glasses, the judge studied the two sides briefly, then returned to his notes. Davey sat stiffly at my side. I had the impression that she had quit breathing.

"The alimony and attorney fee questions are difficult and painful ones," the judge continued. "On the one hand, Mr. Alden obviously feels aggrieved by his recent prosecution and has naturally focused his bitterness on his wife, his chief accuser in that tragic case. He can hardly be expected to accept lightly the idea that he has an obligation to support her.

"On the other hand, Mrs. Alden is obviously in need of financial support—especially at this time. She is not employable right now, not only because of her lack of skills but also because no one would hire her with these charges hanging over her head. Yet somehow she must finance a criminal defense and a divorce action.

"It is clear to this court that the Alden family enjoyed a high standard of living compared to the average Laffler County resident. Mr. Alden's resources are considerable. Therefore I am ordering temporary alimony in the amount of one thousand dollars a week. In addition, Mr. Alden is to keep in effect all medical and hospitalization insurance as well as the automobile insurance on the Cadillac automobile titled in her name. Finally, I am ordering that Mr. Alden pay an initial attorney fee of ten thousand dollars in this divorce action."

"Your Honor, I respectfully protest," Masters said in a tone that was anything but respectful. He was on his feet, looking outraged. He was faking it. He had won the crucial fight over temporary custody.

"I've made my ruling, Counsel," Olenik said with deceptive mildness. "Are you continuing to argue?"

"No, Your Honor," Masters said humbly. Apparently he knew exactly how far he could push this judge and realized that he was close to the limit. He and Alden vacated their table as the next case was called. Alden looked confused.

Davey and I followed them into the corridor. I felt a grim pleasure at their unhappiness over the ruling, but I knew that they'd won the big one—the one that Davey wanted so badly.

"You okay?" I asked her.

"I think the judge was trying to be fair," she replied in a small voice. "He is right about me. I really don't have much of a future."

"That's not what he meant. He was talking about your chances of getting a job right now."

"I guess he just—"

"That will prove to be an illusory victory, Brenner," Masters said from behind me. Davey stopped talking. Her hand went to her mouth. I turned to find Masters glaring at me. Alden was standing behind him.

"What—"

"If you think Joel will pay one cent of alimony to this bitch, you're crazy," Masters said. He stepped up close to me to take full advantage of his bulk and height. Again I resisted the impulse to retreat. Although I was certain that it was all for show, the aura of violence about him was all the more menacing because it was so calculated.

Alden moved closer to Davey. "We don't have to fight like this, Davey," he said. "I don't know what all this stuff is about your lawyer, but you must know how I feel about you. Didn't your lawyer tell you—"

Masters cut him off by stepping between him and Davey.

"Joel still thinks he's in love with your client," he said. "He isn't thinking straight. She plays the virtuous mother while running around dropping her pants for anybody who asks. If she wants money, you pay her, Brenner. She may as well get paid for what she does best."

This time I did not take the bait. "Keep this up and I will be filing a grievance against you, Masters. Your performance today is the slimiest I have ever seen."

Masters smiled sweetly. "Don't start counting your client's alimony yet," he replied. "Ask yourself whether the judge is going to put Joel in jail for refusing to pay while his perjuring wife is free on bond."

With that angelic smile still on his face, Masters walked off down the hall with his client in tow.

I turned to Davey. The despair that I had seen in her face when she was in jail had returned. I was both concerned and curious about the effect on her of Masters's nasty remarks.

"I warned you that I'm not much of a divorce lawyer," I said cheerily.

"You weren't any more dishonest than the rest of them," she replied with a distracted smile.

"Thanks. That made my day."

"You're welcome."

She wasn't kidding.

Masters was too smart to have his client defy a court order. Within a few days Davey received her first support check from Joel. Besides, there was mileage for Joel in playing the role of the oppressed husband. The day after our appearance in front of Olenik, the *Detroit Times* carried a snide piece by Ripley that portrayed Joel as an oppressed husband forced to pay alimony to an adulterous liar of a wife. It was a neat hatchet job.

A few days later a check arrived at the office for the ten thousand Olenik had ordered in attorney fees. Masters and Joel were taking no chances. The influx of cash suddenly catapulted me from the ranks of court-appointed lawyers to retained counsel. Scott, although he loved money, was unimpressed.

With support assured, Davey was able to find an apartment in Richfield, a suburb of Detroit about halfway between Kirtley and St. Clair Shores, where her mother lived with Julie. She visited Julie every morning and usually spent the afternoons with Ann at the clinic or at the lake.

I accepted the news of her move with mixed feelings. I cherished the few hours I spent with Davey. When I could get away from the office, we managed to cram in some golf, fishing, tennis, and just hanging out together. But the downside I had feared was there: I was becoming unhinged in Davey's physical presence—too conscious of her every gesture, too fascinated by the loose strands of hair on the back of her neck when we played tennis, too taken by the occasional mysterious hint of a smile on her small, restrained mouth.

I recognized that I needed some distance. I had to redouble my efforts on her perjury case. The trial was coming up, and Scott, apparently resentful of every minute I spent on Davey's problems, was piling work on me. As far as I could tell, my efforts had increased the flow of cash into the firm, but with alimony owed to two ex-wives and an insatiable lust for buying, Scott was always short of money. Between his files and Davey's cases, I was overloaded, but I welcomed an opportunity to clear my head with legal work. I tried hard to make Davey a legal problem and nothing more. I tried.

Now that I was in the divorce case, I could attack on a new front. I wasted no time in sending out a demand for production of business records and a notice for the deposition of Joel Alden. It felt good to take the offensive again.

13

SYDNEY MASTERS GRIPPED THE LECTERN SO TIGHTLY WITH HIS MASsive hands that I thought he was about to pick it up and throw it across the courtroom. His face expressed disbelief and outrage that the judge had not summarily tossed me out of court.

Judge Olenik was unimpressed. Peering at us over his reading glasses, he shook his head slowly and looked again at the divorce file on the bench in front of him. Squabbling lawyers were one more annoyance he was required to suffer every day of his judicial life.

"I don't understand your objection," he told Masters. "Mr. Brenner has the right to take your client's deposition."

"It's a ruse to get around the rules in the criminal case," Masters said. "He knows that he can't take depositions in the criminal case. Not only that, he's also demanded thousands of financial records from Mr. Alden's various companies. He's threatening to bring these businesses to a standstill with these discovery demands."

I found myself enjoying Masters's anger. With his client not present, it seemed a wasted performance, but it was entertaining and I liked the idea that maybe it wasn't all acting; maybe I really had gotten to him.

Masters was correct, of course: I was using the divorce case to get information that would be denied me in the criminal case. I wanted to poke around in Joel Alden's finances and personal life to find anything that might assist me in defending Davey.

"Judge, you can't let Mr. Brenner harass Joel Alden this way. Mr. Alden is an upstanding member of this community who has been done a great wrong by this woman."

"I can appreciate Mr. Alden's concern," the judge said thoughtfully. "Being accused of a heinous crime would test any man. Maybe—"

I jumped to my feet and interrupted.

"Your Honor, Joel Alden is attempting to obtain custody of his daughter. It is our position that he is not morally fit to be the custodial parent and in fact poses a real danger to the child."

I did not have to explain. Olenik and everybody else in the courtroom knew what I was talking about. Olenik still looked hesitant. I plunged ahead.

"I have the duty to question him about his personal life. His character is very much at issue in this divorce case. And his financial picture is highly relevant also. He is a wealthy man, and his affairs are complicated. Mrs. Alden has always been kept in the dark about his finances. We need a clear picture of his assets."

Masters looked as if he were about to demolish the lectern.

"This is nothing but harassment," he shouted. "Mrs. Alden is not going to get any share of Joel Alden's estate because she is going to prison. This discovery nonsense is a waste of time."

"He hasn't even complied with my requests for the financial records," I shot back. "And then he has the nerve to bring this motion to limit my discovery."

"That's outrageous—"

Olenik had a flaw common in judges who are nice guys. Decent and sensitive himself, he cringed at the idea of a lawyer, armed with a court order, inflicting more pain on a man who had already suffered greatly. He smiled sadly at me. "I don't know, Mr. Brenner . . ."

"Your Honor, you have a duty to protect this child. If you deny my motion, you may be handing an innocent little girl over to a child molester. I can't fight for her if you are going to handcuff me."

It was blunt, it was unfair, it was risky. But I was desperate. I had to gamble on Olenik's reputation for fairness and patience.

Olenik put his hand up. "Please be seated. You too, Mr. Masters. Let's take a calm, rational look at this situation."

Masters was obviously ready to launch into another diatribe, but he thought better of it and took his seat. I sat down too. After a long pause the judge continued.

"It so happens that we have two lawsuits wending their way through the court system, following parallel courses," he said. "In the perjury case there is limited discovery, as we all know. But in the divorce case, wide-ranging discovery is permitted and even encouraged.

"The more people know about their assets and the strengths and weaknesses of their cases, the more likely they are to settle their differences. They can then get on with their lives, with great savings in time, money, and bitterness, not to mention the fact that settlement frees the court of the burden of a lengthy trial.

"Now, I am aware that criminal attorneys frequently use a related civil case as a vehicle for discovery, but so long as it is not abused I see nothing objectionable in the practice. I am going to allow the deposition of Mr. Alden."

"Your Honor, I'd like to have the deposition scheduled sometime after the perjury trial," Masters said. "I'm not arguing with the court, but I see no reason why we have to rush discovery when the criminal case may resolve most of the issues."

I was on my feet quickly. "He is arguing with the court, Your Honor. I have this deposition scheduled in four days and all the arrangements have been made. And I need the documents I've requested."

"My client has urgent business out of town," Masters said.

"They've had plenty of notice, Judge. This is the first I've heard of any inconvenience to Joel Alden."

Judge Olenik smiled at Masters.

"Have your client there," he said softly. "And provide Mr. Brenner with the financial records he's requested."

"I think we should limit the scope of the deposition," Masters argued. "I'd like a protective order that—"

"The answer is no," the judge said, even more softly. "Have your client there at the scheduled time, and turn those documents over to Mr. Brenner within twenty-four hours."

Masters knew his judge. The softer the voice, the more danger to the lawyer. The deposition would go forward.

If patience were the only virtue, Joel Alden was a saint. Although his eyes glowed with resentment, he managed to keep his feelings under control for the first three hours of his deposition. His answers were as vague and unhelpful as possible. Masters had prepared him well.

After a short break we took our seats again in Masters's conference room. Joel sat at a long table flanked by Masters and the stenographer, a young woman with a rigid professional air. I sat across from them.

When the stenographer nodded her head, I continued.

"Mr. Alden, I want to ask you now about a man named Terrence Sinclair. Do you recognize that name?"

"I do." Alden leaned back in his chair and smiled for the first time. For three hours he had dodged and weaved his way through questions about his business operations. Now he could talk about Davey's infidelity.

"Do you recall that he appeared at the first trial?"

I intended to keep him on a short leash by asking leading questions. Otherwise he would eat up the whole day cataloguing Davey's sins.

"Correct. He told us that—"

"I know what he said. I want to ask—"

"Let him answer the question," Masters demanded. "You can't cut him off just because you don't like the answer."

It was an old ploy: make mincemeat out of a deposition by constant interruptions and objections. Confuse the questioner and make the transcript unreadable. I had kept things on track for the first three hours, but Masters did not give up easily; he was also a patient man. Fortunately, I could exercise that virtue too.

"The objection is noted," I said. "Mr. Alden, when did you first hear the name of Terrence Sinclair?"

"I don't remember."

"Was it before your wife went to the police about you and your daughter Julie?"

"I'm not sure."

"Then it would be fair to say that you may have known Dr. Sinclair before the charges were made by your wife?"

"You're putting words in his mouth," Masters said.

Joel got the message. "I heard about Sinclair only when I learned that my wife was sleeping with him. That was after she accused me," he said.

"Then it is your sworn testimony that you were not aware of the existence of Terrence Sinclair before your wife brought charges against you?"

"That's correct," Joel answered, glancing impatiently at his watch.

"Do you know if your attorney, Sydney Masters, had any connection with Sinclair before Mrs. Alden accused you?"

"Not that I know of."

The deposition so far had produced nothing of value in the criminal case. Masters had delivered seven boxes of financial records, but he had turned them over late, and I had not had time to read them all. During the first part of the deposition I had forced Joel to outline for me his financial holdings, occasionally questioning him about a tax return or corporate record, but all of that was window dressing for the divorce case; my real interest was in uncovering something that might help me in the criminal case. And that meant getting down and dirty.

"Mr. Alden, do you have a sexual preference for young children?"

Looking as if he were about to reach across the table and grab me by the throat, Masters shouted, "Don't answer that. That's outrageous."

"And it's also relevant," I yelled back. "The question is whether your client is a pedophile. That's what this case is all about. If you refuse to answer questions on this issue, I'll adjourn the deposition and schedule an emergency hearing in front of Judge Olenik."

My sharp reaction made Masters hesitate. Bully that he was, he relied on intimidation and won many a point that way. But it hadn't worked with me, and he was not eager to go in front of Olenik again.

"I'll answer the question," Joel interrupted. "I insist on answering it."

Masters shook his head in disgust but let his client go ahead. I had the feeling that he was acting again. He and Joel had rehearsed that very question.

"The answer is no," Joel said. "I have no sexual attraction to children. Not now, not ever."

His face flushed, Joel glared at me and spoke with such manly outrage that I almost felt guilty for asking. I had to force myself to recall that he had virtually confessed to me that night in his house. If he had the same effect on the jury, we'd be finished.

"Do you recall a conversation we had at your house a few weeks ago?"

"You asked to come out and see me. I didn't know at the time that you were violating your ethics rules, or I wouldn't have agreed to see you."

I couldn't let his lie pass, but neither did I want to get bogged down in it. "You and I both know that your statement is not true," I said, "but, in any event, didn't you argue in favor of sexual relationships between grown men and young girls?"

"That's a damnable lie. You came to my house and accused me of all kinds of vile things."

Masters looked smug, sitting across the table from me. Another rehearsed answer.

"Is photography a hobby of yours?"

"I take a few snapshots now and then. I wouldn't call it a hobby."

"Have you ever had in your possession photographs of naked children, including children engaging in sexual activities?"

Joel's eyes narrowed. "Another of Davey's lies, no doubt. No, never. I've never had such pictures."

I reminded myself to be careful. Although Masters knew my game plan and I'd lost the element of surprise, there was no point in tipping my hand further.

I consoled myself with the thought that I had accomplished one purpose of the deposition. I'd wanted to get a feel for what kind of witness Joel would make in front of the jury. I had my answer. He would make a good witness for the prosecution.

To hide my frustration, I bent over the box of Alden Construction records I had brought with me. Not only had Masters delivered them late, but they were so jumbled that it would take days to get them in any kind of order. Not that I really gave a damn about his finances; what I needed for Davey's criminal trial was dirt.

I was about to terminate the whole interrogation when a document caught my eye. Almost as an afterthought I'd brought it along; it seemed out of place among the records of Alden Construction and the other entities that made up Joel's empire.

"What is the Terra Group?" I asked as I lifted the paper from the box at my feet. I knew about Alden Construction Corp., Alden Overland Trucking, JMA Truck Leasing, Inc., Laffler Sand & Gravel Ltd., and Alden Ready Cement Co. The name Terra Group seemed vaguely familiar, but it had not come up earlier in my interrogation.

Joel stiffened in his chair and looked carefully at Masters.

Masters sat in silence, inscrutable—but I knew I'd hit a nerve.

Suddenly Masters reached over the table and snatched the document from my hand.

"That's got nothing to do with Joel's business," he said, sliding the document into his leather briefcase on the floor beside him. "It belongs to another client of mine. It got sent with Joel's papers by mistake."

My first reaction was to leap across the table and recapture my document, but I thought better of it. Olenik had already warned me against self-help, and besides, Masters was twice my size.

Instead I looked hard at Masters and in a calm voice demanded that he return the document to me. When he just sat there smiling, not deigning to reply, I turned to the now wide-eyed stenographer. Feeling slightly ridiculous, I said, "May the record reflect that the counsel for the plaintiff, Sydney Masters, has just grabbed a document from my hand and refuses to give it back. It is a document that was turned over to me as part of discovery. I am entitled to the document and will bring the matter to the attention of the Circuit Court at the earliest opportunity."

Masters's reaction stunned all of us. He jumped to his feet and yelled at the stenographer, whose professional composure was by this time completely undone. "Let the record reflect that counsel is mistaken or outright lying when he says the document bears the name of my client."

Despite her loss of aplomb, the stenographer dutifully kept taking notes as Masters ranted on.

"It is the property of another client, and I will not have my integrity impugned in this manner. Counsel is totally out of order, and I intend to bring this matter to the attention of the court and the Grievance Committee."

I stood up.

"This deposition is terminated," I said. "We'll see you in court."

Driving back to the office, I was unable to manage a smile at our comic ending. I had apparently stumbled onto some shady deal of Joel's.

Nothing would have given me greater pleasure than to lift up that rock and see what crawled out from under it, but I had to focus on the criminal case. Sadly, mere crookedness by Joel in his business dealings would not be enough. I had to expose Joel for the monster that he really was. Somehow.

14

RALPH MILES RAISED A PEDANTIC FOREFINGER TOWARD THE CEIL-
ing. "It's not enough for the prosecutor to show that Mrs. Alden made
conflicting statements," he said. "He's got to prove the contrary
proposition—the contrary of the statement that she made under oath.
In other words, he's got to show that Joel did not molest his daughter."

"Big deal. Joel's going to admit it?"

I loved to tease Ralph; everybody did. But because something about
Ralph seemed to bring out the bully in people, I took special care to
use a light touch. For his part, Ralph always took such kidding in
good spirits; it was impossible to offend him.

We were sitting in the library with a pile of books the day after
Joel's aborted deposition. I'd drafted Ralph to assist me with research
in an effort to find legal support for my plan to pillory Joel Alden. We
weren't having much luck.

"Technically, it's irrelevant whether Joel Alden is a molester,"
Ralph said. "What is relevant is whether Mrs. Alden saw him molest
their daughter as she testified."

"A distinction without a difference," I scoffed. "Give me a chance
to show that Joel Alden is a pedophile and Davey will walk—that I
can guarantee."

"You have no real evidence of that, and Kane will never allow you to go on a fishing expedition. He might ignore the distinction if you had something solid to go on, but he's not going to just sit back and allow you to tar Joel Alden again, not after the fiasco of the first trial."

I yawned and stretched, gestures that I knew masked the tension that was building up in me. Trial was approaching, and it looked as though I had neither the facts nor the law on my side. If I could prove that Joel Alden was a molester, or even a dirty old man who was drawn to children, no jury on earth would convict Davey Alden. That much I was convinced of.

But what if I could not get past Kane to the jury to make my argument? What if he barred any attempt to make Joel the bad guy? It would help to be able to pull some cogent legal arguments out of my briefcase. And of course I needed more than legal theories: some evidence might be nice too. It was a measure of my desperation that I kept bouncing outlandish legal theories off the ever-patient Ralph.

"What about some sort of duress theory?" I asked, looking hungrily at the books Ralph had been perusing. "Along the line that Mrs. Alden was faced with a legitimate fear that her husband would hurt their child and had no choice but to destroy him to save the child. It so happens that's what actually occurred."

"Michigan does recognize a duress defense in a perjury case," Ralph answered, "but it won't work in your case."

"Why not? It's the truth."

"Because Mrs. Alden had too many other options. For one thing, she could have just filed for divorce and fought for custody of the child."

"Christ, the more we try to put a legal framework around the thing, the worse it seems for us."

"I guess the fact is that there is no justification for perjuring yourself." Ralph added, "Your idea of coercion might mitigate the sentence, but it would not justify an acquittal."

I looked hard at Ralph. "Do you believe her story?"

Poor Ralph. He believed in me.

"I don't know. When you think about it, it doesn't sound plausible. I find it hard to accept—"

"Davey Alden *cannot* be convicted," I said slowly. I spoke as if by sheer force of will I could make Ralph share my faith in Davey. If I could not convince him, how could I persuade a jury? And if I failed to win over the jury, Davey would go to prison and Julie would become Joel's. Failure was not an option.

"Have you given any more thought to moving for a change of venue?" Ralph asked.

"A waste of time. You've got to make an attempt to pick a jury, and you can be damned sure Kane will frame his voir dire so that we get one. Besides, with Joel being a local big shot, he's bound to have pushed a few people around and made a few enemies. I'll take my chances here."

"Maybe they'll call Joel Alden as a witness. Then you'd get a chance to impeach him."

"You think Holtzman will really call him?" The faint scent of blood had my nose quivering. Near starvation always enhances the senses.

"Holtzman always goes for overkill. He's cautious to a fault. Besides, this will be Joel's chance to seek his vindication publicly. Holtzman can hardly deny him that opportunity. If only we had some evidence . . ."

"I have nothing," I added. "Not one goddam thing. Not a single arrow in my fucking quiver."

A sudden, irrational anger seized me. I pushed my chair back violently and stood up, spilling a pile of books onto the floor. Some of my irritation was directed at Ralph Miles, not because he had done anything but because he was handy, the bearer of bad news, and a natural scapegoat. Poor Ralph. His eyes, made unnaturally small and weak by his thick lenses, swelled in surprise.

In truth, I was angry at everything human—at the law, at myself, at Davey Alden, at everything that made the world the stewpot of lies that it was, had always been, and always would be.

"Goddammit, Ralph. I've got to get that argument in front of the jury—and I'm going to do it. I'm also going to find some evidence that will prove that Joel Alden is a damned pervert. If I have to, I'll go with Davey Alden alone and put her on the stand and make the jury believe her. They'll acquit her. Do you know why?"

"Why?" Ralph asked obediently. We both knew I could not put Davey on the witness stand.

"Because it's common sense. I took a look at the Michigan Criminal Jury Instructions the other day, and do you know how many times the judge tells the jurors to use their common sense? Four times, goddammit. That's what this is all about—just plain common sense. You keep thinking up legal theories and I'll throw them at Kane, but in the end I'll get the message to those jurors, no matter what that pompous, silver-haired fuckhead says."

With that stirring outburst of rhetoric, I slapped Ralph on the shoulder and marched out. On the way to my office I recalled the hoary old maxim: when you have the law on your side, cite the law; when you have the facts with you, emphasize the facts—but when you have neither on your side, pound the table.

Despite my efforts to maintain a balance, the trial of Davey Alden was becoming the Omega point in my life. In a few weeks Davey would go before a jury, and her fate—and Julie's—would be sealed. Beyond the trial there was nothing that mattered to me.

I fretted over my inability to find something that would destroy Joel Alden, for that was what it came down to. Davey had no defense in the law, but if I could make Joel the real defendant in the trial, she might walk out of that courtroom a free woman. I pressured Ralph to find something—anything—in the law that I could throw at Kane and Holtzman, if only to sow confusion. I planned to depose Terry Sinclair in the divorce case, but he had disappeared; I hired a private detective to find him. Because Joel Alden did not look or act like a child molester, I consulted with a University of Michigan professor to see if he could testify about the profile of the man who sexually abuses children.

I began to resent the other cases that intruded upon my preoccupation with Davey Alden. Explaining that he had to fly to California with a client, a grinning Scott Sherman handed me a file that was scheduled for trial the next week. Fortunately the plaintiff caved in the day before trial, and I was able to settle cheap. Then I had to fly to Denver for two days of depositions in a chemical spill case.

Inexplicably, although I saw her frequently at Ann's, I did not discuss the trial with Davey in any depth. She was at Ann's almost every other day, and I usually joined them for dinner. I wanted to brief her on Joel's deposition and other events, but the right moment to talk business never arrived. We cooked steaks and chicken on Ann's brick barbecue, and Ann and I unsuccessfully tried to convert Davey to the joys of the martini (she preferred caffeine-free Diet Pepsi). Once, Davey was able to bring Julie out to Ann's overnight. I tried to stay away, but the skinny, freckle-faced four-year-old would have none of it. She insisted that I be the one to read her *Charlotte's Web* at bedtime.

Away from Davey, I spent almost every waking moment thinking about her trial. In her presence, the cloud of concern lifted and I was free to find pleasure in the moment—the laughter and conversation, the way she would toss her head when amused and then smile self-consciously when she caught me watching her.

One evening I stopped by her apartment on the way home from Detroit and asked her to join me for dinner. I said I needed to talk to her about her case. She agreed and left the room for a quick change.

I was surprised at how quickly she'd been able to make the two-bedroom place look like a home. From the Oriental rug on the hardwood floor to the little decorative birdhouses on the mantel, it was the work of a creative and confident hand.

Over dinner at The Wharf, one of those relaxed suburban restaurants where a tie was out of place, we savored the nutlike flavor of grilled whitefish and drank a fine Spanish wine. Davey had changed from jeans to a black pantsuit that accented her paleness and red hair.

I found myself telling her about my marriage and how Sheila and I had been the odd couple among our friends, she the dedicated servant of enlightened capitalism, I the janitor who cleaned up after that system. The novelty of Sheila and me as a couple—fuzzy-headed liberal and crisp career woman—had certainly been one of the things that brought us together, and many of our friends no doubt nodded sagely and put it down to the fact that opposites attract. Certainly there was superficial truth in that cliché.

I told Davey that Sheila's choice of me was only an enigma until one realized how competitive she was, and what a respite I was for her. I was no threat. I had dropped out of her world. Somehow we needed each other. I did not tell Davey that my mistake was in believing that her need, like mine, would last forever.

Davey listened to me and sometimes talked about herself, but only later did I come to realize that her little confidences, seemingly so revealing at the time, were throwaways, the kind of information a spy is taught to give away under torture in the hope that the enemy will be satisfied. She revealed nothing important about herself.

But I was blind to all that. I talked about myself endlessly, and she listened attentively. Then, embarrassed, I awkwardly changed the subject to books. I kidded her about the way she identified with all the tragic women figures in literature—Desdemona, Anna Karenina, Madame Bovary. Victims of love, all dead tragically, I told her.

"You're leaving off my favorite—Ophelia," Davey said.

"'Favorite' is a strange word to use for Ophelia. She was mad, or she became mad, and she killed herself."

"No, she died accidentally. She fell into the stream."

"Yes, and she floated, singing, until she sank."

Davey stared down at the table and quoted: ". . . but long it could not be / Till that her garments, heavy with their drink, / Pull'd the poor wretch from her melodious lay / To muddy death."

"Another gloomy story of a woman betrayed," I said.

"No, there was happiness, even gaiety, in her madness. She handed out flowers and sang silly little songs."

"I don't remember it that way." I regretted having launched the conversation. I was reminded that there were deep and unknowable currents in this attractive married woman who sat opposite me, this woman whom I'd sworn to save, and I reminded myself that it was not for me to explore those currents.

I made an effort to discuss her legal matters, but the hour was late and Davey's interest seemed mere politeness. Once again she was leaving it all in my hands.

There was an awkward moment when I stood outside her front door again. "I'll call you," I said just before she closed the door. I meant that I would call her to talk business.

On the drive home I recalled that some of Ophelia's silly little songs had been bawdy. Later I looked one up.

> *Quoth she, before you tumbled me,*
> *You promised me to wed.*

He answers:

> *So would I ha' done, by yonder sun,*
> *An thou hadst not come to my bed.*

15

"WOULD YOU LIKE A CUP OF TEA?" ASKED BRENDA FOREMAN, POINT-ing to a pewter pot on her desk. I declined and she poured for herself. She was a matronly woman who would have looked natural hosting an afternoon bridge party or a meeting of the League of Women Voters. In fact, her business was rape.

Brenda Foreman was the executive director of WAR, which stood for Women Against Rape. She was a pleasant-faced woman with short gray hair in her late forties or early fifties, the kind of woman you watched your language in front of. So much for comfortable stereotypes. Crime, like war, tends to stir the pot up a bit.

"If you'd called first, I might have saved you a trip, Mr. Brenner," she said. "I really don't know how I will be able to assist you."

The voice was pleasant enough, as was her demeanor, but I sensed a definite frostiness. Which of course Scott Sherman had warned me about that very first day. Davey's startling confession on the witness stand did not endear her to people like Brenda Foreman. But with less than a month to go before the trial, I had to look in every door.

"It was kind of you to see me without an appointment, Ms. Foreman."

"Please, you can call me *Mrs.* Foreman," she said. "I am a traditional woman who is happily married and proud to be associated with my husband's name."

"Mrs. Foreman it is, then," I replied. "I'm the attorney for Davey Alden—"

"I know who you are, Mr. Brenner. I read the newspapers and listen to the gossip around town. That's why I said I did not see how I could help you."

"I'm not certain I understand."

"Don't *misunderstand*, Mr. Brenner. I only meant that I know who you are and I appreciate that as Mrs. Alden's lawyer you'd like WAR to assist you. Unfortunately, because our past association with Davey Alden was . . . well, let's say disappointing . . . we're not in a position to assist you."

"I get what you're saying, but could I at least tell you what it is that I want? It may not be much of a burden after all."

"I really don't see . . ." She looked at her watch and then back at me. "Very well, if you'll be brief and if you would please keep in mind that I cannot—simply cannot—get involved in the Davey Alden case again."

"I understand that one of your therapists—I believe her name is Andrea Swanson—interviewed and counseled both the Alden child and Mrs. Alden."

"Yes, that is correct. Andrea is one of our best therapists. But what—?"

"I think it would be helpful if I could talk to her and perhaps review her notes on her talk with the child."

"How could any of that be helpful to you now? Now that Davey Alden has confessed to lying about the whole thing?"

"What if I told you that Davey Alden did not commit perjury, that she may have invented the details to get people to believe her, but that she told essentially the truth?"

"That would mean Joel Alden really is a child molester."

"Exactly."

"I would say the same thing I've been saying all along. I cannot help you."

I had a difficult time masking my impatience. By this time, of course, I believed in Davey Alden and easily forgot that apparently Ann and I were the only ones who did. Even her own mother did not believe her.

"Never say never. Why not?"

Brenda Foreman stood up with the obvious intention of terminating the interview. I remained sitting.

"For one thing, that information is privileged—"

"Mrs. Alden can waive the privilege."

"Not for the child if she does not have custody."

"She has joint legal custody. That gives her the right to the information."

With a sigh she sat down again. "Mr. Brenner, I'll be blunt with you. WAR is dependent on the good opinion and financial support of this community for its survival. Our goal is to educate the public and those who dominate our social, legal, and economic structures— mostly men, by the way—away from the myth that women cry rape or child abuse at the drop of a hat. It's been a long and arduous task, believe me.

"Just when we have been making progress, along comes a Davey Alden and threatens to set us back decades in our public relations. I don't know if we'll ever get over the harm she has done. Our funding is already being affected."

"Yes, but don't you—"

She held up her hand and silenced me. "That's not all. Prosecutor Holtzman and Judge Olenik sit on our board of directors. Unless we have the strong support of law enforcement in this community, we have little hope of success—and at present we do enjoy that support. I'm not going to jeopardize the work of this organization for one woman."

"Even if she's innocent?"

"You're her lawyer. I would expect you to say that. I respect your role. Please respect what I have to do."

"You do know that I can get a court order requiring Andrea Swanson to divulge that information?" I said.

"Do what you have to do. We will of course honor any court order. But let me ask you this: Are you certain that Mrs. Alden is telling the truth this time?"

"Very certain."

"I ask because we discovered the hard way that Davey Alden has trouble with the truth. She alters the truth regardless of who she hurts. Be careful, Mr. Brenner. Be careful."

This time I stood up with her. We shook hands. She had a right to be cautious. Davey Alden was a threat to all that she held precious. She was a goodhearted person who could not afford to take a risk.

What if I got a jury of Brenda Foremans? Solid citizens who could not take a chance on Davey Alden. Good, sensible people who would nod in agreement when the prosecutor argued that the community could not afford to be fooled a second time. I shuddered as Brenda Foreman closed her door behind me.

I stared suspiciously at the two bluegill fillets on my plate. "You're sure these things are edible? No restaurant I've ever been in had these on the menu."

Ann slapped at my head with her spatula. I ducked just in time. We sat at her kitchen table, preparing to consume our catch after a morning of fishing on our lake. Ann fished, I rowed. When we returned to shore, eight hand-sized bluegills hung from her stringer. Within minutes they were filleted, sprinkled with seasoned bread crumbs, and sizzling in a big black frying pan.

"Don't tell me your dad never took you fishing," she said. "You really were deprived, boy."

"We fished a lot. Big charter boats, and we caught a hell of a lot bigger fish than these minnows."

In the end I ate not only what was on my plate but four more fillets besides, washed down with a nifty white Zinfandel that Ann had found on sale at the supermarket. Then we sat on Ann's patio, sipping coffee and staring at the afternoon sun shimmering on the lake.

"I wish Davey could see this," I said. It was less than a week since I'd taken Davey to dinner at The Wharf.

"I told her today wasn't a good day to visit."

"You what?"

"I needed to talk to you."

I looked into Ann's dishrag of a face. I didn't like the way she was looking at me. I preferred that she hide her concern for me behind a mask of jeers and insults.

"I don't think I'm going to appreciate this," I said.

"I think you're falling in love with Davey, and I don't think that's a good idea right now."

"Love—the most abused word in the language."

"Don't change the subject."

"You worry too much. I'm all right. So I've noticed that she's an attractive woman. That doesn't mean I'm not in control."

"Good to hear that. She's lonely and fragile, Jack. I'm afraid that if you're not careful, you could damage her badly—or yourself. She's got strange depths to her, and you're not as sophisticated and worldly as you think."

"And you are?"

"I've been around."

"This from a woman who's practically been a nun?"

Ann laughed and sipped her coffee. "Stay focused, Jack. She's a married woman, and that means something to a lot of people. It's obvious you two are attracted to each other. But now is not the time. You can't be her lawyer and her lover both. If you think you can, you're fooling yourself and cheating her. A moonstruck lawyer is about as good as a surgeon with the shakes."

"I'm not her lover."

The resentment that stirred inside me convinced me that Ann was right on. I was slipping under Davey's spell. Everything about her—the polite beads of sweat on her brow when we played tennis, the freckles that played hide-and-seek on her face, the secret well from which her femininity flowed—all were sources of wonder and discomfort for me. Each day I imagined that her eyes were a different shade of blue and that the variations had some meaning I could not yet fathom.

"I can take care of myself—and her."

"Spoken like a real hunk of a man."

"I didn't mean it like that. I'll watch it. I'll be careful."

"Good. Davey's not like other women you've met. Sometimes I think she's a thousand years old. I can't explain it."

I knew what Ann meant, and I couldn't express it either. Davey was impossible to define, a butterfly flitting away to another part of the garden whenever I got close, maddening in her ability to evade attempts to capture her essence—one minute an oblivious innocent, the next a woman who seemed to know all the depths of good and evil.

"I hear you," I said.

"I knew you would."

"So where do you get off lecturing me on mere human love?" I said brightly. "This God of yours is so demanding that I can't imagine you losing your head over something as frivolous as a man."

"Spoken with the arrogance of youth and the ignorance of a modern pagan. You don't know the half of it, Brenner."

"Don't tell me," I cried with mock horror.

Suddenly she was serious, and sad.

"Once when I was a young doctor in Africa—yes, I was young once and not so bad looking—I fell in love with a married doctor quite a bit older than me. He wouldn't leave his wife and I wouldn't have allowed him to even if he'd wanted to."

She sat there wrapped in her memory for only a moment. Then she shook it off and fixed me with a stare. "So don't you tell me that I don't know anything about life and love, Mr. Brenner. I've been there and back."

"Sorry about that." And I truly was.

"But you're right about one thing," Ann added with a rueful smile. "When God sets His sights on you, there's no escaping Him."

"You don't seem the type for a vocation or whatever you call it."

"I'm not. I'm aware that I don't exactly exude reverence or piety. I tried to tell God that, but He wouldn't listen. He has his own ideas about things. At least they didn't involve a convent."

We both laughed.

Ann and her God. Usually I start to squirm if people say God is telling them what to do. Not with Ann. Just so He didn't try to tell me what to do.

16

FOUR DAYS LATER I PAID THE PRICE FOR NOT PLAYING BALL WITH Bob Ripley. Larry Semczyk had warned me about a feature that Ripley was working on for the Sunday magazine section. The weekend after Ann and I had our talk, she called me over for Sunday breakfast and showed me the article. I sat on her patio and read it while my coffee turned to acid in my mouth.

Ripley's piece was one of those against-the-grain pronouncements that invariably arise to counter current wisdom and provide the conflict that is the lifeblood of the media. After years of exposing and hammering away at the hidden shame of sexual abuse of children, someone at the *Times*, perhaps Ripley himself, had decided that it was time to balance the scales and suggest that things had gone too far.

With the Alden case as its anchor, Ripley's Sunday magazine feature explored the upsurge in reported cases of abuse in the previous decade, wondered whether it was the result of more reporting to police or an actual increase in incidents, talked of the hysteria that often accompanies high-profile cases (failing to note that it is the media that usually fans the flames), lamented the malice that leads some women to make false accusations in divorce cases, and pointed out that social workers and police rarely are adequately trained in how to interview highly suggestible children.

"I wish she didn't have to see it," I said to Ann. "God, how I wish she didn't have to see it." Davey had spent the night at Ann's and had risen early to minister to Ann's flowers.

"She'll handle it all right. She's tougher than you think."

Ripley quoted a half-dozen fathers, among them Joel Alden, who claimed to have been falsely accused of molesting their children. He also provided a forum for Fathers Against Interrupted Relationships to sound off on the unfairness of the system. And of course no such article would be complete without experts to lend credibility to its theme: that scheming women were taking advantage of the current hysteria to destroy innocent men. Two Ph.D.s were called upon to pontificate on that thesis.

A striking color photo of Davey graced the front page of the magazine. The photographer had apparently snapped her as she was entering the courthouse during her husband's trial. It was a layout editor's dream. Her striking beauty, those wild red curls, her lithe step as she bounded up the courthouse steps—everything suggested a woman of passion and strength, impatient and uninhibited, capable of anything.

"It shows how a picture can lie better than a thousand words," Ann said. "I ought to get on the phone and ream that editor out. Better yet, I should go down there with a horsewhip and teach all of them some manners."

"And help them sell more papers? Forget it."

Above the photo of Davey on the front page was the headline CHILD SEX ABUSE: CRISIS OR WITCH HUNT? On an inside page, Ripley's story appeared under this headline: A SMALL TOWN SEARCHES ITS CONSCIENCE. Although he played around with the Salem idea throughout his piece, Ripley was careful to avoid saying outright that the sex-abuse crisis was overblown. After all, the idea was to titillate, not offend, the reader. Besides, Ripley's six innocent men might just be liars.

Ripley used less than a thousand words to portray Davey as the archetypal designing woman, as treacherous as she was beautiful. He mentioned the dentist from Southfield and carefully laid out the prosecutor's theory about why Davey had lied on the witness stand: to get Joel out of the way so that she could keep his wealth while she pursued her sordid affair.

Even I managed to get some free publicity. After resurrecting my "Jack the Ripper" nickname, Ripley generously described me as a "wily veteran of the rough-and-tumble Cook County court system, noted in the past for its big city inefficiency and corruption." That little tidbit, juxtaposed with mention of the missing lover, Sinclair, seemed to suggest that I was hiding him. Then came Ripley's *pièce de résistance*:

"Veteran observers of the Laffler County court scene find Brenner something of a mystery. They are puzzled by his tactics. Because his client's alleged perjury was on the record in open court, it is felt that Mrs. Alden's chances of avoiding a conviction on that charge are virtually nil. Nevertheless, Brenner has refused to discuss a plea bargain that could save his client years in prison."

"Listen to this," I said, and read to Ann, " 'Equally puzzling is the nature of Brenner's relationship with his client. After he managed to get Mrs. Alden out of jail on personal bond, Brenner moved her in next door to him in a lakefront home north of Kirtley. Neighbors and residents of Kirtley have seen them together, driving around the community on weekends and on occasion shopping together at local stores.' "

An old lawyer once told me that the only bad news is your obituary, and as far as lawyers are concerned, I'd found that to be true. Let the newspapers paint a lawyer as a shady manipulator, and the world will beat a path to his door. I would survive, but I was not so sure about Davey. Harsh reality had a way of catching up to her with a vengeance.

I was also worried about the effect such an article would have on potential jurors. I had ruled out a motion to change venue as a useless gesture. Now I would have to give it more thought.

Finally, I wondered if I'd dropped the ball with Ripley. If I had been a little more cooperative, things might have turned out differently. Why had I taken such a dislike to Ripley, who was no more obnoxious than half the reporters in Chicago, with whom I got along well enough? What if I'd returned his phone calls?

I looked down at the bitter brew in my cup and wondered if it was too early for a martini.

I found Davey in Ann's flower garden. She wore jean cutoffs and an oversized Michigan State sweatshirt with white letters almost worn off. Her chin and one bare knee were smudged. I handed her a cup of coffee and squatted on the lawn next to her. She sat cross-legged, facing me, and sipped her coffee with a grateful smile.

"Read the Sunday paper yet?"

"A little," she said. "I wanted to get outside before the sun got too hot. I just love the cool of a summer morning."

"Did you see Ripley's piece? He stuck it to us pretty good."

"I saw it and decided not to read it. What you don't know won't hurt you."

I reached over and rubbed at the dirt mark on her knee. Her skin had the cool of the morning still on it. With my thumb I rubbed the spot on her chin. She took my hand and squeezed it.

"You should read it," I said.

"Why? I can't do anything about it."

I intended to say that we shouldn't be seen together around town. That even with Ann along people would gossip. That even Ann was worried. That maybe I'd been indiscreet. I said nothing.

A few days later, on my way back to Kirtley from another court appearance in Detroit, I called Davey and suggested dinner at The

Wharf, the lakeside restaurant we'd dined at before. She said she'd call to reserve a table on the deck at water's edge. We agreed that a lakeside dinner was a good way to bid farewell to the summer.

I had barely left Detroit when black clouds took over the sky. By the time I pulled into the parking lot of Davey's apartment complex, it was raining hard. I was reaching to turn off the engine when a laughing Davey opened the passenger door and slid into the seat beside me. She was drenched and dripping water all over my car seat. The long white pants and yellow T-shirt she wore were plastered to her skin.

"Forget the restaurant," she said. "I'm going to make you the best meal you've ever tasted. It's the least I can do after all you've done for me."

"You're nuts," I said. "Only a fool would run out in this downpour without an umbrella."

"I love the rain. It makes you feel so clean."

"Now we're both going to get soaked."

"Let's stay here. I love sitting in a car on a rainy day," she said with a mischievous smile. She sat facing me with her legs pulled up under her chin, twirling a curl with a finger, her head resting against her window. Her wet hair seemed darker, almost brunette. The car smelled of wet clothing and Davey's scent.

We watched the rivulets of water on the windshield. It was warm and humid inside the car, and after a while I became overly conscious of Davey's presence. As if sensing my unease, she slowly sat up and moved closer to me. Very carefully she placed a hand on my knee and looked me in the eye. Her smile and the laughter in her eyes challenged me.

"I'm starved. Where's that food?" I said, opening my door. I jumped out into the rain and ran to open Davey's car door. Together we ran the thirty yards to the door of the apartment building.

As we ran up the stairs, Davey grabbed my hand and held it until our wet hands slipped apart. Inside the apartment we paused and caught our breath. Davey laughed at the way I stood stiffly in my wet things.

"I've got to get out of these clothes," she said. "Why don't you make us a drink. I'll have a Chardonnay. While you're at it, take a look on the counter. We're having shrimp and garlic pasta."

I found the alcohol in a cabinet above the sink and made myself a martini. I opened a bottle of wine from the refrigerator and poured a glass for Davey. On the cutting board were little piles of sliced vegetables—mushrooms, red peppers, asparagus. In a bowl on the stove next to a covered pan were large peeled shrimp. The pan contained a steaming broth.

"My favorite outfit," Davey said from behind me. I turned and saw that she was wearing a white terrycloth robe. Her feet were bare. She had brushed her hair back.

"There's a robe for you on the bed," she said. "You're soaked too."

"I'm okay. It's drying fast."

She smiled and reached above me on her tiptoes to take dishes from the cupboard. Her wet hair brushed my face. I stepped aside but instinctively reached out to steady her as she pulled a pile of plates from a shelf. The terrycloth felt warm. She laughed and almost dropped the dishes when I touched her. I stared hard at her and she responded by looking down, suddenly shy. A little smile played around her lips.

While I sipped my drink, she set the table and lit the two candles there. Then she dimmed the lights over the table. My feelings must have been written on my face, for she raised a forefinger in a gesture that told me to be patient. Then she came over to me.

I took her in my arms and crushed my lips against hers. She responded and then suddenly stepped back. Her robe fell open. She had nothing else on. She came to me again and pulled my tie loose, then started to unbutton my shirt. I pulled her to me and my arms closed around her body under her robe.

"You've got to take these wet things off," she whispered.

Suddenly, for reasons forever beyond me, I came to my senses. I stepped back and closed her robe. I held her at arm's length. I was calm and lucid.

"Davey, this can't be," I said.

"I'm not pleasing to you?"

"It's wrong. It can't be."

She stared without comprehension. Then, slowly, she raised her hand to her mouth, looking at me as if I were a stranger. She tightened the robe protectively about her and fastened the belt. Then, with a sob, she turned and fled into the bedroom.

I stood there for a long time watching the bedroom door. Intuitively I knew that I must not go to her. I decided to leave. Somehow I knew that neither of us would mention this night. It would be the same as before.

On the drive home I cursed myself for a fool. I had been seeking Davey out, finding any excuse to be with her, enjoying her company. The man of reason was a prisoner of his feelings. She was lonely and confused. That explained her seductive behavior. All that had to end. Too much was at stake. This time I meant it.

17

THE WORD AMONG THE LAWYERS WAS THAT KANE DID NOT PLAY golf or follow any college or professional games. His only sport was tormenting lawyers. Standing before his bench a few days later, I felt like a worm impaled on a hook.

"Tell me again what your motion is all about," Kane said with an amused smile, looking over my head at the gallery of lawyers sitting around waiting to be heard. It was motion day, and His Honor was about to provide entertainment to the assembled members of the Bar.

"Very simply put, Your Honor, I want to call an expert to testify about the profile of the child molester—or, more precisely, the lack of a profile," I said.

Holtzman sat at the prosecutor's table with his chair pushed back and his legs crossed. Now that Kane had singled me out for sport, he could relax.

"In a trial for perjury, you want to call an expert on child molesters?" Kane furrowed his brow in mock bewilderment and dragged each word out so that by the time he finished he had everyone in the courtroom, including me, wondering what kind of fool would bring such a motion. Several of the lawyers chuckled. I took solace in the knowledge that Ann, sitting in the front row, wasn't laughing at me. I was happy I'd told Davey she didn't have to come to court with me.

I replied carefully. "Mrs. Alden is charged with lying when she testified that her husband was a child molester. I want to prove that he is in fact a sexual abuser of children, and I need an expert to offset the impression that just because Joel Alden doesn't look like a sex offender, he isn't one."

Holtzman unfolded from his seat and stood up. "I would remind the court that Joel Alden isn't on trial here, his wife is," he said with an air of tolerant amusement. "Her lies are the only issue in this case."

Kane waved the prosecutor back into his chair.

"The lack of a profile? You want to call an expert who's going to say that he doesn't know anything?"

That got a laugh not only from the lawyers but from almost everybody in the courtroom. I had known from the start that my motion was a long shot, but with Kane's reputation of being anti-prosecutor, I considered it worth it.

"I want the jury to understand that child molesters fit no particular profile. They look and act pretty much like everybody else. They can be CEOs, doctors, lawyers, even judges."

Holtzman didn't bother to stand up this time. "This is nothing more than a tactic to divert attention from where it belongs—on the defendant, Mrs. Alden."

Kane ignored Holtzman. "Who is this witness?"

"Dr. Benjamin Silver, a psychiatrist who teaches at the University of Michigan. He will testify that there are basically two types of child molesters—the regressed abuser and the fixated type. They are often very successful people—"

"Did you bring a copy of his curriculum vitae?"

Kane looked happy when Holtzman's mouth dropped open. Although I was the primary butt this morning, the judge enjoyed toying with lawyers from both sides.

I hastened to the bench and delivered a copy of Dr. Silver's credentials to the judge. With an occasional thoughtful glance at Holtzman, all the while smiling at some little secret, Kane went over the document.

Finally he tossed the paper aside and, with an impatient glance at the many lawyers still waiting to be heard, said, "Motion denied."

The next case was called, and I was shouldered aside before I could even gather up my papers. Ann, muttering something about blackrobed idiots who think they walk on water, walked out into the hall with me.

"At least we created a record," I said.

"What does that mean?"

"In case there's an appeal. We might make something of Kane's denial of my motion. You never know."

"You're not going to appeal anything, because when the jury hears the truth, you're going to win this case."

The next day Ann appeared in my office. I'd told her about Joel's shady dealings in something called the Terra Group. Apparently she'd gone right to work on it.

Sherry's voice was strained. "There's a person out here who claims she's a doctor. She insists on seeing you *now*."

It was just the sort of thing Sherry expected of me. She was convinced that she was the anchor that kept the firm from drifting onto the rocks; she was also of the opinion that my coming aboard was a threat to the firm's high-class image.

Ann came through the door with an elderly man in tow. Dressed in green work pants and shirt, he nervously fingered a tan Carhartt hat; he had the furrowed face of a farmer. When he hesitated in the doorway, Ann ordered him into one of the chairs in front of my desk.

"Charlie's got something I think you ought to know," Ann said, plumping herself down into the chair next to him. "He's just sold his farm."

"Charlie's a volunteer," she added, reaching over and patting the old man on the hand. "He's an angel. He's retired, and he comes down once a week to the clinic to comfort the poor souls in their last days."

I found it hard to picture Charlie holding the hand of a wasted AIDS victim in the heart of Detroit. He looked as though he might never have left Laffler County.

"You're looking for legal advice?" I asked him.

"I don't know why I'm here," Charlie responded irritably. "Ann grabbed hold of me—damn near kidnapped me—and brought me over here. I don't need any advice from any lawyer. I seen enough lawyers in my time."

Ann laughed and slapped him on the shoulder. "Shut up, you old fool." Then to me she said, "Don't be put off by Charlie. His last name is Walker, and his family has been here a hundred years. Now his wife is gone and all his kids are grown. He thinks he's supposed to act bitter, but he can't quite pull it off."

"Five kids, and not one of them a farmer," Charlie said. "Not that I blame them. Farming is dead in this county. Tax you out of existence."

I nodded in sympathy, afraid to respond for fear that it would set off a diatribe. It was a familiar refrain in growing areas like Laffler County. The farmers were the first casualties of progress. Land values went up but so did the taxes, and soon the farmers had no choice but to sell off to developers.

"Charlie used to own fifteen hundred acres in Avon Township," Ann said. "Over the years it got whittled down, and he sold the last seven hundred acres about three months ago."

I must have looked bored or impatient, for Ann fixed me with a stare and said, "Now listen up, Clarence Darrow. My time is too valuable to waste, and I wouldn't be here unless this was important."

Charlie looked at her with admiration. Anyone who could tell a lawyer off like that deserved to be followed to the ends of the earth, even to Detroit.

"Tell him who bought the last of your farm."

"Some guy from Detroit. He said he represented a developer who wanted to hold—"

"No, Charlie. Tell him whose name ended up on the deed."

"Oh. I thought it was awfully odd the way these people worked, so I went down to the Register of Deeds office."

"What did you find there?"

"The guy from Detroit was just a front man. But I knew that all along. He said he represented a developer who wanted to hold the land until—"

"For God's sake, Charlie, tell him the name of the man whose name ended up on the deed."

Charlie looked put out over being deprived of an opportunity to tell his story at his own pace, but he obeyed.

"I went and looked, and the deed was put in the name of a man named Sinclair. His full name is Terrence Sinclair."

Ann looked at me with raised eyebrows.

"Isn't that the dentist? The one who claims he was in cahoots with Davey before she brought those charges against Joel?"

"Yes, but—"

"Hold on. Now, Charlie, tell him what else you discovered."

"They transferred the property again. I thought I was selling it to Landnet Developers, but then this Sinclair guy's name shows up on a deed. Then a few months later my farm got transferred to some corporation I never heard of."

"What name?"

"The Terra Company, or something like that."

Ann grinned and said, "Isn't that the company that came up in the deposition of Joel Alden? Remember?"

"I sure do."

"If Sinclair knew Joel or Masters before meeting Davey, it puts a new slant on things, doesn't it?"

I was still trying to absorb it all.

She stood up. "Charlie, give Jack the copies of the deeds we got at the Register of Deeds. I went with him to get copies. And I found something else fishy too. Someone is buying up a lot of land in the north part of the county. Sinclair's name is on at least three other deeds."

"This could mean that Sinclair was a plant," I said. "I don't know. I'll have to think about it."

"Well, get going on it," Ann said, beckoning Charlie out of his chair. "Charlie and I have been up since dawn doing your work. Now it's your turn to get busy."

I looked at the file Scott had dumped on my desk just that morning. He'd neglected it, and the client was screaming for his contracts.

"I don't know how I can thank you," I said to Charlie.

"Don't thank me, thank her. I tell her something, and next thing I know she hauls me in here."

Ann headed for the door.

"Come on, Charlie, time to head for Detroit. You've still got time to save your immortal soul. You need to make up for all your past sins."

"What sins?" Charlie muttered.

"How about just being a mean old man?" Ann said just before she closed the door.

I sank back into my chair and sat there attempting to make sense of it all. Then I called Semczyk. I told him about Terra and my suspicions. He whistled softly when I mentioned the link between Joel and Sinclair. He promised to look into it.

The flashing lights of the police car behind me stabbed obscenely at the darkness, filling my car with blinding light. I was headed home to look over the Terra Group documents Ann had copied for me. And now—what? I hit the brake pedal and pulled the Volvo over to the side of the country road.

I slid the electric window down and awaited the officer. At such times I usually affected an air of patrician disdain, but that's all it was:

an affectation. Like the rest of mankind, I cringed at the knock in the middle of the night.

In my sideview mirror I saw the officer exit the black and white sheriff's vehicle. The officer was Deputy Gilbert F. Rollins.

"Well, well, if it isn't my old friend, Lawyer Brenner," he said, shining a flashlight at my face. I blinked and shaded my eyes with my hand.

"What do you want, Rollins? I'm in a hurry."

"In a hurry, are we? Too bad, too bad. Let's see your driver's license, registration, and proof of insurance."

"What for? I wasn't speeding."

"You were weaving. You crossed the center line three times before I stopped you."

"This is bullshit harassment, Rollins."

"I smell alcohol on your breath. You're slurring your words, and your eyes are bloodshot. You've been drinking. Please exit the car."

I thought of the martini I'd just finished at the Andan Tavern and felt a spasm of fear clutch at my innards. I was confident that I was not drunk and any fair blood test would prove that. But I was equally confident that Rollins didn't care whether I was drunk or not. He had something bigger in mind: resisting and obstructing, the crime that covered a multitude of police sins. Get in a few licks and then claim that the suspect was resisting arrest, something to explain the black eyes and bruises.

"You ever heard of pretext stops, Rollins?"

"Exit the car, sir. Now."

It was either that or be dragged through the open window. He was primed, eager. I opened the door carefully and got out. Rollins stepped back, keeping his light on my face.

"Now for some roadside tests. You're going to touch your nose with your finger, count backwards from one hundred, walk heel to toe. Sound familiar?"

"I'll decline the invitation. Let's run a breath test and see if your phony drunk-driving stop will stand up."

"First the roadside tests."

"You can stick your sobriety tests, Rollins. The law doesn't require me to take them—in case you hadn't heard. You're making a big mistake, my Neanderthal friend. Joel Alden can't pay you enough to make this worth your while."

"A little more respect, Mister Lawyer. I'm tired of your faggy ways."

Rollins was simple and that made him easy to read. I noted that malice had replaced the cool professionalism in his voice, also that he was not insisting that I produce my driver's license so that he could call the dispatcher to check its validity. Apparently he did not want to create a record of our encounter. I was about to be taught respect for the law.

"You're stupid, Rollins."

I think that caught him by surprise. His intentions were transparent enough. I should be quaking. A warning bell began clanging distantly in the cavernous spaces of his mind. "You've fucked this one up good, Rollins. Your boss Joel Alden isn't going to like you anymore. You'll be lucky if you don't go to prison for this one."

His flashlight moved closer to my face. For a moment I thought he was going to hit me with it, but he was searching my face for the reason for my continued cockiness. Things were not going according to plan.

"Why don't you look inside the car?" I continued. "I was dictating on my car phone and left it on when you stopped me. Every word we've said has been recorded back at my office."

The flashlight swung away from my face and searched the front seat of my old Volvo. Its beam found my car phone and fastened on the green blinking light. With a muttered oath, Rollins reached inside and yanked the receiver out through the window, ripping the cord loose from the permanently mounted base. For a moment I thought he was going to smash it into my face.

"Everything is on tape. You're in deep shit, but it's nothing compared to what will happen to you if you do anything more stupid."

Now I was truly afraid. A cornered rat will attack, and Rollins, below the rat in intelligence, was feeling cornered. He began caressing his holster.

"Use your head. You didn't call the stop in, so it's your word against mine."

Rollins was silent for a moment. Like an outdated computer, his brain ground away in an attempt to salvage something from a situation that had gone bad. Finally the flashlight clicked off and he tossed my car phone into the front seat.

"It's your word against mine, Brenner. No one is going to believe you—I'll take care of that. And your faggot trick with the car phone won't work because you can't prove it's my voice."

I did not argue with him.

"Next time you won't get off so easy. I'm watching you, and before this is done I'm going to nail your shyster ass good."

Then he turned, walked back to his car, and drove away, spraying gravel onto me and my battered old car.

I was lucky. We had no dictating equipment at the office that was accessible by car phone. In fact, I'd never activated the car phone after leaving Chicago. The flashing green light meant nothing.

18

"I'M SURE GLAD YOU DON'T SMOKE," SCOTT SAID AS I TEED MY BALL up. "The way you drink martinis, one flick of the Bic and you'd go up in flames."

I ignored his insult and teed off. My ball flew straight and true down the fairway toward Riverbend's seventeenth hole, got a good bounce, and ran a long way on the green grass. It was my only decent drive of the day.

"I talked to Sheriff Kramer about your run-in with Rollins," Scott continued. "Kramer says Rollins wasn't even on duty Friday night and they can account for all of their cars. He says you must have imagined the whole thing. He's not exactly excited over it. No one got hurt."

"Let's get this straight," I said. "It happened."

I placed my driver back in the bag and jumped into the cart. Although a 250-yard drive went a long way toward making up for almost three hours of slicing, dubbing, and hacking, I'd had enough golf for one day. The only compensation was the crisp early October air and the profusion of fall colors on this Sunday morning.

"That's all you found out?" I asked as Scott placed a tee into the scarred ground.

Scott shrugged. "That's what Kramer told me. It couldn't have been Rollins."

"We'll see."

Scott took a practice swing and then stepped up to his ball. When he had settled in and it seemed that the world had fallen silent watching him, he took his club back with silken smoothness. Then he came down on the ball with a swing that was all fluid motion and concentrated power. The club met the ball with a click, and the ball sailed on a line toward the red flag 440 yards away, landing about where mine had finally stopped rolling, and continuing its journey for another ten yards.

"What the hell," I grumbled as Scott jumped into the cart. "I thought this was just a friendly game between two old fraternity brothers."

"When you start hitting the ball like that, I have to start watching my back, you sandbagger."

I parked the cart and we took our second shots. Still stewing over the Rollins cover-up, I sliced my shot off to the right of the green near a bunker. Scott's six iron sent his ball soaring onto the green about fifteen feet from the pin.

"You'll be okay even if you're in the bunker," Scott said as we approached the green. "As I recall, you were always pretty good with your sand wedge."

"When the going gets tough, the tough get going."

Scott's laughter, so filled with youthful zest, took me back twenty years and made it easy to imagine we were playing a U. of M. course in Ann Arbor when we should have been boning up for finals.

His next comment turned the morning sour again.

"Speaking of the going getting tough, I was talking to our esteemed prosecutor the other day about you and your Davey Alden case," he said.

Good old Scott. I should have known he had something on his mind when he overrode my excuses and dragged me out to Riverbend.

"What are you doing talking to Holtzman about the Davey Alden case?" I asked, not too pleasantly. I could see my ball in the bunker, very close to the overhang.

Scott tee-hee-heed at the sight of my ball and pulled his putter from his bag. I grabbed my sand wedge and putter and headed for the trap.

"Holtzman says you're too personally involved and both you and your client would be better off if you got out."

"Too involved? I take all my cases seriously. Isn't that what we're supposed to do? Or have you forgotten?"

Scott moved to the pin as I threw my putter onto the grass next to the green and trudged into the bunker. He reached up and held the fluttering flag close to the pole. I took up a position next to the ball, wiggled into more solid footing, and studied the distance to Scott and the pin.

"Don't get huffy with me," he said. "I'm only carrying a message— and expressing my own concern for an old buddy who doesn't seem to know which end is up these days."

I stepped away from my ball. "Don't forget that you got me into this case. Your concern wouldn't have anything to do with wanting Joel Alden as a client, would it?"

Even from twenty-five feet away I could see the smile go out of Scott's eyes. I wondered if I was about to trigger one of his notorious Jekyll-Hyde transitions. In the short time I'd been with him in Kirtley, I'd more than once seen him go from grinning fraternity boy to snarling junkyard dog in less than a second. But this would be the first time I had been the cause of it.

"You're talking crap and you know it," he replied, keeping the grin on his face. "Now hit the damn ball before I shove this pole where the sun don't shine."

I put aside my irritation and concentrated on hitting the ball. And hit it I did. It blasted out of the trap in a cloud of sand, rose in a beautiful arc, and came down on the edge of the green in a perfect position to bounce onto it and roll downslope toward the cup. It was a wonderful shot—except that the ball came down on the head of the putter I'd stupidly thrown on the edge of the green, bounced toward me, and dribbled back into the bunker. I was silent. Scott was silent. Even the birds quit singing.

Somehow I finished the hole. I seem to recall that I picked up my ball and threw it onto the green, then three-putted it into the hole, but my memory is mercifully vague on that point.

Scott called a beer break and we sat on a bench at the eighteenth tee. It was almost noon on a Sunday morning, and by any reasonable standard it was good to be alive. Summer was gone, but autumn was just as friendly. I was prepared to be philosophical about life, love, golf, and the practice of law. But then Scott returned to the attack.

"When Holtzman says 'personally involved,' he's not talking about zeal—and neither is your reporter friend Ripley. They are talking about your fucking Davey Alden."

"Go screw yourself."

"We're talking about you doing the screwing, my friend."

"Well, as incredible as it may seem to the likes of you, my friend, I'm not sleeping with Davey Alden."

I wasn't sleeping with Davey, but I wanted to. My noble restraint did not bring with it a holy glow of virtue. I had the worst of both worlds.

Scott could afford to flavor his words with sympathetic humor: he was the one doing the accusing. Sitting on the wooden bench next to him, sipping a can of Bud Light, basking in the warm sunlight, I both loved and feared Scott Sherman. He was my friend forever, my last pathway back to my youth, but I had learned the hard way that those you love pose the greatest danger.

I did not want to lose Scott. Once I had admired him. I remembered his zeal as a young prosecutor; he had believed in what he was doing. When we were young lawyers comparing notes, I had secretly admired his enthusiasm for the law. I wanted to believe in him again, but I had a client to defend.

"What do you know about the Terra Group?"

Scott looked at me. "What's that got to do with anything?"

"I don't know. It's got something to do with Joel Alden. It came up in his deposition."

"Why do you ask me?"

"Because I just remembered why the name sounded familiar. I saw a file on your desk with that name on it."

Scott snorted with impatience. "God, you really are barking up a lot of trees. I told you not to get involved with the divorce case."

"What is Terra?"

"Nothing to bother your pretty little head about. It's a land development group that's looking for a rezoning in Avon Township."

"What's Joel Alden got to do with it?"

"Beats me. I didn't know he was involved. He could be. He's got his finger in a lot of pies. I wouldn't be surprised."

"You're the township attorney, aren't you?"

"That's why I know about the rezoning request. It's on hold right now. It'll probably never get out of the Planning Board. We get a hundred requests like this every year."

I let it go. If I stayed in the divorce case, I'd want to master every one of Joel's business holdings, but right now I had to concentrate on Joel's personal life.

Scott sat with his metal driver in his hands, poking at the ground as we talked. Finally he stood up and carefully lined himself up for a practice swing, but then decided against it. He turned to me.

"Holtzman's right. You should get out of the Davey Alden case."

I closed my eyes. I was a fool for trying to hang on to the past. And for wanting the old Scott back. Life moves on. Everyone seemed to grasp that except me. Sheila understood it. Scott did. I was the pathetic hanger-on. I felt depressed and angry.

"And you wonder why I'm fed up with the law," I said. "Everybody wants me either to plead her or to abandon her. Kane has put it on the fast track. Holtzman and Masters are pressing. You're on my case

about it. I happen to believe Davey Alden is telling the truth about
Joel. What happens to the child if Davey is convicted? And what
about the accused's right to a vigorous defense?"

"Lord preserve me from the idealists," Scott said with a mocking
grin. "I really do get sick of them. They run around trying to make
everything and everybody good—and then, as soon as they soil their
hands on the realities of life, they swing to the side of disillusionment
and cynicism."

"There's a lot to be cynical about," I replied. "I'm talking to
Exhibit Number One."

"You are mistaken, old friend. I thought you were accustomed to
the rough-and-tumble of life in the big city. I can see now that you've
lived a sheltered existence—one where you didn't have to get out and
discover what kind of human being you really are. Our legal system—
and, for that matter, our political system—is great precisely because
it's so tainted—which is to say that it's so human. People argue and
threaten and posture and then finally settle. Nobody gets everything
he wants—nobody should. It's dirty and disorganized, but it works.
The purists like you just don't get it."

"Thanks for the civics lesson," I said. It was a pathetic rejoinder,
but I was accustomed to the moral high ground being my territory,
not his. The problem was that I no longer knew what I believed. I
argued with Scott—but without conviction.

Scott put his hands in his pants pockets and leaned back in his seat
with his legs stretched out in front of him. Above the woods, on the
other side of the eighteenth tee, a pair of mallards beat their way
toward the small lake on the twelfth hole. A fat squirrel ran out into
the middle of the tee, saw us, and scampered back into the woods. In
the distance a church bell rang out a message that no one any longer
understood.

"I'm not a legal scholar," Scott said, watching the ducks disappear
over the horizon. "But I do know that you idealists are wrong when
you study the law as a cup of mystical tea leaves. Our legal system is

not a pale reflection of some divine will. We realists leave that kind of justice for the next world. We settle for the law."

With that, Scott slapped me on the knee and stood up. After stretching, he said, "Come on, one more hole. I'll spot you two strokes and beat your ass. Fifty bucks. What do you say?"

I said okay and found myself parting with fifty dollars in the clubhouse after we'd had a final drink in the bar.

"Think over what I said about you and Davey," Scott said as we threw our clubs into the trunk of his Lincoln. "You're a straight guy and I know you wouldn't want to hurt her—or yourself. Oh, and the next time you get to feeling self-righteous, remember that you're the one screwing a client, not me."

19

"I've been wanting to meet you," Jennifer Calkins said, opening the door wider so that I could enter. She was a fortyish blonde with a good figure and an odd mixture of invitation and sadness in her eyes.

"You don't at all look like I expected you to," she said as she led the way into her living room and directed me into a roughed-up leather armchair. It was a man's chair—a man who, if I recalled Davey's account correctly, was now history. The old chair, smelling pleasantly of pipe tobacco, contrasted sharply with the rest of the decor, which was odorless, expensive, bland. I wondered how a man could give up such a chair—or a woman like Jennifer.

"What did you expect?" I asked when she was seated on the couch across from me. She wore a cream-colored knit outfit with leg-hugging slacks.

"I expected someone more uptight. I heard you came from a big Chicago law firm, and on the phone you sounded so formal—stuffy, actually."

"I hope I haven't messed up your schedule. I could have talked to you on the phone."

"I wanted to meet you. I wanted to see what Davey was getting herself into."

"She's already into a lot of things—mainly trouble."

"Are you trouble?"

"Lawyers are always trouble," I said.

She smiled mischievously, but I did not believe her smile. Her eyes told the truth. She had lost something important and was hoping that I was returning it.

"What kind of man are you, Jack?"

"Dull. Very dull, I'm afraid."

"You need a drink to loosen you up. I made a pitcher of Bloody Marys—the perfect drink before noon."

Smiling brightly, she rose and walked with silken steps toward the kitchen, glancing back quickly just to see if she could catch me staring at her. She was not disappointed.

But it was no good. Neither of us had what the other was searching for. We were fellow searchers, that's all. I stood up.

"I don't want a drink, Jennifer."

She stopped abruptly and turned back toward me.

"I just thought—"

"I want to talk about Davey. That's all."

She retraced her steps and sat on the couch with her arms folded across her chest. "I'm glad. I really didn't want to—well, you know, get into anything more. Sometimes I get tired of that stuff. You know what I mean?"

"I know exactly what you mean."

I returned her smile and suddenly the air was purged of tension, sexual or otherwise. We both relaxed. Now we were just two people about the same age and with more in common than anyone would have guessed.

"You want me to help you," she said, "but I'm not sure I can. I know too much about Davey."

"Like what?"

"Well, she's strange. She plays the role of the naive schoolgirl, but she isn't that at all. She's just not—"

She paused and with both hands carefully brushed back her shoulder-length hair. I could see the hesitation in her brown eyes. She looked at me for help.

"I'm not really comfortable talking about her like this," she said. "Davey is my friend."

"She's my friend too. And I'm her lawyer. You can help both of us by telling me the truth about her—whatever that is."

"I know they're trying to make her look like a bitch. But she didn't care about Joel's money. That wasn't it at all."

"Davey says you introduced her to Terry Sinclair."

She smiled sadly. "That's not quite true, I'm afraid. After my divorce I started hanging out at some fancy singles places in Bloomfield, and she came with me a couple of times. One day Terry showed up and she introduced him to me."

"Before she brought the charges against Joel?"

"Around that time. I'm not sure."

"It's important. Try to remember. When did she introduce him to you?"

"I can't be sure. I think it was after she brought the charges. But she acted like she'd known him for a while."

"Tell me about Sinclair."

"A hunk. He called me and we went out a few times."

"Davey didn't mind?"

"She said there wasn't anything between them."

"Was there?"

"He said there was. He likes to brag that way. He fancies himself a real stallion."

I paused and she brightened. "Hey, I've got coffee. It's good Guatemalan. How about a cup?"

When I agreed, she bustled off to the kitchen. I leaned back in the old leather chair and listened to the clink of cups in the kitchen. I wondered what it would be like to belong somewhere again. In a few minutes Jennifer was back again with a tray. She smiled warmly when I expressed my pleasure after tasting her coffee. When she was seated again, I looked into the darkness of my cup and pressed on.

"You said you knew too much about Davey. What else do you know?"

She looked unhappy again. "I know they want to make Davey out to be a real tramp—like she was cheating on her husband all the time. It wasn't that way at all."

"She didn't cheat on her husband?"

Jennifer frowned. "I didn't mean that. Technically, she did. She slept around a lot, but it didn't mean anything—not like it did for me. I can't explain it. I was screwed up by the divorce, you see, and I was desperate for somebody to love me again. I did all kinds of crazy things that I regret now. I wanted to feel alive again, but with Davey it was different. She was driven by something else. It all seemed so cold to me. She never took it home with her afterwards."

She paused and sipped her coffee, studying my face over the cup to see how all this was registering.

"This doesn't make any sense, does it?" she said. "I'm only making things worse for Davey. All I can tell you is that it wasn't as bad as it looked. She had no emotional attachment to these men. That makes a difference, doesn't it?"

I sat in the chair of Jennifer Calkins's ex-husband and I wanted to stay there forever. I did not have the energy to lift myself from it and go on with the business of lawyering. I liked drinking coffee with Jennifer. I liked Jennifer.

"Don't you think it makes a difference?" Jennifer repeated.

"I don't know. But I know the jury won't like it."

"I was afraid of that. That's why I didn't tell anybody about Davey last time. No one asked me anything and I didn't volunteer. Besides, I had no use for Joel Alden. He helped destroy my marriage. He set Frank up with one of his secretaries. It was the last straw."

Her words were bitter, but time had tempered the message. She no longer cared enough about Frank to hate him, but habit required that she react violently whenever his name was mentioned.

"I'm glad you didn't tell anyone," I said, forcing myself to my feet.

"You're not going, are you?"

"I've got a lot of work to do." The trial was less than two weeks away.

"I wish you could stay."

Her voice and eyes were so filled with her loneliness that I was embarrassed for both of us. Like me, she was adrift and needy, and she longed for the company of people who would not force her to play a role. So did I.

I paused in the open doorway on the way out.

"You knew Davey pretty well," I said. "Do you think she was capable of plotting with Sinclair to frame her husband?"

Jennifer looked at me a long time before answering.

"I wish I knew," she said. "On some days the idea is laughable, but at other times I think Davey Alden is capable of anything."

"That pretty young thing at the front desk couldn't take her eyes off me," Davey said the next day. "What have you been telling her about me?"

"Absolutely nothing, which of course makes you all the more intriguing," I replied. "After all, you are a bit of a celebrity."

She refused to be placated. "I suppose so. But all I want is to get my daughter back and have this nightmare behind me."

"All in good time," I said. "But first we have the little matter of a trial. I need to talk with you again about some of the details of what happened with Joel. I have a lot of questions—things that may come up during the trial."

She sat stiffly in a red dress that had a long pleated skirt. "What's wrong? We've been over all this before. Why couldn't we talk out at the lake?"

"Because a stuffy lawyer's office is just what we need—stuffy referring to the office, not the lawyer. It keeps our minds on our work."

Usually I knew how to talk to clients. I knew when to advise, when to bully, when to persuade, and when to shut up and just listen. Once a trial becomes unavoidable, the idea is to get the facts—no more slipping and sliding—and settle on a strategy. I thought of Brenda Foreman and Jennifer Calkins, and I realized how little I really knew about this woman. I had not seen her since our rainy-day encounter, but I knew she would say nothing about it.

Davey's expression settled into one of sullen resignation. It was another first in our relationship. She was angry at me, even mistrustful. Another Davey? Or was she merely reacting to something she had spotted in me? Or was it my silence since the scene in her apartment?

I looked down at some notes I'd written on a legal pad. The yellow legal pad was a godsend at times like these. Its appearance was like the sounding of a gong, warning all present that serious business was about to commence.

"Let me start out by asking you whether anybody else knew that the specific accusations you made against Joel were false. Did you confide in anybody?"

"Who could I tell? All the people we knew were Joel's friends first."

"The answer is no, you told nobody?"

"Nobody."

"How did you come to select the details of the two incidents? You testified that one involved you coming home unexpectedly from shopping and finding Joel on the bed and holding Julie. How did you come up with that one?"

"Do we have to talk about this?"

"Yes, we do." Her eyes were welling up, and there was a catch in her voice. I was grateful that I'd chosen the office for this conference. Things were too warm and fuzzy out at the lake.

"I read it in a magazine—or perhaps it was a book. Or maybe I just made it up out of my imagination. I don't recall."

"Something as important as that, and you don't remember?"

She dabbed at her eye with a Kleenex that she took from her purse. "You do enjoy being the Grand Inquisitor, don't you?"

"You may have to testify. I don't think you should, but I want you to be prepared just in case. Syd Masters butchered you last time."

"I know. Why should anybody believe me this time? We're just wasting everybody's time. We're deluding ourselves."

That silenced me for a while. She was right. Standing alone, her testimony was not enough. No one would believe her. Ralph didn't. Brenda Foreman said she was a liar. If Jennifer Calkins was called to testify, she'd destroy Davey. The only people who believed her were a foolish old woman and a fuzzy-headed lawyer.

"Where did you get the details?" I asked. "In going over the transcript, I couldn't help noticing how detailed you were—what Joel and Julie had been wearing earlier that day, what Joel was saying to Julie while you stood outside the bedroom door listening, what time of the day it was, what the weather was like outside—lots of details."

"I don't know where I got the details. I don't remember. I just can't recall."

"Say that one too many times in front of the jury, and you will lose all credibility."

"You want me make up an answer? Is that what you want?"

I decided to move on.

"What about the second incident?" I asked, looking down at the notes I'd made from the trial transcript. "You said that Joel was in the bathtub with Julie. Again you seemed to remember all the details— the little things that give texture to a story and enhance credibility. Do you recall where you got those details? Did anyone help you invent them?"

"I made them up. Why can't you accept that? Do you think I lack the imagination to create a story from nothing?"

She was pleading, angry, frightened. I had conducted hundreds of such interviews, and I had a sixth sense about when a client was not telling the truth. Listening to Davey, I felt an all-too-familiar unease moving about in my gut.

"Did you prepare your testimony with Holtzman, the prosecutor? Did he go over with you what you planned to say on the witness stand?"

She hesitated for a moment, as if attempting to see where the question was leading.

"We talked about it, but he made it clear that I had to tell the truth."

"But he suggested that you might phrase things differently. He gave you a better way to word your responses. Correct?"

"Yes. That's what happened."

I jotted down a few notes. The phone buzzed. I told Sherry that the client who insisted on talking to me immediately would have to wait. I sensed Sherry's disapproval of my priorities. As Sherry and I talked, I watched Davey. She was upset, but not so much that she could contain her curiosity about my office. No framed pictures to remind me of home and hearth. Only my degrees, my license to practice, and a few antique law books for decor. She dabbed at her eyes a few times and made an attempt to discipline an unruly lock.

"Tell me again about Jennifer Calkins, the gal who introduced you to this dentist guy—the lover."

"Terry Sinclair was never my lover."

"How did you meet him?"

"Jennifer called one day after I brought the charges and said she knew what a terrible ordeal I was going through. She said she had a friend who had gone through almost the same thing. Would I like to meet him? Maybe it would help to talk to someone who knew what it was like."

"And you never were intimate with Terry Sinclair?"

She looked deep into me with those unfathomable blue eyes of hers, but she did not hesitate.

"Never."

"And you're certain that you never met him before you brought charges against Joel?"

"I'm certain."

"Was there anything at all romantic about the relationship?"

"Not on my part."

"What about him?"

"He never hit on me, if that's what you mean."

I studied my notes, covering a sudden, awkward awareness of her bodily presence—her legs, her wrists, her hair, everything.

"I've met with Jennifer Calkins and she says it was the other way around. You introduced her to Sinclair."

Davey met my gaze evenly. "Jennifer may remember it differently. She wouldn't lie. But that's not how it was."

"Jennifer also says that you ran around on Joel a lot. That you slept with a lot of men."

I thought she might protest or at least look indignant. Instead she smiled sadly and said, "Jennifer is a very troubled woman. The divorce broke her up quite badly. I don't know why she'd say something like that. She may be projecting her own conduct onto me. I don't know. I don't think she would consciously lie."

Davey's answer made me study her more closely. It was disarming in its loyalty to Jennifer, sophisticated in the way it analyzed her, and quite possibly a masterpiece of duplicity.

"Tell me about the time you went to a motel with Sinclair."

"Where is this headed?" she asked wearily.

"This is business. Tell me about the motel."

"There's nothing to tell. I believe it was the second—maybe the third—time I met him. We'd go out for dinner and just talk. He seemed very sincere about offering a shoulder to cry on. One time he called and said he was staying at the Holiday Inn in Farmington and asked if I could meet him there. I went there and knocked on the door of his room. He asked me in while he got his jacket. Then he used the bathroom for a few minutes and we left. That was all there was to it."

"Did you see any luggage in the room? Did he explain why he was staying at a motel so close to home?"

"No, he offered no explanation. I didn't ask. I don't recall seeing any luggage, but maybe I've just forgotten."

"What was the similar experience he is supposed to have gone through?"

She looked thoughtful. "He said that his ex-wife was living with some guy who had molested his eleven-year-old daughter. He said he was out of his mind and wanted to kill the boyfriend. Eventually, he said, he agreed not to go to the police if the guy would move out. And that's how the matter was settled."

"You said he was sincere. What else was he?"

"Well, he was very taken with himself, I can tell you that. He was quite a handsome man, a bit of a pretty boy. The kind who expects women to fall all over him—and they usually do."

"Weren't you surprised that he didn't try to get you into bed?"

"A little, maybe. But I gave him no cause to believe I'd be receptive. I was very much alone during that period, and I needed someone to talk to. I'm certain that's all I conveyed to him."

She paused and smiled tentatively at me. "Can I ask you a question now?" When I shrugged, she went on, "Is it possible that Terry Sinclair was a plant—someone sent by Joel to trap me and lie about me?"

I stared at her. "You have a good imagination," I said.

"Is it possible?"

"Tell me again about how you found out about Joel—I mean how he was attracted to children. What tipped you off?"

She looked down at the floor, and when she finally decided to answer, her voice was flat and lifeless.

"When we had sexual relations, he treated me like a little girl. That's what he called me, 'my little girl,' and he . . . he wanted me to shave . . . my pubic area so that I would be his little girl. He stopped calling me that when I got pregnant and Julie was born. Then, when she was no longer an infant, after she started walking, he started to refer to her as his 'little girl' in the same tone of voice. Once he caught me staring at him and he laughed—and it was an evil, knowing laugh. He knew that I suspected and it didn't bother him. In fact, it seemed to make things all the more titillating for him."

"I need something concrete. Suspicion is not enough."

"It is for a mother protecting her child."

"It isn't in a court of law."

"Then the law is wrong."

"Right or wrong, it's the way things are going to be at your trial. You told me about a letter you found, and some photos of children."

"Yes, a letter from his daughter Melanie accusing him of sexually abusing her for most of her life. It was written just before her suicide. I saw the letter. The prosecutor said it wasn't admissible evidence, so I couldn't mention it at Joel's trial. Besides, it disappeared."

"Holtzman was probably right about that. It would be hearsay. Not admissible."

Davey shook her head. "The law doesn't make sense."

"That's a debate for another day," I said. "Tell me again about the photographs. They were typical porn shots of children?"

"I don't know what typical is, but they were filthy."

"One man's filth is another's art. What exactly did they show?"

"A young girl—seven or eight years old—lying on a bed without any clothes on, but in a pose that did not reveal any of her intimate areas, except her breasts, which were unformed. It was the context that made it so chilling. Others were horrible—children in sexual poses with each other or with an adult male. I remember feeling sweaty and faint. God, it was awful. And then Joel walked in on me."

"That's when you threw the pictures at him?"

"Yes, and he slapped me." For a minute she was angry, but her anger seemed to frighten her. It made her shrink back into her seat. Her voice became flat again. "When I called him filthy-minded, he laughed at me and said no one would believe me. He challenged me to go to the police, and said they would never take my word over his, that he knew everybody worth knowing among the police. Not only would they not believe me, but he would throw me out and have Julie all to himself."

"Did he admit abusing her?"

"He implied it, but he never came out and said it. The idea was that he would do what he wanted when she grew up a little more. Some of it is vague . . . I think I may actually have passed out at some point."

"Did Joel have any friends who were out of the mainstream—not Riverbend people, not business associates, but people he kept away from his day-to-day friends?"

She thought for a minute. "Not that I can think of. No, I can't recall seeing anybody like that around. Why do you ask?"

"Birds of a feather flock together."

"I don't remember anybody like that."

I leaned back in my chair. We were going to trial soon, and so far I had nothing—only the word of Davey Alden.

"You never slept with the dentist?"

"You asked that. Is that a business or a personal question?"

"Just answer it, please."

"No—never."

"Never," I repeated absently, wearily.

20

I KNEW I WAS OUT OF LUCK WHEN JUDY CUSMANO REJECTED FILET mignon and said she preferred spaghetti. And when she turned down my suggestion of a bottle of Chianti, I knew my hopes for the evening were as dead as the fish on display in her supermarket.

"All right, Cusmano, what's his name?" I demanded when Judy stopped in the dairy section to study the expiration dates on the milk cartons.

"There's no one else, silly man," Judy said with that slow smile of hers. Dressed in jeans and a Hard Rock Cafe T-shirt from New York, with her black hair curling down over her shoulders and her large dark eyes laughing at me, she was particularly desirable this night.

"I wouldn't be offended, you know," I insisted as I took a carton of milk from her and placed it in the cart. "I know I'm not the only man in the world. What the hell, we're both grownups."

"That's awfully adult of you, Jack, but there really is no one."

"Then what's wrong?" I asked, instantly regretting the pique in my voice. "Is it that I didn't call ahead or something?" Many of our best times together had started just like tonight, with my impulsively hunting her down at the supermarket on her regular Thursday shopping expedition. Maybe she thought I was taking her for granted.

Maybe she sensed the truth: that I wanted to use her to put some distance between myself and Davey Alden.

"Don't be silly," she replied, taking over the cart and pushing it down the gleaming aisle toward the canned goods. I fell behind while I considered my long-range prospects. Endangered but not desperate, I decided. I caught up with her just as she reached for a can of tomato paste.

"I thought we had an understanding. No demands, no ties, no regrets."

She handed me two cans of tomato paste to put in the cart. "I don't regret anything, Jack. I hope you don't. I've had some wonderful times with you."

A tart response died on my lips when I saw a fragile elderly couple turn into our aisle. They seemed lost and confused amid the profusion of things to buy in this glittering emporium. When the wife stopped to peer at the labels on the green beans, the husband stared at us hopefully, as if about to ask us directions out of this place.

"If there isn't anybody else—and I recognize your right to find somebody else—how come I'm getting the bum's rush?" I whispered. "I thought we could rent *Casablanca* and watch it tonight while we finish off a bottle of Chianti."

Judy tossed a can of mushrooms into the basket and headed down the aisle. I trailed behind with the cart. We turned the corner, and the smell of freshly baked bread enveloped us. I hungrily caressed the paper wrapper over a still-warm baguette, but caught myself before I threw it in the basket. I followed Judy over to the hard rolls.

"The problem is that they grow stale if you keep them too long," Judy said. Then, seeing my doleful look, she added, "I mean the rolls, not you, you silly man."

I started to grab her arm but thought better of it. "Cut it out. What's happened? This doesn't have anything to do with the Alden case, does it?"

"Not directly."

"Then it has something to do with Davey Alden. You're jealous. You've been reading all that garbage and you're jealous."

Again that slow smile. "Don't be an ass, Jack. I thought you knew me better than that. Although I might ask what brings you here tonight, but I won't. You don't owe me anything—nor I you."

"I'm surprised you would let Davey Alden undermine our relationship like this."

"It isn't Davey. It's you. I don't hear from you for weeks, and then suddenly you appear, grinning at me over the cabbages. You're really no different from all the other saps she comes on to. You forget that I've seen her in operation. Apparently you like them girlish, jiggly, and helpless."

"I'm sorry if I hurt you."

"You didn't hurt me. You disappointed me."

Judy smiled again and turned to place an eight-pack of Diet Pepsi in the cart. Then she took a place in the short line at the only checkout counter open. In front of us was the older couple we'd seen in the canned goods aisle. While his wife sorted through her coupons, the old man stared at us with a mixture of curiosity and amusement, wondering perhaps what anyone so young had to be unhappy about. I dropped my voice again to an insistent whisper.

"You can't say the sex was bad," I said. "Go ahead. Say it. You can't."

"No. I can't say that, but that's not the point. Sex is a reflection of a relationship—not the whole of it."

"For Christ's sake," I said through gritted teeth.

"It happens to be the truth," Judy replied with a hint of irritation in her voice. That and the way she jerked the basket away from me gave me hope. Anger I could manage; what I could not handle was reasoning calm. I pulled the basket back. Judy turned her back on me.

When our turn came, I placed Judy's goods on the counter and watched as the conveyer carried them to the checkout clerk, a big-haired, gum-chewing blonde. She too looked at us with curiosity. Apparently our feelings were emblazoned on our faces like soup-can labels. I kept quiet while the clerk rang up the purchases and bagged them, but I returned to the attack as we headed out the door.

"I thought we had something good going," I said, carrying the two bags, which, I noted sullenly, contained the makings for a dinner that I would never taste.

Judy stopped at her Mustang hatchback and unlocked the back. I put the grocery bags inside and turned to her. The night air was cool. She looked at me with an expression I could not define; I hoped it was not pity.

"I'm going to try celibacy for a while, Jack."

Holding her by the shoulders, I looked into her face.

"I can't believe I'm hearing this," I said. "What happened to the liberated woman?"

"I'm taking one more step on the road to liberation."

"Celibacy?"

"For a while. Until I get my bearings."

"Bearings? Of all the people I know, you're one of the few who does have her bearings. You know who you are and what you want."

"Knock it off, Jack. You're a sincere fraud—the worst kind."

"Couldn't we at least talk about it?"

"We both wanted a simple relationship—sex—and now we've found out it's impossible, or at least I've made that discovery. You pretend to be simple—a good, old-fashioned, horny guy—but you're anything but simple. You're deep and strange and screwed up, just like everybody else, and a really good guy. You made me want more. In the beginning all I wanted was a simple libertine. You had to go and spoil it by being the kind of guy you are. I realized I wanted more."

"No spaghetti dinner?"

That earned a grudging smile.

"I think best not."

"Maybe good sex is incompatible with friendship," I said gloomily.

Judy's laugh was like the final few notes in a favorite melody. "Don't say that. When I'm done with my celibate phase, I'll demand the best of both worlds."

"You've been so quiet, Counselor, that I thought you'd quit and headed back to Chicago," the voice on the phone said.

I had no trouble matching a face with that patronizing tone: Ripley.

"If it isn't the Big Bad Wolf himself," I said, leaning back in my chair and placing my feet on the desk. "It must be a dull news day to have you checking with the hicks in the hinterland. What can I do for you?"

"Do I sense a slight lack of cordiality, Counselor? Perhaps a little coolness? Could it be that my journalistic efforts have been less than pleasing to you and your client, the lovely Mrs. Alden?"

"Cut the shit, Ripley. You did a hatchet job on us and you know it. That's what we get for failing to lick the boots of the mighty Fourth Estate."

"Any chance that you might settle the case, work out some sort of plea bargain?" he asked. "Holtzman thinks he's got you cold on this one. He's going to try the case himself."

Ripley deserved tripe, and that was what I gave him. "Prosecutor Holtzman is a formidable adversary, and it will be an uphill battle even to hold our own with him," I said, delighting in what I imagined was the look of pain that must have crossed his face.

"I hear that you've got some sort of wild defense—like you're going to find the smoking gun and prove Alden really did molest his kid."

"So that's what you hear?"

"Any truth to it?"

"Attend the trial and find out my strategy there. Besides, what you're talking about could be slandering poor old Joel Alden. You can print what you want, but leave me out of it. I'll do my talking in the courtroom."

Ripley and I jousted a few minutes more, and then he got off the line. I spent all of two seconds upbraiding myself for my bad attitude toward Ripley. It was useless and dangerous to antagonize him, but I could not help myself.

Leaving my feet on the desk, I stared at the documents that I'd been working on before Ripley's call. I was drawing up an agreement for a business client who was following my advice to buy out a competitor. The client, a golfing buddy of Scott's, was willing to pay two hundred dollars an hour for careful work. Unfortunately, I was not in a mood for careful work on Scott's files.

I picked up the phone and called Larry Semczyk at the *Chronicle*. Off the record, I gave him a brief summation of my game plan. I said I intended to prove that Joel Alden was a child molester, a pedophile, and that would be enough to get Davey acquitted. When he pressed me, I had to admit that I didn't have much to work with. I did not tell him that I hoped he would print something that might offset Ripley's poison; I was hoping he would do something to replant the idea that Joel Alden was a molester.

Before I could get back to work, Sherry buzzed with a call from Cal Berger, the investigator I'd hired. A retired State Police detective, Berger had a square head and a bull neck, with a barrel body to match. His appearance masked a cool, efficient, and honest intelligence. We'd hit it off immediately.

"Got your man," he said.

"Super. Where'd you find him?"

"At work."

"At work as a dentist?"

"Just got back from overseas. Seems like he went on an extended vacation just about the time the subpoenas were being typed up."

"Did you talk to him?"

"Didn't try. I figured I'd save him for you. Couldn't take the chance of scaring him off. Might go to ground again. Your best bet is to waylay him at his office. He's got appointments all afternoon on Monday. I checked."

Despite setbacks with WAR and Jennifer Calkins, I harbored hope, born of desperation, that somehow talking to Terry Sinclair would produce something to help Davey. Holtzman's theory that Davey had tried to frame Joel to clear the way for a paramour was the glue that held the prosecutor's case together. If Sinclair didn't come through for the prosecution, or if I could destroy him as a witness, we might stand a chance.

Sinclair was on the prosecutor's witness list, but he had not testified at Joel's trial, so there was no way of knowing what he would say under oath. I couldn't go to trial without some idea.

"What about Sinclair's ties to Joel Alden or Syd Masters?" I asked Berger. "Anything on that?"

"I was waiting for you to ask. No ties to Alden, but get this. Eight years ago Masters defended Sinclair on a rape charge. Seems he was doing bad things to women patients while they were under anesthesia. One of them complained, but Masters got him acquitted. There were rumors of a dozen other women ready to come forward, but Masters made life so miserable for the one gal that nobody would speak up after that."

"So Masters could have something on Sinclair."

"That's what it sounds like."

"If only I could get that in front of the jury."

Berger chuckled. "Wouldn't it be grand. But that's your bailiwick."

"Maybe we can parade the other women in front of Sinclair. Can you get their names?"

"Not so far. My contact in the prosecutor's office retired, and no one can seem to find the old file with all the names. Kind of strange."

"All right. What about Joel Alden? Anything on him?"

"Nothing. If the guy's a pervert, he's been discreet about it. I checked out some pretty sleazy sources, and not a thing."

"Well, that's good about Sinclair. Think you might still turn up something on Alden?"

"I doubt it. I'll keep looking, but I hate to take your money for nothing."

"Well, send me your bill so far. Let me know if you come up with anything else."

Now that I knew where to find Sinclair, I found myself caught between curiosity and hesitation. I had to know Sinclair's story. I had to know, but I did not want to know.

21

TERRENCE SINCLAIR, D.D.S., WAS A HANDSOME MAN WITH WAVY black hair, a Tom Selleck mustache, and the sort of lean body that took work to maintain. Only the petulant mouth hinted at the weakness of character that often afflicts men who are handsomer than they need to be.

The Grosse Pointe Woods waiting room of Dr. Sinclair did not smell or look like a dentist's office. The genuine leather couches and chairs in his waiting room reminded me of a downtown personal injury lawyer's office—except that in the downtown offices the clientele was poor and black and smelly. Here they were white and wore Polo and their antiperspirants never quit.

Getting past the receptionist turned out to be the easy part. I put on the pained face of a Scotland Yard detective and, selecting my words with Victorian delicacy, mentioned that I was there to see the doctor about "a matter of the utmost discretion involving a lady of his acquaintance."

In a few minutes I was seated in his private office, the one you get to see if your dental care plan exceeds five thousand and you look as if the cost might be more painful than your aching teeth.

"What the hell is this all about?" Dr. Sinclair demanded as he closed the door behind him. He was holding the business card I'd handed to the receptionist. At six feet plus, he loomed over the chair in which I sat. An eyebrow was arched in annoyance.

I didn't believe him for a minute. He was scared. I had the feeling I wasn't the first man to appear on his doorstep wanting to talk about delicate matters.

"Take it easy, Doc," I said. "I'm not here to spoil your day. I'm just a lawyer with a problem, and you're the man who can help me."

Looking unsoothed, he took a seat at his desk. He glowered at me. "What kind of problem?"

"I represent Davey Alden."

"Davey who? I don't know anyone by that name." Were those little beads of perspiration along his hairline? Had that frown eased just a bit upon learning that I was not an irate husband?

"Don't try to shit me, Doc. You've been dodging subpoenas for her trial for a month."

The doctor looked pained by my crassness. Normally, I like to believe, I'm not particularly crude with strangers, but something about Sinclair, perhaps his Grosse Pointe pretensions, brought out the mugger in me. I resented the expensive furnishings, and in particular I disliked the airy Japanese flower print on his wall. That Davey had been able to stand more than five minutes of his company I found hard to believe.

"Oh yes, that miserable child-abuse case they tried to drag me into."

"Then your memory is refreshed?" I tried to keep the sarcasm out of my voice.

"The situation would be hard to forget. Especially the lady."

The last comment was made with a smile that was part leer and part question. It asked if I wanted some inside stuff about "the lady," and said he'd be happy to oblige. It would be man-to-man stuff—the kind of material usually shared in the locker room or around a tavern table over a third pitcher of beer.

"Was there something about Mrs. Alden?"

Terrence Sinclair, D.D.S., leaned back in his chair, barely able to conceal his relief. "You bet there is," he said, looking at his watch. "Look, I'm in the middle of a filling. How about if I meet you in a half hour across the street at the Coat of Arms and we'll have a drink and talk about it?"

"Good idea," I said, rising when he did. It was a lousy idea, but I had no choice. I would have preferred to talk then and be done with him. I'm fussy about who I drink with.

The Coat of Arms did not date back to the Middle Ages, but it did predate my appearance on earth. A plaque just inside the door said that it had been a blind pig during Prohibition. Alcohol still seemed to be its main preoccupation, but I noticed a chalkboard that announced the day's food specials—broiled whitefish with dill sauce, prime rib with fresh horseradish, linguine with clam sauce (red or white).

I took a seat at the bar. The predominant color in the place was red—red leather trimming the bar, red seats in the booths, red tablecloths on the tables. A huge portrait of a reclining nude hung behind the bar.

With its shady history and a decor that cultivated an air of disrepute, it was just the kind of place I liked: tacky but expensively so. It was only three o'clock and there were fewer than half a dozen other patrons there.

When Sinclair arrived, he ordered a beer and directed me to a booth away from the ears of the bartender. A cream-colored sport jacket had replaced the blue lab coat, and under the jacket he wore an open-collared raspberry shirt from which protruded a mass of black chest hair.

"So you want to know all about the lovely Davilon?" he asked. He was in his element: talking about women.

"If there's something that is helpful . . ."

Again the pirate's grin.

"I gather that you were, shall we say, intimate with Mrs. Alden," I said. I remembered to grin conspiratorially.

Sinclair stroked his mustache. "They had me there. That was not the most pleasant experience—sitting there waiting to be called to the witness stand to talk about plunking somebody else's wife. Especially when the poor sap is sitting right there."

"You knew Joel Alden before?"

"Never met him."

"What about Syd Masters?"

"That prick? He did a little legal work for me once. Set up my PC and stuff. He's a hotshot attorney around these parts, you know. You'd think he'd treat an old client better, but no, he subpoenas me and tells me he's going to roast my balls unless I tell all about Davey and me."

"Did he have something on you? Something to blackmail you with?"

Sinclair looked as if he was about to take offense, so I changed the subject. I wanted him to keep talking. Maybe at trial I could figure out a way to impeach him with his prior rape arrest.

"When is the last time you talked to Syd Masters or the prosecutor about this case?"

"Not since the first trial. Frankly, I've been out of town for a while. Somebody said it probably would be settled and I wouldn't have to testify. I don't need that kind of trouble."

Good news. Masters had not been able to reach him and polish his performance for trial. The bad news was that every question I asked would be relayed to Masters when he finally did get his hands on Sinclair.

"I'm puzzled about something. Your name shows up on several deeds for the purchase of land in Laffler County. The deeds were drafted by Syd Masters. Are you a business partner of his or something?"

Sinclair stared at me and then down into his glass of beer. Finally he said, "I was just doing a favor. Masters said he needed someone to take title to the land. It was just sort of a pass-through deal. A straw man, I think it's called."

"Why do a favor?" I asked, smiling, keeping it light. "I thought you didn't know anybody in Kirtley and didn't like Masters."

Sinclair showed his teeth in a wolfish grin. "Maybe I was a little hard on Masters. Actually, he and I go back a long way. When he needs a little help like that, I don't mind lending a hand. No big deal."

"I see. So it was just as a favor for Syd Masters."

"Yeah, I was in his office one day on another matter, and he asked if I'd agree to act as a straw man."

"It was my understanding that you knew some of that Kirtley crowd, and that's how you met Mrs. Alden."

"Not so. I met her in a bar. To be sure, it was a high-class Bloomfield watering hole, but a bar nonetheless. She was there with a girlfriend—they always are—and I took her to a hotel that same night. It was an evening of earthly delights, believe me."

"Who was the girlfriend?"

"Beats me. Horsey-looking bitch a few years older than Davey."

"Does the name Jennifer Calkins ring a bell?"

"Nope." He drank some of his beer and studied me.

"You're certain that Jennifer Calkins didn't introduce you to Davey Alden?"

"Very certain."

"Have you ever had a child who was sexually abused?"

"God, no. I've never had any children—not that I know of." Again the boys-will-be-boys grin.

"Did you ever tell Davey that you did?"

"Look here, Brenner. Davey and I spent some wonderful times together, and if she wants to deny me now, that's fine with me. But if they put me under oath I'll tell the truth. Nobody is going to nail my ass for perjury. I saw what happened to her."

"Did you meet her before or after she accused her husband?"

"Before. About six months before."

"You certain about that? Could it have been after?"

"Nope."

"What makes you so certain?"

"Because she tried to get me involved in her little scheme. She asked me to help frame her old man."

I looked away from him and saw my face in a mirror across the aisle from us. I took pains to hide what I saw from Sinclair.

"What exactly did she ask you to do?" I asked.

"I don't recall exactly, but I didn't like the smell of it. I told her to count me out."

"But you can't recall precisely what she asked you to do?"

"No details. Sorry about that."

"How many times did you actually meet with Mrs. Alden?"

"Come on, Brenner. What's the difference? I don't remember. It must have been four or five times. Christ, I don't know. I laid her more than once . . . let's put it that way."

He took a swig of his beer.

"Where did these meetings take place?"

Sinclair sighed and looked at his watch. "I've got a lady waiting for me," he said. He drank the rest of his beer and started to rise. I put my hand on his arm and stopped him.

"One last thing, Doc." He sat down again with an impatient frown.

I leered at him and said, "Wasn't her tattoo something?"

I watched his eyes look inward to search his memory.

"I don't remember a tattoo," he said doubtfully.

"It's a work of art."

I was insisting, leaving no way out—all the while grinning and leering so hard that I feared my face might shatter like a mirror.

I overdid it. His eyes went hollow with suspicion. He stared at me.

"What's your game, Brenner? She doesn't have a tattoo. I don't know what you are talking about."

He squeezed out of the booth and stood there looking at me. The suspicion had turned to disappointment. He thought he'd had my admiration and envy, which were the two things that really counted in his world of disposable women. He had misjudged me.

"She doesn't have a tattoo," he said. "I remember her well. The lady is a little weird in bed. Don't try to talk to her about it after-wards—she goes bizarre on you. And the tears—she cries a river every time you do it. She's different in a kinky sort of way."

He left. I stared at the table. I dipped my fingers into the little pud-dle left by his beer glass. It reminded me of the tears on Davey's face the night she came to my bed. It reminded me of her wet pillow.

22

THE HUMAN MIND IS A MERCIFUL ORGAN. LIKE THE BODY, IT IS often able to isolate and encapsulate a dangerous invader. It rallies the defenses for a counterattack. It buys time.

After Sinclair left, I sat at the bar and drank a martini. Mercifully, my mind was on automatic pilot. I had a job to do. I'd talked to Sinclair. Now I needed to see if we could get help from Evelyn Alden, Joel's ex-wife. Any witness is merely a plus or minus for your side, nothing more. Sinclair was a minus. Maybe Evelyn would be a plus.

I fished a notebook with Evelyn Alden's telephone number from the inside pocket of my jacket. She lived in St. Clair Shores, just a few miles away.

I found the public phone near the men's room and dialed the number. On the third ring someone picked up the receiver, fumbled it, and finally mumbled a greeting. It was a woman's voice—Evelyn Alden. I told her who I was.

"I don't know any Davey Alden. Never heard of him."

"It's a she, Mrs. Alden. Davey Alden is the present wife of your ex-husband, Joel Alden."

"Joel, that son of a bitch."

"Yes, and I'm representing Davey Alden—"

"Yeah, now I remember. I read about it in the paper."

"I need to talk with you, Mrs. Alden. I'm in the area and could be there in ten minutes."

"I can't help you. I'm too busy." She had the deep, furry voice of an alcoholic.

"Please, Mrs. Alden, I'm desperate to talk to you. I know you're busy and I'll only take a few minutes. I promise."

I doubted that being busy was her problem. From what I'd heard, getting from one martini to the next was the only problem she had. Still, she was entitled to her illusions, and no doubt one of hers was that there were not enough hours in the day.

"I haven't got anything to say to you, Mr. Brenner."

"Please, you're our only hope. Davey Alden is going to prison unless you help us."

She hesitated before answering. "I'll talk to you, but I can't do you any good. Do you understand that? *I can't do you any good.*"

"I understand. I really do." No one could do me any good. Not she. Not Brenda Foreman. *I can't do you any good.*

Evelyn Alden had a well-traveled face that was a trail of sorrows. She had obviously been beautiful once, and, surprisingly, despite a river of martinis over the last thirty years, she was still comely. Equally surprising was her ability to move surely and gracefully as she led me into her living room.

"Have a seat, Mr. Brenner. May I pour you a martini?" She pointed to a half-filled pitcher on her coffee table.

I accepted her invitation to sit down but declined the martini. As she freshened her drink, I looked around. Joel had done well by her. The furniture in her apartment was elegant and expensive, the oil painting on the wall was an original Zawisa, and the knickknacks were chosen by an interior decorator with plenty of someone else's money to spend.

We made small talk for a while and then I steered us toward the point of my visit.

"Thank you for agreeing to see me. I know you're busy."

"I felt sorry for you."

She took a seat on a chair across from the sofa I occupied and crossed her legs. She wore navy blue slacks with a pale blue blouse. Were it not for the aura of irremediable sadness that emanated from her, she would have looked a dozen years younger. Her medium-length brown hair had a healthy sheen, and she had managed to retain her figure even into her fifties. *Matronly* was not the word for her.

"Why do you feel sorry for me?"

"Because you cannot beat Joel Alden. He'll destroy you and your client."

"Why do you say that?"

"Joel always gets his way. He never loses. I know. I've seen him operate."

"And you're Exhibit Number One?"

"What's that supposed to mean?"

"I'm asking if he's destroyed you too."

"I mind my own business when it comes to Joel. I stay away from him. As long as the alimony checks keep coming in regularly—and they do—I don't make waves for him."

"He's bought you off, then." I waved at the plush furnishings. From the beginning I'd sensed that being nice to her would get me nothing.

"I don't like the sound of that, Brenner."

"I'm going to be blunt, Mrs. Alden. You have no reason to care what happens to Davey Alden, but you should care what happens to Joel Alden—this is your chance to see that justice is finally done."

"I'd like to see that bastard brought down a peg or two," she said, without hope.

"We're being given another chance to see that the truth comes out, but we need your help."

"There's no way that I can help you." She picked up her martini glass and stared into it, not liking what she saw there. Her own image? The past? The future?

I leaned back in my chair and sighed. I wished I'd accepted her offer of a drink.

"For your daughter, then," I said. "Will you help for the sake of your daughter? I'm talking about Melanie."

At the mention of her daughter she began to wilt in front of me. I'd meant to sting her, to put some life into her, but she was dying another death before my eyes, one of a thousand that she'd already suffered in the prison in which she was living out her endless days.

"My daughter is dead," she said, looking up from her glass. "My dear, sweet Melanie died a long time ago." A vague smile of remembrance played around her mouth, but in her eyes there was muted horror.

She looked sharply at me. "It was cruel of you to mention her to me—in the same breath that Joel Alden's name was mentioned."

"But that's precisely the point. This trial is an opportunity to avenge what happened to your daughter. I can't leave Joel out of the picture. He's the one who made it the ugly picture that it is."

Evelyn Alden abruptly stood up. Her passivity had been replaced by a desperate wildness. She was determined not to hear anything I had to say about her daughter and Joel. Simple humanity dictated that I leave her alone. But I was a lawyer, and having a client exempted me from the rules of simple humanity.

"You must go now. I've had an exhausting day."

"You can't blot out the truth with a pitcher of martinis, Mrs. Alden," I said. "You have an opportunity to do the right thing. For God's sake, woman, Joel Alden raped your daughter. You can't hide from that any longer."

I was wrong. She *could* blot out the truth—whatever it might be. She awoke to the truth every day, but by midmorning the truth was mercifully fuzzy around the edges and by noon it was firmly entombed. The rest of the day was tolerable then.

With a snarl, Evelyn Alden hurled what remained of her martini in my face.

"Get out," she said. The hand that held the empty martini glass was trembling violently. "Get out of my house, you pig."

Calmly I pulled my folded handkerchief from my back pocket and wiped my face. Most of the drink had hit my suit jacket and striped tie. I dabbed at the stains and looked at her.

"I'm sorry, Mrs. Alden. I am truly sorry."

"I'll tell you something, mister. I hate Joel's guts—but he never touched my daughter. Never! Someone is feeding you a pack of lies. I would never have permitted it. Now get out before I call the police."

I got up and left. As I closed the door behind me, I could see her standing there. The cocktail glass had slipped from her fingers onto the thick carpet at her feet. I wondered how much of our meeting she would remember in the morning.

I reminded myself that I had a duty to my client. That was what made *my* days tolerable. That is how I entombed the truth. The problem with the truth is that it never stays dead. It always rises again.

23

FOR ME ANGER IS COLD, NEVER HOT. IT SLIPS INTO MY SOUL THE WAY a chill enters a room—gliding in under a door, washing over the furniture, penetrating everything. That's when I understand what it means to be coldblooded.

On the drive to Davey's apartment, I had no thoughts and no feelings about her. I had no plan of action; no imagined dialogue played in my head; no passions bucked and heaved against the restraints of reason. My Volvo ticked off the miles relentlessly until I was pulling into her parking lot. Her Allante was parked outside her apartment.

Her face lit up when she saw me. Yesterday that look would have carried me for a week. I brushed past her and stood looking around the apartment. Tasteful, just like Joel's other wife.

"You're just in time for a thrilling soup-and-sandwich combo," Davey said.

"Sounds like a little bit of heaven, but no thanks."

"I'll put everything on hold in case you change your mind."

"I'll take a martini."

I took off my jacket, pulled my tie loose, and took a seat at one end of the beige couch. Through the kitchen doorway I watched Davey put away her dinner preparations and begin mixing me a drink. She wore faded jeans, a red cotton top, and flat black shoes. She had the habit of concentrating so hard on whatever physical task she was performing that she became oblivious of anything else; it was useless to try to talk to her at such times.

She handed me the martini and took a seat at the opposite end of the couch, a few feet away, curling her legs under her.

"Our moment of truth approaches—soon the trial," she said with a wry smile.

"*Your* moment of truth—to be precise," I said.

"Yes, that's correct," she said with a quick, worried look into my eyes, seeking reassurance and not finding it. "You said you wanted me to go over the jury questionnaires," she added, gesturing toward the stack of documents on the coffee table.

"Did you get a chance to go through that pile?"

"I started to—but I couldn't see the point of it. What are we looking for?"

"Hope—we hope to find hope."

"Of course there's hope. Where there's Brenner, there's hope."

I noticed how under my close scrutiny she pulled her legs tighter under her. When she spoke she looked straight ahead, occasionally darting a nervous glance at my face. We sat in silence for a while. Finally she uncurled her legs and sat upright.

"Sit still," I said. "You must have a case of opening-night jitters." I touched the bare skin of her forearm with a finger wet from my glass. She shivered and I laughed.

"I don't like it when you drink," Davey said, standing up to face me, folding her arms across her chest. In a lighter tone, she added, "What about the questionnaires? What will they tell us?"

"The kind of people we don't want on the jury—the self-righteous, the engineers, the computer freaks—anybody who wants two plus two to add up to four."

"We don't want jurors who like things to make sense?"

I laughed loudly and too long. "Not in your case, my dear. Not in your case."

Davey moved over to her sound system and began sorting the CDs scattered around it. "What difference does it make? I thought the jurors were chosen by lot. I never knew we had a choice as to what jurors we get."

"I told you. Each side gets to knock twelve jurors off the panel— without giving any reason. Color of hair, occupation, political loyalties . . . anything you don't like."

I drained my glass and joined her at the stack of CDs. I held on to my empty glass, finding something reassuring about its coldness and bulk in my hand. I stood close to her and touched her arm again. She moved away.

"What's wrong with you, Jack? You're acting strange. Did something happen today?" Her eyes seemed light blue tonight, the way they always did when she was alarmed or worried.

"I talked to Terry Sinclair."

"Was he able to give you anything to go on?"

"He gave me plenty to go on, I'd say."

"Let's hear it."

"Not so fast," I said. I took a seat again on the couch and slapped an invitation on the cushion next to me. "Let's get comfortable first. I want us to be nice and cozy."

Davey took a seat in a chair across from me. "I'm comfortable right here," she said. "Did you get a chance to see Evelyn Alden too?"

"I talked to both of them. And Jennifer Calkins too, but you knew about her. I learned a lot."

"What did they have to say?"

I got up from the couch. "You sure you don't want a drink? It'll relax you. It may help you to calm down."

I started to walk over to the kitchen to refill my glass, but, quick as a cat, Davey was out of her seat and taking the glass from my hand. She led the way to the bottles she'd left on the counter.

"I'll do that," she said. She began pouring the Boodles into the glass. When she slowed down I grabbed her hand and kept the bottle tilted over the glass to make certain that a generous measure got poured.

"Make it yourself, then." She stepped back and watched me finish making my drink. "I'm beginning to think you're the one who needs to calm down. You must have gotten an earful today."

"That I did, that I did."

"Well, quit peering at me over your glass and tell me what's wrong."

"Evelyn Alden says you're a liar, and so does Jennifer Calkins. Terry Sinclair says you're the best lay he's ever had."

We stood in the kitchen next to the counter and stared at each other, I with an asinine grin on my face, Davey looking stunned. She seemed suspended between tears and a display of anger. I could not help but admire her acting skills.

"What do you mean?" she asked slowly.

"Just what I said. Evelyn says you're lying, that Joel never molested Melanie. And my old drinking buddy Terry says you tried to snooker him into your little plan to do in your husband. Not only that, he was full of tales of a Thousand and One Nights of carnal delights with you."

My sense of righteousness demanded fear and shame from her. I got a show of anger instead.

"Either your old drinking buddy was drunk or you were, and judging from your present state, I'd say it was you," Davey said. "And that probably can also be said of Evelyn Alden, who, if I recall correctly, drinks almost as many martinis a day as you do."

"Very clever," I said, "but you can't blame me for wondering if I was the only one to resist your charms. Maybe I should have taken my turn."

"You bastard," she said, and started to push past me. I grabbed her arm and drew her toward me, but I quickly released her when I saw her tears. Etched on her face were all her thoughts about me—anger, disappointment, and, finally, at long last, fear. She stormed into the living room and threw herself onto her chair. She sat there with her face averted and partially covered with a hand, as if blocking out a light shining in her face.

I sat on the couch again and sipped my drink.

"I suppose I should be happy that you're not trying to lie your way out of this one," I said. "Maybe that's progress."

Davey said nothing.

"I really don't expect clients to tell me the truth, you know. So don't feel bad about lying to me. It's built into the defense—sort of a margin of error, the way they do in the political polls. In fact—this may amuse you—I'm surprised when a client doesn't lie. It sort of screws things up when they don't, if you know what I mean."

"I didn't mean to lie," Davey said in a small voice, not looking at me, not moving. "I had to, I had no choice."

"Not lie? Christ, you don't know how *not* to lie. Is it all a lie? Everything? No. Don't tell me. I don't want to know. Oh, don't worry about your case. You'll get a defense worthy of the name. I'm not in the least affected by my client's lack of candor. True, it may make things a little difficult, but, what the hell, it's all in a day's work for an old pro like me."

"You don't know how it was, how it is," that small voice said again. "I never intended to deceive you, I never did."

"The road to hell is paved with good intentions, my dear," I said.

24

Judy's smile was so welcoming that I was tempted to forget the grim business at hand and try to persuade her to spend her lunch hour with me in carnal bliss. More than once I'd caught her like this at noon in the parking lot of the Department of Social Services, which was housed in a building as colorless as the county jail.

"Miss me?" I asked after we finished exchanging hugs. I held her hands in mine.

"Of course, you dope."

"Ready to run away with me?"

She politely but firmly retrieved her hands. "You didn't waylay me like this to satisfy your lustful desires," she said. "I know you too well. It's about the Davey Alden case, isn't it? You need help. I can see it in your face."

I explained that WAR wouldn't let me talk to Andrea Swanson, the therapist who was seeing Julie and Davey. I doubted that Julie had given Andrea anything that I could use in court, but it was a loose end that needed tying up. I could get a court order, but I might end up with a hostile witness. I recalled that Judy knew Andrea, and hoped that she could persuade Andrea to meet with me.

"Do you have permission from Davey to talk to her therapist?"

"I've got a written release that covers both Davey and her daughter. There's no legal impediment. I doubt that Swanson can help me, but I've got to be thorough."

"I'll try. I'll ask her this afternoon."

I said that if Andrea would agree to talk to me, I would meet her at Jack's Landing, a restaurant on the outskirts of Kirtley. The food was lousy and the coffee worse, so we would be assured of a measure of privacy.

I considered asking Judy to lunch but thought better of it. I watched her little blue Mustang pull into the noonday traffic. She did not look back.

"Smoking or nonsmoking?" demanded the waitress, swooping up a stack of menus and sizing me up for the seat next to the kitchen. The tag on her faded blue uniform said her name was Pat. She looked as if her feet hurt and I was to blame.

"Do I need a reservation?" I asked, grinning at the rows of empty tables. Two men sitting next to a window that looked out onto a lake were the only other customers.

"A wiseacre, eh?"

"Hey, you must have grown up in Chicago," I said. "I haven't been called a wiseacre since I left. It makes me homesick."

"I grew up in Detroit. I dunno what you're talking about," she replied. But my cheerful impudence had struck a chord somewhere. Unsuccessfully resisting a smile, she led the way to a window table on the water, far enough away from the only other customers to ensure privacy.

"There'll be two of us," I said. "I'm expecting a lady."

"Ha! What lady would be seen in a place like this with the likes of you?" she said, slapping the menus onto the table.

"One that's never met me before."

"That I believe, that's for sure."

I laughed. When she grinned back at me, she looked years younger. I liked her.

"Coffee? Or are you ready for something serious?"

"Just coffee."

"Whatever you say." I watched her stalk off. The smile on her face was probably the first time that day she had shown her teeth in anything other than a snarl. Good old me, the smile-maker of Laffler County. Come to think of it, it was probably my first smile of the day too.

Andrea Swanson arrived before my coffee did. She was a lean woman, perhaps in her early forties, with a gray face and no makeup of any kind. In place of paint on her face, she wore a mask of perpetual concern, which today, I discovered, was more than mere habit; it took me only a few minutes to discover that she was very uneasy about our meeting.

"WAR would kill me if they knew I was here meeting you like this," she said.

"War is hell."

"Please don't make a joke of it."

"I'll try."

My friend Pat arrived with the coffee and left with Ms. Swanson's order for a Diet Coke. I ignored the mocking grin that appeared on Pat's face when she saw who I was meeting. Andrea Swanson was not the stuff of afternoon assignations.

"Did you bring the release from Mrs. Alden?" Ms. Swanson asked. "I need the original for my files."

I pulled the document from my pocket and handed it over to her. She studied it carefully and then placed it in the large black purse on the floor next to her chair. I'd gotten Davey to sign all kinds of releases, never knowing what secrets I might need to delve into.

"Do you know who I am?" Ms. Swanson asked. "I mean, do you know what I do? What kind of work I do?"

"You're a social worker or therapist. You were evaluating little Julie Alden, I believe."

"I'm a certified psychiatric social worker and I'm employed by WAR. I provide therapy for victims of sexual abuse, usually women and female children, but sometimes young boys too. I did see Julie Alden, but, more important, I also met with Davey Alden. You want to talk to me about Julie, but I have information about Davey Alden that you should know. I hope you can appreciate that I'm caught in the middle. I happen to like Davey a lot. I also like my job and I would like to keep it."

"What do you have that's so important for me?"

She studied my face for a moment as if wondering how much I knew. "How well do you know your client, Mr. Brenner?"

"Apparently not well enough."

"What do you mean?"

Like most lawyers, I was ambivalent about mental health professionals: they promised more than they could deliver. Yet lawyers and judges regularly swallowed their skepticism and relied on them in making all kinds of decisions. They were the only game in town.

"I keep making new discoveries about my client," I said cautiously. "She's a constant source of surprise. Bluntly stated, I've gotten burned by her more than once."

Ms. Swanson nodded. She seemed to gain confidence from my little confession. Her colorless face appeared to draw life from my disadvantage.

"That's understandable, Mr. Brenner. Davey Alden is a hard person to know. For one thing, she is a compulsive liar—yes, I can see from your reaction that you had some inkling of that—and, for another, she is pathologically promiscuous. She can be incredibly manipulative and deceitful."

"Jesus," I said.

"I'm sorry if I shocked you, but I believe you have an urgent need for this information. I believe you need to understand Davey Alden."

"I'm trying to beat a perjury case. I don't see what my client's Freudian anxieties have to do with getting her acquitted."

Ms. Swanson's smile was loaded with irony. "Freud missed the boat on women too, Mr. Brenner, but I'll save that for another day. My information can't help you in your trial—it can't be used. But there are things you must know about Davey Alden if you are to defend her to the fullest."

Outside our window was a patch of grass and a canal that led to a small lake. The summer was long gone. The water looked black under the somber sky. An empty bird feeder attached to a huge oak swung in the fall wind. A few rust-colored mums, hanging on like the last guests at a party, huddled under the bird feeder.

"What kind of things?"

Ms. Swanson's smile was patient. "Did she ever tell you anything about her childhood?"

I rolled my eyes but nonetheless dug back into my memory. "I recall that she was an only child and that she excelled in high school. She was a cheerleader and won a scholarship and all that. Ideal mother and father, it would seem, except that Mother sides with Joel in the current troubles, which I find very unusual. Other than that, quite a typical suburban life. Didn't like college all that well and got married too young after her father died."

Those were some of the facts I knew about Davey. I doubted that I knew much that was true about Davey Alden.

"Are you aware that Davey grew up as her father's lover? That by the time she was a teenager she was his full sex partner, and that the relationship lasted right into her college years? That at fourteen she had an abortion arranged by her father, who got her pregnant?"

In the silence that followed, while Ms. Swanson's words seeped into my understanding, all my senses suddenly seemed sharpened. I heard the clink of silverware and low laughter from the table across the room, I watched a blue jay land on an oak branch and stare resentfully at the empty feeder, and I could smell the various sauces bubbling in the kitchen. I saw that Andrea Swanson wore contact lenses, and I noted that her eyes were green and sensitive, the kind that register pain easily.

"What the hell are you telling me?"

"That Davey Alden was sexually abused by her father, not once but continuously, right up until his death. That Davey Alden's childhood was as far from normal as can be imagined, and that the consequences have been far-reaching and tragic, beyond even what an intelligent and sophisticated lawyer like you could comprehend, Mr. Brenner."

An intelligent, sophisticated lawyer like me. I'd heard it all, of course. Like a priest sweating in his confessional, taking upon himself the sins of his flock, I had sat across from defendants, hundreds of them, perhaps thousands, and listened to them catalog perversions and offenses against other human beings. Heinous murders, mutilations, crimes against children—things that most animals would never do to each other.

Nothing about people, even myself, could surprise me. That's why the strength of my revulsion at Ms. Swanson's revelation was a surprise. Disgust rose in my gorge like a piece of bad meat. And, God help me, some of it was directed at Davey.

"Mr. Brenner, I can imagine what you must be feeling now," Andrea Swanson continued. "I'm not being glib when I say that. You're her lawyer, but you're also her friend. I know what a terrible shock this must be to you. I felt you had to know."

"It's kind of difficult to absorb," I admitted. I wondered how much she knew about Davey and me. I said brusquely, "But I don't see how this plays into the trial. Her background is one thing. Whether Joel Alden molested his child is another question entirely."

"Is it?"

"If anything, it may make things worse for her. It may be an explanation for why she made a false accusation against her husband. She could be mentally unstable—no doubt she is—after a childhood like that. In fact, that's what you've just told me. She is a liar—a promiscuous liar."

"She's a crippled human being as a result of the abuse she suffered. There's no doubt about that."

"Then suspicion about Joel Alden could be nothing more than the product of her crippled mind."

In the dim recesses of my soul I could hear a silent scream of anguish building—and a terrible indictment being drafted against me. But how could I have known? *How could you* not *have known?* said the accuser. *You have eyes but you do not see.*

Andrea Swanson answered me with a question. "Do you believe Davey?" she asked.

"Once I did. Now I don't know. She's lied about so many things."

"Let me tell you about those lies. Most of the time she doesn't lie. She is not a compulsive liar in the sense that she lies about everything for no reason whatever. Davey lies about her promiscuity—the two are inextricably intertwined. She lies because she must at any cost cover up her sexual activities."

I did not respond. I was looking inward, into the murky depths where I saw things I did not like.

"She doesn't have any choice, Mr. Brenner. Lying is what you do when you're raised the way she was. The adult you love and trust tells you that you must say it didn't happen, and you do what you're told. It becomes a way of life. After a while the line between fantasy and reality becomes blurred and you don't know what's real and what's not. Young children often confuse that line anyhow. For someone like Davey, it becomes something you carry right into your adult life."

"What about her mother? Didn't she know anything?"

"In her heart she did. Davey made efforts to tell her what her daddy was doing to her, but the mother shushed her and told her that she was making up stories. She didn't want to believe her daughter. People are shocked to learn that many mothers react that way. Forced to choose between their marriages and their children, they choose their marriages."

"But why believe Joel over her own daughter? Joel wasn't her husband. She chose him over her own daughter."

"The fact that Davey's mother believes Joel rather than her own daughter follows the pattern of a lifetime. I'm not at all surprised by her lack of faith in her daughter—just as I'm not surprised that Davey often does not know what is real and what isn't. All her life she's been told by the people who count that her senses and memory are lying to her."

"But what about when she grew up? When she was in high school and, for Christ's sake, in college?"

Andrea Swanson sighed. I saw that she was not as detached as she should be. She suffered along with her patients.

"We have to be careful about blaming the victim, Mr. Brenner."

"I'm not blaming Davey."

"Good. I knew you wouldn't make that mistake."

"What I meant was that I'm amazed something did not come out at least by high school. I've handled hundreds of such cases, and in my experience the crime is discovered well before then."

"Perhaps, but you would have to know something about what a giant Davey's father was to her. On the surface, he was a kindly husband and father, but he totally dominated Davey's mother and Davey, his only daughter. His manipulative nature allowed him to pursue his evil program for years by jerking them around like puppets. He became obsessed with Davey and was determined to control her life totally. He was also ambitious for her. This meant that she must succeed in anything she attempted—school, extracurricular activities, social life—except, of course, dating, which was his exclusive province."

"Why the promiscuity?"

I feigned professional detachment, but I had no doubt that Ms. Swanson saw through me completely. I didn't care. I trusted her now. I wanted to confess to her. I wanted to tell her about how I desired Davey Alden.

She frowned and took a sip of her Diet Coke, the arrival of which I had not even noticed.

"*Promiscuous* is a word loaded with moral condemnation," she said thoughtfully. "I meant that she engages indiscriminately in sexual activities with men she happens to meet. I attach no moral judgment to my description of what she does."

"That doesn't explain her behavior," I said. "I'm looking for a why."

"I would think that would be obvious. Davey Alden grew up believing that the way to please a man was with her body, sexually. As a little girl—four or five years old—she was learning that the way to succeed in the world—keep in mind that virtually all of that world consisted of her father—was to please her daddy. Her mother just was not a factor. When Davey grew older her whole sense of self-esteem depended on whether she was pleasing to her father, and of course that meant sexually satisfying him. Later that would mean any man who had power over her, anyone from whom she needed something."

There was something obscene about dissecting Davey and laying out the pieces of her psyche on a table to paw over. But I could not stop.

"What about Sinclair?"

"She's not telling the truth when she says she met him after going to the police about Joel. She knew him before, and discussed her fears with him, but I believe her when she says she did not attempt to involve him in her accusation."

"And the other men? You say she's always been like that?"

"Periodically, when she was away from her father in college especially, and later when Joel's influence over her waned. So it was not a constant thing, this promiscuity. It only flared up when she needed reassurance, and she went after reassurance in the only way she knew how."

I was not totally ignorant on the subject. The impact of sexual abuse on the behavior of its victims often came up in criminal cases. Experts frequently were called to the witness stand to explain why child victims failed to report being molested. I knew about the problems of incest survivors: bed-wetting, sexual acting out, feelings of suffocation, low self-esteem, blocking out of childhood memories— the list went on and on. It was all abstract knowledge, of course, the subject matter of testimony and cross-examination, and since I was a defense attorney I was predisposed to skepticism about such testimony. The list was so long that almost everyone could find a symptom or two that applied to oneself. Study hard enough and you too can be a victim.

But this was reality: the abstract had been made concrete in my own little corner of the world.

"You asked if I believed her about Joel," I said. "I said I didn't know. Right now I can't afford to believe her, not after all that's happened. Yet I do believe her about Joel, and have almost from the beginning. I just do."

And it struck me why I believed. It was the nude painting of Davey in Joel's den. The eyes in the painting were not Davey's, not the eyes of a woman at all, but those of a child—a child's eyes in the naked body of a woman. That was what made the portrait obscene.

"I believe her too," Ms. Swanson said. Relief flooded her face and softened her features; it was then that I realized that she was actually quite beautiful. Her sympathetic eyes lent their character to the rest of her face, making it all the more striking because it was so plain and unadorned.

She went on, "It was not mere coincidence that Davey married Joel Alden. Or that Joel Alden found Davey. Men like Joel Alden are predators—"

"And he was looking for someone like Davey—a victim."

"Correct. It is amazing how the predator can spot the vulnerable prey. They say that a wolf will come face to face with a moose and in an exchange of looks will know whether the moose is injured or old or sick, or whether the pack should move on and not risk attack. It's that way with child molesters. Some sort of acutely sensitive antenna assists them in locating victims. A child molester can walk into a room and home in on the one woman who will be vulnerable to him, a woman who has children and who, more than likely, was a victim of sex abuse herself as a child. Such men are masters at insinuating themselves into households that contain a supply of victims."

"And Julie was next on Joel's roster of victims."

"Davey was attempting to break the cycle. She did make up those stories about Joel, but she had knowledge, both intuitive and practical, of Joel's proclivities. And she had no reason to trust authority—the police, the legal system, anyone. After all authority—her father and mother—is what betrayed, abused, and abandoned her. She had to take matters into her own hands. She may not have been correct or wise, but at least she acted to save her daughter."

"And if she is convicted, she will have lost the battle," I said, half to myself. I looked up at Andrea Swanson. "Does Davey know that you and I are talking?"

"No. I didn't call her after I agreed to meet you. She called the other day, and it was all I could do to keep her from total despair. She told me about your confrontation. She also told me that you're not like other men and that she has feelings for you. She's very confused right now. When you sent word, I decided that I had to talk to you."

"You feared I would give up on her."

"Something like that."

"Sometimes—"

"You don't owe me any explanations, Mr. Brenner. You know about Davey now. You can't use any of this at trial. If her childhood history were to become public knowledge, it would kill Davey. You can't use the information—but at least you know now."

We shook hands outside the restaurant and I watched her drive away in her little red Escort. Maybe there was hope for the world after all. Evil was everywhere and most of the time seemed to be in the ascendancy. It was hard to see how one or two Andrea Swansons could make a difference. A legion of Andreas probably would change nothing. But her existence gave rise to hope. Hope keeps us going.

25

I waited outside Davey's apartment for her to come home. When she arrived, I asked to come in. My stripping away of her lies had accomplished its purpose. I had made her afraid of me.

"Sit down, please," I said, indicating her couch. "We have to talk."

Davey took a seat on the couch where I'd touched her arm and made her shiver. I sat in the chair that I'd left her sitting in that night. I was determined to keep my face neutral, sensing, as I did, that some of the emotions seething within me might only degrade her further.

"What do you want?" she asked, her voice and face as passive as mine.

"I had a talk with Andrea Swanson today," I said. "Remember her?"

"Of course. I took Julie to her. I saw her just the other day."

"You needed some therapy yourself," I said gently.

I saw a new kind of fear building in her eyes. This is what I'd hoped to avoid. I had caused enough pain.

"She talked to you about me? She told you things about me?"

"She told me about you and your father. She felt it was imperative that I know."

Suddenly she was the prey discovered in her hiding place, instinctively freezing, suspended between flight and concealment. Horror spread over her face like a blush.

"Why? Why did she have to tell you anything?"

"She believed I could defend you better if I knew all about you. You signed a release. Davey, I want to—"

I stopped. Her body seemed to draw into itself, almost into an upright fetal position, with an arm held stiffly up to her face. I wanted to approach her but thought better of it.

For a long time I sat there watching her silent agony. Neither of us spoke. I had not intended to be cruel. I was getting to the heart of the matter in the only way I knew how. There was no time for a delicate unfolding; our trial was upon us.

"Talk to me about it," I said. Outside, the approaching night was stealing the light from the day, casting the room in shadows. Davey did not answer me. She was rigid.

"I want to share this with you," I told her silent figure. The words tasted like chalk in my mouth. I sounded like one of the psychologists and social workers I liked to ridicule.

Still Davey did not respond. I half expected her to tumble over on the couch and lie there in her fetal position. I was paralyzed myself. More light leaked out of the day, and shadows began to take over the room. Davey seemed to be waiting for something. I waited with her.

Then she began to speak. So tiny was her voice that I missed part of what she said and had to lean forward to catch the rest of it.

"Share? Are you going to live my life with me? What could you possibly know about a life like mine? I don't—"

"I can try. Don't shut me out. I didn't understand. I was cruel, vicious."

In the gloom I saw her move slightly. I reached over and turned on a light. She appeared less rigid, but she stared past me out the window.

"Share *this* with me," she said in that voice from the netherworld. "A little girl fucking her father when she is just seven years old—or even younger—"

"Davey, you don't have to—"

"Be quiet. You want to know why I don't trust anyone—not even you? Why I rely on no one but myself? You said you wanted to share this with me, remember?"

"Yes, but why—"

"You must hear it. You asked to share. Maybe you can really share it, take some of it on you, but I doubt it. Did you know—no, I suppose Andrea didn't tell you—that when I was eight my father brought home a vibrator that he taught me to use so that he could watch me pleasure myself? And when I was only ten he got a dildo so that my vagina could be stretched to the right size for his comfort and convenience. How about that, Jack? Are you sharing all this?"

She did not wait for an answer. I sat and listened, telling myself that I could take it, that I was no stranger to such horrors.

"Where was my mother? She was right there. Oh, not standing over the bed watching us, but she knew. She knew all right. My mother, from whose flesh I am made, she let it happen. When I was five I went to her and told her about Daddy and me, not ashamed or injured, but bragging as one rival to another. I was stealing Daddy away from her, I thought. And she told me that I was dreaming, that it had never happened.

"Later, when I was six or seven, and he hurt me, I complained to my mother and she got angry and told me that I was a silly girl who was making up bad stories and that if I was not careful she would wash my mouth out with soap."

"Don't, Davey, please don't," I whispered.

"They say that some girls grow up and can't remember. Well, I remember everything. No blocking out for me. I remember details, lots of details."

And details she gave me—until my guts convulsed and burned with . . . what? Revulsion? Yes, of course, but . . . recognition? The grinding knowledge that in every human lurks dreadful possibilities, and that, as much as we deny it, people like Davey's father and Joel

Alden are every bit as human as we are. On and on she went, and I listened in sweaty silence until I wanted to cry out for relief.

"My father and I even had music in common. We both loved Rod Stewart and a line from one of his songs became our code word. When he called me 'Angel,' it meant he wanted to have sex with me. I was twelve or thirteen then. 'Come on, Angel, spread your wings and let me come inside you.'"

"Oh God," I said.

"And my mother never had a clue. She says I was lucky to have had such a wonderful father."

"Let me get you something," I said when she paused for breath. When she did not respond, I started to get up.

"Sit down," she ordered. "We're not finished. Can you imagine what it is like to grow up and suddenly realize that you are not like other little girls, that you have secrets, big secrets, that you cannot share? No innocent flirtations with the boys in the eighth grade because there is no innocence anymore, not for you.

"And you know what? My daddy made me happy to be his little girl, his special possession, the only one who could really make him happy. Oh boy, did I know how to make him happy. And that made me happy. He did not have to threaten me to keep me quiet. Oh sure, he let me know that our secret could not be shared with the rest of the world. No one could understand, he told me, and the bad police would come and hurt him if I ever told anyone. This was our special thing that made us superior to the rest of humanity."

"But when you got older?"

It just popped out.

"Don't you understand?" she said with bitter defiance. "I didn't *want* to tell anyone. He was my father, for God's sake."

"Davey, I'm sorry. You were a victim."

"So they say. Did you know that when I was in college my father used to drive up to East Lansing in his van and we would have sex in the bed in back? By then I had some different ideas, of course, but that did not stop him. And someone like me does not learn to say no to her lord and master. I and the father were one. He was in me and I was in him."

"Davey, don't. That's all in the past now."

"In the past? How little you know. My father lives on in Joel Alden. Talk about a resurrection. My father died and rose again. He lives. Hallelujah. And I am being born again. Don't you see? I will live on in Julie."

The eerie voice had turned hoarse, and it came from a place deep inside her. In hell the flames are cold, and despair is their fuel.

She fell silent. Her gaze was fixed on the window beyond my head, but it was dark outside and there was nothing to see.

I couldn't think, but I did act. I slowly slid from my chair and half fell and half crawled across to Davey, sitting like a statue on the couch. I knelt at her feet, but I did not touch her.

"You have to believe what I'm going to say," I told her. "You're surrounded by love. By my love and that of many other people, including Ann. Nothing has changed now. Knowing about what happened to you does not change my love for you. There, I've said it. I've fallen in love with you, Davey. You have no more need for secrets. You can let go now. You're going to be free. I know the worst and I love you."

"Do you, Jack?" she said in a voice so full of resignation that I wanted to weep. She smiled sweetly at my little speech and I dared to reach up and take her hand in mine. Her smile said that it would be nice if such things could be true, but it was all right if they weren't.

For once in my life I had spoken honestly and unguardedly, with no thought of consequences, no lawyerly weighing of alternatives.

I had hope. And Davey had none.

"I'll never let Joel get Julie. I promise you."

"I believe you, Jack. I believe you." She was comforting me. The story demanded a happy ending and she wanted to make me happy.

Her sweet resignation chilled me more than anything I'd heard on this day of horrors.

I stood up and pulled Davey to her feet and took her in my arms. We stood there holding each other for a long time. Then she gently disentangled herself and, holding my hands, smiled into my face. She brushed my lips quickly with her own.

"You should go now," she said. "I'll be all right."

26

THE HONORABLE FRANCIS X. KANE DID NOT OFFER US A CUP OF coffee from the silver pot that adorned his immaculate desk. I took my seat across the desk and watched as he filled a delicate china cup for himself. I wondered whether Holtzman also was put out by the judge's bad manners. From his deferential grin, I gathered not. Apparently I was the only one who had overslept and skipped breakfast.

"Well, Jack, how are you acclimating to Laffler County?" asked the judge, sipping his coffee with a contented smile. "How do you like life in God's country?"

"I can't complain," I said dully. I found it difficult to respond to his ersatz charm without the stimulus of caffeine coursing through my veins. The events of the last few days had taken their toll.

"A great place to practice law, I can tell you that," continued the judge, ignoring my lack of enthusiasm. "As you may know, I practiced law in a lot of courthouses here in Michigan—and in quite a few in other states too—and you'll not find a better bunch of lawyers than right here in this county."

"So I've noticed."

"Isn't that right, Brad?" With that the judge emitted a machine-gun burst of manly laughter that refused to die a natural death. It went on and on, demanding a response. Holtzman obediently joined in, and the two of them rat-tat-tatted in unison. I did not understand the joke, or think that anything was funny, but still, to my everlasting discredit, I found myself smiling appreciatively in His Honor's face. I may even have made a sound to go with the smile.

Finally the judge fell silent and carefully brushed back an errant white lock. He had taken off his jacket. His white shirt, starched just right, had two buttons on the pleated cuffs. I did not need to see his shoes to know that they glistened.

"Down to business now, gentlemen," he said. "This is our last chance to settle this matter before trial, which is scheduled for next Tuesday. No one is really planning to try it, are they?"

I raised my hand, guiltily. Holtzman glared at me. The judge's friendly eyes turned to ice.

"He wants a trial," Holtzman said.

"This doesn't sound like one that should go to trial, Brenner," the judge said. "You're an old hand, or so I'm told. From what I've heard of this case, you haven't got much to defend. You must know that."

Holtzman grinned triumphantly at me. All lawyers are in favor of a strong judicial hand in resolving cases short of trial—until that heavy hand comes down on them. Then they talk about lazy judges who refuse to try cases.

"Judge, when you take a closer look at the case as I have, you'll realize that she does in fact have a chance, an excellent chance, in front of a jury."

Judge Kane smiled unpleasantly. He looked at Holtzman and then back at me. The smile dissolved into the half-amused look of a father whose patience is about to give out in the face of squabbling offspring.

Holtzman jumped in. "Defense counsel seems to have an unrealistic view of his chances at trial, Your Honor. I've tried to talk some sense into him, but he won't listen. The last thing that Mrs. Alden needs is a trial. It would be a waste of the court's time as well as the prosecutor's."

Holtzman's heavy-handed attempt to make me look like the bad guy was in the time-honored tradition of an in-chambers conference with the judge. The posturing differed little from what went on in the courtroom.

"I realize that the court has a busy docket, but I take offense at the prosecutor's suggestion that the court's docket should dictate my decision on whether this case should be tried or not. I know when a case should go to trial and when it shouldn't."

Kane looked at Holtzman and frowned.

"Have you made any offers, Brad?"

"We certainly have, Your Honor. A two-year cap for a life offense. That's more than reasonable."

"This is the first time I have heard that particular offer," I said when the judge turned his deepening frown toward me. "The last offer I heard was a plea on the nose and a five-year cap."

"Two years doesn't sound unreasonable, Jack, and it's a cap. Not more than two years or she can withdraw her plea. Besides, I can sentence her to less than the cap. Maybe you can talk me into going light on her."

"I understand all that, Judge. It's a super deal—unless Joel's a molester and gets custody of the child, which he will if she's convicted of perjury."

Holtzman made a growling sound. "For Christ's sake, Brenner. Haven't you read the transcript yet?" He rolled his eyes and looked to the judge for assistance.

The prosecutor had managed to press the right button, for the judge leaned forward in his chair and fixed me with a stare that demanded an explanation.

"I hear rumors, Jack," he said. "I hear you're going to make a circus out of this case." That word again. Kirtley apparently had a vocabulary the size of a thimble.

"I have a client to defend, Your Honor. I can create doubt about whether Joel Alden did in fact sexually abuse his own child."

"She admitted on the witness stand that she lied about that, did she not?"

"Yes, she did."

"Well?" he replied with a wink at Holtzman.

I would not have been surprised if he'd added, "I rest my case."

Holtzman sat back in smug silence. He'd managed to turn the judge and me into adversaries while he sat on the sidelines. I could not attack the judge, but the prosecutor was fair game. I looked at Holtzman.

"If the prosecutor had done his homework," I said, "he would know that he had the burden of proving that Joel Alden did *not* molest his child. He can't convict Mrs. Alden just because she made conflicting statements. Take a look at *People v. Cash*."

The prosecutor's mouth fell open in disbelief. "She admitted that she lied by saying that Joel Alden sexually abused his own child," he said. "Are you suggesting that you are going to be able to show that he did?" He looked at the judge, awaiting a cue, unsure whether he should react with derision or outrage.

"Perhaps you should explain yourself, Counsel," the judge said with a scowl. "How exactly are you planning to defend this case?" A minute ago I was "Jack." The use of the impersonal "Counsel" did not augur well.

"I've got more law, Your Honor," I replied. "There's also *People v. McCann*, which—"

"Now look here, Brenner. I have fifteen hundred cases a year to handle, and damn few of those will ever get to trial. I'm not going to waste the taxpayers' money messing around with a case just because some big city hotshot is trying to build a reputation. I read the papers. I know all about this case."

"What exactly *do* you know about this case, Your Honor?"

I did not raise my voice, but there was a lot of restrained anger in it, and I did not care that he could spot it, which is generally not a good attitude when you are speaking to a man who can summarily jail you for contempt. Still, I had learned long ago that a bad judge does not respect a respectful lawyer. Good lawyering often requires skating on the thin ice of contempt.

Holtzman crossed his legs and shifted to a more comfortable position in his chair, the better to enjoy the show, no doubt.

"I know only what I read in the newspapers," Kane said cagily. His outburst had been meant to intimidate. He was aware that he might go too far and risk a disqualification. I was hoping that he had.

"With all due respect, Your Honor, it sounds as if you have already made up your mind about this case. Perhaps you should recuse yourself."

The judge placed his elbows on his desk and made a little tent with his fingers, over which he gazed at me with amusement. A judge he might be, but no mere referee role for him. He preferred the parry-and-thrust of legal combat.

"I certainly will not recuse myself, Mr. Brenner. I have a duty to control my docket and not waste the taxpayers' money. Furthermore, I am charged with the responsibility of overseeing the ethical conduct of attorneys who appear in front of me. And I must say that what I hear and read in the paper raises serious questions not only about your strategy in defending this case, but also about the nature of your relationship with your client."

"If you're talking about Ripley's nonsense, then I'm disappointed in you, Judge. He's pissed because I didn't play ball with him."

"That may well be, my friend, but the profession is blackened when the reputation of a member of the Bar is called into question, especially as it relates to a woman client. Perhaps you should consider handing this case over to someone who is not so personally involved."

There it was. I'd dared to challenge his ability to preside over Davey's trial, and now he wanted me off the case.

"Mrs. Alden and I have a professional relationship," I replied coldly. "I do not know what kind of gossip the little town of Kirtley may be wallowing in these days, but I am not about to let gossip and malicious rumor dictate how I defend a client. Nor am I going to let myself be intimidated into pleading a case out just because the powers that be find it inconvenient—or embarrassing—to go to trial."

"Take it easy, my friend," the judge said. "No one is trying to intimidate you. By all means, have your trial if that is what you really want. I doubt that a trial is what your client needs, but you and she must be the judges of that."

With that, he briskly opened the file and studied its contents. I had fended him off, but at what price?

"How long a trial are we talking about?" he asked Holtzman, who looked startled and then disappointed. He had been counting on the judge to bring me in line.

"Our proofs will take a day or so," he said.

"I don't imagine that I'll have a lot of cross for the prosecutor's witnesses," I said, "and I haven't decided whether I'll call my client."

"I'd love you to," Holtzman said. He knew that I wouldn't dare call Davey. I would have to win the case on cross-examination.

"If you have any last-minute pretrial motions, file and schedule them no later than next Monday," Kane said. "I'll expect your voir dire questions on my desk by tomorrow at five. We'll start the jury selection promptly at eight-thirty. I'll handle the voir dire myself. I'm expecting a short trial. We'll take an hour for lunch and go until about four each day. I do not tolerate tardiness. I expect the attorneys to be prepared and to make their objections succinct and to the point. Any questions, gentlemen?"

Neither of us had any questions, so the judge stood up, terminating the meeting. He was his usual jovial self as we departed. He even told a joke. I managed a responsive grin and left with a comradely wave. Holtzman stayed on to join in the command performance of hearty laughter.

*   *   *

Bashful in face-to-face encounters, Larry Semczyk lost his inhibitions on the phone and was a smooth-talking pro. But this time he could not hide the undercurrent of excitement in his voice.

"You've really put me onto something," he said. "I've spent two weeks looking at deeds and talking to farmers in Avon Township."

"Anything for the Fourth Estate."

I sounded playful but I was still seething over my clash with Kane. On top of that, Scott had sent a message through Sherry that he wanted to see me about Davey's case.

"My editor has assigned me to it almost full time. That and Mrs. Alden's trial."

"What can you tell me?"

"Anything you want, so long as you promise to be discreet."

"Understood."

"It looks like somebody is quietly planning to put a huge toxic waste landfill, probably the biggest one in the country, right here in Laffler County. It will handle PCBs, polychlorinated biphenyls, the nasty stuff they used in industry for so long."

"You've got all this nailed down?"

"Not yet. It's what we suspect. Somebody is buying up a bunch of farms in the north part of the county. We think the idea is to secretly assemble the land and then push it through the township so fast that nobody has a chance to mount any opposition. It's a big story."

I smiled. Davey's trial was important. A garbage dump was not.

"You'll have to excuse me," I said, "but I'm a city boy and I don't see what's so big a deal about a landfill."

Semczyk laughed. "You would if they were planning to build a toxic waste dump next door to you. We practically had an armed revolt in Dresden Township last year when someone proposed a landfill there—not a toxic one, just a regular one. Nobody wants any kind of landfill next door. People will go berserk when they hear it involves PCBs."

"Don't the federal and state governments check it out first?"

"Sure, but who watches the watchdogs? This thing is worth millions and millions. If someone influential like Joel Alden is involved, things can be expedited and maybe even overlooked."

"You're hinting at some sort of corruption."

Semczyk paused. I could tell he was wondering how much he should tell me, and that gave me a sinking feeling. I recalled that Scott was the attorney for Avon Township, where almost all of the farms were located.

"This is where it gets touchy," Semczyk said. "We've had our eye on a couple of board members in Avon Township for some time. Nothing concrete, but if these guys are corrupt, this is a ready-made situation for bribery. A speedy approval could be worth millions for the developers. For all we know, the skids are already greased."

"What about Sinclair?"

"Like he said, he may just be a straw man. I don't know much more than you told me."

"I'd love to tie him to Joel Alden. The deeds I saw are dated well before Davey made her accusations."

"I checked out the Terra Group. It's a partnership with a lot of names I never heard of, but I spotted some that have ties to Alden. Maybe all of them do. You won't find his name on any of the documents, but I have a hunch that Joel is up to his neck in this thing. I'll bet it's his project."

"Well, let me know if you find anything I can use."

Semczyk paused again.

"There's one more thing. I hate to mention it. But I owe it to you to say something."

I did not respond. After a wait, Semczyk filled the silence.

"My boss thinks Scott Sherman may have something to do with it. I'm going to look into it. I thought I'd better warn you."

"I hear you," was all I could think to say.

After I replaced the receiver, I stared at my Michigan Law diploma for a long time.

"No big deal," Scott had said.

"Time to cash in your chips and get out of the game, my lad. Even the Old Fox can't beat these odds."

"So now crazy Don Quixote is the Old Fox."

I tried to keep the sarcasm out of my voice, not altogether successfully. There was just enough truth in Scott's gibe to bring out my stubborn streak.

"You're my hero, lad. If there is anyone who could have pulled this one off, you're the one, but you should have cut a deal when you had a chance. Now you're up to your eyebrows in shit, with no way out."

We sat in his office. For once his desk was neat. Except for my handling of Davey's case, he was pleased with the way things were working out with me in the office. Just a week ago I had hammered out a $250,000 settlement in an auto negligence case in which the carrier had reserved a cool million. Insurance companies are not known for their gratitude, but this one was glowing with appreciation for my skills.

"What's your point, Scott?"

"You've got to get out of the Davey Alden case. You've managed to polarize the situation to the point where no deal is possible, and you've also pissed the judge off."

"As usual, Scott Sherman hears everything first."

"I make it my business to know what's going on—especially when it can affect my pocketbook."

"Davey Alden can pay her bills," I said. "Olenik ordered Joel to cough up the money for her legal costs. You don't have to worry about money in this case."

"It's not money. I can't afford to let you waste your time on the Alden case. You're too valuable. I mean it. I'm talking about a partnership—you and me. I'm telling you, guy, that there's no limit to how much money we can make if we play our cards right."

"What about Davey Alden? Just dump her?"

"You can't do her any good. Let's be honest. You got a case of the hots and you lost your head. Do her a favor. Get out and let somebody cut the best deal they can for her. Holtzman doesn't want to try this case. It's still possible to work something out."

"I'm not looking for a deal. This one goes to trial."

"What the hell kind of defense could you possibly have?"

I gave him an Old Fox smile. I wanted Holtzman and Joel to know what they were in for. Apparently Scott was the pipeline between us.

"I'm going to let them prosecute Davey for perjury while I put Joel on trial as a child molester. When I get done with him, no jury will convict his wife."

"Where are you going to get evidence that Joel is a molester, and even if you find it, how the hell are you going to convince Kane to let it in?"

"Wait and see."

Scott got up and walked around the desk, taking a seat on the edge so that he towered over me. "You're not listening, son. Get out of the Davey Alden case. You're not the man to handle it."

"As I recall, you're the one who got me appointed—or had you forgotten?"

Scott looked old and ugly at that moment. "It wasn't your trial skills, my boy, that got you appointed. I suggested you because I figured you knew how to cut a deal. No fuss, no muss. Little did I know that you'd end up thinking with your dick."

"Does this have anything to do with the toxic waste dump? Is that what this is all about? Are you going to sell your soul for the Terra Group?"

I regretted the words as soon as they left my mouth. I had promised Semczyk that I would be discreet.

Scott went from angry to icy cold in an instant.

"Look, I'll make it plain and simple. Get rid of the Davey Alden case, one way or the other, or we can forget about a partnership. I need you, but I don't need you that bad."

"Fuck you."

"Think about it, Jack. With me you've got a chance. You were a lost soul when I took you in out of the rain. You don't want to go back to defender work. You need the salary I pay you. It's time to grow up."

27

"So the judge despises you, the prosecutor has an airtight case, and you can't find any evidence that might help your client. Other than that, how do things look?"

"I think you've got it." I wondered if Ann appreciated how close we were to true gallows humor.

We sat in Ann's living room the night before Davey's trial, Ann on her couch while I sprawled in a brown leather chair with my feet on an ottoman. Maggie lay on the floor between us, snoring. Outside, it was raining and occasionally a gust threw the rain against Ann's picture window.

"Maybe I'm blind," I said. "The judge, the prosecutor, even my own partner—all of them think I should get out of the case."

Ann held the brandy snifter in front of her and studied its color.

"Davey's case getting to you?"

"If you're suggesting I have cold feet, forget it."

"Don't get touchy, buster. What's the problem?"

"I just told you. Maybe I'm not seeing things straight. You said as much a few weeks ago. Maybe we should cut a deal."

"Spoken like a true lawyer. You get a case worth fighting for, and you want to save face and cop a plea."

Maggie raised her head and studied our faces. I liked to think it worried her to see the two people she loved most fighting. But maybe we were just disturbing her sleep.

"Look, you're not the one who has to take it to trial. You don't have to face the jury, and if we lose, you sure as hell won't be the one to look Davey in the eye and say 'sorry about that.' Why don't you stick to slicing people up and leave the lawyering to me?"

"Don't you dare compare our professions, you numbskull."

"Spare me the healer-of-the-sick routine."

"As usual, you miss the point. We doctors are glorified car mechanics. You lawyers are the ones who have the opportunity to reach for grandeur."

"Grandeur, no less. I'm flattered."

"Don't be. You lawyers blew your chance to achieve justice a long time ago. You let the adversary stuff get out of hand. Maybe it was the good old American competitive spirit that did it. But you blew it."

It was an old argument between us. Ann had a fixation on justice. In the end things were always evened up. Things were never just the way they were. She insisted that things could be changed for the better—that even lawyers could be redeemed.

"How did we blow it, pray tell?"

"When you decided that you could get up in front of a jury and advance a version of the facts that you knew was false. Oh, I know all about the idea that a criminal deserves a vigorous defense. But it's one thing to use the rules to make sure some poor devil doesn't get railroaded, and another to lie to the jury."

"What's all this got to do with Davey?" I asked.

"Davey's best defense is the truth. You don't have to lie. You get the truth in front of the jury and you will prevail."

"More of your God talk?" That was my fallback position when things weren't going well. Disqualify Ann because of her faith in a God of Good Intentions.

"I haven't mentioned God, but now that you have, I see no reason why He should be left out of the equation."

I sneered, but with Ann my mockery lacked sting. She was one of the few credible religious people I'd ever met. Her God was just there, an integral part of her life, a presence who did not have to be mentioned with every third breath.

Another thing I liked was that her conviction allowed for doubt; she could see the reasonableness of my position. Of course, that had its downside: it spiked my liberal smugness.

I got up and walked into the kitchen area to find the brandy. I poured myself an inch or two and did the same for Ann.

"What's God going to do for Davey?" I said when I was seated again. Maggie came over and laid her head on my lap.

"Don't worry about God. The question right now is what *you're* doing for Davey. It sounds to me like you're thinking of turning tail."

"I'm just trying to paint an accurate picture. The fact is that I haven't come up with anything to prove Joel is a pedophile."

"Why can't Davey just get on the witness stand and tell the truth— why she did what she did? Surely the jury will see she had no choice."

"They won't listen to her, not after Sinclair testifies. Holtzman will portray her as a conniving country club bitch just the way Ripley did. Besides, I don't think she'd come across well. If she breaks down, it'll look like acting. If her childhood comes out, it may look like she's imagining things. I can't put her on the stand."

Ann snorted. "You're talking like it's hopeless."

"Not hopeless but sure as hell uphill."

"That Sinclair is a liar. You've got him cold on those deeds. That'll take care of him."

"It'll help cast doubt on his story, sure. With some of the things I've come up with, I can inflict a lot of little cuts but not the fatal gash. We can't get around the fact that Davey lied under oath. It's right there on the record in the first trial. The only way around that is to convince the jury to go against the law and decide that Davey was justified. That means proving Joel's a child molester."

Ann patted her lap and Maggie moved over to her.

"My poor, poor baby," Ann said. She was looking at Maggie, but I knew she was talking about Davey, who had given me permission to tell Ann everything. Since then they'd become closer than ever.

Looking into Maggie's adoring eyes, Ann asked, "Why does God permit so much evil in this world He made? Why does He allow so much suffering? Why do the innocent suffer the most?"

I was no longer sneering.

"You always say it's because He gave us free will. And I always ask how a loving God could be so cruel as to make us free to do such horrible things."

"Yes, you always do say that," Ann said sadly. It was late and she looked tired. "And I always respond that there's always enough goodness in the world to hold the evil in check, if only barely. God does not abandon us."

We both smiled when Maggie stretched, yawned, and slumped back onto the floor in a blissful heap. Dogs do not suffer from the future.

"What the hell," Ann said suddenly. "I'm starting to sound like you. You've said a hundred times that juries are unpredictable. In this case you've got to trust that they will sense the truth. That'll be your job. If you give them the truth, they'll do the right thing."

28

In the Midwest, once you get outside the big cities, away from places like Chicago and Detroit and Cleveland, the courtrooms reflect the earnestness of the jurors who serve there. They are honest places filled with scrubbed, shiny faces, glowing with good faith and rectitude. The sincerity, as Davey and I entered Judge Kane's courtroom, was almost palpable.

Davey gave a little gasp at the sight of so many people in the courtroom, and hesitated for a moment in the doorway. Then, before I could take her arm, she threw back her shoulders, raised her chin, and walked ahead of me to the defense table. She wore the same gray suit she'd worn the first time we met in court; she called it her lucky suit because on that day I had gotten her out of jail.

I sat Davey down at the table and began to remove the books and papers from my briefcase. We were the first arrivals, and I could hear the whispers of the crowd and feel eyes boring into my back. Without looking, I also knew those eyes were already beginning to evaluate Davey. In the crowd were seventy-five potential jurors.

I sat down and began to talk quietly to Davey, less concerned with what I said than with creating an impression of serious but not panicky concern. That's the way it would be from now on: every move and word weighed for the impression it would make on the finders of fact, the twelve citizens good and true who would decide Davey's fate.

I opened a law book and pretended to read. The buzz created by our arrival faded, and the awkwardness caused by our presence was starting to concern me when the courtroom door opened and Brad Holtzman entered with Sandra McClellan, my sour-faced opponent in front of Judge Kashat, along with a meaty-faced sheriff's detective I'd seen a few times around the prosecutor's office.

McClellan was there for the women's vote. Should Davey take the witness stand, McClellan would be the one to beat up on her during cross-examination. Her very presence at the prosecution table carried a message: even women should be outraged by Davey Alden's perjury.

Holtzman and McClellan were conservatively dressed in dark suits. With my brown tweed sport jacket, darker brown wool pants that needed pressing, and penny loafers, I'd opted for the warm teddy bear look, even loosening my drab tie and unbuttoning the collar of my tattersall shirt.

Holtzman, sporting his before-the-big-game grin, came immediately to our table and shook my hand, while nodding courteously to Davey.

"Last chance to take our offer," he said, sotto voce. "Plead straight up with a two-year cap. Offer withdrawn once the judge walks through that door."

I did not get an opportunity to reject his offer, for just then Judge Francis X. Kane entered the courtroom. The bailiff was Deputy Gilbert F. Rollins, and as he swaggered into the courtroom just ahead of Kane, he smiled at Davey and me. My insides crawled at the sight of him, and the sick bile of paranoia rose in my throat. Was this Holtzman's little joke? Had Rollins asked for this assignment? I struggled to look unaffected by his presence, determined not to give either of them the satisfaction of a complaint from me.

Once the judge was seated, a grinning Rollins told the rest of us to take our seats. Besides the seventy-five veniremen, there were fifty or so eager spectators seated in the courtroom and another fifty waiting impatiently in the hall. Ripley's articles had drawn them like flies.

When the room had quieted down and the judge had given an almost imperceptible nod, the seventy-year-old county clerk, Ralston Nash, who made a personal appearance in the clerk's seat only in high-profile cases, intoned solemnly, *"People of the State of Michigan versus Davilon A. Alden,* Number one-eight-nine-nine-three-dash-FC." The ritual continued with the lawyers putting their appearances on the record and indicating that they were ready to proceed to trial.

Sounding like a game-show host warming up the audience, Kane explained the workings of the Circuit Court, making certain that the jurors understood how hard he worked and what great shape his docket was in. He said that the voir dire process consisted of asking them questions about their qualifications as jurors.

"Now let me tell you something about this case," Kane said, breaking into a conspiratorial grin. "But I suspect that many of you already have heard of or read about it." An eyebrow arched into a question mark and the jurors laughed dutifully. Of course they knew about the case. Laffler County had been talking about little else for months.

"The charge against Mrs. Alden is perjury. The People accuse Mrs. Alden of coming into this court and swearing under oath that her husband sexually molested their daughter. The prosecutor charges that she testified under oath knowing full well that the accusation and her testimony were false and that she is therefore guilty of perjury. Mrs. Alden pleads not guilty to the charge. It is the duty of the prosecutor to prove guilt beyond a reasonable doubt."

I did not look at Davey, but as the judge went on, wooing and educating the jury, I caught a whiff of scent from her—a splash of cologne on her wrist, or perhaps just her hair spray, and with it came an intense wave of . . . what? . . . melancholy, love? Whatever it was, I suppressed it and concentrated on Kane's performance.

". . . means that the scales are actually tilted in favor of a defendant in a criminal trial in America. The prosecutor must upset this presumption of innocence by presenting to you evidence that proves guilt beyond a reasonable doubt. It is not enough if he proves that Mrs. Alden *might* have done it, *could* have done it, *possibly* did it, or even *probably* did it. He must prove guilt beyond a reasonable doubt or you must acquit the defendant."

I had to give the devil his due: Kane did a good job in giving the jurors the fundamental principles of criminal law.

My real concern was that the very air we breathed was poisoned against Davey. Joel Alden was a prominent citizen, Davey had embarrassed the community, and the winds of public opinion, fanned by the media, were blowing against her. Kane, political animal that he was, could not help but be influenced by these things, but, more important, the jury would be too. Even if Kane tried to be fair, it might be too little too late.

The judge went on to tell the jury that Davey did not have to take the witness stand or produce any evidence whatsoever, and they could not hold her silence against her. But she could testify if that was what she chose to do. Then he turned to the question of press coverage.

"I am aware that there has been extensive media coverage of this case. We'll be questioning you about what you have read or heard about this case. I instruct you now that you must put aside anything you have read, seen, or heard in the media. You must base your decision in this case only on the evidence that is duly admitted in this courtroom—not on streetcorner gossip or what the newspapers or television report from people who are not under oath or subject to cross-examination."

Suddenly the judge frowned. Staring hard at the jurors, his handsome face the essence of dramatic righteousness, his voice rising to stentorian heights, he said, "Now I want you to do something. Look at the person next to you—yes, take a good look. That person next to you is a stranger. You are assuming that he or she is a juror. But how do you know that? You don't. For all you know, that person is a witness in this case or a relative of someone connected to this case. That person may be eager to talk to you about this case, *to prejudice you by telling you one side of this case.*"

Just as suddenly, the judge's cheerfulness returned.

"That is why I know you will follow my instruction not to discuss this case with anyone, including your fellow jurors, until the time comes for you to deliberate."

Many of the jurors grinned back at the judge. I tried to memorize the faces of those who looked too relieved. For what I had in mind, I needed stubbornness. I would try to get rid of the eager-to-pleasers.

"Now I will call upon the attorneys to introduce themselves and mention the names of any witnesses they plan to call. Please listen carefully to see if there is anybody you know among the witnesses who may be called in this case. We'll start with the prosecutor, Mr. Holtzman."

Holtzman stood up and faced the jurors. He told them who he was, introduced McClellan, and mentioned the names of the five other assistant prosecutors who worked for him. He then read the list of witnesses he expected to call. It included the names of Joel Alden and Terry Sinclair.

Kane smiled at me. "Now, Mr. Burr— . . . ah . . . Mr.—ah yes, Brenner. Perhaps you might care to mention any names that may be important to your case."

A juror or two snickered at the judge's mischievous smile. I stood up and introduced myself and told the panel that I was practicing law with Scott Sherman and Ralph Miles in Kirtley. Then I had Davey stand up and face the jurors while I introduced her as my client, Mrs. Alden. She smiled shyly and sat down.

"I have not decided whether it will be necessary to call any witnesses in this trial," I then said, turning back to the judge. I had provided Holtzman with no witness list. I had no one. Only Davey, and she couldn't testify.

Then Clerk Nash began to select jurors for our trial. He reached into a box that looked as if it had once held shoes and drew out a slip of paper.

In about ten minutes there were thirteen people in the jury box, and Kane started his voir dire. Among the eight women and five men were three full-time homemakers (the judge drew a laugh by warning the men not to say that their wives "stay home and do nothing"), an executive secretary, a bookkeeper for her husband's plumbing business, a woman mail carrier, a waitress, a woman CPA, three salesmen, a driver of a Pepsi truck, and an engineer for the Chrysler Corporation.

The judge then started down a list of questions designed to flush out prejudices and incompatible attitudes, but the way he phrased them telegraphed to the juror the right answer. "Mrs. Kendall, do you think you can be a fair and impartial juror in this case despite the fact that your house was broken into three months ago?" "I believe I can, Your Honor."

One of the salesmen was released when it turned out that his daughter had scheduled a midweek wedding the next day in Connecticut and he had plane reservations for that night. "I think it's fair to assume that they expect you to be there," Kane said. "Families are kind of funny that way." He led the hearty laughter that followed.

As jurors were excused, new names were drawn and the questioning resumed.

As always, the juror interrogation appeared to be searching and complete, but in truth the law indulged in a polite fiction on that score. Although the voir dire usually managed to skim off the screwballs and the obviously biased, there was a line beyond which the lawyers and judge customarily did not pass, for it was understood that almost every juror could be disqualified if pressed hard enough. Most of the questions were really an explanation of the law—followed by a promise from the jurors to follow that law.

No one was surprised when almost all the jurors admitted that they had read about the case in the *Laffler Chronicle* and the Detroit dailies—and no one believed the waitress when she insisted that she had never heard of the case. The engineer was thrown off after he told the judge he had made up his mind about the case on the basis of what he read in the papers. All the other jurors swore that they had not made up their minds and could ignore the media coverage, basing their verdict only on the evidence duly admitted in the courtroom. No one really believed them either.

After almost an hour of questioning by the judge, three of the jurors had been excused for cause—the engineer, the salesman giving away a daughter, and a housewife with a severe hearing problem.

It was no secret that I wanted as many women on the jury as possible, the younger the better, while Holtzman would push for men and conservative older women. Despite the jurors' renunciation of bias, we believed that certain types of jurors were predisposed to think in certain ways. Engineers and accountants are precise and often demand impossibly accurate proofs; union workers tend to resent authority; older women are hard on younger women who get themselves into tight sexual situations; women with young children more easily identify with victims and their families in a child molestation case. Some lawyers swear that these predilections can be scientifically verified, but for most of us they are little more than superstitions and might just as easily be based on eye color, hair style, or weight (and in fact often are).

I now had nine women on the jury, six of them under forty and only one of those unmarried. Five of the nine had children around Julie's age. However, each side now had twelve peremptory challenges.

"I believe that I have conducted a searching voir dire of this jury, gentlemen," Kane said. "Do you have any additional voir dire?" It was clear that he expected us to say that we were satisfied. In case of an appeal, the record would then be free of any complaints about our inability to ask the jurors questions ourselves; the judge's in-chambers declaration at the pretrial that he would handle voir dire himself was not part of any official record. Holtzman dutifully declined to ask anything further. I was tempted to try my luck but decided that I did not want to risk being chastened in front of the jury; the judge's forgetting my name had already put me one down. I said I had no questions.

"Any peremptory challenges for the prosecution?" the judge asked.

"The People will thank and excuse Juror Number 23, Mrs. Kresnak," Holtzman replied, smiling an apology at a young mother I'd hoped to hang on to. Mrs. Kresnak sat in stunned silence for a moment before she realized that she had been kicked off the jury. Then she rose and blushingly left the courtroom.

Holtzman and I continued to move jurors in and out of the box like pawns in a game of chess. Each new juror had to undergo a vetting by Kane. At one point, having used only five of his twelve challenges, the prosecutor passed, the first step in an attempt to get me to exhaust my challenges before he did, thus leaving the final choices to him. I was tempted to pass also, thus finalizing the jury selection, but there was one older woman on the panel who I wanted to excuse. I used a challenge to get rid of her.

Holtzman passed again, but I had a bad feeling about the electronics company executive who had just been seated. I used a peremptory, and the maneuvering continued. Gradually the courtroom was thinning out as jurors were excused and departed. I looked around to get a feel for who was left and saw Judy Cusmano and Andrea Swanson sitting among the spectators.

Juror Number 57, Doris Ann Whiting, was called and took the place of the executive. She was a well-groomed, gray-haired woman in her fifties. Voir dire revealed that she was married to a Ford Motor Company engineer, had three grown children, no grandchildren, and was attending Wayne State University almost full time in the hopes of obtaining a degree in English literature. She looked intelligent and interested.

"Pass," Holtzman said.

"We are satisfied with this jury, Your Honor," I said. Holtzman looked surprised, as did the judge. I still had five challenges left, but I was convinced that we were as well off as could be hoped. The jury consisted of seven women and six men. Five of the women were young mothers, two of them full time. The sixth was a single female student working on a degree in marketing. The final woman was the last juror chosen, the fiftyish college student. One of the thirteen would be drawn off by lot just before the jury started deliberating.

Of the six men, four were under forty. One of the other two was a gentle retiree who looked as if he might feel sorry for Davey. The final male was an enigma—the Pepsi driver who was one of the first chosen to sit in the box. I'd noted on the questionnaire that he had been a Teamsters union steward some years back. The truck driver stereotype suggested that he would be more sympathetic toward a male victim in a case like this, but the union involvement might mean that he disliked the police and would favor the underdog, especially since Joel Alden was an employer and a community big shot. He was the biggest question mark on the panel. I was playing a hunch with him.

"Ladies and gentlemen, you have been selected to serve as jurors in this case," Kane said. "I will now ask you to stand and take an oath to do your duty as jurors."

After swearing the jury, Kane read them preliminary instructions, explaining the procedure we would follow from opening statements to closing arguments. Then he adjourned the trial until the next morning at 9:00 A.M. so that we could put the finishing touches on our opening statements and line up our witnesses. He told the jury that he did not expect the trial to last more than a day and a half.

The dark night of the soul for lawyers comes when preparations are as complete as they will ever be and the lies told to clients and yourself come back to sit on the edge of the desk and stare you in the face.

I sat at my desk late into the night and assured myself that Davey was the one person I had not misled. Others, myself included, but not Davey. I had explained the law and was satisfied that she understood, and the facts, well, she knew them better than anyone.

Plain and simple, she was guilty of perjury. My job was to make certain that things were not plain and simple.

Ann was entitled to her belief in ultimate justice, but the present was my concern. If her God were judging, Davey and Julie would be safe, but He had left things in the hands of frail human beings, and jurors were the most fallible of all.

Ann to the contrary, I could not have a simple faith in the law, and I did not have her God to fall back on. The irony of my situation was not lost on me. I had left criminal law to escape the obfuscation and moral ambiguity endemic in that field. Now those very tactics and traits were once again my weapons of choice. All in the cause of truth.

So I went over my notes and research a second and third time and tried to anticipate every legal argument and factual development, rehearsing every imaginable scenario for possible weaknesses in Holtzman's case. If I got Davey acquitted, it would be in cross-examination, and it would be because I had sown doubt among the jurors. I had no one to call to the stand on Davey's behalf; I had to win my case with the prosecutor's witnesses. I had to slice them up so badly that no jury could take a chance on convicting Davey.

Finally, when the only wise thing left to do was get some rest, I turned off my lights and closed my door. Passing Scott's office, I noticed that he'd left the antique lamp on his desk lit. I turned it out and was almost to his door when I paused. On an impulse I turned back and relit the lamp. I searched Scott's desk and credenza for the Terra Group file I'd seen on his desk. It was not in his office.

Still in the grip of my impulse, I went to the outer office and searched the filing cabinets and the secretarial desks. Nothing. Then I remembered Scott's computer and his fascination with the latest technology. I went back into his office and turned on his Micron, sitting in his chair as it came to life. In less than a minute I was into his hard drive and looking at file names. I caught my breath when the Terra Group name scrolled up into view.

The file was locked. The computer was demanding a password. I tried a dozen—the first names of all three of his wives, the names of his children, his mother's first and maiden names, even the name of his dog. Then I recalled why he wanted to live so close to Ann Arbor. After six strikes I got it: Go Blue.

What appeared on the screen was a rough draft of a document that appeared to be a partnership agreement. The principals included Joel Alden and Masters and four other names I did not recognize.

Scott's name was there too, not as a partner but as a consultant. The document provided a huge annual fee for him if the group successfully constructed a landfill in Avon Township. The agreement did not mention that Scott Sherman was the attorney for Avon Township and supposedly dedicated to representing the best interests of its citizens.

I shut off the computer and turned off the light. I stood outside the office for a long time with my hand on the door handle. Then I got in my car and drove home and tried to get some sleep.

29

HOLTZMAN WALKED OVER TO THE DEFENSE TABLE AND JABBED AN accusing finger at Davey.

"This woman is an adulteress who concocted a vicious lie," he said. "She is a cunning perjurer who would stop at nothing to get rid of her husband. A divorce was not good enough. She wanted him in prison. That way she could have his money for herself and her lover."

I wanted to grab Holtzman's finger and rip it off. Instead I jumped up and protested to the judge.

"Your Honor, I object to this blatant attempt to inflame the jury. The prosecutor is stooping to intimidation and humiliation. He knows he has no case—"

"I object!" Holtzman yelled. "He has no right to interrupt my opening—"

"Both of you be quiet," Kane ordered. He glared at us for a moment and then went on, "Mr. Brenner, if you have a *legitimate* objection, be so kind as to state it succinctly. We do not need a speech. Do you understand me?"

"Yes, sir."

"And as for you, Mr. Holtzman, we could use a little less finger-waving." Looking back at me, he added icily, "We are off to a bad start, gentlemen. I am warning you right now that I will not put up with your nonsense during this trial. These jurors and the court expect a professional effort from the two of you." The last remark was made with a winning smile at the jurors, who responded with appreciative smiles of their own.

Holtzman and I both thanked the judge, each of us hoping the jury would believe that it was the other guy who'd been reprimanded. I sat down and Holtzman returned to the lectern to continue his opening statement. He seemed a little less rabid as he sketched for the jury what he intended to prove.

Ralph was right about Holtzman. He was overcautious. He told the jury that not only was he going to present official transcripts of the aborted trial of Joel Alden, but that he would also present live testimony from people who'd heard Davey perjure herself. To prove motive, he would bring in Terrence Sinclair. Then he would top off his proofs with the testimony of Joel Alden, who would convince them beyond any reasonable doubt that he was an innocent man and that Davey Alden was a perjurer.

Davey had visibly paled at Holtzman's accusations. I had coached her on how to behave during the trial—how to sit, how to look concerned without appearing shocked or angry, even how to look at me so as not to fuel speculation about our relationship. She had made an effort to tame her hair that morning. She did not look like Ripley's Sunday-magazine adulteress.

Still I was worried. Since our appearance in the courtroom, and especially since Holtzman's attack, she'd settled into a state of resignation close to indifference.

"When the evidence has been presented and you have heard the law that you must apply to this case, I am convinced that you will find the defendant guilty of perjury," Holtzman was saying. "You will have no choice."

The prosecutor collected his notes and returned to his seat.

"Do you wish to make an opening statement now, or do you wish to reserve it, Mr. Brenner?" the judge asked.

I stood up, but I did not answer Judge Kane's question immediately. The courtroom whisperers and fidgeters fell silent. The stenographer sat with her fingers poised over her machine. Kane's questioning look started to turn into a frown.

Holtzman's smug confidence had irritated me, and perhaps the jury too.

"Your Honor, I will make an opening statement."

I walked over to the jury box and stood only a few feet from the front row of jurors. I had no notes. I let my face reflect the worry I felt.

"In this case, ladies and gentlemen, nothing is what it seems. For the most part, all of you have lived normal lives, but for the next few days you will inhabit a shadowy forest filled with twisted desires and perverted impulses. I ask that you listen patiently to the evidence and then vote your consciences.

"When you go into that little room back there to decide on your verdict, it will only be you and your consciences. The prosecutor, the defense lawyer, the judge—none of us will be able to make the choice for you. That will be your job, and no one else's. So powerful is the role of the jury that no one can tell you what you must decide. No one can second-guess you."

I paused and looked reproachfully at Prosecutor Holtzman.

"Don't let anyone tell you that you have no choice. The evidence in this case will be such that you will have to make many difficult choices. Don't let anyone steal that responsibility from you.

"That's why you're here—to make choices. You are not a rubber stamp brought here merely to endorse the prosecutor's viewpoints. You will have a choice.

"All of you have lived a number of years—you are mature adults— and you bring a variety of life experiences with you to this trial. With

maturity you have learned that things are often not what they appear—
that it is a mistake to jump to conclusions."

I let my eyes roam over the jury, seeking eye contact, willing my
faith in Davey into their hearts and minds.

"For those of you who have children, you know all about there
being two sides to any story"—I allowed myself a little smile, and several jurors responded in kind; one even nodded her head—"and you
know better than to punish anyone before you have had an opportunity to gather all the facts.

"*Appearances are deceiving.* That maxim is especially important in
this case. I have said that you will be entering a foul, twisted world. I
am talking about the sexual abuse of children. No one understands
the mind of the child molester—the pedophile. He lives in a world
so far different from our own that sometimes the testimony of the
tiny victim—and that of the mother—seems incredible. You have no
experience with that world, and you will find some things hard to
believe.

"There is danger in your innocence. Because you cannot imagine
such crimes, you may believe that they could not—did not—happen.
That could lead to a miscarriage of justice.

"I can ask no more of you than that you give my client a fair trial.
You will learn in this trial that she did certain things for which the
prosecutor seeks to have her condemned. Wait until you have heard
all the evidence. Things are not what they seem. There will be a natural tendency to start to make up your minds as the evidence comes
in—especially when it appears damning, as some of it no doubt will.
Resist that temptation. Wait until you have heard all the evidence.

"I believe that if you listen carefully to the evidence in this case,
you will not only have reasonable doubt, you will have *no doubt* that
Mrs. Alden is innocent of these charges.

"I thank you."

I walked back to the defense table and sat down without looking at
Davey. My opening statement was conjured out of thin air, and the

judge and I and the prosecutor all knew it. Worse than that, it promised things that I could not produce. In the end, Holtzman would put Joel Alden on the witness stand and the two of them would have the last word. Holtzman knew this, which was why he didn't object to my slippery attempt to twist his words. He could afford to wait.

The evidence for the prosecution unfolded with the same inevitability as a march to the gallows. Sandra McClellan led off. She called Judge Olenik's stenographer, Grace Fuller, who took the witness stand and identified the transcript of the trial of Joel Alden. McClellan had her read aloud to the jury those portions in which Davey untruthfully told how she had witnessed Joel sexually abusing Julie.

Then came the reading of the cross-examination of Davey by Syd Masters. Just as the witness started to read that portion of the transcript, Masters, as if on cue, entered the courtroom. A deputy made room for him in the back. I noticed that among the crowd were Bob Ripley and Larry Semczyk. I wondered how many other reporters were present. I looked for Ann, who, so far as I knew, was the only supporter we had. She was not there. I had not seen her since dinner the night before. I missed her. I knew that Davey needed her there too.

During the reading of the transcript, Davey sat next to me with her hands folded on the edge of the table. Her hands epitomized her: frail, delicate, easily broken. Not the hard, scheming bitch Holtzman and McClellan were presenting to the jury.

McClellan had softened her look for the trial. Her blouse had a frilly collar, and she wore gold earrings and a gold bracelet. For a moment I thought the pink on her cheeks was artificial, but then I decided that it was simply the competitive spirit surfacing.

The next witness was Judge Olenik's court clerk, Sally Katowski, a trim, middle-aged woman with a no-nonsense air. She essentially told the same story as the transcript, with frequent references to that document to refresh her memory. It was overkill, but it served to back up the dry transcript with a live witness. Jurors liked the real thing. I liked it because I got to cross-examine a live witness.

"Am I correct in assuming that you had an opportunity to watch Mrs. Alden while she was testifying?" I asked.

"I saw everything. I was only a few feet away from her."

"Now, Ms. Katowski, I want to ask you about Mr. Masters."

"Objection," McClellan protested, remaining seated. "Mrs. Alden is on trial here, not Sydney Masters."

"How in the world is that relevant, Counsel?" Kane demanded.

"Your Honor, I believe that the tactics and demeanor of the cross-examiner—in this case Mr. Masters—is relevant to show why Mrs. Alden reacted the way she did. I believe that I can show that she was intimidated into answering some of the questions the way she did."

"That's nonsense," McClellan said. "Mrs. Alden committed the crime on *direct* examination. I see no—"

"I'll let you proceed," Kane said. He was giving me leeway, but his manner told the jury that he thought little of this tactic. Since Davey had in fact lied, I did not think much of the tactic myself, but I could not pass up an opportunity to cross-examine a witness. Besides, any chance Davey had rested on winning the sympathy of the jury, and I had to start somewhere.

"Do you recall Sydney Masters cross-examining Mrs. Alden?"

"Yes, I do."

"Are you familiar with Mr. Masters and his courtroom technique? Does he appear in your courtroom very often?"

"Yes, quite often. We see him a lot in Circuit Court."

"Would it be fair to say that Mr. Masters is known for his aggressive manner?"

The slight smile that played around Ms. Katowski's mouth told me I'd hit pay dirt. Court staffs usually have definite opinions about the lawyers they have to deal with; it was unlikely that Masters's scaly personality made him a beloved figure in the courthouse. I also had a hunch that Ms. Katowski did not like to see a male lawyer abuse a woman witness, even if she was a perjurer. Masters would have enjoyed playing with Davey as if she were a fly—pulling off her wings before smashing her. The trial transcript could not convey that picture; I was hoping that Ms. Katowski could.

"Aggressive? I think you could say that. Mr. Masters is known as a very aggressive attorney."

"Was he aggressive with Mrs. Alden during the testimony we have just heard read in the courtroom?"

"I think you could say that." Again that slight smile.

"Now, Ms. Katowski, tell us what you mean when you say that a lawyer is being aggressive. In what way was Sydney Masters aggressive toward Mrs. Alden?"

McClellan rose in protest. "Your Honor," she began, drawing out the words, "I must object to this. Where is counsel going with this? I repeat: Sydney Masters is not on trial, Mrs. Alden is."

"I'll overrule the objection," Kane said wearily. He was giving me enough rope to hang myself, but I suspected that he had enough of the defense lawyer in him to be curious about how far I could carry this attempt to put Masters on trial. It was a variation on an old defense theme in criminal cases: when you have nothing else, put the police on trial.

"In what way was Sydney Masters aggressive toward Mrs. Alden that day?"

"Well, he stood very close to her. He's a very tall man—a huge man—and he kind of leaned over her. That was one thing."

"What else did he do that seemed aggressive?"

"Well, he kind of badgered her, if you know what I mean. He wouldn't let her complete an answer."

"Did you find his manner intimidating—considering that you were only a few feet away from the both of them?"

McClellan could not take any more. "Objection as irrelevant, Your Honor. How this witness felt about Mr. Masters's manner is irrelevant."

"Sustained. I think you've about exhausted this topic, Mr. Brenner. Please move on."

Somehow I'd earned the title of "Mr. Brenner." A promotion from the condescending "Counselor." I decided to quit while I was ahead.

"No further questions."

McClellan could not let it rest. After a whispered conference with Holtzman, she asked, "Sally, isn't it true that Mrs. Alden told Mr. Masters that she lied on her direct examination—that she had made the whole thing up? That's what she said, isn't it?"

"Yes. She admitted that she had lied about the sexual abuse."

"You are not saying that Mr. Masters intimidated her into saying that, are you? She wasn't forced into anything, was she?"

"Not that I could see."

McClellan settled for that. She knew I was boxed in. If my plan was to put Davey on the witness stand and have her insist that Masters had bullied her into recanting her charges against Joel, then I'd done a good job of laying the groundwork for her testimony. But Davey would not be testifying.

Kane called a lunch break. The prosecutor had just two more witnesses to go: Terry Sinclair and Joel Alden.

30

"Dr. Mahoney brought her into the office just a few minutes ago," Ralph said. "I put her in the library and hotfooted it down here."

"Good thinking," I said. Just as Kane ordered a lunch break, Ralph and Ann had stormed up the courthouse steps with talk of new evidence. The mystery of Ann's disappearance was solved: she had gone after Evelyn Alden and brought her to Kirtley.

We were in a small conference room just outside the courtroom. Ann looked like yesterday's leftovers. She sat holding Davey's hand.

"What the hell is this all about?" I asked. "You're gone all night, and now you show up looking like roadkill and babbling about new evidence."

Ann wrinkled her nose at me and said, "I was doing your work, buster. I knew Evelyn Alden must be holding out on you, and I decided to take matters into my own hands. With a little bedside manner and a whole lot of martinis, I managed to come up with the smoking gun."

"What is it?"

"A diary kept by Joel Alden's daughter. The girl who killed herself."

"Where is it?"

"Back at the office. She'll give it to no one but you."

"Did you see it?"

"Enough to know it's dynamite."

"All right," I said. "I'll meet with her over the lunch hour. You take Davey to lunch and if it turns out to be nothing, I'll meet you there in a half hour. If I get tied up, I'll see you back here at one-thirty."

"Maybe I should go with you," Ann said.

"You go with Davey," I said.

"What do you suppose the diary means?" Davey asked.

I didn't answer. I left her to Ann.

Sherry's blue eyes flicked in the direction of the library. I found Evelyn Alden among the piles of books Ralph had left there. She sat at the long table staring straight ahead, barely noticing our arrival. In her hands was a small volume that she held tenderly, as if it were a prayer book.

"Hello, Mrs. Alden," I said, taking a seat next to her. Ralph sat down across the table from us. I did not ask her how she was; she was obviously in hell. My first thought was that she was still drunk, but then I decided that at least part of the problem was that it was noon and she was still sober.

I looked down at the book she held. On its cover at the top was a white cat whose tail curled downward to form two words: My Diary. It was tattered and swollen from having gotten wet somewhere.

"I would never look at it," she said, following my eyes down to the book. "I put it in the bottom drawer of my desk the night Melanie died. No one ever saw it, not the police, not Joel, not even me—not anyone. I never looked at it. Not ever. In all these years, not one time. Not until Ann came and talked to me."

Her eyes searched mine to see if I had any explanation for why she'd never looked at Melanie's diary.

"Is he going to win again?" she asked. "Joel always gets everything he goes after. No one can stand up to him. There's no stopping him."

"Did you bring that book to show me, Mrs. Alden? Did you want me to see it?"

Abruptly she placed the small volume on the table and slid it over to me. I stared at it—suddenly afraid to touch it. The torments visited on Evelyn Alden had come out of those pages, and I wanted no part of them.

"Did you think that this diary would help me in Davey's trial?" I asked.

Evelyn Alden stared at me. The lines on her sleepless face ran down from her eyes like erosion scars.

"You must read it to find out," she said simply.

I opened the book. Some of the pages were torn out, and many others were unreadable because of their soaking. I had heard somewhere that Melanie's body had been found in a bathtub. Had the diary been found with her? I could not find it in me to ask Evelyn.

I opened to a readable section in the middle of the book. Melanie must have been about twelve or thirteen when she wrote it. The handwriting had the graceful sweeps so characteristic of girls of that age. I read long passages about school—teachers she did or did not like, observations about other girls and how they dressed and acted around boys, complaints about parental insistence on good grades—all the concerns expressed by schoolgirls since the beginning of recorded time.

Then a passage at the end of a day's entry caught my eye.

Daddy came again last night. I told him that I didn't want to but he just laughed. I am glad that my periods started so that sometimes I can say no.

So matter-of-fact was it that I'd almost skipped over the entry. There was more.

I love Daddy so much I cannot understand why Mother is so mean to him, so cold to him. He tells me that he has only me and that only I can make him happy. I know that I can make him happy. He taught me how to love. What secrets we have!!! What would all those silly girls in that stupid math class think if they knew what I know? They never will. They are so immature! They act as if they are women already. I am the only one who is already a woman. They know nothing but they act as if they know everything.

I waded through all the teenage trivialities—the gossip, the petty jealousies, the enthusiasms, the youthful misperceptions. Schoolgirl innocence served up on a bed of grown-up sordidness. I felt no outrage; my feelings were at the saturation point. I read on with a sad, detached curiosity.

Last night my sounds almost woke Mommy up. Sometimes I wonder if she knows. She got up and went to the bathroom but did not come into my bedroom. What a surprise she would have gotten!!!! Dad thinks it is time for me to learn 69. He thinks my boobs are better than most grown women he knows.

I flipped ahead to the end of the volume. Like the earlier parts of the diary, the entries were sporadic and difficult to place in time. Many pages were water-stained or smeared. Sometimes she mentioned school events that made it possible to estimate how old she was. Toward the end she appeared to be about fifteen years old or so. The tone was markedly different from the earlier entries.

I hate him. God (who I don't believe in), how I hate him. Why can't he leave me alone?????? Last night I tried to say no and he hit me (he is a fucking bastard!!!) in the face and told me I couldn't say no. Someday I will get even. I will tell somebody. If only I could. He knows everybody and they all do what he wants—even the police and the judges. He says they would laugh at me and put me in a juvenile home. I would like to kill him sometimes. Maybe they would then hang me or shoot me!!!!!!!!

I slid the book across to Ralph. While he leafed through it, I got up and grabbed an ashtray for Evelyn, who was fumbling in her purse for a cigarette.

"How can we get it in?" Ralph asked when he had finished.

"It's hearsay. But we've got to find a way."

"We've got some crash research to do. It's too good not to use."

"Agreed—but we've got only thirty minutes."

I remembered Evelyn Alden. "Mrs. Alden, I'm going to send you out to lunch with one of our secretaries. Mr. Miles and I have to study some law to see how we can use your daughter's diary."

Evelyn Alden nodded absently. Now that we had the diary, she seemed to have lost interest. I caught Sherry before she left for lunch and gave her the assignment of wining and dining Evelyn. I put a two-martini limit on the lunch tab.

31

HOLTZMAN HIMSELF CONDUCTED THE DIRECT EXAMINATION OF THE
prosecution's bombshell witness, Terry Sinclair. It was a bravura performance. He was almost apologetic as he led the witness through a
tale of passionate trysts in seedy hotels; he seemed actually embarrassed and left many questions unanswered in what appeared to be a
triumph of delicacy over duty.

Then came the mushroom cloud.

"Did Mrs. Alden ever talk about her husband?"

"She couldn't stand him. Wanted to get rid of him."

"Did she talk about divorcing him?"

"Once or twice—but she came up with a better idea."

Holtzman paused to let the suspense build. He wrote something in
the notebook on the lectern. For an instant his eyes met mine, and I
could see smug anticipation in them.

"What do you mean, 'a better idea'?"

"She wanted to fix it so her husband would go to prison. That way
she could divorce him and get everything. She wanted me to go along
with it, but I wouldn't."

"What did she plan to do?"

"She wanted to accuse him of a crime. She called him an old pervert who would deserve whatever he got."

"Did she say what she planned to accuse him of—what crime?"

"It was something about child abuse—molesting a child."

"Is that what she said? Molesting a child?"

Sinclair seemed suddenly uncertain. He looked hopefully toward Sydney Masters, who was now sitting in the front row of the courtroom.

"Something like that."

"Can you remember anything specific? What crime she planned to accuse him of?"

"Molesting his own child, as I recall."

"What did she want you to do in this little scheme of hers?"

"I'm not sure. We really didn't get that far. I told her right away to count me out."

Sinclair remained vague about the details, and Holtzman was smart enough to move on before it began to sound as if he was impeaching his own witness.

When my turn came, I rose to the task with a relish that was more personal than was seemly in an experienced attorney.

"You told the prosecutor that you met Mrs. Alden sometime before October first of last year, but you didn't say how you met her. Tell the jury how you claim to have met her."

"Actually I met her through an attorney, Sydney Masters, who did a little legal work for me. He introduced me to Joel Alden and his wife. Masters wanted me to invest in a real-estate development and invited me for dinner at the country club. That's where I first met Mrs. Alden."

I cursed myself for not taking Sinclair's deposition. Coached no doubt by Masters, he was free to say anything he wanted; it would be his word against mine. I was angry and suspicious. Why the new story?

My anger got the better of me. "Do you recall that you and I met just a couple of weeks ago, Mr. Sinclair?"

"Yeah, vaguely."

"Didn't you tell me that you'd met Mrs. Alden in a cocktail lounge?"

"I said something like that."

"And now you're changing your story?"

"Not at all. I knew her before we met in the bar. Like I said, we met at the country club. I could tell she was bored with her husband. She was coming on to me, so I called her the next day and asked her to meet me at a bar, an out-of-the-way place I knew about."

Holtzman had not asked how Sinclair first met Davey. It had been left for me to stumble through that door. I could not help but turn and look at Holtzman with a mixture of grudging admiration and distaste. I had no doubt that Sinclair was lying; I could only speculate about what Holtzman knew.

"And you claim you slept with Mrs. Alden at a motel on the same night you met her, and that was before October first of last year, the date she went to the police and accused her husband, correct?"

"That's right."

"You are certain about that?" I asked, taking a copy of a Master-Card charge slip from my pocket and placing it on the lectern in front of me. Sinclair's eyes followed the document and remained on it as he answered.

"Yes, I'm pretty certain."

"And your testimony is that you checked into a motel—I believe you said it was a Holiday Inn—with Mrs. Alden on the first night you met her. Isn't that what you said?"

"Yes, I said that." Suspicion clouded his face, just the way it had when I had asked about a tattoo in the Coat of Arms. His dislike and distrust of me needed no words. He watched the paper on the lectern as if it were a leper.

"And you are certain of that?" I picked up the paper and moved it to another part of the lectern.

"Yes."

"Could you be mistaken about that, Doctor? Is it possible that you met Mrs. Alden later—much later—than October first? Are you certain that you do not want to change your testimony?"

"Certain? Yes, I'm certain. I do not want to change anything. I'm telling the truth."

I picked up the charge slip and held it up. "I want to ask you one last time, witness. Are you certain that you met Davey Alden before October first of last year?"

"I think so. Yes, that was it—about that date."

"Wait a minute now, Doctor. Just a minute ago you were certain that it was before October first that you met Mrs. Alden—in fact, you were certain that you were intimate with her before that date. Now you do not seem so certain."

"I can't be certain of the exact date," Sinclair protested, his movie-actor face a portrait of false outrage. "Where were *you* on October first of last year? How can anybody answer that question?"

Sinclair was a fear biter. He was certain that every question I asked was a deliberate trap, and he wanted to get back at me. He could be dangerous; that last rhetorical question was made with a pleading look for support from the jury.

"You can answer it by starting to tell the truth, Doctor. I'll settle for the truth anytime."

"Objection, argumentative," Holtzman said.

"Sustained."

"Thank you, Your Honor. The truth will do just fine, Dr. Sinclair. You were so certain about that date just a few minutes ago. Is it your testimony now that you are uncertain when you met Mrs. Alden?"

"You could say that," Sinclair replied with a sigh of exasperation. He watched me put the MasterCard slip back into my pocket. It was a receipt for an oil change for my old Volvo.

Then, perhaps sensing that he had been tricked, he added, "I don't see what the big deal is."

"Your Honor, I do not see the relevancy of all this," Holtzman interjected.

I jumped in before the judge could rule. "I'll tell them what the big deal is, Your Honor. Mrs. Alden went to the police and accused her husband on the first of October of last year. If the good doctor met her after that date, their relationship could hardly be a motive for her to lie, which is what the prosecutor wants this jury to believe. I—"

"You've made your point, now get on with it," Kane said.

"Thank you, Your Honor," I replied.

Then I announced, "In any event, the witness does not know when it was that he met Mrs. Alden." I was unable to resist a smile when I saw Holtzman squirm as he pondered whether to protest again. He decided to let it go; too many objections would make him look as though he had something to hide.

"Now let's talk about your claim that Mrs. Alden tried to enlist you in a plot to frame her husband. Who else was present when she made that proposal to you?"

"No one. We were alone."

"Where were you?"

"At a restaurant . . . no, we may have been at my place."

"You're not sure?"

"I can't remember exactly."

"Now wait a minute, Mr. Sinclair. Are you saying that this woman attempted to get you to commit a crime—frame an innocent man—and you can't even remember where it took place?"

Sinclair's eyes flicked to Masters. I turned and stared at Masters, praying that the jury had noticed it too.

"It was in a restaurant. I remember it was in a restaurant."

"What restaurant?"

"I don't remember . . . I'm not sure."

"How many times do you claim that you met Mrs. Alden?"

"I don't recall—about four times, maybe five . . ."

Again his eyes darted over toward Masters. Anger and disgust began to simmer within me. I believed Davey's claim that she had never tried to enlist him in her scheme.

"Who do you keep looking at, Mr. Sinclair? That man over there"—I turned and pointed at Syd Masters—"can't help you. He's Joel Alden's lawyer. He doesn't have the answers."

Holtzman jumped in. "This is outrageous. Mr. Brenner is badgering the witness."

"The witness should tell the truth, not what Joel Alden's lawyer wants him to say," I snapped. "Oh, I forgot. He's your lawyer too, isn't he, Dr. Sinclair?"

"Get on with it, Counsel," Kane ordered.

I took a deep breath. I needed to keep my cool if I was going to help Davey. Rollins stared hard at me, savoring the idea that the judge might find me in contempt and order me taken into custody.

"Tell me about the Terra Group, Mr. Sinclair."

Sinclair smiled at me. "It's a real-estate development project that I made a small investment in. The plan is to hold the land and eventually build condominiums."

It was smooth. Masters had already anticipated my use of Terra to link Sinclair to Joel. Now Sinclair was presenting himself as an investor, a business associate of Joel, no mere straw man. Yes, he was tied to Joel; that was how Davey was able to meet and seduce him.

"So you're a business partner of Joel Alden?"

"I'm not sure what his role is. There are a lot of investors and I'm not acquainted with all of them."

"You're a business partner of Joel Alden, and just by coincidence, Sydney Masters was your lawyer too."

"Masters did some legal work for me a long time ago."

"Didn't he represent you on a criminal charge?"

"Objection! This is irrelevant."

"Your Honor, I have a right to show possible bias on the part of a witness. Sydney Masters—"

"Objection sustained. Move on, Counsel."

"But this witness was—"

"You heard me."

It was dizzying. I had gone for the jugular, fully intending to bring out the rape charge against Sinclair, a charge on which he had been acquitted. It probably would have caused a mistrial and possibly landed me in jail. For a moment it had seemed worth it. I cleared my head and took aim again.

"How many times do you claim you met with Mrs. Alden—had sex with her?"

"About three times. Something like that."

I shook my head in mock disbelief. "Are you asking this jury to believe that this woman asked you to commit a crime when she hardly knew you—had met you only a few times?"

"That's the way it happened."

"What did she want you to do? Specifically *how* would you contribute to this grand conspiracy? What was your role?"

"It never got that far. I told her I wasn't interested. No amount of money was worth it."

"Could it be that all Mrs. Alden did was tell you that her husband was a pervert and belonged in prison? That she was so desperate that she turned even to the likes of you for help?"

"The likes of me told her no deal. She offered to share her old man's money with me. I told her to look for somebody else."

"And you want us to believe that this woman was so smitten with you that she offered you a fortune—millions of dollars—but that your conscience prevented you from even thinking about her offer?"

"That's what happened." This time Sinclair's answer came out as a snarl. The pretty boy was showing his ugly side. The glory of cross-examination: character will out.

"Tell me, Mr. Sinclair, are you as certain of all these facts as you are of when you first met Mrs. Alden?"

"I'm sure."

I turned away from the lectern and sat down next to Davey. Holtzman breathed a sigh of relief, which was cut short when I jumped up again.

"By the way, Mr. Sinclair, did you report this criminal scheme to the police?"

Sinclair glared. "I didn't."

"Surely you called Joel Alden on the phone and told him?"

He was silent.

"No further questions."

I sat down.

Holtzman did some ineffective redirect concerning the October first date but managed only to confuse Sinclair. He finally sat down, looking unhappy.

Actually he had done well with Sinclair. Even if the jurors doubted the really damning parts of Sinclair's tale, the mere fact of Davey's relationship with him seemed to say so much about her character, and in the final analysis, character was what this trial was all about. Character is what every trial is about. It is always relevant. That's why the law is so afraid of it.

When Kane called a ten-minute recess, I left Davey and Ann in one of the conference rooms and went to find Ralph in the Bar Association law library. Ralph was poring over *Michigan Courtroom Evidence*, a fat looseleaf volume in a maroon binder. He was not liking what he found there. I joined him in staring at the book.

"It can't be all that bad," I said.

"It isn't good, that's for sure," Ralph replied, blinking as he looked up. "I can't figure out a way to get around the hearsay aspects of this. The diary is an out-of-court statement that you want to offer for the truth of its contents. The dead girl can't be cross-examined about her statements. Kane will never let it in."

"Just get me something," I said. "If necessary I'll bullshit Kane and Holtzman on excited utterances or something. That diary is it for us. Either we get it in front of the jury or Davey may just as well kiss Julie and her freedom goodbye."

32

JOEL ALDEN STEPPED UP BRISKLY FROM THE BACK OF THE COURT-
room and raised his right hand to take the oath. Everything about his
manner—the sorrowful set of the mouth, the impatient scowl, the
deep breath he took before sitting down—said that he would have
preferred to be anywhere but here, preparing to administer the coup
de grace to his wife, the mother of his child.

Playacting or not, the effect was striking. Joel Alden was the flesh-
and-blood embodiment of Davey's crime.

I knew the jurors and spectators would be looking for Davey's reaction as her husband took the stand—and I worried. Where I saw
dazed resignation, others might see indifference or even callousness.
Reporters invariably described a failure to shout or scream as reacting
"impassively." Decoded, it meant a lack of feeling or remorse.

Standing at the lectern, Holtzman took his time, carefully estab-
lishing Joel's deep roots in the community, his leadership role in community affairs, his successful operation of a business that employed
several hundred citizens in Laffler County—all the things Davey had
attempted to destroy when she concocted her tale of perversion.

"Can you tell the jury how you met your wife?"

"Davey was a waitress at the Riverbend Country Club."

"How old are you and how old is Mrs. Alden?"

"I'm fifty-eight and she is thirty-two."

"And you have been married for ten years?"

"Affirmative."

"I know this is difficult, Mr. Alden, but could you tell me? Were you in love with your wife, Davey Alden?"

"I loved her. I still do. I don't know what went wrong. I must have failed her somehow. Somehow I could not satisfy her needs."

In his everyday life, Joel was the rough-hewn man among men, but today he was the suffering cuckold whose wife's youthful passions demanded more than his aging loins could deliver. I had no doubt that it was Masters who had crafted the role, just as he had no doubt written most of the script for Sinclair. Holtzman might think he was in charge, but in the end he was just another actor, and in a supporting role at that. Syd Masters was the producer and director.

"Did your marriage to Davey Alden produce any children?"

"Her name is Julie. She's named after—"

"How old is Julie now? What is her birthdate?"

"She is four. She was born—well, she was born in July. She was born July fourteenth, four years ago. That would—"

"How did you first become aware that your wife was making allegations of sexual abuse against you?"

"A cop came to my door. That's how I became aware. Actually, I was in my office and two detectives from the sheriff's department came and questioned me about what Davey was saying. I told them the truth. I—"

Holtzman had Alden tell how he was shocked and humiliated by the charges and the need to deny them to the two detectives, both of whom he'd known for years. Then came the limbo while he waited to see if the prosecutor's office would decide to charge him formally with criminal sexual conduct. Finally there was the arrest, the booking, the fingerprinting, and the jailing until he could arrange for bond.

I recalled Scott telling me how Holtzman had been salivating at the thought of the publicity that the arrest of a big shot like Alden would generate. Now the only juices flowing from the prosecutor were ersatz tears of compassion for Joel the victim. Forgotten now was Holtzman's hasty decision to prosecute before a thorough investigation. That was one of the things the jury would never hear about.

"And of course you were cleared of all charges in a trial earlier this year?"

"Affirmative. Davey got up on the witness stand and perjured herself, but then she got tangled up in her lies and my attorney proved beyond a shadow of a doubt that she was nothing but a liar."

"How did it make you feel to be accused—"

"Objection. Your Honor, the defense will concede that Mr. Alden did not enjoy being accused of sexually abusing his daughter. But that is not the point of this trial. The prosecutor is making a blatant bid for the sympathy—"

"Sustained. Please proceed on to other matters."

"The case against you was dismissed?"

"I was cleared of all the charges. I was found innocent."

I could not let that one pass either. "Your Honor, I really do have to object and ask that Mr. Alden's answer be stricken. Mr. Alden was not found innocent of the charges. There was merely a dismissal."

"And I object to these repeated interruptions of this witness's testimony," Holtzman responded hotly. "The defense lawyer is quibbling, and he knows it. Mr. Alden could never be charged again with those crimes."

"That's because of a technicality," I shouted. "It would be double jeopardy. Even if he—"

"Gentlemen, let's cease the bickering and get on with the case," Kane said with an impatient wave of his hand at Holtzman, who was almost frothing at the mouth. Turning to the jury, Kane said with affected weariness, "The jury is instructed that no verdict was ever delivered in the previous trial, but it is also true that Mr. Alden can never be brought to trial again on the same charges. You are to disregard the lawyers' statements on the whole issue."

Kane's instruction was as likely to confuse as clarify things for the jury, but at least they'd been told that Alden had not been found "innocent." It was little more than a distraction, but I was desperate, and lawyerly obfuscation is a time-honored tradition in the courtroom.

As I resumed my seat, I noticed Ralph had come in and was sitting in one of the chairs behind the counsel tables. In his hands was the Michigan evidence book, which he clutched so tightly that it looked as though he was determined to choke the right answers out of it. He smiled grimly at me and shook his head. Nothing yet.

Well aware that Joel Alden was the human focus of his case, Holtzman stretched out his appearance on the stand. I feared that the jury was reading Alden exactly the way the prosecutor wanted: the older man whose heart had turned foolish over a beautiful young woman.

"Let me direct your attention to the dates of March fourteenth and May third of last year," Holtzman continued. "Do you recall the testimony about those dates?"

"Those are the times Davey said I molested Julie. It never happened. It's all a damn lie."

"After Mrs. Alden made her accusations, did you attempt to reconstruct the events of those two days?"

"I sure did. On both of those days I was working in my office at home. She deliberately picked days when I was home so that I couldn't prove I was somewhere else."

"Do you even remember seeing your daughter Julie during the time you were working at home those days?"

"On March fourteenth I was in my office at home all day until I left for a three-o'clock appointment. I may have seen Julie at breakfast, but I don't even recall that."

"What about the May third date?"

"I know I was home working—going over some bid figures and trying to get away from the damn phone—but that's all I recall. I can't say for sure about anything that day—except that it's a heinous lie she's told."

Holtzman paused and stared at the ceiling for a moment. Then he left the lectern and walked halfway to the witness. Again he paused for dramatic effect.

"I'm going to ask you directly, Mr. Alden. I know that you have suffered a lot, but your ordeal is almost over. Did you ever sexually abuse your daughter Julie on March fourteenth or May third?"

Joel Alden took a deep breath and sat up stiffly in his chair. The waiting and the delays were over; this was his opportunity for revenge and vindication. It was his chance to make things right.

"I never did such things to Julie. I never sexually abused my own daughter. I am not that kind of person. I would never do such a thing. I'm incapable of such a thing. My wife lied, and she'll lie again if she gets the chance."

"No further questions," Holtzman said.

Ralph tapped me urgently on the shoulder and handed me a scribbled note.

"I think he just opened a door," he whispered. I glanced at the note and shoved it into my pocket.

Joel Alden displayed just the right combination of concern and outrage as I stepped forward to cross-examine him. It is the guilty who act unconcerned on the witness stand. Knowing that we are all guilty of something, the innocent are afraid, and jurors, who fear condemnation like the rest of us, identify with that fear.

"Mr. Alden, you said on direct examination that you are twenty-six years older than your wife," I said.

"That's right." He might be concerned, but just under the surface, visible to all, seethed a barely restrained defiance.

"How long did you know Davey Alden before you married her?"

"I dunno. A couple of years. She was a waitress at the club for a couple of years during the summers."

"So she was a young college student when you met her. Is that correct?"

"I guess so. Yes."

"If she is thirty-two now and you've been married for ten years, and you knew her for two or three years before that, then she must have been about twenty when she first drew your attention. Correct?"

"I guess that would be about it."

"And you would have been forty-six years old. You were forty-six and she was twenty, maybe even nineteen?"

"About that."

I sneaked a look at the jury. I had to be careful. I was attempting to make a not-too-subtle and rather nasty point: he liked them young. It could backfire.

"Was this your first marriage?"

"No. I was married before."

"You were married before? What was the name of your first wife?"

"Evelyn."

"How long were you married to Evelyn Alden?"

"We were divorced two years before I met Davey, if that's what you're getting at."

"I'm not getting at anything, Mr. Alden. I just want you to tell the truth. How long were you married to Evelyn Alden?"

"Twenty-five—no, twenty-six years. Too long."

"Too long? I gather it was a bitter divorce."

"Not really. She got what she wanted. I recognized my obligations and provided well for her."

"What was the cause of the divorce, Mr. Alden?"

Holtzman rose to his feet. "I don't like to interrupt counsel, but what is the relevance of this line of questioning?"

"I'll withdraw the question," I said quickly.

"Were there any children born of your marriage to Evelyn Alden?"

"We had a daughter. She died."

I saw his eyes flick in the direction of Syd Masters, who had appeared in the courtroom again. As casually as I could, I moved sideways to block Joel's view of Masters. I wanted to deny him the comfort of eye contact with his personal attorney.

"What was your daughter's name, Mr. Alden?"

"Melanie. Her name was Melanie."

Out of the corner of my eye I saw Holtzman stirring.

"You said your daughter died. How did she die?"

"*Your Honor,*" Holtzman protested, "this is cruel beyond belief. Mr. Alden has already suffered at the hands of this defendant. Now her attorney—"

"This is a crucial area, Your Honor," I said. "I assure the court that I will be able to tie it up so that its relevance becomes clear."

I hoped that the very intensity of my plea might somehow make Kane realize that something was up, that I was not merely harassing the witness, but he was insensitive to the subtleties of my style.

"Objection sustained. For the life of me, Mr. Brenner, I cannot see how this is relevant to these proceedings here today. I am ordering you to move on to a new subject."

Kane was getting revenge for my insistence on going to trial.

"Your Honor, I would ask—"

"Get on with it, Mr. Brenner. Either get on with your cross-examination or sit down."

"With all due respect, Your Honor, I would ask that I be allowed to bring up a matter outside the presence of the jury."

Holtzman let out an exasperated grunt. Kane glared at me. I could feel the curious eyes of the jurors on me. I hoped they were not also hostile eyes.

"I will not tolerate unnecessary delay and frivolous interruptions of this trial," Kane announced with a look that had withered many a lawyer. "I have made my ruling. Are you going to stand there and continue to argue with me?"

I walked back to counsel table and stood there facing Joel. A gloating Holtzman looked at me with pity, perhaps thinking that I was beaten and about to sit down. Instead I removed the diary from my briefcase and went back to the lectern. I held the diary up for the world, including the jury, to see.

"Were you aware that your daughter Melanie kept a diary, Mr. Alden?"

Joel did not answer immediately. From the corner of my eye I could see Holtzman leaning over and whispering with McClellan. As Joel and I stared at each other, his mask suddenly slipped and he looked at me in the same way he had when I visited him in his home. Just as love can be conveyed in a fleeting glance, so can evil, and Joel's look displayed all the evil embedded in his soul. Sadly, only I could see it.

"Well, Mr. Alden?"

Holtzman was starting to move, lumbering to his feet, ready to object.

"Would you like to read your daughter's thoughts, Mr. Alden? How a little girl feels when she has been sexually abused by her father year after year until there is no joy left in life—until death seems the only way out?"

Holtzman, halfway to his feet, sank back into his chair for a moment. No one stirred in the courtroom. Then Holtzman was bellowing his outrage, struggling to his feet, his chair skidding back almost to the bar. Kane's eyes were arched in surprise and shock.

"I have *never* . . . this is the most . . ." Holtzman sputtered. "Your Honor, I move for a mistrial."

Kane kept his head. His face a model of impassivity, he instructed Rollins to remove the jury and waited patiently until the door closed solidly behind them. Rollins returned a few seconds later and stood by the door.

"You've got about ten seconds to tell me why I should not hold you in contempt of court," Kane said.

I was both intimidated and elated. For the first time in the trial, I had some real control over events. Bully he might be, but Kane was savvy enough to know that he had to permit me to create a record, and if he held me in contempt he probably would wait until the verdict was in before sticking it to me, unless of course he granted a mistrial, which was unlikely because it meant coming back another day and starting all over again.

Upon such a frail reed of reasoning rested my hope of escaping the clutches of Rollins, who stood by the door savoring my plight. I decided to brazen it out. If my head was going to end up on a pike, I might as well have it happen in the presence of the media, including Semczyk and Ripley.

"Your Honor, I asked this court to give me a hearing outside the presence of the jury. You ordered me to proceed ahead and that is exactly what I did—in front of the jury. Now you seem to be telling me that I did wrong."

Kane looked like a candidate for the Heimlich maneuver. His face reddened and he looked as if he was having trouble breathing. I decided to press on while I was still allowed to speak. I picked up the diary and held it up so that the whole courtroom could see it again.

"I just learned of this piece of evidence this afternoon, Your Honor. It will change the complexion of the whole case. The diary is truly a hand from the grave. It describes in revolting detail how for years Joel Alden sexually abused Melanie, the daughter of his marriage to Evelyn Alden. It is a dramatic and conclusive piece of evidence that can lead to no verdict other than an acquittal of the defendant."

Holtzman, finally gathering his wits about him, exploded out of his seat like a fighting cock. He accused me of bad faith, malpractice, dishonesty, unethical conduct, and contempt of court.

"In twenty years of the practice of law, this is the vilest display of dirtbag lawyering I have ever seen," the prosecutor raged. "Mr. Brenner is making a mockery of these proceedings and is blatantly contemptuous of this court."

Again I held up the diary for all to see. "I believe that the prosecutor will sing a different tune when he sees the contents of this diary, Your Honor. It is a horrifying record of one of the worst crimes of mankind—incest. I've never seen anything as damning in all my years in criminal law."

"It's also hearsay of the worst sort," said Holtzman. "This girl is dead. I can't cross-examine her. To allow this diary to come into evidence would be unfair to the prosecution. I've never even seen this document. I have no idea what's in there."

For one breathless moment I thought Kane was going to declare a mistrial or rule that the diary was hearsay and order that the trial continue without further discussion. I was not prepared to sit down meekly, and just as I thought I could hear the cell door sliding open again, Kane looked out over the audience and apparently saw the reporters scribbling in their notebooks. I was saved.

"Gentlemen, this is a matter that we should discuss in chambers."

As the judge left the bench in a swirl of black cloth, I noticed that Joel Alden was still sitting in the witness box. We had forgotten all about him, but he had not forgotten us. Collecting my papers, I looked up and caught him in an unguarded moment: he was staring at Davey and me with eyes filled with fear and malevolence. If only the jury could have seen him.

33

"I HOPE YOU BROUGHT YOUR TOOTHBRUSH," KANE SAID OVER HIS shoulder as we followed him into his office. "I'm not sure how many the jail has in stock."

He tossed his black robe carelessly onto one of the chairs that formed a semicircle around his desk and took his seat. We sat around his desk. The robe lolled there obscenely, next to McClellan, half on the floor, mocking the majesty of the law.

"Just hear me out, Judge. That's all I ask."

"This is contempt of court, pure and simple," Holtzman said. Kane silenced him with a wave of his hand. Fixing me with his alpha-wolf stare, he studied me for a long minute before speaking.

"I can assure you, Brenner, that if this is a cheap trick you'll be behind bars before the day is out and you'll have your ticket pulled here in Michigan. When I get done with you, I doubt that Illinois or any other state will allow you to practice there either. Do I make myself perfectly clear?"

"You have made yourself clear, Your Honor, and now it's my turn. Look at this diary and you'll see what I am talking about."

Holtzman kept at it. "It's hearsay, Judge, and I object to your even looking at that piece of garbage. Look how ripped up it is. It looks like someone fished it out of a sewer somewhere."

"Oh, be quiet, would you, please," Kane said. "How am I going to rule on its admissibility unless I read the damn thing?"

That's exactly what Holtzman did not want. "For Christ's sake, Judge, the woman admitted in open court that she was a perjurer. She's probably a forger as well."

"That may be so—but I still have to review the evidence to see what it is that we are dealing with," Kane said, snatching the diary from the hand I had reached across the desk.

"Even if it's genuine, it's still hearsay," Holtzman continued. He was desperate that the judge not see the diary. Anything could happen once that threshold was passed.

"How in fact did the girl die?" Kane asked, recalling that the question had never been answered. He sat frowning at the white cat on the cover of the diary—suddenly hesitant.

"She committed suicide," I said. "A few years after the divorce."

"How do we know she wrote this document? Even if it's relevant and not hearsay, how will you authenticate it?" He was looking for reasons to delay delving into the mind of the dead girl. I recalled my own reluctance in the law library with Evelyn Alden.

"That's exactly our point, Judge," McClellan interjected. "How can they—"

"I have the mother of the dead girl here to testify that she saw the diary in the girl's bedroom and recognizes the handwriting."

"The bitter ex-wife of Joel Alden," McClellan scoffed. "She hates Joel so much that she would do anything to destroy him."

"That goes to its weight—not its admissibility."

"Well, I'll look at it, but if it's not admissible, I don't give a good damn what it says," Kane finally said. "And, frankly, I see no way for you to get around the hearsay rule."

Kane started reading the diary, flipping through the pages, pausing from time to time to read a passage more carefully, letting nothing show in his face. While he read, I studied the scribbled memo that Ralph had handed to me just as I started to question Joel Alden. In it he had written, "They've put Alden's character into evidence. We should be able to rebut same." The note also cited a Michigan case on character evidence in similar situations.

While the judge read, I looked about his office. On the credenza behind him was a color photo of his family: a wife, two daughters, and three grandchildren. The absence of sons-in-law made me wonder about their standing in the Kane tribe. On the wall were two prints of hunting scenes—one showing a duck hunter and his retriever, the other of two English pointers locked up on a covey of quail. The hunting scenes reminded me of my father.

Finished, Kane handed the volume to Holtzman, who thumbed through it as if it were contaminated, grunting every now and then at a particular entry. After a brief review he handed it to McClellan, who skimmed it and then placed it in no-man's-land—on the edge of the desk, equidistant from all four of us.

Kane leaned back in his chair and straightened his tie. "Very interesting and very unpleasant reading, but that doesn't mean that the jury gets to consider it or even hear of it," he said. "It looks like you're out of luck, Brenner."

"It's hearsay, no two ways about it," Holtzman said, his voice swelling with assurance, believing he'd heard the last word on the subject.

I knew that it wasn't that simple. Kane had to be appalled by what he'd just read. I also knew that he had a defense lawyer's mind and might buy a plausible legal argument in favor of letting it in. And, finally, I knew that on a close question he would check the prevailing winds.

"Judge, you know as well as I do that this piece of evidence should come in," I argued. "The rules of evidence are meant to reflect the wisdom and common sense of the law. If there is any common sense—not to mention justice—in the law, the jury will hear about the diary. They have a right to know what kind of man Joel Alden is."

"That's an emotional argument, not a legal one," Kane said. "I really see no way around the hearsay rule. The girl who made these statements is not here to be cross-examined, and you clearly are offering the diary for the truth of its contents. That's hearsay by any measure, and you can't satisfy any of the hearsay exceptions."

When it came to evidence, McClellan was quick. "Not only that," she said, "but the diary does not bear directly on the issue he wants to use it for—whether Joel Alden molested his daughter Julie, as his wife testified. It relates to a totally different charge of sexual abuse involving another daughter. So you've got not only a hearsay problem but also a relevance problem."

Leaning back in his chair again, Kane held his hands up in a gesture of surrender. He was absolved; the rules were the rules. Holtzman and McClellan maintained a discreet silence.

"I'm not ready to concede the legal issue yet, Judge," I said, "but let's go back to the common-sense argument for a minute. The law is not stupid. When something like this diary arises, there must be a way to get it before the fact finder—otherwise the law *would* be stupid."

Kane's look of tolerant amusement told me that I was not impressing him, but I was just warming up. "Please understand me. You have a practical problem too. I saw several reporters out there, and there may be others I do not know. They heard me describe the contents of the diary. There's no way to keep the news that Joel Alden sexually molested another daughter out of the press. Nor the fact that the daughter later committed suicide. If you keep the diary from the jury, the public is going to hear about it anyway—and so will the jury when this trial is over. If that happens, this case will smell worse than it does now."

He understood me, all right, and so did Holtzman. Elected officials know that a good press means a satisfied public, and they will do almost anything to keep the busy bees of the media pollinating the public with favorable news. They understood me all too well—and they hated me.

"This is the most outrageous attempt at blackmail I've ever seen," Holtzman yelled. "Not only is Brenner contemptuous of this court, but he's practically criminal in his behavior. Judge, we can't be intimidated by suggestions that we have to curry favor with the media."

Kane fixed me with a sardonic smile. We understood each other completely. Finally he said, "You are priceless. First you attempt to corrupt the rules of evidence, and now you suggest that this court should compromise its integrity by considering the impact all this may have on its public image."

He frowned and shook his head slowly. "What I ought to do is declare a mistrial and throw you in jail for contempt of court. And you can be damn sure I would disqualify you from representing your lady friend next time. But I'm not going to give you the satisfaction of a mistrial. I'm going to finish this trial and deal with you later on."

He was not the first judge I had offended, but he put on the most convincing display of outrage. Had I gone too far? Was it possible that the man might risk all for principle? Not a chance, I decided. But I kept my expression respectful and attentive.

Kane was not through. "I assure you that any decision I make on this evidence will be based solely on the law and not on any personal consideration," he said stiffly. Then he peered at me and added, "No matter what my personal feelings about your conduct may be, I have an open mind. I will give you two minutes to make a last legal argument to support your position. I don't want any more of your emotional bullshit, Brenner. I will listen to legal arguments and that is all."

Holtzman, surprised by the reopening of the door, cleared his throat and started to protest, but thought better of it. The noise he made sounded like a frog.

"Your Honor, the hearsay is a problem," I said. "But there's another way that the diary can be used that would satisfy both the ends of justice and the rules of evidence."

"What is that, pray tell?" Kane said.

"Judge, this diary is character evidence. We want to show that Joel Alden molested Melanie so that the jury will believe he's the kind of character who would do it again—this time to Julie. If we succeed, we'll certainly create a reasonable doubt about Mrs. Alden's guilt. Granted, you normally can't use character evidence that way, but—"

"And it shouldn't be permitted now," McClellan interrupted. "You can't use evidence of bad character to prove guilt."

"But it's permitted when the other side introduces evidence of good character—as happened when Joel Alden testified. We should—"

"We did *not* put Joel's character into evidence," Holtzman cried. "We absolutely did not. That is a false statement."

I looked down at my notes of Joel's testimony and quoted, " 'I am not that kind of person. I would never do such a thing. I'm incapable of such a thing.' If that isn't putting character into evidence, I don't know what is," I added.

"It is not, absolutely not," Holtzman sputtered. "Joel added that himself. It was inadvertent. Besides, the defense failed to object, and it's too late now. I am objecting to their use of character evidence."

Kane stroked his jaw. "Well, MRE 405 does allow inquiry into specific instances of conduct," he said. "But usually we are talking about an *accused* putting his character into issue. The prosecutor can't do it, but a defendant may."

"Joel Alden is not the accused, his wife is," McClellan said.

"Joel's guilt or innocence is an issue in this trial—and in that sense he is an accused," I said. "Joel testified that he has such a good character that he could never commit such a crime. We must be allowed to prove that he does not own a good character, and the diary is our way to do that. Judge, take a look at *People v. Vasher*. It's a recent case, and it's almost exactly our situation here." I handed the judge the photocopy of the Michigan Supreme Court case that Ralph had handed me.

"He can't do it, Judge. It's not allowed by the rules, and that's that." Holtzman tried to sound authoritative, but he sensed the issue was slipping away from him. He stared resentfully at the pages I'd just handed the judge.

"It's a tough one," Kane said thoughtfully, looking at the *Vasher* precedent. "I can't imagine letting the jury take the diary back into the jury room with them."

I saw where he was headed. "Then just let me ask him about his conduct with the daughter who committed suicide. I should be allowed to ask questions about the information contained in the diary. The diary wouldn't have to come in as an exhibit."

"He wants to get that diary in the back door—something he can't do through the front door," Holtzman said.

I drove in for the layup. "Judge, you have enough to hang your hat on if you want to let me use that diary to cross-examine Joel Alden. You've read that diary, and you know it's the right thing to do. You don't need me or the press or the public to tell you that. Let the jury make the decision as to Davey Alden's guilt or innocence, but give them the facts. Don't sweep anything under the rug."

"He can't do it, Judge," was all that Holtzman could manage. He looked at McClellan. "Sandra—"

McClellan shrugged irritably. "If the damn diary is the real thing, maybe . . ."

Her voice trailed off. Holtzman and I stared at her. I wanted to kiss her.

Kane stood up and turned away from us, looking out the window of his second-floor office onto the grounds of the county complex. Most of the trees were naked to the oncoming winter. Gray clouds stretched to the horizon. On the windowsill was a small statue of the blindfolded Lady Justice, and the judge toyed with the scales in her hand as he talked.

"You never know what is going to come up in this business," he said, speaking more to himself than to us. "Poor old Joel Alden," he said. "He escapes a conviction for molesting his little girl, and just when it looks like he's got his good name back, the sky falls in. Joel Alden, a pervert? What the hell is this world coming to?" He turned and grinned at us, cynically, with eyes to match. "Not that I've made up my mind on Joel's guilt, you understand."

He turned and leveled a disgusted look at Holtzman. "Leave it to our prosecutor's office to foul its own nest again. Once this diary stuff hits the fan—and it will, even if I don't let it in—Joel Alden can kiss what's left of his reputation goodbye. And if the wife doesn't get convicted of perjury, our prosecutor had better hope the voters have a piss-poor memory."

Shaking his head, the judge returned to his desk and sat down. Then he gave me a wink. What the hell, it said, we both think like defense lawyers. And there was always the matter of the press.

"I'm going to let you cross-examine Alden on the events described in the diary," he said. "But the diary itself cannot come into evidence as an exhibit. The jury doesn't get to read it. And you're stuck with the answers Joel gives you. No rebuttal witnesses."

"I can't believe it," Holtzman said. "You said you were going to keep it out."

"I'm not afraid to change my mind when I'm wrong," Kane said piously. "I like to think that I'm big enough to reverse myself when the law or facts require it."

Evelyn Alden came through for us. With the jury still out, I put her on the witness stand and had her identify the diary. Apparently the two-martini limit was the right prescription for her; she was calm and lucid, and she came across as more sorrowful than vindictive. She told the court that Melanie had kept the diary for years, and that as a mother she had respected her daughter's privacy. Even after her daughter's suicide she had refused to read it. She admitted that she had hidden the diary from the police. She had retrieved it from the bathtub where the girl's body was found.

"Was there a reason why you refused to read the diary after Melanie's death?" I asked. "Might it not have yielded a clue to her reason for taking her own life?"

My question was accusing, and I immediately regretted asking it.

"I was afraid to—I just couldn't. I put it in a drawer and never told the police about it."

I let it go at that. Holtzman blundered about on cross-examination, but could not change the simple fact that Melanie's mother said the diary was authentic. Fortunately for him, the jury would not hear Melanie's mother; her only role was to show Kane that the diary was what I claimed it to be.

After hearing the testimony, Kane confirmed what he had told us in chambers: I could ask whether Joel Alden had molested Melanie, but I could not tell the jury of the existence of the diary. I could use it only to formulate questions. Any violation of his ruling would be a contempt of court.

Kane also made clear that he was expressing no opinion about the truth of Melanie's allegations—or about the guilt or innocence of Davey.

Our judge had an eye on the exits. Juries were unpredictable. Holtzman's sure thing was losing its luster of certainty.

34

When Scott showed up I was not surprised. It seemed inevitable that he would appear for the final act of Davey's story. He had been there for the opening, and it was fitting that he play a role in the finale.

"I couldn't let Jack Boy face the baddies alone," he said to Davey and Ann. "Besides, it's time to haul in the big guns—me."

Kane had ordered me to make a copy of the diary for the prosecution, and Scott found us in a conference room while Ralph was off laboring over that task. When Davey and Ann smiled gratefully at Scott's offer to help, I did not join in.

"Your concern is touching," I said. "It wouldn't have anything to do with a call you received from Masters, would it?"

Scott was unable to take his eyes off Davey. I could see why. Under the grinding pressures of the trial, she seemed more and more reduced to a fragile essence, a candle flickering in a delicate glass shade, exquisite, lovely. In the face of such luminous beauty, men hold their breath.

Scott took a seat across from the two women and waved at me to join them at the table. I remained standing.

"I did get a call," he said, finally answering my question, still staring at Davey.

"I got a call from Holtzman," he said. "They're willing to talk about a plea. You've been giving them a good pounding."

"And he's just beginning," Ann said. "Jack's about to rip the mask off Joel Alden and let the world see the slime underneath."

Scott looked at me.

"Why you?" I asked. "Why call you?"

My old friend shrugged. "As a sort of mediator, I guess. Maybe a neutral party can open up avenues of communication."

"Jack doesn't need any help," Ann said.

"Jack's the greatest," Scott said. "That's why I've got him working for me, but that rascal keeps all the prettiest clients for himself. I'm jealous."

Davey said nothing. I had no idea what she thought of all this, but I liked the way she was looking at me.

"How can you be neutral?" I said. "We're in the same law firm, and that means you're working for Davey too."

"I was speaking generally," Scott said, with a twist of his mouth. He turned again to Davey and added, "No one can be neutral when it comes to some things."

"Cut the shit, Scott," I said. "Are you here as Holtzman's messenger boy?"

I wondered if Davey and Ann saw the way his eyes hardened when he turned to answer me. He studied me for a moment before asking, "Are you sure you're doing the right thing?"

"You mean the diary?"

"You'll do a lot of harm with that little book—and all to no avail. You can't really avoid a conviction and you know it. The only thing you will accomplish is to blacken Joel Alden's name even further."

Ann spoke up. "Blacken Joel's name? It *should* be blackened for what he's done."

Scott shook his head slowly. "You have no idea of the damage you will do," he said to me. "If you use the diary and your client gets convicted, Kane will hammer her good for using such tactics. I'm talking about prison time. And you'll do Joel Alden irreparable harm. Last but not least, Jack, you'll screw yourself up so badly that you'll be useless to me from now on."

"What the hell does that mean?" I said.

"Are you willing to risk having Davey go to prison?"

"We're willing to take whatever risk is involved."

Then, in one of those slick turnabouts that so often left the opposition sputtering, Scott was suddenly his affable, imperturbable self again.

"Hey, what are we quarreling about?" he asked. "Our job is to cut the very best deal we can for our client, and that's exactly what I think we can do here." He was appealing directly to Davey and Ann. "If we all stay flexible, both sides can go home happy. That's the system working at its best."

"You're a dreamer," I said.

"All you have to do is meet with Holtzman and Masters. What can you lose?"

Anger welled up in me. "What the hell are you holding back?" I said. "If you know of some deal being offered, out with it."

Scott shrank back in mock terror. "Holtzman and Masters want to talk, and they're ready to cut a deal."

"Why Masters? Has Holtzman handed the prosecution over to him?"

"I can handle Masters. I'm one of the few lawyers in this county who can. He wouldn't dare pull the crap on me that he dishes out to the other lawyers. We understand each other."

"What kind of deal are they talking about?" Ann demanded. She too had picked up an odor.

Scott addressed his reply to Davey. "We're talking about the best of all worlds. Walk out of court a free woman."

"They'll drop the charges against Davey?" Ann asked.

"I don't know the details. Maybe she'll plead to a misdemeanor or something."

"That's not good enough," I said. "If she's convicted of anything, she'll lose the custody battle."

Now it was Scott's turn to act impatient. "That's been thought of. I don't know the details. I'm not working for them."

Of course we agreed to meet. Although it was too good to be true, stranger things had happened in my career. The diary was gift enough, the miracle I had been hoping for, but now it was just possible that Joel, realizing that his reputation could not survive another onslaught, had persuaded Holtzman to offer a deal.

A short time later I found myself sitting with Ann and Davey across a table from Holtzman, McClellan, and Masters. Scott remained standing. I wondered if he had trouble deciding which side of the table he belonged on. Joel Alden was not there.

Holtzman got down to business.

"Mrs. Alden pleads guilty to a misdemeanor with a recommendation of no jail by the prosecutor. I'm sure Kane will go along with that recommendation."

"What about the kid?" Scott asked. "They want to know about the custody of the little girl."

Holtzman had the good grace to look uneasy. Linking resolution of a criminal case to settlement of a divorce was fraught with evil possibilities. "I'll have to defer to Mr. Masters on that question."

Masters was even more direct. "She pleads guilty to a misdemeanor and Joel drops his custody fight. She gets the kid and a generous property settlement. It's over."

"That's the whole deal?" I asked.

"Not quite. We get the diary and all copies."

I felt Ann's grip on my arm.

"That's all?"

"One more thing."

When I did not respond, Masters continued, "I understand that you haven't blabbed to the press about the diary's contents. They only know generally that there's a diary with some lurid allegations. That means the only outsider who's read it is the judge. Am I correct?"

"Except for Evelyn Alden."

"We're not worried about her."

"Then you're correct. Only the prosecutors and the judge have read it."

Masters looked unblinkingly at me. No word was uttered, but I felt currents of communication pass between Masters, Holtzman, and Scott. The three of them knew what was coming.

"One last item," Masters said. "You must personally tell Kane that the diary is a fake—that you were duped. We will not say who faked it, but the inference will be clear."

"Evelyn Alden," Ann said, grabbing my arm again.

Masters looked at Ann but made no response.

Scott took up the slack. "The prosecutor sincerely believes that the diary is in fact a fake," he said. "All you really have to say to Kane is that you suspect the diary may not be authentic. No one can really be sure. Evelyn Alden is not exactly a reliable or unbiased witness."

"What else?"

"An affidavit from you to the same effect," Masters said. "We want something in writing to satisfy the press. They know about the diary, but they don't know the details. As far as they'll ever know, it was another lie by another of Joel's wives. The diary itself and all copies will be deep-sixed."

"What more could Davey ask for?" Scott said, beaming at her. "She walks free and wins custody of Julie and enough money to be secure the rest of her life."

I looked across the table. Holtzman seemed satisfied that he had safely distanced himself from any unsavory details. McClellan, who had not said a word, was unreadable; her sour expression was unchanged. Masters wore a poker face. Scott, still standing, seemed genuinely pleased with his role as deliverer of Davey.

I thought of Evelyn Alden, who lived in an alcoholic stupor most of the time and probably had already forgotten about the diary. Then there was Davey, who would get what she wanted: her freedom and her child. And, finally, there was Jack Brenner, who was only too happy to sell his soul to save this particular client, and who would get the better of the devil in the bargain, the market for lawyers' souls being somewhat depressed these days.

Ann was ready to fight. "Evelyn is telling the truth about the diary," she said. "What about the next child Joel Alden molests? When are we going to stop him?"

I ignored her. As a lawyer, my obligation was to my client, not to the whole world. I did not look at Ann and I did not look at Davey, who sat silently on my left, listening to me, relying on me, trusting me. I would make the decisions. We were within reach of all that we had worked for, and if ever there was a time for clear-headed thinking, it was now. My job was to save Davey and Julie, period.

"No visitation with Julie, ever," I said. "And no contact with Davey."

If there was a meter to test the air for the collective effect of sighs of relief, it would have gone crazy. Scott and Holtzman smiled, and even Masters's stone face seemed to relax a little. Only McClellan looked unhappy, as usual.

"No problem," Masters said.

"We all go home happy," Scott said.

A few housekeeping details were discussed. Nobody thought that Kane would be a problem. He would pretend to be irritated but would secretly be relieved. He would agree to recess the trial until we had all the paperwork typed up and signed.

Holtzman and McClellan stood up.

Davey whispered a concern into my ear.

"Mrs. Alden wants assurances that Joel will be barred from any contact with Julie, not just formal visitation," I said to Masters.

Masters looked as if he was about to quibble, but before he could say anything, McClellan spoke for the first time.

"I don't think you'll have to worry about that," she said. "Family man that he is, Joel's already found a new one."

"A new what?" I asked.

"Didn't you hear? Joel's going with a divorced woman who has two young daughters—preteens, as I recall. I hear he just dotes on those two girls. They're little cuties. He's just crazy about them."

Next to me, Ann emitted a low moan. I stared at McClellan. Her face was as it always was: eternally unhappy. The other faces in the room seemed out of focus.

"You have a real death wish, don't you?" Scott said, watching Holtzman and the others stalk off down the hall. "Being a winner makes you feel guilty. Losing is what you do best. You just had to go and turn down the deal of a lifetime."

"Win some, lose some," I said, but my heart wasn't in it.

"You get hold of some crazy idea about saving the world, and you never let go. It's your way of feeling superior to the rest of us. Any normal person would settle for belonging to an exclusive club or just looking down on hillbillies, niggers, and queers. Not your kind. You've got to feel morally superior."

"I don't feel superior—morally or otherwise," I said.

"The hell you don't. You and your zealous missionary friend. I wonder if either of you even gave a thought to Davey Girl—what was best for her. You're the one who told Masters to stick it. Davey didn't make the decision. You and that old woman did."

Scott was furious, barely able to restrain himself from physically striking out at me. I was angry too, but also sad. Which is not to say that I was silent. I was just sad enough to speak the truth.

"You're not pissed about my moral pretensions," I said softly. "This isn't even about landing Alden Construction as a client. This is about the Terra Group and a landfill that is going to make you a millionaire. Davey's case is the only thing standing in the way. And you want me to sell her out."

"Since when is winning considered selling out? You had everything your client could hope for right in the palm of your hand, and you threw it away. What were you thinking of? Tell me that. At least tell me that."

"I looked at your computer file, Scott. For God's sake, does the money mean that much to you?"

Scott laughed at me. "You're goddam right, money's important. You found out in Chicago how far your noble thoughts took you. What were you thinking?"

I thought of Semczyk and the investigation I'd instigated.

"I was thinking about what a fool I am," I said.

"Tell me something I don't already know."

"I'm a fool because I keep thinking that your kind of lawyering isn't what it's all about. That maybe—just maybe—justice is bigger than Syd Masters and Frank Kane and Scott Sherman and all the others who cut such a wide swath through the legal system. That's why I'm a fool. I think too many crazy thoughts—like I'm going to win this trial, that the jury isn't going to convict Davey."

Scott shook his head. "What a pity. What a fucking pity. We could have made sweet music together, Jack Boy. We could have made real money together. Christ, what a fuckup."

I had no more noble thoughts. I had a trial to finish. I didn't need Scott's recriminations and lamentations. Yet I felt guilty about disappointing him. I wanted his approval. My sense of loss overshadowed even my disgust at Scott's descent into criminality. Fuckup indeed.

"Sorry about that," I said.

"Remember I said you would make yourself useless?" Scott said.

"I remember."

"Well, you're useless to me now. I can't use you anymore. You're out of a job as of this minute, my friend, and Ralphie Boy is off this case—unless he wants to join you in the ranks of the unemployed."

Sandra McClellan and I arrived at the courtroom door at the same time. I moved to open the door for her, but paused with my hand on the handle.

"I don't know whether or not I should thank you for what you did back there," I said.

McClellan stared impatiently at the closed door. She looked as if she might slap my hand away and open it herself.

"Don't thank me for anything," she said. "My job is to help send you to the showers, and that's exactly what I'm going to do. If I still have a job. Don't read anything into anything."

I opened the door and followed her into the courtroom. As she passed me, I whispered into her ear.

"If I get sent to the showers, you're invited, Sandra. I can't think of anyone I'd rather take a shower with."

I could not see her face as she walked ahead of me into the courtroom. I doubted that there was a smile on it. But I knew there was a smile somewhere inside there.

35

I KNEW SOMETHING WAS WRONG AS SOON AS JOEL ALDEN TOOK THE witness stand for my cross-examination. In his eyes I saw a half-concealed smugness that made me uneasy. It should also have made me cautious.

"Tell me, Mr. Alden," I said when the jury had returned. "You have described yourself as a good family man—a father who loves his children. You are a man who would never abuse a child, sexually or otherwise. Am I correct?"

"That's a fair statement."

"Oh, come now, Mr. Alden, it's more than a fair statement. It's the truth, isn't it?"

"Yes sir, it is the truth." It was frustrating. I wanted the jurors to see his malice and arrogance, but Joel was too smart to fence with me openly.

"We have been talking about your child Julie. Now let's talk about Melanie, your daughter from your first marriage."

"Yes sir."

"How did she die?"

"She committed suicide."

I paused to let that sink in. A hush fell over the courtroom, the kind of silence that comes upon the jungle when a predator is on the move.

"How did she kill herself, Mr. Alden?" I asked in a hoarse whisper, aware that several of the jurors were reacting with distaste at this line of questioning.

For just an instant, before the mask of pained concern fell in place again, I saw another flash of hatred in Joel's eyes. "She took an overdose of pills and drowned in the bathtub," he said slowly. "It was after the divorce. She was in her mother's custody."

"Do you know why she committed suicide? Did she leave a note or anything?"

"Her mother didn't find one, so far as I know."

Walking over to the defense table, I shuffled through the papers there as if looking for a particular document. I noticed that Davey was watching and listening closely. I picked up a sheaf of papers and returned to the lectern.

"Are you saying that you have no idea why your daughter Melanie committed suicide?"

"I have no idea."

"No idea at all?"

"None."

"Do you recall receiving a letter from Melanie a month or so before her death—a letter that she wrote and sent to you here in Kirtley? Do you remember such a letter?"

"There is no such letter." He knew we did not have the letter because he had destroyed it.

"Wait till I describe the letter before you rush to deny receiving it, Mr. Alden. Or do you already know that there is something damaging in the letter?"

"Counsel is arguing with the witness, Your Honor," Holtzman protested.

"Gentlemen, please," Kane said mildly. He almost sounded apologetic. The diary apparently had shocked him into something resembling neutrality.

"Isn't it true that your daughter Melanie—your sixteen-year-old daughter—wrote you a letter in which she accused you of sexually molesting her for almost all of her life?"

"That's not true."

"What's not true, Mr. Alden? That you got the letter or that you sexually abused your daughter Melanie?"

"Neither. I mean, neither of them are true. I never touched her and she never sent me such a letter. It just isn't true."

"Isn't it a fact that your current wife"—I walked over to Davey and pointed at her—"found that letter and read it? And that you went into a rage and took the letter away from her and destroyed it? That you laughed at her and struck her? That from that moment on she knew that her child would never be safe from you unless she did something. That—"

Holtzman stopped me. "If counsel wishes to testify, why doesn't he take an oath and get on the witness stand? I object."

"Sustained."

"You did get a letter from Melanie just before her death, didn't you?"

"I did not. It's a lie."

"Are you saying that Melanie never wrote you a letter accusing you of sexually abusing her?"

"That's exactly what I'm saying."

I picked up my papers and tapped them on the lectern to align the pages.

"And so if someone were to testify that your wife found such a letter and that you took it and destroyed it, that testimony would be a lie?"

"That's right."

"What about the photographs, Mr. Alden? Do you recall that Davey Alden was outraged by the photographs of child pornography she found in your den?"

Holtzman was on his feet. "Your Honor, may we approach the bench?"

We huddled in front of the bench, and Kane turned off his microphone. "Brenner never mentioned any letter or photographs," Holtzman fumed. "The only thing we talked about was that damn diary. This is nothing but a cheap trick."

"This is fair cross-examination," I responded with equal heat. "I—"

"Get your answer and move on," Kane whispered. "You're not entitled to beat him over the head with unfounded accusations."

We returned to our positions, Holtzman's victorious look telling the jury that he had just successfully taken me to the woodshed. I kept my face expressionless. Kane was correct. Unless Davey testified, the letter and photos were only unfounded accusations.

"Please answer the question, Mr. Alden," the judge said.

Alden studied me up and down before answering. When he spoke, his voice was quivering with hurt and anger. "There were no pictures. That's nothing but another one of her lies."

I shuffled some more papers.

"Are you aware of any other writings by Melanie accusing you of sexually abusing her?"

"I heard that you and Davey have come up with another lie."

I smiled. "You heard? You and your attorney have been talking about your testimony, haven't you? Did you rehearse your testimony with Mr. Holtzman? Or was it with your personal attorney, Mr. Masters, or both of them?"

This time I caught him unprepared—with a cheap trick. He looked as if he had been caught bribing the highway commissioner. And over nothing. The prosecutor and even Masters had a perfect right to talk to him about his testimony so long as they did not tell him what to say—which of course is exactly what I wanted to suggest.

"What did they tell you to say?" I added while Joel struggled for an answer. When Holtzman started to object, I quickly said, "I'll move on to something else, Your Honor."

Ignoring Holtzman's disgusted look, I went over to the defense table and picked up the diary. I studied it for a moment before returning with it to the lectern. All was silence again. The final stalk was about to begin.

"Your testimony is that you never sexually assaulted your daughter Julie and you never sexually assaulted your daughter Melanie?" I said, picking up the diary so that Joel could see it. He knew what it was. The jurors did not—not yet.

"That's what I said." He watched the diary closely as I handled it: I was the snake charmer and it was my cobra. His gaze drew the attention of the jury to it.

I opened the small volume to a page Ralph had marked. I looked up at Joel several times as I read to myself. Joel licked his lips and waited for my question.

"I want to draw your attention to a night twelve years ago or so, Mr. Alden. It was a Christmas Eve. Melanie was about fourteen."

"I don't recall," he said.

"Let me refresh your memory. Do you recall that on that Christmas Eve when you visited her in her bedroom—something you frequently did, it would seem"—I hurried on when it appeared that Holtzman was bestirring himself to make an objection—"do you recall the purpose of your visit?"

"I don't recall such a visit."

"It was the night you introduced your daughter to mutual oral sex. You mean you don't recall that?"

Behind me a sigh, almost a moan, spread through the courtroom. Out of the corner of my eye I saw Holtzman cringe and then recover to shake his head in dismay at my tactics.

"It never happened. That's nothing but a filthy lie."

"I agree it's filthy, Mr. Alden. The question is whether you did such a thing. You are aware that before she died your daughter Melanie said you did that very thing on that very Christmas Eve?"

"It's a lie."

"Very well. I'll move on to another incident."

"Object to the word *incident*," Holtzman said, jumping to his feet. "There is no evidence whatsoever that any of these ugly innuendos are true. They are nothing but figments of counsel's feverish imagination."

For once Kane seemed at a loss. The parameters of his ruling on my use of the diary were ill defined. I intended to take every advantage of that vagueness. The jury couldn't read the diary, but it was obvious that I was using the diary to question Alden.

"Please move on," Kane responded with an annoyed look at both of us.

Again I leafed through the diary until I found a page marked by Ralph. I read the entry silently and from time to time looked up thoughtfully at Joel. Finally my question came.

"Let me ask you about a July Fourth—apparently when Melanie was still only fourteen or fifteen. Do you recall anything memorable about a July Fourth holiday?"

"Nothing."

I looked down at the entry made by his dead daughter. I maintained my façade of polite professionalism. Distaste, disgust, contempt would all have been acceptable emotions under the circumstances, but they were too easily overdone. One false note and the cobra could turn and bite me.

I looked up at Joel with a puzzled frown. "Isn't that the occasion when for the first time Melanie managed to reject your demand for sexual intercourse? She dared to say no to you? Don't you recall that?"

"No. That's a disgusting lie." If only he would respond with the same malevolent look I'd seen earlier in the trial. Anything but this all-too-believable portrayal of repressed pain and outrage.

"Don't you recall that you slapped Melanie in the face and that she had to tell her mother and the whole world that she got her black eye playing softball?"

"Another lie. I did not have sex with my daughter that day or any other day."

"Not that day because for the first time she said no—and you hit her in the face."

"Not so. I would never have done such a thing."

I sneaked a look at the jury while I pretended to study the diary. They were revolted by what they were hearing. Was their revulsion directed at Joel or at me? Who could tell what the jury saw? Joel Alden's mask was composed of layer upon layer of lies—and peeling off one layer only revealed the next. Even if a juror saw through one lie there was another one demanding to be believed.

Holtzman was being uncharacteristically patient. He did not want to prolong things. Soon, he knew, Kane would have to cut me off.

"You say you would never do such a thing, Mr. Alden," I continued. "You are not that kind of person, you told us. Then how do you explain your daughter's accusations? Why would she accuse a loving father like you of sexually molesting her, time after time?"

I turned to Holtzman and stared at him challengingly—daring him to object. He did not move a muscle.

"Why would she do such a thing, Mr. Alden?" I insisted. Then I went further. I walked over to the witness box and stood only a few feet from Joel and the jury. I held the diary up for Joel and the world to see.

As if this were the cue he'd been waiting for, Joel started to speak, answering my question with one of his own.

"Didn't Evelyn tell you that Melanie was a very sick girl?" he said. His voice was dull—as if the memories evoked by my questioning were covered by scar tissue and no longer capable of making him feel anything.

"Melanie was under psychiatric care for many years before her death," he continued. "She was even in an asylum for a while. She imagined all kinds of things. She accused me of terrible things—all kinds of unspeakable crimes. We didn't know where to turn. I think that's why our marriage failed. We took to blaming each other. In the end, neither Evelyn nor I could stand the stress."

Now I knew why Joel looked smug taking the stand.

"What was the name of her psychiatrist?" I asked. When you fall into quicksand, you struggle even though you know that only makes things worse. You cannot help yourself.

"Doctor Melvin J. Fleischman. He's in Ann Arbor. I have his address and phone number if you think you'll need them."

"What hospital was Melanie admitted to?"

Joel sighed and rubbed at his face. "I think it was a children's hospital connected with the University of Michigan. It was years ago. I can't be sure what year. But I'm sure that they would have the records."

I looked at Davey. Her eyes when they met mine were full of trust and encouragement, making me wonder if she knew what had just occurred. I looked away quickly. Joel Alden sat quietly before me awaiting my next question.

"And you want this jury to believe that Melanie's accusations were all the result of mental illness—not that your abuse caused her to lose her mind. Is that what you want this jury to believe?"

"Yes—because it's the truth."

"And you never saw fit to mention her illness in any of my earlier cross-examination?"

"You were the one asking the questions."

"The real truth is that your sexual abuse of Melanie is what drove her into mental illness, isn't that correct?"

"Absolutely not."

"No further questions."

I sat down. I was exhausted. I had no energy left with which to do further battle. I had no weapons left. The news of Melanie's mental illness might have spiked the one weapon I had.

Holtzman asked a few questions so that he could have the last word. Joel Alden stepped down from the witness box. Holtzman announced that he would have no further witnesses. The prosecution was resting. Kane called a recess.

As soon as I saw Ralph's face, I knew the answer to the question that had kept me stalling an impatient and angry judge for the last hour. The downturned curve of Ralph's mouth told me all that I needed to know: Joel was telling the truth about the extensive psychiatric treatment that Melanie had received in the years before her death.

"That bad?"

"Evelyn was pretty well into the sauce," he said, "but I gather that it was a pretty severe diagnosis—schizophrenia. She was kind of vague. Frankly, I couldn't make sense of a lot of what she said."

"I forgot to ask her anything about Melanie seeing a shrink," I said.

"You didn't have much time," Ann said impatiently. "I suggest you and Ralph quit whining and decide what your next step is going to be. You're both out of a job, so you've got the time to concentrate on winning this case."

I exchanged a quick smile with Ralph. Nothing like a layperson telling the lawyer to get hold of himself. And it worked. Like a good air freshener, her admonition purged the air of the despair that hovered in the room like stale cigarette smoke.

"Stick to your witch-doctoring and leave the law to us," I said. "With Kane breathing down my neck, I don't need you kicking me in the behind."

"What did you get on the psychiatrist?" I asked Ralph.

"He died a couple of years ago."

Davey shook her head and asked, "Could you be mistaken on how bad it looks for us? Maybe the jury did not believe Joel."

"We have to assume the worst—and I don't think we'll be far off," I replied. "Our best shot was that diary, and they managed to blunt it with Joel's testimony that Melanie was suffering from delusions. It looked like a sure thing for us, but now I don't know. We don't have time to dig up evidence to counter Joel's statements—and apparently no such evidence exists. The shrink is dead and Evelyn Alden is drunk most of the time."

"Then we don't have much choice, do we?" Davey said.

I did not have to ask what she meant. We had not talked about it, but I knew what she meant.

"Choice about what?" Ann asked, studying our faces.

Davey was calm, almost serene. "I've got to testify after all. In my heart I knew that it would come to this."

"With the diary I thought we had it locked up," I said. "Now I don't know. Melanie's mental illness is a wild card. I may have fouled it up by telling Davey to reject their deal. Now she's got to testify."

Ann looked alarmed. "Now wait a minute. You're the one who convinced me that Davey could not under any circumstances testify. She cannot tell a lie, and the truth will do her in. I don't understand."

Davey's sudden grasp of the realities was unsettling. "Jack knows that we probably will lose if we go to the jury as things stand now. We have nothing more to lose by my testifying. I will tell the truth. I will admit that I lied at the first trial, and I will tell the jury why I had to do it. They can believe me or not. I will be no worse off than I am now. And there is always the possibility that the jury will believe me and let me go."

She gave me a self-deprecating smile. "Have I got it right, Jack?"

"You've got it right." I stared at her pale face.

I turned to Ralph. "Go down the hall and tell the judge's secretary that we will be presenting a witness after all. That's all you have to say. Tell her I need about fifteen minutes to talk to my witness. Then hang around and keep them off my back for about a half hour."

When Ralph had departed, Ann looked hard at me and said, "Are you sure, Jack? I don't want to scare Davey, but you yourself said that the prosecutor would butcher her if she took the witness stand. And you, Davey? Are you up to a cross-examination by that lout Holtzman or that McClellan woman?"

Davey reached over and patted Ann's hand and then held it. "I'm scared. But it seems right. I lied, and now I will tell the truth."

"And the truth shall make you free," I said bitterly.

"Don't sneer," Ann said.

I sat down next to Davey and held her hand.

"Do you want me to go back and see if I can cut the same deal?"

"It's too late."

"Maybe not. I know how to get off my high horse and crawl when I have to."

"I didn't mean that. You were right to tell me to turn it down. Joel has found some new victims. I'd rather die than let Joel harm another child. The diary will stop him. It has to."

"It may not."

"It will."

We sat in silence for a while. Then Ann and Davey stood and hugged. Before she left us alone, Ann turned and said, "Kick butt out there, Brenner. Teach them a lesson."

I sat down again with Davey. "We've got fifteen minutes to get ready. Holtzman is going to throw every weapon in his arsenal against you. He'll try to make you wish you were never born."

Davey's enigmatic smile reminded me how little I knew her. Despite all that had happened between us, she was a mystery still.

"I've wished many times that I had never been born," she said. "Now I want to live. Mr. Holtzman can't do me any harm."

Deep inside, I too had always known it would come to this: Davey testifying. Like Scott's unexpected appearance, there was a symmetry in it that made it inevitable.

36

WHEN DAVEY WALKED SERENELY TO THE WITNESS STAND, I FAL-
tered for a moment, doubting myself, wondering whether I could go
through with the secret decision I had made. I had no choice, I told
myself.

Davey paused in front of the clerk and raised her right hand to be
sworn. As she promised to tell the truth, her voice was so soft that I
could barely hear it, but when she stated her name after taking a seat,
her words were firm and clear.

Dressed in a navy blue suit with a white blouse, tentative in her
movements, ethereal in her presence, she was anything but the
seductress of Holtzman's opening statement or the siren of Ripley's
imagination. The jury, prepared to meet a temptress, was instead
confronted with a vision of chaste young womanhood.

Very carefully I had Davey relive her initial testimony at Joel's
trial. Each time she answered a question, she obediently leaned forward to speak into the microphone, just as the judge had instructed
her. With me as her guide, we picked our way through the minefield
of her perjured testimony. She was pale but determined.

"Now, Mrs. Alden, you have just described your testimony at the
trial of Joel Alden," I finally said. "I want you—and I know this is

difficult—I want you to tell this jury whether that testimony was the truth."

Davey took her time answering my question, but there was no hesitation in her response. She turned and looked into the faces of the jurors.

"What I said at that trial was not accurate. I made up the details of the two incidents that I described. None of the details were true. They never happened."

"Then is it accurate to say that you lied to the jury?"

"No. That would not be accurate—or fair. I told lies, but I was telling a larger truth. I believed then and I believe now that I was justified in doing what I did."

There was not a sound in the courtroom. Even Kane had abandoned his customary aloofness and was listening intently.

"How can you say that you lied and yet also say you were telling the truth? How can both of these things be true?"

"Because Joel Alden is a child molester. I found out what he was like and I knew that I could never prove it, so I pretended that I saw him molesting Julie. I did it because I knew that Julie would be his next victim. I would have taken any risk to save her. I may be guilty in the eyes of the law, but I should not be convicted of any wrongdoing."

People held their breath. This was defiance. Far from throwing herself on the mercy of the court, Davey Alden was defying the law—and at the same time demanding justice, telling the world that there was no justice in the law if it chose to condemn her. As frail as a leaf, so pale that she was almost transparent, so earnest that her life force seemed to flow out of her into each word she uttered, she was demanding the unthinkable.

"How did you discover that your husband was a threat to your child? In other words, how did you find out that he was attracted to young children?"

I steered her through her story of stumbling upon the dirty pictures in Joel's desk in the den. I made her describe the photographs in revolting detail. I brought out how Joel had laughed and sneered at her and finally struck her. How he had created in her a feeling of helplessness by suggesting that he controlled everyone to whom she might turn for assistance. How everything he said was calculated to convince her that she could do nothing to stop him from possessing the body and soul of their young daughter.

Following my instructions, she faced the jury and told her story, and I knew that for the moment, for perhaps only this moment, the jury had entered into Davey's world and was living her horror with her. I also knew that the spell would pass and that shortly Holtzman would have his turn and that after that the judge would instruct the jury on the law—and that there would be no comfort for Davey in the words the judge would speak. The law does not make allowances for perjurers.

"Now, Mrs. Alden, I want you to tell this jury how you knew what kind of details to include in your story to make it believable. How did you make these invented incidents seem so real?"

When Davey looked puzzled, I plunged on. She had no inkling of what I was about to do. I spoke slowly so that there was no chance she could misunderstand me—or that Holtzman might miss it. Despite my earlier misgivings, I felt nothing. I was doing what had to be done. It was my duty.

"I'm talking about Angel. Do you understand me? Don't you remember telling me about Angel? I want you to tell us about spreading your wings."

I watched impassively as Davey's face took on the haunted look of the betrayed. I paused for only a second—long enough to make certain that Holtzman had taken it all in—before jumping in again.

"I'll withdraw that question," I said quickly. I knew with sickening certainty that Holtzman had seen the lure and would go for it.

"I want to ask you now about Terry Sinclair," I continued. "That dubious gentleman testified that he'd had sexual intercourse with you on more than one occasion. I believe he wanted this jury to believe— he wasn't really very certain about it—that all this took place before you went to the police and accused your husband. The prosecutor would like to suggest that your relationship with Terry Sinclair was the motive for your going to the police—in other words, you wanted to get rid of Joel Alden and have his money while he rotted in jail—"

"Your Honor, is this final argument?" Holtzman objected, this time playing the good sport, willing to treat my transgressions with humor. Now that Davey had in effect admitted her perjury he could afford to enjoy himself; the judge would clear up any ambiguity in the minds of the jurors.

"Is there a question somewhere in there, Mr. Brenner?" the judge asked. There was a stir among the spectators.

I asked my question. "Did you meet Terry Sinclair before or after you reported Joel to the police?"

Stunned by my earlier betrayal, her eyes filling with mistrust, Davey managed to collect herself and go on. "I met Terry Sinclair after I went to the police about Joel. He had nothing to do with my decision to accuse Joel."

"Did you have a sexual relationship with Sinclair?"

"Yes."

"Did you at any time attempt to persuade Sinclair to assist you in your plan to report your husband to the authorities?"

"Never."

"Did you ever talk to Terry Sinclair about your husband's money and suggest to him that he might share in it if your husband went to prison?"

"Absolutely not."

"You heard Sinclair testify that he met you at the Riverbend Country Club and that he was a business associate of your husband. What is the truth of the matter? Where and how did you meet Terry Sinclair?"

"We met at the Fairfield Inn in Bloomfield. I was having lunch with a girlfriend and he came up to us and started talking. I never met him at the country club. And I am not aware of any business connection he has with Joel."

"Why did you have a sexual relationship with Terrence Sinclair?"

In the little time we'd had after deciding that she would testify, we had prepared for that question. There was no way that she could tell this crowded courtroom what forces directed her life; she did not know herself. The jury would have to settle for our prepared answer.

"I was lonely and afraid. Terry Sinclair seemed to understand," Davey replied woodenly. "As far as I was concerned, I was already divorced. I could not stay married to a man like that. Terry's sudden appearance in my life seemed like a gift from heaven. I was vulnerable at the time and ready to believe in anyone or anything."

"Can you think of a reason why Sinclair would say that you tried to get him to help frame your husband?"

She looked past me at Sydney Masters and shuddered visibly.

"I don't know. I do know that Terry was threatened by Joel's attorney. Terry told me that himself. He said he was told that he would be ruined if he did not cooperate."

I left the lectern and stood at the defense table, looking down at the array of documents and notes spread out there. Davey had told her story. Standing alone, it was not a particularly believable story, but coming from Davey it rang true—or so I thought. Was it enough? Enough to cause the jury to ignore the law? I doubted it. We needed more—and for that we had to depend on Holtzman.

"No further questions."

37

HOLTZMAN WAS NOT THE FOOL OF MY ADVERSARIAL BIAS. HE WAS A scarred veteran of countless courtroom clashes, and in most of them he had emerged victorious. He could handle juries. When he chose to turn on the charm, it flowed in irresistible waves. He was smart enough to know that Davey's admissions on the witness stand did not give him carte blanche to beat up on her. Like me, he sensed that her story had struck a chord with the jury. He would try to destroy her, but he would do it with a rapier, not a bludgeon.

He was acutely aware that even now he could lose the game. When the door to the jury room closed, those twelve citizens could do what they wanted, and prosecutors do not get to appeal an acquittal.

"Good morning, Mrs. Alden. If I remember correctly, you were the victim in the last trial and your husband was the defendant. Now it seems that your husband is the victim and you are the defendant."

Holtzman's smile as he looked at Davey was disarming; she returned it tentatively.

"I want to be clear about your testimony so far today, Mrs. Alden. I want to make sure we get the truth this time. All right?"

"All right."

"You never saw Joel Alden sexually abuse your daughter, Julie. Correct?"

"That is correct."

Holtzman smiled reassuringly. "But you testified under oath in the case of *People versus Joel Alden* that he had—that you saw him sexually abuse Julie on two occasions—March fourteenth and May third of last year? That's what you testified?"

"That is correct."

"You were under oath, were you not?"

"Yes."

"And your testimony was false, wasn't it?"

"I know, but—"

"That's a simple yes or no, Mrs. Alden. Did you know that your testimony was false? A simple yes or no, please."

"Your Honor—" I started to object.

Kane would not hear of it. "I think she can answer that question simply, Mr. Brenner."

Holtzman's voice hardened. "Mrs. Alden, your answer, please. Yes or no?"

"Yes."

Holtzman's triumphant look announced that he was tempted to call it a day and sit down. But something was nagging him. It had been too simple. No verdict other than guilty was possible. Still, there was the diary, irrelevant and explained away by Joel, yet a nagging mosquito bite still. And the woman did not act guilty; she had the nerve to sit there and look like a victim.

Holtzman was wary. Had he missed something? Or was the danger in pressing forward? One question too many and victory might dissolve into disaster; he had seen it happen to many a lawyer. But if he missed something? He returned to the lectern.

"How many times did you say you had sex with Dr. Sinclair altogether?"

"I didn't—I mean, no one asked me . . ."

"I'm asking you now, Mrs. Alden. How many times did you and Terry Sinclair have sexual intercourse?"

"I don't know. Maybe two or three . . ."

"I assume that some of them were after Joel Alden was arrested, correct?"

"I don't recall. I think—"

"So while your husband was stuck in the Laffler County Jail, you were in a warm bed with your friend Terry Sinclair. Isn't that correct?"

I jumped up. "Mr. Holtzman is attempting to belittle and humiliate Mrs. Alden, Your Honor. This isn't cross-examination, it's assault and battery."

"I'm tired of you gentlemen bickering," Kane said irritably. "I am also tired of speechmaking by the two of you. We are almost at the end of this trial. Save your speeches for your final arguments."

"Thank you, Your Honor," Holtzman said. He turned to Davey and asked, "Did you and Terry Sinclair ever discuss what the two of you would do together when your husband was convicted and sent to prison?"

"We never talked about such things. I mean it was—" She looked exhausted and confused. I had warned her about Holtzman's cunning and possible brutality, but I was helpless to ease her suffering—nor, in the final analysis, did I want to. It was necessary.

Holtzman left the subject of Sinclair and turned to Davey's tale of catching Joel with child pornography. He pressed her for details: dates, times, where else she had been that day, what she and Joel had been wearing, the whereabouts of Julie when the confrontation took place—all the while managing to suggest to the jury that she was lying. Then he would switch back to Sinclair, only to return shortly to the photographs again. It was meant to confuse Davey—and it did.

Several times Holtzman caught her in inconsistencies and trumpeted them about the courtroom. Still, Davey clung to her story. And although Holtzman moved around the courtroom with a triumphant air, I sensed his frustration. The harder he tried, the less Davey sounded like a criminal. But he pressed on. He had to.

Davey was close to collapse, and Holtzman took full advantage of her weakness and attempted to make her look inconsistent, selective in her memory, willing to say anything to save herself. At times during the cross-examination I wondered if we might have to carry her out of there—and the worst was yet to come.

Holtzman walked over to the detective sitting at counsel table. During their whispered conference I saw Holtzman shake his head vigorously several times and glance up at Davey, who sat stoically awaiting the outcome of their conversation. She did not look at me.

Finally Holtzman finished his discussion and returned to the lectern. With his gold pen he made a few notes on a legal pad and looked up at Davey.

"Tell us about Angel, Mrs. Alden," he said with a smile that said her secret was out. "What does that have to do with all those convincing details at the first trial? We want to hear how you spread your wings."

Davey stared at Holtzman. I was grateful that she did not look to me for help. In the back of the waiting courtroom someone cleared a throat, and it snapped like a firecracker. In the deepening silence, Holtzman's appearance of amused superiority began to look strained.

Still Davey did not answer. Looking straight ahead, unblinking, she seemed not to be aware of our presence. A nervous finger twirled a strand of hair. Once I saw a hint of a smile play about her lips and I saw her lips move.

I saw all this and I wanted to stand up and object, to bring it all to an end for her. I feared that I had driven her to the brink of madness—but I did nothing.

Whatever Holtzman saw, he did not like. "Come now, Mrs. Alden, perhaps you did not hear me. I asked you about the meaning of the word *Angel*. What does 'spread your wings' mean? Please let us in on your little secret."

Still she did not answer. Kane must have seen her smile, for suddenly he reddened and leaned toward the witness box. In a voice that did not contemplate even the possibility of disobedience, he said, "I am directing you to answer the question, Mrs. Alden. What is Angel?"

Davey did not even acknowledge the judge's presence. She continued to look toward Holtzman, but what she saw was anyone's guess. A lone tear began its journey down her face, a tear like the one I'd seen that first day in the Laffler County Jail. It spoke volumes, but there was no one there who could interpret—except me, and I could offer no help.

Just when my restraint was beginning to weaken, Davey uttered something that no one heard. Kane, who had half risen to threaten her, sank back into his seat, relieved that he did not have to face total disobedience after all. He nodded curtly at Holtzman, handing the ball over to him.

Holtzman handled it deftly. "I'm sorry. I did not hear you. Could you repeat that, Mrs. Alden?"

Davey's voice was barely audible. "It's a line from a Rod Stewart song," she said.

"From Rod Stewart, no less," Holtzman responded, covering up his surprise with sarcasm. "Did Mr. Stewart help you invent your phony story about Joel Alden molesting his own daughter? Who is Angel? Did an angel tell you what to say? Did an angel spread his wings over you and tell you what to say in court?"

"'Spread your wings and let me come inside you.'"

"That's the line in the Rod Stewart song?"

"Yes, that's it."

Closing her eyes, she sang softly, "'Come on, Angel. Spread your wings and let me come inside you.'"

"What in the world . . . Your Honor, I would ask the court to direct the witness to answer the question. She is being evasive."

Kane had been around enough to spot a quagmire when he saw one. Holtzman could get himself out of this one.

"Perhaps you could rephrase the question, Mr. Holtzman," the judge said.

I decided to get involved after all. "Your Honor, Mrs. Alden is not being evasive. The prosecutor is being abusive. She is doing the best she can."

"She is not answering my question," Holtzman snapped, happy to have someone other than a fragile woman to vent his frustration on.

"Why don't you ask questions instead of yelling and making speeches?" I said.

"It was a code word my father used when he wanted us to have sex," Davey said. "When he called me *Angel*, I knew what he wanted. He wanted sex with me. He wanted me to spread my wings and let him come inside me."

Holtzman, like everyone else in the courtroom, was too stunned to say anything for a long time. Then all he could manage was, "Sex? Your father had sex with you?" Finally he asked, "What does that have to do with this case?"

It was my opportunity to slip the stiletto in. "Your Honor, it has everything to do with this case. The prosecutor asked how Mrs. Alden could manufacture such convincing details of child sexual abuse. Now he knows."

For the first time in the trial, Kane had nothing to say. He stared at me. Holtzman reddened as he contemplated the consequences of his failure to leave well enough alone. He'd been had.

"Are you trying to tell this jury that you were sexually abused as a child?" Holtzman shouted, his face contorted with fury. He was striking out blindly, determined to club Davey into submission. "Yet another lie? Is there no shame in you at all?"

I started to rise but thought better of it. Davey had to suffer for a little while longer.

"Have you no shame?" Holtzman pressed.

"Shame?" Davey asked, as if amazed at the question. "Do I have shame?"

"That's what I asked."

Suddenly Davey straightened up in her seat and brushed back a wayward strand of hair. I saw the telltale pinpoints of red in her cheeks: she was not only alive, she was defiant.

"I have lived with shame every day of my life, Mr. Holtzman. I am ashamed now of who and what I am. I don't remember a day that I have not lived with shame and fear. Even as a very young child I knew something was wrong—even though I idolized my daddy and thought he could do no wrong. I—"

"I didn't ask for a speech." Holtzman interrupted loudly, overriding Davey's frail but surprisingly intense voice. "Your Honor?" he pleaded to the judge.

"Just answer the question, witness," Kane said.

"So much for your shame," Holtzman said with a sneer. "Are you saying you were sexually abused as a child and that's how you knew how to describe sex abuse when you decided to lie about Joel?"

"Those details happened to me," Davey said. This time her voice quaked. The defiance of a moment ago was gone, a flare-up amid dying embers. Now she seemed played out, suspended between the horror of memory and a merciful exhaustion.

"I lived every one of those details myself," she added. "I could never forget them. There is not a day that I am free of those memories, hundreds and thousands of them."

Her sudden weakening seemed to bring out the predator's instinct in Holtzman. "And those memories—real, imagined, or fabricated—are what you used to falsely accuse Joel Alden?"

"I used what happened to me, yes."

"And your accusations against Joel Alden were false. You perjured yourself. You're not changing your story on that, are you?"

"I found out what Joel was like. It was only a matter of time before the details became true for Julie. I could not wait until then."

"You admit you lied on the witness stand after being given an oath, don't you?"

"Yes. I lied."

"Now, about the sexual abuse of you by your father—he is conveniently dead, isn't he?"

"No. Not conveniently. He is just dead."

"And you're trying to make us believe that your father sexually abused you during your childhood—and no one ever found out?"

"No one ever found out."

"Are you saying that your mother did not know what was going on?"

"Yes."

"Why didn't you report him? Tell us that."

Davey looked at the prosecutor with that same otherworldly expression on her face. "I loved my father, Mr. Holtzman," she said simply. "I loved my father."

"You loved this man you claim made your life a living hell? Is that what you want us to believe?"

Davey looked at him with pity. "He was my father. I loved him no matter what he did to me. At times I hated him for what he had taken from me but at the same time I loved him for what he had given me."

Davey was beyond cleverness, past caring what effect her words might have on the jury or anyone in the courtroom. I wasn't certain she was even aware of where she was anymore.

"I thought I was receiving a wonderful gift from him, Mr. Holtzman. When I was a very young girl and even an adolescent, I thought that he was a god—and that what he did to me was good for me. He wanted to create in me an appetite for such things."

"You mean you *enjoyed* sex with your father?"

Holtzman was not a cruel man, but in his mind, fired as it was by prosecutorial self-righteousness, Davey Alden was not only a liar, she was evil and had to be destroyed at any cost. He had lost his head.

Holtzman's question hit Davey like a jolt of electricity. She stiffened and looked at me and then at Holtzman. A cry of torment welled up from deep inside her and died just before it touched her lips. She straightened up in her chair and almost stood up.

"*Enjoy* it?" she said in a voice that was a whispered scream. "Do you know what it is to be introduced to sexual pleasure when you're only seven years old? I'm not talking about mere sex, Mr. Holtzman. That started much earlier for me—at three or four, so early that I can't recall any first time. I'm talking about a father teaching his daughter the joys of sex when she is just seven years old."

"Now, Mrs. Alden—" Holtzman protested, overwhelmed by the torrent he had loosed.

"You asked if I enjoyed the sexual experiences my father gave me, didn't you? I'm going to answer your question. You are a man, Mr. Holtzman, and you will never understand in a thousand years—but I am going to answer your question."

"Mrs. Alden—"

"Be quiet. You wanted an answer. I *did* learn to enjoy sex with my father. Is that what you wanted to hear? I was his sexual toy from the time I was a little girl. Details? I remember lots of details, hundreds of details. I remember my father penetrating me time after time—every orifice, with every instrument imaginable. He taught me to spread my little wings and fly with him. I recall him giving me my first orgasm—and our first mutual orgasm, oh, that was quite a day. I—"

Holtzman could hardly talk. "Your Honor—" he begged.

Like everyone else in the courtroom, Kane sat transfixed. At the sound of the prosecutor's voice he cleared his throat and turned to Davey—whether to silence her or not, I do not know. I was on my feet before he could find his voice.

"Let her talk, Judge," I said.

Kane's mouth fell open in surprise. In all his years on the bench, I am certain, no one had ever talked to him like that. If he'd had an opportunity to collect his wits, his wrath would have known no bounds, but he did not get the chance. Almost as if the interruption had never occurred, Davey continued her soliloquy.

"He was proud of both of us. I think I was thirteen then. I remember that the sheets had a flowered pattern and that there was a border of little bluebirds on the wallpaper where it met the ceiling.

"I liked it. God forgive me, I did enjoy it. For a time I saw myself as my father's favorite—his mistress of pleasure. By age fourteen I was a skilled lover—knowing how to give and receive pleasure. I was wise beyond my years in the matters of the flesh."

Davey closed her eyes and sat tensely in her seat, her hands clenching and unclenching in her lap. Some internal struggle was being waged as we waited. No one made a sound. Then she opened her eyes and looked at Holtzman again. When she spoke again, her voice had lost its coating of tears; instead it was heavy with loathing—of the prosecutor, of mankind's need to lick the earth, of herself.

"Now do you see where I got the details, Mr. Holtzman?" she asked. "Do you want more? Have I answered your question? Is your curiosity satisfied?"

Holtzman did not respond to her interrogation. Davey sat unmindful of her surroundings—dried up, brittle, ready to splinter into a thousand pieces at the slightest pressure. And the courtroom seemed to respond to her peril: mere silence was replaced with a hush.

"I have no further questions," Holtzman said quietly.

From the look on the prosecutor's face I could tell that he was tasting ashes. He had stepped through a door that I had deliberately left ajar; in his eagerness he had violated an elementary trial maxim: never ask a question to which you do not already know the answer.

I stood up.

"We rest," I said.

38

THE EARNEST, DANGEROUS FACES OF THE JURORS GAZED BACK AT ME. Sincere, dedicated citizens, but human, merely human, and that was their curse as well as their glory. On these frail human beings, so subject to the limitations of memory, education, and unacknowledged biases, rested the fate of Davey Alden.

"And so we come to the end of our journey," I said. "When we began I warned you about the dark path this trial would follow. I did not mislead you. It was all that I feared and worse.

"Together we have traveled across a nightmarish landscape of twisted desires. Sometimes you must have wondered if you would ever see the light again. If you would ever feel clean, innocent again.

"Yes, ladies and gentlemen, you will see the light again, and yes, you will be able to regain the sense of decency that made your lives bearable—and innocent. You have seen the face of evil and you've been changed by that encounter, but after the trial you will go back to your safe world of trust and decency.

"Not so Davey Alden. There is no trust or decency in her world. The face of evil haunts her days and nights, and there is no rest for her, for she has been violated by evil, penetrated to the core of her being. In every corner of her dark world lurk her—and our—worst fears.

"Yes, ladies and gentlemen, you can return to your world, but Davey Alden cannot."

I stood in front of the rail just a few feet from the jury, so close that I could touch them. McClellan had made the prosecutor's closing argument. She had stressed cold facts and hard law. I had no law and few facts on my side. I had only the truth.

"The prosecutor has told you that you must follow the law and put aside sympathy, and the judge will tell you that too. They are correct. You must not base your decision on mere sympathy. You must follow the law."

I paused and turned away from the jury to survey the courtroom. Davey sat at the defense table, facing me and the jury, gone away, not reacting. I might have been talking about someone else. Behind her, Ann waited grimly. And taking it all in was the public: fascinated, titillated, its hot breath filling the courtroom.

I turned back to the jury and said with a touch of anger, "Yes, you must follow the law. But the law is not some cold formula that you can apply with mathematical certainty. It demands a human heart. If you apply the law coldly, you will not render justice. You must apply it humanly. You are human beings, not computers. And it is from your human hearts that justice will come—if it is to come at all.

"Fortunately, members of the jury, the gap between law and justice in this case is more apparent than real. Yes, you must follow the law, but I believe that you can harmonize the demands of both law and justice. And when you do that, I have no doubt that you will acquit Davey Alden.

"I said that you will not be able to convict Mrs. Alden. How can I be so confident?

"Because Davey Alden is an innocent woman.

"Davey Alden is not only innocent of these charges, but she is the embodiment of betrayed innocence. She is every woman who has ever been oppressed and abused and persecuted. She is every little girl who has had her childhood stolen from her by a monster disguised as a father or grandfather or friend.

"I say that she is innocent—in every sense of the word. She survived a satanic father, a corrupting adolescence, and a nightmare of a marriage—and she remained innocent. Davey fought the evil that sought to despoil her. She, the victim eternal, stood up to evil. When evil appeared in the form of Joel Alden to threaten her child, she put aside her passivity, her role as victim, and fought with the courage of a lioness."

I paused. I did not know where to go next. My hesitation was the opening Holtzman had been waiting for.

"Your Honor, I really must object," he said. "Mr. Brenner is telling the jury to ignore the law and acquit his client because she is some sort of symbol of oppressed womanhood. I object and ask that the jury be instructed to disregard Mr. Brenner's argument."

"You're coming close to arguing jury nullification, Mr. Brenner," Kane said sharply. Then he turned to the jury:

"Jurors, I am the one who tells you what law you must apply. Anything a lawyer tells you about the law that conflicts with what I instruct you must be ignored. It is true that your decision in this case is final, but you must follow the law as I explain it to you."

I looked into the eyes of the jurors and said, "In plain words, what the judge has said is that you can acquit Davey Alden no matter what the law says. You *can*, but you *may not*. It's your call, and what you say is the final word on the subject. In short, no matter what anyone tells you, you can bring back any verdict that you feel is just."

The gods were smiling on me that day. I was telling them to make up their own law. But instead of coming down on me, Kane turned to the jury and said, "I repeat, ladies and gentlemen, that you must follow the law. And you will get the law—the correct law—from me, not from Mr. Brenner. Move on, Counsel, and if you misstep one more time, I will react severely, I assure you."

I moved on.

"Davey Alden was fighting for the safety of her child, and in her own way she was telling the truth—a truth that transcended the particulars of her testimony about what Joel Alden did or did not do."

I walked through the evidence with the jury, minimizing Davey's infidelity with Sinclair as best I could, discrediting his testimony, belittling the prosecutor's theory that Davey had tried to enlist Sinclair in a plot against Joel. I went over Davey's testimony about Joel's appetite for children and relived with them her confrontation with him over the letter and the photos.

I was suddenly afraid. How could these sincere, well-fed citizens of Laffler County enter into the mind of a Davey Alden? I closed my eyes and stood there like that in front of the jury for what seemed like a long time. To the jury it may have seemed that I was praying. Finally I opened my eyes and said, "What is the truth of any event? What is the truth of anything that happens in life? Is it merely the sum of all the facts? Do we have the truth when we have all the facts? I don't think so.

"Don't we reach the truth by finding out what the facts *mean*? Isn't that why we talk about some facts being the *true facts*? Facts in isolation have little or no meaning. Facts understood in context make an event glow with the light of understanding. It is only then that we can say that we have found the truth."

I walked back to counsel table and filled a paper cup with water. Davey watched me with the same courteous, detached concern as before. I wondered what she was thinking and feeling at that moment—if anything. I had used Holtzman to violate her one more time. I sipped my water and returned to the jury.

"My point, ladies and gentlemen, is this: you should look to the meaning of what Davey Alden said about her husband at that first trial. What is the meaning of Joel Alden? Is he a molester of little children? Does he prey on little girls as his wife has testified? Was little Julie next?

"If you believe the testimony of Mrs. Alden here today, then I submit to you that you must conclude that she was not lying when she testified against Joel Alden in that first trial. She told the truth about him. She manufactured details, but what she said on that witness stand was the essential truth—he is a pedophile who stalks little girls and sexually abuses them.

"Trust your instincts. Be guided by what you know intuitively about this case. Listen to the voice of reason, but hear what your heart says too. We must find the truth here. We must find the *meaning* of what has happened in the lives of these people."

My voice dropped to an anguished whisper.

"You have visited the chamber of horrors that was Davey's childhood. Now do you understand where she got the details to flesh out the charges she made against her husband? Can you understand? Did she have to wait for something to happen? Wasn't the future already present for her?"

I said many other things and finally it was time to stop. Suddenly nothing I'd said seemed honest or effective. I'd spun a silver web of words with which to capture the jury—and I had failed. Out of nothing I had created nothing. I stumbled blindly on.

"We have talked about the Aldens—Davey, Melanie, Evelyn, and of course Joel Alden. There is one Alden who has been mentioned but about whom we have not said enough.

"I am talking about Julie Alden—a beautiful, red-haired little girl of four. It does not take much imagination to predict who will get custody in the divorce if her mother is convicted of perjury.

"Ladies and gentlemen, I do not envy you your heavy burden of responsibility. Your decision here will ripple outward from this courthouse and touch many lives—for good or for ill.

"What I ask of you is courage. If you have courage, then nothing, not even the law, can stop you from seeing the truth and acting on it.

"When you reach the truth in this case, you will find Davey Alden not guilty. She is innocent if anybody is.

"I thank you."

39

WHEN I WAS TEN YEARS OLD I WENT HUNTING WITH MY FATHER AND he shot a grouse. I picked it up alive and could find no wound. Suddenly it went limp and died in my hands. Shock, my father told me. Sometimes lightly wounded game died from the shock of being handled by humans. Childishly, I blamed myself for the death, convinced that the little creature had died because I had touched it.

I had the same feeling about Davey as we sat in the conference room awaiting the verdict. There were a thousand things I wanted to say to her, yet when Ann went to make a phone call and left us alone, I could find nothing to say. I wanted her to trust me again. I wanted to tell her that I'd had to destroy her on the witness stand in order to save her. But words stuck in my throat; even my thoughts seemed counterfeit in the face of such devastation. Instead of speaking I sat next to her and took her hand from her lap and held it between mine. It felt cold and lifeless. I wanted to kneel in front of her and lay my head in her lap.

"Understand that I love you," I said finally. "Everything that I did here today was for you. And we're going to win. I know it. Every ounce of my being knows it. I've had hundreds of jury trials, and I know when I've scored. Davey, listen to me, we're going to win it. The jury is going to acquit you. You will be going home to Julie."

And I believed it. I was confident—as much as one could ever be with a jury—that Davey's testimony and the diary had done their job. I'd seen several of the jurors nod their heads during my closing and then sit marble-faced for McClellan's rebuttal. I believed . . . because I wanted to believe.

I moved closer and held her face in my hands.

"Davey, please come back to me. I will make things right again. You can't give up now. Julie needs you. I need you."

At last she responded, not with words but by raising her hand from her lap and laying it on mine. Her eyes met mine and there were tears waiting in them, but she did not cry. She had learned long ago that tears did no good.

As grim as a firing squad, the jurors filed into the courtroom.

I searched their faces for some clue. All of them looked straight ahead. No quick glance at the defendant, no encouraging smiles, no tears. All I could tell was that they were not happy with their decision.

One of the male jurors clutched the folded verdict form in his right hand, telegraphing his role as foreman, their elected leader, the man to whom they looked for guidance. I tried to read something in his details: Stephen Coleman, Juror No. 78; tall, thin, balding; under forty; an accountant; wore a jacket and tie every day; rumored to be friendly but reserved when the jurors socialized over lunch.

He was not one of the jurors I was counting on.

"Please be seated."

Kane waited for us and the fifty or so spectators to take our seats. They were all there: Joel Alden, Sydney Masters, Scott Sherman, Bob Ripley, Larry Semczyk, even County Clerk Ralston Nash, who always managed to materialize out of nowhere for the big moments.

When the rustling and coughing had subsided, Kane nodded at Clerk Nash.

"Would the foreman of the jury please rise and identify himself by name and number?" Nash intoned.

Juror Coleman rose, cleared his throat, and gave his name and number. Holding the verdict form in both hands well away from his body, he stood awaiting further instructions.

Kane explained that he wanted the foreman to deliver the verdict by reading from the form. Then he looked at Davey and me and said, "Please rise to receive the verdict of the jury."

I stood up and helped Davey to her feet. She was almost weightless. I took her hand briefly in my sweaty, slippery palm and squeezed it. Then we stood at attention facing the jury.

Kane frowned at us and turned to the panel.

"Please deliver the verdict, Mr. Foreman."

The foreman cleared his throat again and read:

"Count I, perjury, we the jury find the defendant not guilty.

"Count II, perjury, we find the defendant not guilty."

I enfolded an uncomprehending Davey in my arms. I held her until I feared that I was crushing her. Then I handed her to Ann, who stood just over the rail, weeping with joy. People were talking all at once, and Kane was pounding his gavel to restore order.

After things calmed down, the prosecutor and I thanked the jurors for their hard work and Kane excused them. He then formally adopted their verdict and discharged the bond. Finally, after glaring one last time at me, he adjourned court and left the bench.

I turned to Davey. People were all around her asking questions. Ann joined us at the counsel table and ran interference for me as I guided Davey through the crowd and out of the courtroom. At one point I thought Ann was going to straight-arm Ripley, who persisted in asking Davey how the verdict made her feel.

We took refuge in one of the conference rooms, a place to hide until the crowd thinned out. Ann stood guard outside.

I knelt in front of Davey's chair and took her hands in mine. "It's over, Davey," I said. "We won."

She smiled wearily.

"We couldn't win but we did," she said.

40

"Somebody wants to join the party," Ann said, following Evelyn into the room and closing the door. Evelyn's eyes glittered with excitement. She had been drinking.

I could not help but recall my first meeting with Evelyn. Now she had something besides the memory of a dead daughter to live for. Now she had revenge.

"Did we bury that scumbag this time?" she asked. "Did we do the job right this time?"

"We got him, all right," I said. "We're home free."

"Did I bring enough in to hang the bastard?"

"You did more than enough. The diary was just what we needed. It did the job."

My approval pleased her, and her happiness became a little less brittle. "We did the right thing," she said to Davey and Ann. "I knew it would be all right."

A look of smug satisfaction spread over her face.

"I read the diary and knew it was just like what happened to Melanie," she said. "That's exactly what she went through and how she would have said it. That's just what Joel did to her—the bastard."

A sliver of ice sliced its way into my heart. I wanted to leave. I looked at Ann and Davey. I did not want to hear any more.

"Of course it's what Joel did to her," I said. "It was Melanie's diary."

Cunning crept into Evelyn's face. "If you say so," she said.

"*You* said so. You told me it was Melanie's diary and you repeated that under oath in the courtroom."

"It worked, didn't it?"

I was out of breath and had to hang on to the table to steady myself. I glanced desperately at Ann and Davey.

"Are you telling me that it was *not* your daughter's diary?"

"It might well have been."

I grabbed her roughly by the hands. "Goddammit, what have you done? The diary is a forgery?"

"Not at all, you silly man. It's real."

"Is it Melanie's diary?" I shouted at her.

"Not exactly."

"For God's sake, whose diary is it?"

"Davey's."

Ann sank into a chair next to Davey. "I don't believe it."

I stared at Davey. She returned my gaze evenly. No one spoke for a long time.

Continuing to stare at Davey, I finally said to Ann, "Don't you see? Davey gave Evelyn the diary and they passed it off as Melanie's. They duped you, me, the jury, the whole world."

"Don't be a fool, Jack," Ann said. "Evelyn doesn't know what she's saying half the time." She turned to Evelyn. "Tell him he's got it all wrong, dear. Tell him."

Evelyn looked confused, vaguely aware that somehow she had done something to spoil the party. She did not respond.

"I don't believe it," Ann repeated.

"But it's true," Davey said. Deathly pale, her face full of shadows, she spoke so softly that I had to lean forward to catch what she was saying.

"It's true," she said again.

Ann's face sagged.

"Oh, Davey," she said.

I sat down in a chair across from Davey, close enough to touch her. The scene reminded me of the first time I had laid eyes on her in that small, hopeless room in the jail. We had talked about truth.

"I had no choice," Davey said.

"What does that mean?" I said.

"Without the diary there was no chance that the jury would let me go," Davey said. "*With* it, we had a chance. You said you needed something more, something that could prove Joel was the monster that I know he is."

"You forged the diary?" Ann asked.

"It's my diary. I wrote it when I was young. It's the story of my childhood—but it was Melanie's story too."

"My poor dear," Ann said.

"How could you?" I whispered. "You've ruined everything."

Davey did not flinch. "I'd lost all hope. Nobody, not even you, Jack, could save me. I had to help myself, the way I always do. I went to see Evelyn and talked to her about Julie. I asked her to help me save her."

"I'll be damned," Ann said. "I thought it was my idea to go to Evelyn. I was set up. I'll be damned."

"You don't get it, either of you," I said angrily. "For God's sake, this is more fraud and perjury, and this time Davey's made us a part of it."

"I'm sorry," Davey said.

She looked at me with tenderness in her eyes—either that or pity.

Her eyes were blue and dark, and I could not see into their depths. I had the feeling that if I could penetrate those depths I would have lived ten thousand years.

Epilogue

ON THE SHORES OF LAKE MICHIGAN IS A TOWERING SAND DUNE
that looks out across a sheltered bay toward two islands a few miles
away. It is a place of incomparable beauty, and as is so often the case
with beautiful things, there is a tragic tale just beneath the surface.
The place is called Sleeping Bear Bay.

I drove the two hundred miles there the week after the trial to join
Ann in a condominium at The Homestead, a manicured resort in the
forest on the edge of the bay. Ann had browbeaten a friend into letting us use it for a few days. Its second-floor balcony overlooked the
water. It was November, and we had the resort virtually to ourselves.

According to Chippewa legend, a mother bear, escaping a raging
forest fire in Wisconsin, attempted to swim Lake Michigan with her
two cubs, but lost sight of them in the stormy waters. The mother
bear reached shore and waited there for her cubs. They never came.
Taking pity on the mother, the Great Spirit Manitou covered her
with sand as a monument to her fidelity. Then Manitou raised the
two cubs from the water as two islands. The faithful mother is known
today as Sleeping Bear Dune, and her cubs are called North Manitou
Island and South Manitou Island.

In the summer the legend adds a hauntingly sweet flavor to a visit to the area. November is another story. Then the blue waters of the bay turn gray and hostile, and a visitor stares at the massive dune and begins to understand things that can only be hinted at when the skies are bright and the waters friendly.

I spent a lot of time on the shore looking out at the dark outlines of the Manitou Islands, studying the endless whitecaps, listening to the crash of the surf. Ann said that from the balcony I looked like a piece of driftwood on that thin ribbon of beach.

"You still licking your wounded pride?" she said after one of my walks. Still wearing my parka, I sat at the fireplace warming my hands. Ann wore sandals and green scrubs that doubled as pajamas.

"California doesn't have weather like this," I said.

"You're going to take your weather with you, I'm afraid. You keep this up and it'll rain the rest of your life."

"You're imagining things," I said irritably.

Instead of replying, Ann poured a fresh mug of French roast and brought it to me. She joined me in front of the fire. The coffee burned going down. I took off my parka.

"All right, so Davey fooled us all," Ann said. "It was wrong, immoral, unethical. So what are you going to do about it?"

"Nothing."

"Exactly. You didn't defraud the court. Davey did. You've said you have no duty to hand Davey over to Holtzman and Kane. Now you've got to move on."

"I've just helped pervert justice. Pardon me if I can't treat that lightly."

"Nonsense. What we've witnessed *is* justice. Davey's acquitted, Joel is giving up the custody fight to avoid another beating, and it looks like Semczyk is going to expose him and his landfill cohorts, including that crummy partner of yours. What more could you ask?"

I shook my head in disgust and got up and walked to the sliding glass door that opened onto the balcony. A freighter, one of the last of the season, was passing out of sight behind South Manitou Island. I watched it for a while before answering Ann.

"I could ask for truth."

"Your precious law would have convicted Davey. You know that as well as I do—and that's what Davey knew. Faced with an impossible situation, she took matters into her own hands to achieve a just result."

"You're saying the end justifies the means."

"I'm saying that sometimes God writes straight with crooked lines."

"The 'G' word again."

"You've made the law your god."

"It's all we have."

"All we have, but it isn't all there is. Human law is at best an approximation—a pale reflection—of divine justice. But things can go wrong, and then the law may become an instrument of injustice."

"That's nuts. It's what every kook from the Weathermen to the militiaman argues. God help us."

"And He will," Ann said. She toasted me with her coffee mug.

I thought of another maxim: *hard cases make bad law.* The lesson in the Davey Alden case was that there was no lesson. Sometimes the law is inadequate. Human nature and affairs can be so complex that they defy reason and make a mockery of the law. Some cases, like some people, just fall between the cracks.

"Did you see her before you left?" I asked.

"Of course I did. She wishes you could forgive her. In her own way she loves you."

I smiled.

" 'In her own way.' I like that."

"My dearest Jack, Davey was never yours to lose. She belongs to another world, one that you and I can never understand, a place that we should thank God we've never had to live in. She's been set free, but she doesn't know how to live in our world. She's like a wild animal whose cage door is open but who is afraid to venture out into free-dom. It may be a long time."

I walked back and slumped onto the couch. Ann was studying my face with a mixture of concern and amusement. I wondered how I had fallen so low that I had to be taken under the wing of a garrulous old woman who refused to let me live with my lies.

"Where are we going out to eat?" I asked. "I can't take any more of your home cooking."

"Now, that's the Jack I know."

It was well past midnight when I drove through downtown Kirtley. Snow fell politely, softening the harshness of the deserted streets and sidewalks. It was the first snow of the season, and so softly and gradually did the large flakes accumulate that it could hardly be called a snowstorm.

I wondered what the good folks would think when they awoke at dawn to a clean, white world. Like me, winter was slipping into town quietly. Unlike me, winter was staying.

Heading out Old Plank Road, I clicked the bright beams on for the final few miles. Every house and barn, every dip and bend in the road, was familiar to me.

As I turned into the driveway, I wondered whether the neighbor kid had taken good care of Maggie. Neglected, she would be sure to have taken her sweet revenge by chewing up the furniture. But when I pushed open the door, all was as it should be. After letting Maggie outside, I surveyed the room, mentally cataloging my belongings. Except for a few books and pictures, nothing in the cottage was really mine. When I left on the morrow, the only thing that would mark my passing would be the chewed-up arm on the striped couch.

I slept poorly for what remained of the night. It was one of those nights when you sleep and dream and awaken and then start the cycle all over again. I was in California as a public defender again, and Davey came to me in the night, and turned out to be Sheila . . . Davey was found guilty, no, it was me the jury was convicting . . . Scott Sherman and Francis X. Kane sat across a table from me and watched me eat ! . . . Joel Alden sat in a library and held Julie on his lap, reading to her from a thick book that looked like a Bible . . .

Of such fragments were my dreams, and I was relieved when the dawn came and I could escape the night. Maggie, kept awake by my tossing and turning, slept in while I made coffee. The snow lay outside my window—untouched, chaste, bright.

Despite my restless night, I felt resolute and at peace. I would drop the cottage keys off to Scott and say goodbye; it would be a strain for both of us, and I could almost see the relief in his eyes when I drove off. And there would be something else in his eyes too that I had not seen before—fear.

I would not see Davey again. Another lawyer had taken over the divorce case, and with custody of Julie and a huge settlement in the works, she would be all right. I would keep an eye on her indirectly through Ann. I liked the idea of still having to watch over her.

When I began to pull boxes and suitcases out, Maggie raised her head and questioned me with her eyes. When she received no answer, she stretched and opened her mouth in a wide yawn that said it didn't matter. She understood. The more things change, the more they stay the same.

About the Author

Stan Latreille is a circuit court judge in Michigan. He holds degrees in both journalism and law and has worked as a reporter and editor at the *Detroit Free Press* and the *Detroit News*, as well as practicing as an attorney. This is his first novel.